MW01100685

THE
LAKE TEMPLETON
MURDERS

- A FATI RIZVI
PRIVATE INVESTIGATOR MYSTERY

HS Burney

For my loving husband, who puts up with my wild imagination and crazy ideas, with a patient smile.

HS Burney writes fast-moving, action-packed mysteries set against the backdrop of majestic mountains and crystalline ocean in West Coast Canada. She loves creating characters that keep you on your toes.

A corporate executive by day and a novelist by night, HS Burney received her Bachelors' in Creative Writing from Lafayette College. A proud Canadian immigrant, she takes her readers into worlds populated by diverse characters. When not writing, she is out hiking, waiting for the next story idea to strike, and pull her into a new world.

Contents

CHAPTER 1

Thursday, Dec 12, 2019

Quiet, picturesque towns conceal devastating secrets. They wriggle under the belly of sunny perfection, threatening to upend everything.

Lake Templeton is no different. An ocean-facing oasis off Vancouver Island on the west coast of Canada, Lake Templeton is a tapestry of vacation homes, flanked by shady trees standing guard in the gentle breeze. The acres of private estates are guarded by a small but dedicated knot of locals, the die-hards that claim they will never live anywhere else.

Why are they there? Maybe they're surfing enthusiasts on trust funds that breathe through the sand on their soles. Maybe they're digital nomads that have saved enough after spending years cycling through bug-infested motels in East Asia. Or maybe they're remote workers that can withstand a thready internet connection as long as there's a boat docked outside.

I know why I am here. There's only one reason I find myself in towns like this. A body has washed up on the shore.

No, I am not the police. Police require warrants before they break down doors. I only need a good pair of boots.

I am not first on the scene. My police scanner doesn't extend that far out of Vancouver. But where my scanner doesn't go, I have well-placed informants.

Less than an hour after I get the news, I am on a ferry to Nanaimo. From there, I key in my GPS coordinates and begin the two hour drive to Lake Templeton. My car wraps around the periphery of the Pacific Ocean, tires skimming over sloping mountain roads, gritty with stale snow mixed with dirt and rock.

I know the Sergeant who presides over the municipality. His office is in the neighbouring town of Otter Lake, population 20,000, nearly four times Lake Templeton's. Sergeant Keller is a long-time mentor, a self-chosen godfather, the one who first taught me detective work. He knew me when I was a wet-behind-the-ears wannabe sleuth stepping gingerly around crime scenes, afraid of knocking things over.

At Otter Lake, the promise of Christmas hangs in the festive air. Storefronts are decorated with wreaths. Streets glisten with gold and green. Red streamers dazzle in the sunlight. People float on the sidewalks without a care in the world.

The entrance of the Sergeant's office is frenetic with activity. No one stops me as I walk in. Sergeant Keller looks frazzled, the craters under his eyes merging into weather-beaten cheekbones. His graying hair is skewed and combed back in clumps, as if he has run his fingers through it rapidly to make it look presentable. His white cotton shirt is stretched taut across a belly rotund with too many greasy late-night meals. It's clear he hasn't slept. He is talking rapidly with a constable, voice raised above the shrill noise of the ringing phone.

I tap my boots on the linoleum floor, dislodging little pieces of slush, and alerting the Sergeant to my presence.

He looks up, blinks, and a vacant confusion descends on his face. He looks at me as if I am a unicorn here to collect its horn.

"Fati? What are you doing here? I didn't call for you."

"You didn't have to," I say, walking in. "I thought you might need a hand."

Sergeant Keller sighs, dismisses his officer with a gesture, and turns to face me. "I won't even bother asking how you found out."

"Good," I say, smiling. "Because I'm not going to tell you."

I make myself comfortable on the scratched wooden chair that faces Sergeant Keller's desk. One leg lists to the side, groaning in protest under my weight. The rickety furniture in the Sergeant's office hasn't been replaced since he was a bouncing lad, filled with fire and idealism, fresh off the academy assembly line.

With resigned reluctance, Sergeant Keller sits down across from me. I pull my iPad out of my shoulder bag.

"Tell me everything."

"Why are you here, Fati?" The Sergeant asks. "Did Alena hire you?"

I carefully write down the name in capital letters. "Alena - and who would that be?"

"She's the mayor at Lake Templeton."

"Ah - so the mayor of Lake Templeton doesn't trust the police to solve the case."

"I didn't say that!" The Sergeant throws up his hands. Shakes his head at me in rebuke. His face flickers with indecision.

I lean forward. "Look, Sergeant, I know you're short staffed," I state. "A murder investigation takes a lot of resources. Vancouver Island isn't exactly murder capital."

"You're overreaching - we don't know what happened yet," Sergeant Keller says. "We have to wait for the coroner's report. But right now, it looks like an accident - or suicide."

"It could be," I concede. "It could also be cold-blooded murder. Come on, Sergeant. You know you can trust me to be discreet. Just let me ask around a little, see what I can uncover. It can't hurt. I promise I won't make you look bad."

The Sergeant gives in. "Fine - go over there. Let me know what you find. They're not big fans of the police at Lake Templeton anyway. Bit of a closed off community."

"I like a challenge," I say with a smile.

The Sergeant looks at me searchingly. His fingers drum across the wooden desk in a staccato rhythm.

"Why are you here, really?" he says. "Is the paid work drying up? What did I teach you about lean times in a PI's life?"

"I know how to find work, Sergeant," I say. "In fact, I'm at the point where I can be selective. I don't take on paid work that bores me."

Sergeant Keller chuckles. "So no more cheating husbands and spendthrift wives?"

"Or lost kids hiding in the attic or office drones digging up secrets to beat each other out on the next promotion."

"Good for you," Sergeant Keller says. "I'm proud." His smile carries the weight of parental pride.

"What can you tell me about the victim?" I ask, abruptly switching gears. It's time to get back to business.

"Sharon Reese, thirty-eight years old, washed up on Culver Beach at Lake Templeton."

"Are you sure the body washed up on the beach?" I ask. "What are the chances she was killed there?"

"Little to none," Sergeant Keller says. "The coroner confirmed that she was in the water for hours. There was mud and debris on her. High tide last night so she washed up to shore quickly. Otherwise, it could've been days or even weeks until she was found."

My fingers move across my iPad, taking quick and efficient notes.

"Time and cause of death?" I ask.

"In progress," Sergeant Keller says.

"Any friends or relatives?"

"None that we've found so far," Sergeant Keller says. "She lived alone. We searched her house. It looks like she either jumped or fell from the dock outside. There's no railing."

"Or she was pushed," I suggest. "What about her phone?"

"We found her ID in her purse but couldn't locate her phone. It's switched off."

"Did you put in a request for a call history?"

Sergeant Keller sighs. "This isn't a murder investigation, Fati. Chances are she tripped and fell. We found evidence of alcohol intoxication. She couldn't have saved herself from drowning."

"Got it," I say. "What can you tell me about Mayor Alena?"

"She's a young woman like you," Sergeant Keller says. "Beautiful. She was celebrating her thirty-ninth birthday last night. Got elected not too long ago. She came from Vancouver. Kind of cold and aloof, in my opinion, but the townspeople seem to like her. Enough to vote for her, at least."

"I see. I'll talk to her and see where I end up."

Sergeant Keller nods. "Make sure I don't get a call from the Super like on your last case."

I grin as I rise. "I'm here to make you look good. You won't regret this."

"I hope so!" Sergeant Keller says, leaning back and lacing his wizened fingers. "You need to find a hobby, Fati. Or a boyfriend."

I bite back a caustic reply. Sergeant Keller is a relic from simpler times when women formed their identities in the shadow of their male protectors. But he has championed me at my worst. He knows me in ways I no longer allow people to know me. I can forgive his tactlessness. Chalk it up to an identity crisis brought about by impending retirement.

"This case *is* my hobby, Sergeant," I say lightly, sliding my iPad back into my shoulder bag. "As you said, I'm not getting paid. As for boyfriends, have you seen the fools that make up the pool of eligible bachelors in this city? No, thank you!"

"Have you tried these new online dating apps?" Sergeant Keller says. "My daughter found the nicest boy on this one called Bubble…"

"Bumble," I gently correct him. I won't mention that I use Tinder occasionally. In ways the traditional, family-values Sergeant would never approve of.

With a final nod, I turn around and march out the door. Lake Templeton is beckoning. And I am answering her call. I can't wait to find out the secrets she has in store for me.

Alena Krutova is the mayor of Lake Templeton. An icy blonde, she has piercing gray eyes that grab everything they rest on and shred it to pieces. She greets me at the entrance of the mayor's office at City Hall. It's the biggest building in the town square, Lake Templeton's watered-down version of a downtown core.

Alena's shiny blonde hair is swept in a side knot. A beige cocktail dress ends at bony knees. Slim legs are encased in sheer pantyhose that sparkles as the light touches it. Buttery leather ankle boots perch on dizzying stilettos. Her makeup is freshly touched up and her face is set in an even, inscrutable expression. Her slim silhouette defies gravity as she sashays over to me.

Sergeant Keller told me that Alena was celebrating her thirty-ninth birthday last night. The party was a lone firework in a town hibernating in the depth of winter. The celebrations were interrupted in the early hours of morning by the arrival of the police. Clearly, Alena did not have time to change out of last night's outfit.

There has never been a murder at Lake Templeton, not in the last fifteen years I've been in this business. As she faces me, Alena is a picture of cold calm.

"The Sergeant called and told me he was sending a private investigator," she says.

No word of welcome and no hint of a smile. Sergeant Keller warned me that Lake Templeton was a tight-lipped community, helmed by a standoffish mayor.

Alena's speech is crisp, each vowel enunciated properly, as if she spent long nights perfecting it in front of a mirror. I can tell she isn't a native English speaker.

I smile. "My name is Fati. I help out the police from time to time. Can I talk to you for a few minutes?"

Alena beckons me with a nonchalant wave of a manicured hand. I enter her office and sit down. The space is stark and minimalist. No photo frames or personal mementos. Either she has no one she cares about or she guards her private life closely. The white walls look freshly painted and beautifully offset her light gray leather chair and silver-accented gray desk. A potted palm sits in the corner, bathing in the shower of sunlight streaming through the floor to ceiling window. The white centerpiece rug is pristine, like the shaggy fur of a Samoyed just returned from a relaxing day at the spa.

"Why have the police engaged a private investigator?" Alena's voice is a taunt. "Can't they handle the investigation on their own?"

"Lake Templeton is a small town, Ms. Krutova," I say, evenly. "I'm sure I don't need to tell you that bodies don't often wash up on its shores. A little extra help doesn't hurt."

"What are your credentials?" Alena's voice is like an ice cube.

"I was a cop for several years," I say. "But I've been solving cases long before then, since I was twenty, fifteen years ago."

Alena nods, lacing her fingers together. Her nails are neatly filed in rounded squares and lacquered with clear polish.

I pull out my iPad. "What can you tell me about the victim?"

"Sharon," Alena says. "She was the Lake Templeton Treasurer."

She looks oddly unaffected for someone who worked closely with the victim. I wait, expectantly. But Alena says nothing more.

"What else can you tell me about Sharon?" I prod.

Alena squares her slender shoulders. "What else do you want to know?"

"Did she have any enemies? Where was she last night? Is there someone you suspect? Who found her body? Did she have a family, friends, acquaintances I can talk to?"

"I shared all of this with the police when they were here," Alena says dismissively.

"I'm asking you to share it one more time - with me." I maintain my open expression and friendly tone, even as my blood curdles at her condescending tone.

Alena is unruffled. "Very well, then. No - Sharon did not have any enemies. She was in her late thirties. She lived alone. Hard worker. Didn't have many friends."

"Was she at your birthday party last night?"

"No - she was invited but she didn't come."

"Her body was found at the beach in the early hours of the morning. Who found it?"

"It was Sergio - Sergio Alvarez," Alena says. "He works with me, here at City Hall. He went out for a run on the beach at eight-thirty in the morning."

I write down the name in capital letters on my iPad.

"Does Sergio run alone?" I ask.

"I think so," Alena says. "He likes his quiet time in the mornings."

"The Sergeant tells me that the victim was drunk," I say. "Did Sharon have a drinking problem?"

"Not that I know of."

"What else can you tell me about the victim?"

"What else do you want to know?"

With an audible sigh, I lay my iPad down on her unblemished desk. "Look, Alena, I will be very honest with you. You can either cooperate with me or you can deal with a swarm of cops all over your sleepy little town. You decide."

The Sergeant's office does not have the resources to swarm the town. It took almost his entire bench strength to process the crime scene and search through Sharon's home. But Alena doesn't know that.

Alena's expression doesn't change. "I will cooperate with you. But you have to tell me what you want to know. We are in shock at this senseless tragedy. Sharon has lived here for over three years. We genuinely liked her. Except... well, in the last few weeks, I started to suspect she was embezzling money from the town treasury."

"Really? What made you suspect that?"

"We are in the middle of a big revitalization project for Lake Templeton," Alena says. "I am not sure if you've had the time to look around, but this town has a lot of potential. We have over a thousand kilometers of waterfront. It's easily accessible from the main island but far enough to be a hidden oasis. We have a stretch of untapped, non-agricultural land that we can develop into a resort to capture international travelers. In recent years, we have caught the attention of some very wealthy investors."

Alena's voice has eased into a practiced sales pitch which I suspect she has recited several times before.

"How much money have you raised for this project?" I ask.

"About twenty million dollars. We have another ten committed from the provincial and municipal governments."

"What is the total project cost?"

"A hundred million," Alena says. "Excluding the new resort which we licensed to a developer."

"Who are your investors?"

"That is confidential information."

"And it's a public private partnership?"

"Yes."

"How much money do you believe Sharon stole?"

"A recent audit of our books revealed a half a million dollars missing," Alena says. "Sharon handled the money on a day-to-day basis. As Treasurer, she had full access to our accounts, both operating and restrained."

"Did you confront Sharon about the embezzlement?"

"No," Alena says coolly. "I wanted to be sure before I accused her. An independent auditor is looking into the matter."

"I'm going to need access to Sharon's office so I can look through her files."

Alena raises one elegant shoulder in a half shrug. "Be my guest. Although the police didn't ask to do that."

I smile. "They sent me."

Another curt nod, then Alena starts to rise from her chair, an unmistakable indication that this interview is over.

"Please be discreet in your inquiries," Alena says. "I do not want to cause unnecessary panic amongst our investors."

"I understand." I close my iPad. "I want to talk to Sergio before I look through Sharon's office. Where can I find him?"

It's a sunny day in Lake Templeton. Its brilliance dulls the memory of the pellets of ice that rained down most of last week. As I walk towards my car, the coastal wind whistles at me and fizzles out as it absorbs into my jacket.

Retail stores encircle the town square like a denture. Most are dimly lit, open but empty. The parking lot is dotted with a handful of cars. Winter isn't peak tourist season at Lake Templeton.

On the way to Sergio's cottage, I reflect on my conversation with Alena. After learning about the Lake Templeton revitalization project, her reticence makes sense. A murder investigation involves big, splashy publicity. It could scare away potential investors. Alena wants this matter wrapped up quickly and quietly. A circumspect private investigator can do that. Not the lumbering police.

I am intrigued by Alena, the mysterious mayor of Lake Templeton. How did she win hearts and minds at the ballot box?

Where is she from? Her accent is beautifully papered over, but unmistakably foreign.

What brought her to Lake Templeton? It's a small pond for a woman so cosmopolitan.

Does she live alone? Does she have family, friends, a significant other?

I make a mental note to find out everything I can about her.

Sergio's cottage is a five-minute drive from the town square. I take the ramp off the Island Highway onto a narrow semi-dirt road which twists into a residential street. Sergio's driveway is hidden behind a canopy of trees. I park on the side of the road, the tires of my Mazda 3 sedan sinking into the slushy mud bank which, just a few days ago, was likely covered with snow.

The house is a squat structure, at least thirty years old, battered by rain, cooked by sun, and bruised by seasons. The exterior paint is worn off in patches, exposing the wood-frame construction. A splintered railing borders the front deck, which appears to list to the side. A sparkling, near-new snowboard and shoes stand sentinel in the spiderwebbed corner of the deck, sticking out like a diamond ring in a garbage chute.

A bright blue Kia hatchback sits in the driveway. Its tires are covered with several layers of mud, each older and crustier than the one above it. My boots smack against a soggy bed of fallen leaves. It's clear that home maintenance is not a priority for Sergio.

The gaudy 'Welcome' sign on the front door hangs slightly askew. As I raise my hand to knock, I notice a movement in the side alley that leads to the back of the house.

"Hello? Sergio, are you there?"

"What? Who is it?" A slim, striking redhead darts into view. In his late-20s, Sergio has regal, almost aquiline features with cheekbones that can cut glass. A smattering of freckles checkers a nose that looks like an 'after' photo from a plastic surgeon's office. As he approaches me, I see that Sergio is gripping a rake in a gloved hand.

I smile and point to his dirty overalls and Hunter boots. "Gardening day?"

He squints at me. "Sorry - who are you?"

I introduce myself. "Alena told me where you lived," I say. "I understand that you're the one who found Sharon's body on the beach this morning."

Sergio lowers his head. Distress stiffens his shoulders. He sets the rake aside and wipes his hands on his overalls.

"Yes," he says. "I'm happy to talk to you. But I already gave my statement to the police. Would you like to come inside?"

I follow him as he pushes open the front door. The inside of the house is chaotic. Haphazardly arranged knick-knacks crowd a TV table. Walls teem with craggy rows of paintings and photos. Multiple throw rugs clash colors on the light yellow fabric sofas in the living room. A dark gray sweater is tossed on a crookedly angled chair along with a checkered muffler. It's a cataclysm of personalities competing for attention.

I sit down on a single-seater sofa, pushing aside a throw rug to make room. "So, Sergio, I understand that you work with Alena at the mayor's office?"

"Yes," he says, perching stiff-backed on a neighbouring chair. Almost immediately, he jumps back up as if scalded. "Oh, I'm so rude - can I offer you tea or coffee?"

"A glass of water would be great, thank you."

Sergio excuses himself to go to the kitchen. I rise to my feet and quickly scan the living room, settling on the framed photographs sitting on the showcase. There are a couple of snapshots of Sergio in snowboarding gear on top of a mountain, an exultant grin on his face.

I grimace. I will never understand why people willingly fling themselves down treacherous mountains, feet strapped to a board. It's a suicide mission.

Or so my parents always said. As immigrants from Pakistan, they were slow to embrace the customs of their adoptive country. My brother learned to ski while in college. But my sister and I still prefer to keep the mountains at a distance, admiring their beauty from the comfort of a cushioned seat at a cafe, hands curled around a mug of hot chocolate.

I focus back on Sergio's photos. He lives alone and runs alone, but he doesn't appear to be lonely. There are several photos with other young people, all smiling, flushed with the high of life. There's a striking older woman with sharp features and high cheekbones. The similarity is undeniable: it's Sergio's mother.

The sound of the running water in the kitchen subsides. The soft squeak of wooden floorboards signals that Sergio is returning to the living room. I slip back in my seat and cross my legs, as if I never moved.

Sergio hands me a glass of chilled water. I accept with a smile and take a small sip. My former colleagues at the police academy would call me reckless for sampling a drink prepared by a potential suspect. Maybe I'm not completely averse to suicide missions, after all.

I reach into my shoulder bag for my iPad. "Tell me what happened this morning."

"I was out for my morning run when I saw her," Sergio says, voice laden with pain. "She was on the beach. She must have drowned."

"Did she live close by?"

"Her lodge is on the other side of Culver Beach," Sergio says. "The police said she was drunk last night. She must have slipped and fallen - it's quite treacherous, the deck outside her lodge. It ices over in the winter. I told her so many times to install a railing."

"So you think this was an accident, not murder?"

Sergio looks taken aback. "Of course! Murder? Why would you think it's murder? Who would want to kill Sharon? She was a lovely person. Very private, but pleasant and helpful to everyone."

"When was the last time you saw Sharon alive?"

Sergio tilts his head to the side, considering my question. "Last week, on Friday, at the council meeting."

"Did you attend Alena's birthday party last night?"

"No," Sergio says. "I wasn't feeling very well."

"Can you tell me where Sharon was, what she did, in the days after the council meeting, prior to her death?"

"She flew to Vancouver to pitch to prospective investors," Sergio tells me.

I feel a stab of frustration that Alena withheld this from me.

"When?" I ask. "And how long was she there for?"

"I think she left over the weekend," Sergio says. "And came back last night…" Sergio stops, squelches his lips together, an expression of suffering.

"Did she do that often - fly to Vancouver for investor meetings?" I ask.

"Not that often," Sergio says. "Once every couple of months, I think."

"Did she travel alone?"

"I think Alena usually went with her," Sergio says. "But I don't think she did this week."

"Why not?"

"I don't know - I think she had another commitment. But you'll have to ask her."

"How did Sharon fly to Vancouver? I didn't see any Harbor Air seaplanes around here."

"Oh, it's a private airline," Sergio says. "It's the only one that flies from Lake Templeton. It's called Pacific Air."

I write it down in capital letters on my iPad. "Does Pacific Air have an office I can visit?"

"I don't know… but I can give you the name and number of the owner," Sergio says. "He flies the plane himself. His name is Aditya. Aditya Roshan."

"That sounds perfect," I say. "I will get in touch with Aditya later today. How long has Pacific Air been servicing Lake Templeton?"

"A couple of years, I think," Sergio says. "We didn't have any plane service before that."

I steer the conversation in a different direction. "How well did you know the victim, Sharon Reese?"

"We worked together," Sergio sighs. "I'm the marketing manager for Lake Templeton. I promote the town and create content for our social media pages. We're trying to get new investors for the Lake Templeton revitalization project. I'm sure Alena told you about that."

"She did," I confirm. "How many investors have you landed so far?"

Sergio shrugs. "You can ask Alena. I don't know."

"Can you tell me anything about Sharon's private life?" I probe. "Friends? Family? Others in her orbit?"

"She wasn't very social," Sergio says. "I don't think she had any family."

The rest of our conversation is uneventful. Sergio has been living at Lake Templeton for just over a year. Prior to moving here, he was a freelancer, working on ad hoc social media projects for various clients. An uncle passed away, leaving him the cottage at Lake Templeton. Unattached and obligation-free, Sergio decided to move and save on rent. After Alena saw his work, she hired him.

I wrap up with Sergio and head to my car. I need to find a motel where I can lay my head down for the night. I have a feeling this case may take a few more days.

On the way, I stop at Culver Beach, where Sharon's body was found. Culver Beach is shaped like a claw, with the shores of Lake Templeton hugging it from one side and the other opening up to the ocean. In high tides, waves batter it from one direction, bringing debris from the neighbouring houses.

It was these waves that carried Sharon once the water besieged her lungs and she stopped breathing. Maybe her killer was hoping that the body would descend to the depths of the ocean, swallowing its secrets. It must have been a rude shock to see the evidence of their crime splashed across the morning papers.

Sharon's body was half-reposed face-down on the wet sand, deposited on the shore like plastic waste. Clumps of hair were caught in the jagged rocks that edge the receding land, one bloated arm flung over a large boulder, as if trying to find a grip. Her legs floated behind her like windsocks. Silk shirt ballooned over the surface of the water like a parachute.

The crime scene has been cleared up. Culver Beach sparkles in the vestiges of the sinking sunlight, sand glinting like diamond dust. The only remnants of the morning's tragic discovery - dried boot prints in the grassy sand, left behind by the police.

The nearest house is walled off by a thicket of trees and is currently empty, owned by a businessman who only spends a few months here in the summers. The beach is quiet, with not even a dog walker in sight. I walk on the sand for a few minutes, shoes in hand, reveling in the quietude. I breathe in the fresh air, slightly briny, and crisp enough to open up my nasal pathways.

No answers will be found here. Not for me. I have limited experience analyzing crime scenes. Even though, as a beat cop, I elbowed my way to many sites above my pay grade, attaching myself to the most brilliant detectives like a barnacle. Thankfully, you don't need to be an expert at crime scene analysis to catch a killer.

And catching a killer is what I do best.

I will answer the plea in Sharon's outstretched arms, still flailing in death as her body collided against the land, unmoored from its watery grave. I will unravel the secrets in the wide eyes and rote responses of Sharon's colleagues. The combative non-responses of Mayor Alena Krutova. And the exaggerated sorrow of Sergio Alvarez, Marketing Manager at City Hall, who claims to only know Sharon as a dear colleague.

I will piece together the puzzle of Sharon's life. Who was she? What was she doing in Lake Templeton? Did she steal a half a million dollars from the City? And did it drag her to an early death, pitched off the deck outside her own home?

What transpired on Sharon's deck last night after the sun sank behind the heavy winter shadows?

The answers hover in the glacial air. They wisp through the fog rising from the lake. They're protected by the dense night, blackening every surface it touches. They're hidden - but I will find them.

I turn away from the beach and start walking towards my car. There's much more to unravel in the mystery of Sharon Reese's death. I am just getting started.

CHAPTER 2

Thursday, Dec 12, 2019

I find a room at the Lakeside Inn, a three-and-a-half-star hotel. There are only four in Lake Templeton, ranging from a
bedbug-infested hole-in-the-wall to a Best Western style mo-
tor inn with a hot tub and gym that goes for four hundred
dollars a night in peak season.

I understand the rationale behind the revitalization
project. Lake Templeton is an untapped treasure. Sea water
that wavers from rich blue to turquoise to deep green. Lush
forests with the famous Vancouver Island cedars that soar
towards the sky. Rocky beaches edged with oil slick rocks
with enough striated sedimentation to make a geologist's
mouth water.

But to attract more visitors, you need places to stay.
You need whale watching tours and snorkeling adventures
and speedboat rentals. And you need civil infrastructure to
support them. That requires money.

My basic room at the Lakeside Inn has a Murphy bed. A small pantry contains an overused stove and a mini fridge. I toss my overnight bag in a corner, power up my laptop, and key in the Wi-Fi password.

In any investigation, the internet is my first port of call. It's quick, convenient, and free. A global data bank of information, a few clicks away. When I was in the police, social media was in its infancy. My traditionalist colleagues mistrusted it. Pooh-poohed its insights. Until it changed the rules of the game. We no longer had to wring information from perps. They came to us willingly with their lives on a platter, told through their online profiles.

I type in 'Sharon Reese.' I click through Facebook, LinkedIn, Instagram, Twitter - nothing. A Google search reveals scant personal information. There are a couple of local newspaper articles about Sharon's volunteer work with BC Children's Hospital.

That's unusual for a woman with no children. Were there other kids in her life, nieces, nephews, maybe? But her colleagues at City Hall said Sharon had no family.

My next search is for Alena Krutova. Her website is littered with photos of a selfless politician whose only aim is to serve the people. A smiling Alena shaking hands with her constituents, leaning in, and looking interested. A somber Alena behind a podium, dressed crisply in silken creams and tans. Alena, one of the people, standing shoulder-to-shoulder, surrounded by adulation.

Alena's Twitter profile has just over five thousand followers - the entire population of Lake Templeton, undoubtedly. She tweets five days a week, Monday to Friday, at eight-thirty a.m., probably when she arrives at the office. Her tweets talk to her key priorities: tourism, amenities, and infrastructure renovation.

In recent weeks, they include updates on the Lake Templeton revitalization project. It will put Lake Templeton on the map as a tourist paradise, in the same rink as its more popular cousins, Tofino and Ucluelet. Plans have been drawn up and architects have finished their rendering. The City is edging closer and closer to its funding goal every day.

I comb through comments and retweets. Sergio is usually the first to comment on Alena's posts, expressing his enthusiasm through colorful emojis.

A familiar name jumps out - Lona Mason. Lona is a popular legislative assembly member in the Vancouver-Fraserview riding. Hails from a high-powered Albertan oil family. Her capstone issue - family law and child rights. Women supporting women in politics? Maybe.

Alena's internet presence is suspiciously whitewashed. So I phone a friend.

George Derby owns a private company that does background checks for large corporations. A former intelligence officer, he took early retirement a few years ago at the ripe old age of forty-five. Now, he enjoys a high-octane life in Toronto, always on-call, running a small but efficient outfit with only twenty employees, all with Mensa-level intelligence, fluent in multiple languages, and with layers upon layers of covert contacts to call to find out anything you want to know about anyone.

George picks up on the fifth ring and greets me pleasantly. It has been some time since I last reached out. When it comes to nosy private investigators, only absence can make the heart grow fonder. I give George a quick rundown on the shifty, ice-eyed Lake Templeton mayor.

"Do you need the full meal deal on this one, Fati, or can you make do with a basic package?" George asks. "We are super stretched these days. It's that new work visa program - background checks on international candidates take so much longer."

"A basic is fine, my friend," I say. "She's not a suspect, not yet anyway, but I think she's hiding something. I need to know who she is, where she came from, whether she was born in Canada, stuff like that. I picked up a hint of an accent, so I think she may be an immigrant."

"I can do a local background check if you need results fast," George offers. "Where is she from? Last name sounds Russian."

"Local is fine for now." I run a Google search on Alena's last name. "Russian, definitely Russian. Or former Soviet bloc."

"Okay - give me a few hours."

I hang up and turn my attention to the City of Lake Templeton's website, expecting to find detailed plans for the revitalization project. But there's only a placeholder with a basic artist's sketch. It looks like it's drawn from a stock photo of an oceanside resort in Cancun.

I move on to Sergio Alvarez. He has a bold internet presence. Not surprising for a social media marketer. One hundred thousand Instagram followers - whoa! I scroll through his recent posts. Artistic shots of the seascapes and panoramas of Lake Templeton. Posts promoting local events, farmer's markets, and craft fairs.

My search on Aditya Roshan, the airline pilot, is pending when my eyes start to cross over. Exhaustion hits me like the rear end of a truck backing out of a driveway. It's time for a cold shower and hot coffee.

As a private investigator, I'm used to operating with little sleep. We thrive on late night stakeouts and answer our phones at odd hours. I take icicle-like showers and mainline caffeine to keep going, sometimes for days at a time.

Later, perked up, hair wet and sipping my coffee, I call Sergeant Keller.

"How are you doing out there, Fati?" he asks.

"Making progress," I say, grimacing at the acrid taste of the hotel brew. Clearly, cleaning the coffee maker is not on housekeeping's list of recommended tasks. "My goal is to solve this before Christmas so you and your team can take off for the holidays."

Sergeant Keller chuckles. "Wouldn't that be a treat. I've been doing this for over thirty-five years and something like this always happens in December - right before Christmas."

"Mayor Alena Krutova is a little slippery," I say. "You weren't kidding about that."

"I warned you."

"It's odd that a woman as posh as her would be headlining a small town like Lake Templeton."

"Isn't that right," Sergeant Keller agrees. "The town's never had a mayor like that before. They elected her about the time the Lake Templeton project got going. A woman who looks like that can attract all kinds of investors."

"I'll stay here for a few days while I work through this," I say. "Do you have an ETA on the coroner's report?"

"Probably by tomorrow," the Sergeant tells me. "Don't be disappointed if it's an accidental death or a suicide. There were no signs of struggle on the body."

I feel a pang of disappointment at the thought. "No one said the victim was depressed or suicidal. She may have been embezzling money from the town treasury, though. That's a possible motive for murder."

"Could be suicide too if she was worried about getting caught," Sergeant Keller suggests.

I begrudgingly agree.

"If it turns out to be a homicide, we will have to call in the forces," Sergeant Keller says gently. "I've put in a request for resourcing with the RCMP Commissioner's office."

My body tightens. Sergeant Keller and I operate on goodwill, borne of a personal relationship. If the full artillery of the Royal Canadian Mounted Police comes in, they will kick me off the case. I need to work fast.

"Did you talk to Aditya Roshan, the airline pilot who flew Sharon home last night?" I ask.

A rhythmic beep interrupts us. It's a call on the other line. I glance at my phone - it's George. "Sergeant, I'll have to call you back. Keep me posted on the coroner's report, please."

I hang up with the Sergeant and turn to George. "That was fast."

"You asked for the discount version," George says. "Alena Krutova is an immigrant from Russia. She arrived in Canada in 2009, little over ten years ago. No criminal record or civil lawsuits. Up until 2015, she lived in Vancouver - had senior roles at BC Children's Hospital, the Vancouver Aquarium, and Science World. She moved to Lake Templeton four years ago - took a job for a charity that works with First Nations communities. She was elected mayor just under three years ago."

"Thanks, buddy," I say. "The only thing on her LinkedIn is her current gig as Mayor of Lake Templeton."

"It seems she's not a fan of self-promotion," George agrees. "She's been nominated for several awards over the years but turned them down."

I contemplate this information while I sip my coffee. Why would Alena work in the not-for-profit sector but turn down the glory that accrues from it? And why run for mayor in a small town like Lake Templeton instead of pursuing a higher profile in Vancouver? Maybe it's the revitalization project. Successful execution would catapult her to the top of the premier's star pupils' list. There's less red tape in a small town. Less opposition. Less pushback. Less bureaucracy.

I need to have another chat with Mayor Alena Krutova. But first, I need to examine Sharon's office and her home.

The police have already been there but they miss things. They're in a rush for results. They want to make a splash for the media. Not me. Like a meticulous craftsman, I take my time. The most important component of a murder investigation is to get to know your victim very, very well.

It's late in the afternoon when I return to City Hall to look through Sharon's office. The tired sun is losing its battle against the slowly rising dark. Its pale light paints tailwinds around the dark clouds that are descending fast, merging into one another, crowding the winter sky.

Alena has changed out of last night's clothes. She is freshly powdered and coiffed, getting ready to give a press conference. Cream slacks suit with soft pinstripes. Kitten heels in luxe patent leather. Hair pinned back, befitting a somber politician addressing her constituents on a shocking story.

A smattering of reporters dots the press room, some idling on their phones and a few staring expectantly at Alena.

Civilians are scattered through the crowd, chattering amongst themselves. An electric hum of activity sizzles the air.

The news of a suspicious death rocking the island town has started to circle the airwaves. Global BC, the biggest regional media company, has picked it up and radio stations across the province are running the story on a repeating loop every fifteen minutes.

I join the disjointed faces spread out across the room. Alena welcomes the crowd with a smile that transforms her face. Her voice is clear and firm, with a calming undertone. Perfectly crafted to win hearts, minds, and votes. She starts talking about the body that washed up on the shores of Lake Templeton.

"At this time, we can share that the victim is Sharon Reese, our beloved neighbor and City Treasurer. The police investigation is underway - they have not yet shared a cause of death, but early indications are that this was a terrible, unfortunate accident."

Accident? My eyebrows shoot up to my hairline at the presumptive statement.

"She told us to keep quiet about the case," someone speaks into my ear.

Startled, I turn to face Marla, City Hall office manager who also oversees reception and serves as Alena's assistant. Marla is a rotund woman, no more than five feet tall. Curly brown hair frames a round face. Split ends stand up in random directions despite the visible deposits of product that stiffen her curls. Marla pushes her black plastic glasses up the bridge of her nose as she regards me with a grave expression.

"Really?" I inquire. "Why?"

"She said it would cause a panic among the townspeople," Marla says in a low, confiding tone.

Or maybe Alena wants to control the situation. Carefully curate the message. Present a facade.

"Does she usually do that?" I say. "Ask you to hide information?"

Marla shakes her head a little too vigorously. "No, of course not. But nothing like this has ever happened before."

"Were you at Alena's birthday party last night?"

Marla seems taken aback at my abrupt question. She nods, tentatively. "Yes, most of us were. Nothing else is happening this time of the year. There's that music show in Otter Lake but that's not for another week."

"Why wasn't the birthday party held at Alena's house?"

"Alena doesn't like having people over at her place."

"Do you know Aditya Roshan, the airline pilot, who flew Sharon back last night?"

"Oh yeah," Marla says. "He's on the City payroll. Flies the mayor and council members all the time. Nice guy - a little weird, though."

I wonder what brought Marla to my side to share secrets. Office gossip or Alena's mole? With a wan smile, I turn away from Marla and back to Alena.

Mayor Krutova is waxing on about the virtues of Sharon Reese and her incalculable value to the Lake Templeton community. Her voice strikes the perfect balance of sorrow, regret, and empathy. She is a leader who will hold the town together as they recover from this unexpected tragedy. She will walk with them, but slightly ahead of them, so she can buttress them from the winds of pain.

"I will keep you apprised on the status of the case, in line with my ongoing commitment to full transparency." Alena closes the call.

A commitment to full transparency. Hardly. I hold back a derisive snort.

Scattered questions arise from the audience in a predictable pattern. The rubbernecker wants lurid details. How long was the body in the water? Are the police sure she wasn't killed on the beach? Was it a jealous lover? Maybe a serial killer? The mother hen wants to know if the town is safe. Will police protection be provided for single women living alone? And the heckler blames it all on the ineffectiveness of the local government.

Shaking my head, I make my way to Alena. She already agreed to let me search Sharon's office - in the interest of full transparency, of course. And I am here to collect on that commitment before she changes her mind.

While Alena wraps up her press conference, I chat with City Hall staff. Twenty minutes later, she ushers me towards Sharon's office.

In a brusque tone, Alena tells me I only have thirty minutes. She has organized a late afternoon team huddle to talk about Sharon's death. A mental health professional has been called. A private investigator loitering around will make people uncomfortable. Hold them back from sharing.

I contemplate pushing back, but ultimately agree. I have a vague suspicion that this is an excuse to brush me off. But protesting would make me appear insensitive, and I need the trust of City Hall staff so I can mine them for information.

Sharon's office is neat and orderly. No errant paper is out of place. Spiral bound documents are organized by type and kept in a locked credenza. City planning records, financial statements, projections, and budgets are collated and organized by date. Permit requests are paper-clipped to their respective approvals. Key correspondence is color-coded by the recipient.

The usual bureaucracy with bloated language that hasn't been changed since the settlers first conquered the native lands and started to form governments.

It immediately strikes me that most of the paperwork makes little reference to the Lake Templeton revitalization project. The three-year financial projections are business-as-usual; expected revenues from the project are not factored in. There are no line items on the 2020 budget for project costs.

The only hint that the project is underway is in the nine-month financial statements as on September 30, 2019. A line item - restricted funds of twenty million earmarked for the project. Investor equity. But the statements are rough drafts; I can tell from the highlighting and the handwritten scribbles in the margins.

There must be a separate folder for the Lake Templeton revitalization project. The project was a prominent part of Sharon's day-to-day routines and performance metrics. And Sharon was meticulous in organizing and retaining information.

Did Alena squirrel away the file after Sharon's death? But why? I suspect she would claim it was to protect the identity of the investors and to safeguard the integrity of the embezzlement audit.

I glance at my watch. Six minutes left until Alena waltzes in on her sky-high heels to show me the door. I lock up the credenza. I will go deeper into the paper trail later.

I turn my attention to Sharon's minimalist physical space. Her desk is uncluttered. The only items on it are her computer, keyboard, and mouse. Nothing else to interrupt her flow. A slate gray scarf hangs at the back of her door, folded over a fawn-colored jacket. A white umbrella with colored stripes is tucked behind the door jamb.

Odd. Sharon's colleagues said she walked to work. She would have put on her jacket and scarf before leaving the office on Friday. It rained that day so she would have taken her umbrella, too.

There are photos mounted on the wall. There's one of a sweating Sharon in shorts and a tee-shirt, at the conclusion of a sole-crushing run. Sharon's colleagues mentioned that she was a marathoner. In another photo, a younger Sharon is dressed in a black ball gown with a modest neckline. Her dark hair is blown out and her face is made up with soft smoky eyes and nude-pink lips. It looks like a formal event, maybe a gala.

I read the inscription. 'YWCA 2009.' Ten years ago.

Sharon is front and center in the photo. Half a dozen people flank her; she's clearly being honored. She holds her award like a bludgeon, looking uncomfortable with the recognition. I make a note on my iPad to do a Google search for the YWCA Gala 2009.

Why was Sharon honored? The YWCA award is for women who have demonstrated outstanding acts of courage. Sharon didn't accomplish anything that noteworthy. Or did she? I have more work to do.

With seconds to go until my thirty minutes are up, Alena strides in. I ask to access Sharon's email and get a glacial look, followed by a curt response. Due to a technical issue, the City's servers are currently unavailable. Undeterred, I tell Alena that I will be back.

Time to head to my next destination - the lakefront lodge where Sharon lived alone.

Sharon's lodge is located a seven-minute drive from City Hall. Forty minutes for a brisk walk or half an hour for a run each way. What demons was she trying to exorcise by working her body to exhaustion every day?

A narrow tree-lined road twirls me around for fifteen minutes before depositing me at the mouth of a dusty pebbled road that opens up abruptly into an expanse of water. The lodge is a solitary structure that rises from the grainy sand and ends in a pier that juts out into the ocean. A small dinghy bobs on the water, tied to a wooden post.

The police have already done a sweep. They found evidence that Sharon plunged off the dock. Scrapes were found matching the heels of her pumps that constricted her bloated, blue-veined feet when she was found.

Why was Sharon wearing heels on the dock last night? She was an avid outdoorswoman. She lived at this lodge for three years. The week's snow hadn't yet melted and last night, exuberant winds brought freezing rain. Sharon would have known the dock was slippery. And dangerous. There was no railing.

And why did Sharon go out on the dock in the first place? It was eleven p.m. Too late for an evening stroll. Did she forget something? Or see something moving outside the window?

Then there's the matter of Sharon's blood alcohol level. If she wasn't drunk, she would have survived. Swam to safety.

There's also the fact that Sharon's body was found wearing a silk blouse and business skirt. Presumably the same outfit she wore to her investor meetings in Vancouver. Why didn't she change out of her work clothes when she got home?

The questions bounce around my brain like ping pong balls as I approach Sharon's house.

The lodge stands on the water, looking forlorn, as if aware that its sole companion is never returning to warm its walls. The chill in the air is deepening as temperatures rapidly drop with the rising darkness. The melodious whistle of the wind blends into the soft slap of waves on the resting shore.

I let myself in through the front door, brushing aside the yellow 'Crime Scene' tape. An artwork of muddy boot prints mars the wooden floors. The police don't clean up after themselves. And Sharon had no one who cared enough to clean up after them. Her colleague, Sergio, was her emergency contact at the health authority.

The lodge is built out of exposed sloped wood. The entrance opens up into a living room decorated with a simple brown leather two-seater sofa and an animal print throw rug. A round analog clock hangs over the 40-inch TV set, reminding me that it's two minutes to six p.m. Every item of furniture stands proud in austerity. Nothing extravagant. Everything basic, functional, and bare bones.

The TV sits on the surface of a low bookshelf stacked with a single row of paperbacks. Curious, I thumb through the books. Someone's choice of reading material can tell you a lot about them.

Sharon liked personal development books. Tomes that offer ground-breaking suggestions for attaining inner peace. Her taste leaned more towards the spiritual than the practical. *Big Magic, The Power of Positive Thinking, The Secret, The Untethered Soul.* I can picture Sharon sitting on her shag rug, cross-legged, cup of herbal tea in hand, lapping up the advice, imagining the 'someday' when things get better.

Was she just a bored personal development junkie? Or was there something clawing at her that she thought these books could fix? Something she could escape by drowning in a bottle?

A title catches my eye. It stands apart, a slap in the face through the sea of serenity. *Should I Swallow the Poison Pill? Survivor Accounts of Escaping Cults.*

I pull out the book. It's a slim hardcover, no more than three hundred pages. The cover is black, typecast in red and white, like a sensationalist newspaper headline. It consists of a messy collage of photos, which look like something mildewy you pull out of an old photo book that has been left in the attic for too long. The author is called Korinne Kendall.

I open the book to find a handwritten inscription inside the title page:

Dear Sharon,

Thank you for being my inspiration for this book. Your story is poignant and unforgettable and I feel honored to be the one to tell it. The world can learn from your strength and courage and I hope that, in a small way, this book will help. You are a dear friend and I feel blessed to have met you.

Love - Korinne.

Did Sharon escape from a cult?

I flip to the inside back cover for the author's photo. Korinne Kendall is a well-groomed, ethnically ambiguous, caramel-skinned woman in her mid-40s. Full lips set in an even expression that looks sultry. Brown eyes pierce through the page, framed by a shoulder-length coif that starts dark at the roots and gradually lightens to wisps of coffee foam. She is wearing heavy makeup and a bright orange front-open shirt that exposes her meager cleavage.

She resembles a Real Housewife more than a writer. I bat away the thought, ashamed that it hopped through my brain.

I shove the book into my shoulder bag. I add 'Google search - Korinne Kendall' to my quickly growing task list on my iPad.

I walk into the kitchen. It's spotless. Light gray cabinetry looks like it's diligently wiped down every day. A well-used stove, a drying rack, a microwave, but no pots or utensils left outside. I open the fridge. A loaf of bread, a brick of cheese, butter, leafy greens, a bunch of carrots, three Tupperware boxes stacked with leftovers towards the back - all well-organized and laid out in a logical arrangement. A carton of milk and two large bottles of apple juice.

I make my way to Sharon's bedroom. As expected, the room lacks personality. A Queen bed is adorned with a bare white sheet and pillowcases.

A down comforter is scrunched up by the foot of the bed, which I assume is the police's doing. All evidence indicates that Sharon was a very tidy person. The bed is flanked by two side tables, one of which has a marble-bottomed reading lamp with a tasseled white shade.

I look through the side table drawers. Old receipts - grocery bills, hardware store, pharmacy. The biggest purchases Sharon made recently were a power tools set, running pants and shoes from Under Armour, and a prescription refill for Ativan, an anti-anxiety medication.

So Sharon suffered from anxiety. Not surprising if she escaped from a cult. But it doesn't jive with the fact that she was drunk the night she died. Sharon was too responsible to mix alcohol and prescription drugs. It's also gnawing at me that I found no alcohol in her home. No wine rack or liquor trolley. No bottle of Jack Daniels hidden inside her pantry.

Sharon's living space embodies a woman with simple tastes. No lavish paintings or high-end furniture. No Persian rugs or luxury cars with titanium wheels. No designer clothes or shoes protected in flannel dust bags.

I am baffled. What would she do with a stolen half a million dollars? If she didn't spend it, where was she hiding it? Banks ask questions about source of funds. If dissatisfied, they would have seized her money, detained her, and called the police.

I make my way to the bathroom. The counters are wiped clean with only a toothbrush and a tube of toothpaste sitting in a holder by the sink. The shower is hidden in a corner behind a polka dotted white curtain. I push aside the curtain to find a tiled wall. A three-tiered caddy hangs over the shower. The shampoo, conditioner, and bar of soap are from a drugstore. It doesn't look like Sharon was a spendthrift in any area of life.

But she was not immune from the universal problem of long-haired women - shedding. I spot a small knot of dark hair in the drain.

There is something else in the drain - something that doesn't belong. A few strands of curly red hair. Unmistakable, very visible red hair. Hair that I saw earlier that day - on Sergio Alvarez, Marketing Manager at City Hall. Sharon's colleague who found her body.

What was Sergio's hair doing in Sharon's shower drain?

CHAPTER 3

Friday, December 13, 2019

Back at the Lakeside Inn, my head is buzzing. I seize my laptop, a woman on a mission. On page four of my Google search on Sharon Reese, the story starts unfurling. Long-buried newspaper stories rear their heads. Puzzle pieces start to join in a recognizable landscape.

Sharon was the sole survivor of the defunct cult, Nation of People.

I vaguely recall the rescue. The story dominated national media for weeks. It was splashed across every newspaper. There were photos of Sharon awash with popping flashbulbs covering her face with her work-worn hands, dark hair strategically positioned to hide behind.

The country wanted more of Sharon. But she was in no mood to give. No TV interviews, no radio appearances, no quotes for local or national newspapers. And then, the media moved on to something else and Sharon gratefully sank back into the shadows. Into obscurity.

She was indoctrinated into the cult at an early age, swept into the madness by her mother, a grieving widow who got caught in the trap of the charismatic, honey-tongued founder, Jefferson Wall. Sharon was seven years old when her mother abandoned her home, defaulted on her mortgage, and stole away in the middle of the night with a shoulder bag and her only child. Personal belongings, including her passport, were left behind. No one could contact her. She and her young daughter became faceless disciples that existed only to please a false god.

The cult resided on a remote corner of the Haida Gwaii Queen Charlotte Islands. And that is where Sharon lived for fifteen years, with no idea that a world existed beyond it.

In 2003, at the age of twenty-two, Sharon left. But you can't call it an escape. She was left standing when all one hundred and seventy-eight followers of the cult committed mass suicide, along with their leader, Jefferson Wall. When the police broke down the doors, Sharon was in an incoherent state - babbling, blinking, and twitching. But she was alive.

In the coming weeks, Sharon struggled to communicate and answer questions. Doctors said she had minor brain damage. The poison that killed her fellow cult members was found in her bloodstream too, but not enough to kill her.

Did Sharon chicken out at the last minute? Did she take a sip of the lemonade instead of downing the whole glass?

No one knew. Not even Sharon. She claimed she couldn't remember.

Sharon only shared inconsequential details about that fatal day at the commune. But she did share what life was like before the suicidal rampage. With Korinne Kendall, eight years after she was liberated.

I pull Korinne's book out of my shoulder bag. The room is inky dark; the only light emanates from my laptop screen. I switch on the table lamp.

It's time to put the author through the digital wringer. I type her name in my Google search bar.

Korinne Kendall was a C list celebrity for several years before she started writing books. She found her fifteen minutes of fame on a reality show, parlayed from a stint as a fitness model. A Google image search shows photo after photo of Korinne, a diminutive, small-boned woman, in revealing bejeweled bikinis, flexing her bloated quads, rock-hard calves, and ropy arms. Her body is shiny with several layers of spray tan and oil and her face is caked with makeup.

Korinne's author website boasts a more demure series of photos. In a cream pantsuit with her balayage lightened hair professionally mussed, bowling ball veneers lined up in a neat row in her toothy, fuchsia smile. In a silk dress with her legs crossed, smoldering at the viewer, bright pink fingertips resting casually on her knee.

Korinne has written three books. The one that sits in my lap is her first - released eight years ago, in 2011. The book has 3.8 stars on Amazon Kindle - unimpressive, really - but over twelve thousand reviews. Whether they liked it or not, people read it. Sensationalist material, voices of cult survivors, the promise of an exclusive scoop, lurid details of lives most haven't lived but are intensely curious about. It was a car wreck, playing on people's deep-seated desire to be horrified.

Korinne's 'About Me' page indicates that she is an author who lives in Vancouver with her fiancé and her dog. She enjoys long walks on Locarno beach.

I click to her 'Contact Me' page. There is a fillable form with an open-text box. No email address or phone number. That's too bad. I am too impatient to send a message into a black hole and await a tardy response that may never come.

I head to social media. Facebook and Instagram are the preferred methods for minor celebrities to share personal details about their lives with fans. I skim through a colorful collage of Korinne's life. Beachy sunsets. Sunrises at Locarno Beach. Korinne with a silver-haired man with a stocky build. Her fiancé. Photos of Lake Templeton - and a cozy, single-story house by the water. One captioned '*Vacation home*'.

And then I find a post that contains the clue I'm looking for.

It's a photo of Korinne and her dog at the beach. Her dog is a milk white, open-mouth Samoyed with fur as pristine as freshly fallen snow.

'On our way to our daily morning walk - grabbed my coffee at Figaro. Need an extra shot of espresso this morning after last night's love from my amazing fans! So humbled.'

In another post several weeks prior, Korinne is holding the same cup of coffee.

'Guys - I highly recommend Figaro. I'm so addicted. It's my favorite spot for my morning coffee. My choice - non-fat caramel vanilla latte. Yum!'

Figaro is a coffee shop located a twenty-minute walk away from Locarno beach. That's where I will track down Korinne. She must live in the area.

I glance at the clock - twelve minutes to one a.m. Time to pack it in and pick it up tomorrow. Begrudgingly, I turn my laptop off. Just a few pages of Korinne's book before I fall asleep.

I plop into bed like a wet rag. I peel off my jacket and kick off my shoes, but I won't bother changing. Sleep is like switching off an overheated phone every few hours to keep it going. Necessary, not fun.

I turn on my bedside lamp and flip to the Table of Contents on Korinne's book, hoping to find a mention of Sharon to guide me to the right page. No luck. The book is a generalized account of the horrors of cult life, interspersed by snippets of interviews from actual cult survivors. But Korinne has anonymized her sources.

My eyelids are getting heavy. The words start to creep into each other. Before I know it, I am asleep.

I snap awake at the sound of my phone screaming in my ear. Sunlight is pushing against the frayed curtains, determined to find its way inside.

What time is it? A glance at my phone shakes me out of my stupor - 10:03 a.m. I slept through my alarm. I must have been out cold.

I swing my feet to the floor. A muscle creaks in complaint in my back. Grumbling, I dial Sergeant Keller.

"Ah - glad I got you," he says. "Coroner's report is back. Cause of death - drowning. No signs of struggle. Given her level of intoxication, we believe she got drunk and fell off her dock. Sorry, Fati. Not what you were hoping to hear, I know."

"I don't buy it," I declare, my voice resolute. "Either she was running away from someone, or they pushed her."

"You've been on the case for a day," Sergeant Keller says. "Why are you so sure?"

"Intuition," I say. "I don't have as many gray hairs as you do but I'm getting there."

"Do you want to tell me what you've found?"

I hesitate. Something holds me back from sharing about the hair I found in Sharon's drain. I have to talk to Sergio first.

"Give me a few more days, Sergeant." I walk to the kitchen, yesterday's socks cushioning the cold marble floor. "Let me sort this out. Don't close the case yet. Please."

The Sergeant sighs, pauses. Then gives in. "Okay fine - three days. Call me and keep me posted on how you're making out."

"Done."

"Remember - I need evidence, Fati," Sergeant Keller reminds me. "Not a hunch. Hard evidence."

"Really, Sergeant? I'm insulted. My time in the academy wasn't *that* long ago."

I switch off.

It's a frigid, sunny day. The snow is hardening and cracking. My tires crunch over gravel as I pull out of the small service road onto the main Island Highway. There is sparse traffic going into town. Most Lake Templeton residents have flown the coop for warmer weather. Every minute or two, a red light slows me down, makes me tap my fingers restlessly against my steering wheel.

After my phone call with the Sergeant, I got a hold of Aditya Roshan, the airline pilot who flew Sharon home the night she died. As luck would have it, he's in town today, and available to chat with me at the Lake Templeton airport. I need to wrap up my business at City Hall quickly.

I arrive a few minutes past eleven a.m. I spot Sergio's car right away, back tires caked with mud. I park my Mazda beside it so I can discreetly peek inside. I consider breaking in and quickly discard the thought. The parking lot is on open ground and although the only human I see is a man with a winter jacket and knit hat walking away in the distance, I don't want to take any chances. Not this early in the case.

The backseat is empty. In the front, scrunched up candy wrappers and a coffee cup sit next to the gearbox. A key chain hangs from the rear-view mirror attached to a season pass for a local ski resort.

At City Hall, there is a small buzz of activity. Marla, the receptionist, is on the phone, talking rapidly, as if narrating a salacious story. A man and a woman are standing by the copier, enthusiastically discussing a hockey game. An older woman in a sweater and knee-length skirt smacks the water cooler as she mutters to herself.

Alena's office is a few steps past reception. The door is ajar. I silently slide past Marla, head held high as if I belong there. She doesn't look at me.

As I approach Alena's office, voices waft out the door. Alena's passionless tone combines with a male voice - it's Sergio. I cannot hear what they're saying. I lean closer - and that's when the rebuke comes like a loving whiplash.

"We can see you, you know." It's Alena.

Sheepish, I push open the door. "Sorry about that. Force of habit, I guess."

"What can we do for you, Ms. Rizvi?"

Alena is dressed in pinstripe slacks that hug her skinny legs in just the right places to make them look lean but not gaunt. A cream silk blouse with an understated gemstone necklace completes the look. Her hair is pulled back into a ponytail. She looks like she just stepped off *Vogue* - office glam edition.

Sergio is wearing jeans and a turtleneck. He looks strained, but cracks a smile as he reaches out to shake my hand.

"I have more questions," I say, taking Sergio's hand.

"My sources in the Sergeant's office suggest that it's an accidental drowning - which is what we told you when we first spoke." Alena cannot keep the triumph from seeping through her voice.

"Now hold on a second. The case isn't closed yet."

Alena raises her shoulder in a half-shrug. Her signature gesture when something doesn't warrant a response.

Sergio jumps in. "Look, Ms. Rizvi..."

"Fati," I correct him.

"Fati…" Sergio continues. "I know you think something's going on here but I promise you - no one wanted Sharon dead. We all liked her."

"But she was embezzling money," I say. "Surely, that raised some ire."

Sergio's smile doesn't waver but it hardens, as if it were bolted on. "No one knew about that besides me and Alena," he says. "And why would we want to kill her? Our necks are on the line. The money's gone. The investors trusted us. Now Sharon's gone and we've no idea what she did with it. We're freaking out over here."

There is a strange undercurrent between Alena and Sergio. They stand apart but slightly leaning into each other. They are not touching but their movements seem coordinated, like one is subconsciously mirroring the other. Could it be the natural camaraderie of two friendly colleagues, the paternalistic warmth of a boss towards her employee, or something more? A clandestine understanding between co-conspirators?

"Are your investors aware that the money has been stolen?" I ask.

Alena turns up her nose. "Of course not." Her voice is a hiss.

"I have to talk to you, Sergio," I say. "Alone."

A sharp glance passes between them. Alena straightens her shoulders, looks me in the eye, and says, "No."

"I was talking to Sergio, not to you," I say, unwavering. "Do you speak on his behalf now?"

Sergio cuts in, looking uncomfortable. "I think what Alena's saying... is that we can talk in front of her. Of course I'm happy to answer your questions. We want to find out what happened as much as you do."

"Do you?" My gaze doesn't stray from Alena. Our eyes are locked in dead heat, neither willing to budge.

Alena crosses her arms. "Of course. What is it you've found, *Ms. Rizvi?*"

Heavy emphasis on my last name, a show of dominance, an obstinate refusal to grant me the familiarity of using my first. She is driving a stake to mark her territory. She will cooperate with me but she will not relent.

I turn to Sergio. "Sergio - this is somewhat sensitive. Are you sure?"

Sergio nods, like a relieved dog wagging its tail to see its owner.

"I found your hair in Sharon's drain," I say flatly, carefully watching his reaction.

His freckles darken against his pale face as the color drains from it.

"How do you know the hair is his?" Alena challenges me, not missing a beat. "Is he the only red-haired person in town?"

"He's the only one I've met," I snap. I turn back to Sergio. "Look, Sergio, I'm sure you didn't mean to hurt Sharon. Please tell me the truth. I'm sure there's a reasonable explanation."

"I didn't hurt her!" Sergio exclaims, looking offended. "Yes - I was at her place. And that *is* my hair."

"You don't have to do this, Sergio." Alena's voice is laden with warning. "I don't see her holding a DNA test."

"It's okay," Sergio says. "I want to tell the truth. I was at Sharon's place. But it's not what you think. See - the thing is, Sharon and I were together. We were... dating."

Alena looks startled. "What are you talking about, Sergio?"

"It's true," Sergio says. "It was very new, so we didn't share with anyone. I was at Sharon's place the night she died. I met her at the airport and drove her home. We had sex, showered, and then I went back to my place."

"And did the two of you drink together?" I ask, trying to wrap my brain around this odd pairing.

"No, we didn't," Sergio says. "I left her place at around nine thirty. Maybe she started drinking after I left."

"Why didn't you stay the night?"

"Sharon was tired," Sergio says. "Her investor meetings in Vancouver didn't go so well. And she had to report back to city council in the morning."

"She didn't want you around to comfort her?"

"As I said, the relationship was very new."

"I see."

"Sharon was a neat-freak." Sergio is starting to ramble. "She liked her things organized in her own way. I'm not like that. I leave my socks on the floor and forget about them. It was better for us to have our own space. Otherwise, we'd just fight."

"Why didn't you tell me the truth yesterday?" I ask. "You must've known I would eventually find out about your relationship with Sharon."

Sergio flushes, avoids my eyes. "I was hoping you wouldn't. No one at City Hall knew. And now that Sharon is gone... I didn't want police to suspect me."

"Because you've seen on TV that the police always suspect the husband or the boyfriend."

Sergio ducks his head in agreement, but stays silent. Several curly red strands fall across his forehead but he makes no move to push them away. I bet most who witness this gesture cannot help but reach out and ruffle his silken hair, as if he were a dog offering his head to be petted.

"Did you tell Sharon about the embezzlement probe?" I ask.

"No, of course not," Sergio asserts. He clenches and unclenches his hands, sees me looking, and relaxes his fingers.

"I trust Sergio," Alena cuts in. "I told him to keep the matter private and I have no doubt he did."

Gratitude flashes across Sergio's face as he looks at Alena.

"Why do you think Sharon stole money from the City?" I ask.

Another cryptic glance between Alena and Sergio. They look at me, Sergio hesitant, Alena guarded.

"We don't know," Alena says. "She never said that she needed money. She lived a very simple life, as I'm sure you are already aware."

"That's right, she did," I agree. "No boats or Maserati's or designer shoes from Holt Renfrew. And I'm having trouble reconciling that with her purported theft of a half a million dollars."

"Maybe she jumped off the pier because she felt guilty," Sergio offers in a helpful tone.

"That won't explain why she stole the money in the first place," I rebut. "Do either of you think it had anything to do with her former cult connections?"

I watch their faces closely. My blunt question is an accusation - why didn't they tell me about Sharon's past?

"I don't think so," Alena says smoothly. "That was a long time ago."

Every word she speaks is invested with her ego. Never wrong. Never apologizing. Never ashamed.

"Sergio - you were dating Sharon," I say. "Did she say or do anything to give you an idea what she planned to do with the money?"

"No, nothing." Sergio shuffles his feet, clasps his hands together, as if to stop their fidgeting.

"Did you initiate the relationship to gather intel on her?" I ask, baldly.

"No way," Sergio says immediately. "I was attracted to her. It happened naturally."

"And you didn't tell Alena about it because you knew she wouldn't approve," I add. "It's clear you two are close."

"I guess so."

"Has Sharon dated anyone else since she moved to Lake Templeton?"

"We can't be sure," Alena responds. "She was a very private person."

"Why did Sharon move here?" I ask. "Her prior experience was in not-for-profit work. Why move to a small town and become a treasurer?"

"I recruited her," Alena says. "I knew her from the non-profit world. She was dedicated and hard-working. I thought she would make a good addition."

"And she was ready to give up the city lights in favor of a quiet life in the sticks."

"She grew up in a cult," Alena states in a matter-of-fact tone. "Life in the city was fascinating for some time, but she was tired of it."

I switch gears. "Let's talk about the Lake Templeton revitalization project. It's critical to your re-election, isn't it, Ms. Krutova?"

"The town is very invested in it, yes," Alena hedges.

"It was a cornerstone of your mayoral campaign," I say. "Your reputation is tied up in it."

"That is why I need to find out what Sharon did with the money," Alena says. "Her death is an inconvenience - for the town and for all of us at City Hall."

"When will the audit be complete?"

Alena raises her shoulder in her signature languid shrug. "They are working on it."

"I'm sure the success of this project will pave the way for an MLA run," I say. "You've hinted at a campaign in the past."

Alena's expression doesn't change. "I have not yet decided whether I will run." She turns to Sergio to bestow a practiced smile. "It depends on when this one is ready to take my reins here in Lake Templeton."

Sergio preens under the praise.

"Oh, so you have a succession plan," I say. "Mayor is a democratically elected post."

"Of course." Alena is indifferent to my insinuation. "I have no control over whether the town chooses Sergio. But I know that under my tutelage, he will be ready to put his best foot forward."

"Everything I've accomplished is because of your guidance, Alena," Sergio gushes.

"I'm curious," I say, turning to Alena. "Why did you come to Lake Templeton to pursue your mayoral aspirations? Why not run in Vancouver?"

"It's hard to get things done in a large city," Alena says dismissively. "Too much bureaucracy."

"Not to mention, way more competition for votes," I add.

Alena offers a curt nod.

"Did Sharon give you an update after her investor meetings in Vancouver?"

"She called me, yes," Alena admits. "She was disappointed. She thought this group was a sure thing. But they did not agree to invest."

"Why not?"

Alena turns up her hands. "Maybe Sharon was off her game. Feeling guilty about embezzling money."

"I would like to review the file for the Lake Templeton revitalization project," I say abruptly. "I didn't see it in Sharon's office yesterday."

Alena bristles at my commanding tone. "How would that help with your investigation?"

"You said Sharon was stealing money from the City," I say patiently. "The project could have something to do with her death."

Strain creeps, unbidden, into Alena's voice. "I can make the file available to you," she says in a clipped tone. "But it will take some time."

"I'd like to see it today," I say, in a tone that brooks no argument. "But before I do that - I have another question for you, Alena."

Alena raises her eyebrows, mouth set.

"Why didn't you go with Sharon to the investor meetings in Vancouver this week?" I ask.

"I had a personal family commitment to attend to," Alena says coldly.

Later, I am seated in Sharon's office with a file folder titled 'Lake Templeton Revitalization Project.' Alena made me wait on a splintered wooden bench at reception for forty minutes. I'm not fussed. Let her have her pound of flesh. Patience is a stock-in-trade of any decent private investigator.

The file seems skinny. I know Alena lightened it before putting it in my outstretched hands. Pulled out the most incriminating information, locked it up, maybe shredded it.

There are details on the financing package for the Lake Templeton revitalization project. It includes bank debt. The borrower is the City of Lake Templeton's corporate partner, a numbered company. The City has provided a guarantee to the Royal Bank as security for the loan. The loan is partially drawn.

That's odd. The project hasn't started. Shovels haven't hit the ground. Only site permitting and initial design work have been completed. So why has the loan already been drawn?

I return the file to Alena with a grateful smile. Her face relaxes when I tell her I am leaving City Hall.

"Who is your next target?" Alena asks, deadpan.

"The airline pilot who flew Sharon home the night she died," I say. "Aditya Roshan."

"Is he in town?" Alena says. "He doesn't live here."

"Yes, he has a flight today," I say. "I talked to him this morning."

"Good." Alena crosses her arms. Sensing that she has had enough of me for the day, I bid goodbye and head to my car.

Suspects can only handle me in small doses. Too much and they collapse under the weight. I apply enough pressure so a suspect makes mistakes but not so much that they close up like a snail under threat. It's much easier to coax them out than to crack their shell.

The Lake Templeton airport is a shipping-container sized box with a vending machine, and a coffee maker that has seen better days. An all-gender bathroom is carved into a corner. A couple of benches provide seating for four people. Aditya meets me in the airplane hangar, a small shed-like structure that can accommodate no more than three mini airplanes.

Aditya Roshan is a tall East-Indian man in his early forties. His white pilot's shirt reveals the physique of someone who stays reasonably active while his small, ill-concealed belly shows that he doesn't hold back from gastronomic delights. His mop top dark hair is starting to pepper with gray. Curly strands flip about in the breeze, some landing in his eyes. He seems oblivious to this irritant. His face is grassed over by dark, five-day stubble and his neatly filed fingernails are chewed at the ends.

Aditya appears preoccupied as he reaches out to shake my hand.

"So, Aditya," I say. "I understand that you flew Sharon to Vancouver for her meeting with investors on Monday and flew her back on Wednesday night. What time did you arrive in Lake Templeton that day?"

"Just after six p.m.," Aditya says. "Our scheduled arrival time was 5:50 p.m. But we ran into some choppy winds."

"I see. And did Sharon leave the airport right after you arrived?"

"She did."

"Was she alone?"

"I don't know," Aditya says. "I didn't see her after she got off on the tarmac. I had paperwork to do."

"And how was her mood that evening?"

Aditya considers my question. "Now that I think about it, she seemed a little tense. I assumed the investor meetings didn't go well."

"Did you ask her about it?"

"No, I didn't. We weren't close."

"But you flew her back and forth to the mainland regularly, did you not?"

"I fly a lot of the senior government people - council members, the mayor," Aditya says. "Sharon didn't talk too much. She was always busy with her paperwork."

"Was she the only person on the plane that day?"

"Yes."

"Mind if I see your flight plan?"

A flash of annoyance crosses Aditya's face. "Sure, I can show it to you. It will confirm what I told you, though."

"Do you usually fly the plane with a single passenger?" I say. "That must get expensive. There's fuel costs, aircraft maintenance, airport fee, and the rest of it."

"I have an exclusive agreement with Lake Templeton."

"Will this exclusive agreement continue once the Lake Templeton revitalization project is complete?"

"I hope so."

"Are you the only shareholder of Pacific Air?"

Aditya's face darkens. "What does that have to do with Sharon's death? Do you want to see my birth certificate too?"

"That won't be necessary." My tone remains cordial. "Is there a CCTV camera at the airport?"

Aditya nods, his scowl starting to fade. He shifts his weight from one foot to the other and clears his throat as if trying to return to equilibrium.

"Mind if I have a look?"

"I don't have it," Aditya says. "You can contact the City to get that footage."

Great. Just what I need. Another trip to City Hall.

"One final question," I say. "Was Sharon drinking during the flight?"

"No," Aditya says. "I don't serve alcohol on my planes."

"She could've slipped a small flask on board."

"Maybe." Aditya scratches the side of his chin. "But I've never seen Sharon drink during a flight."

"Where do you live, Mr. Roshan?" I change track.

The furrows deepen in Aditya's brow. He responds in a blistering tone, "Do you want my home address too? Maybe you can also go and interview my wife."

From even-tempered to combative with the flip of a switch. But I am unfazed.

"I will if I suspect she was in any way connected to Sharon."

"She wasn't," he barks. "I keep my work and private life separate."

"Let me rephrase my question," I say. "You run flights here fairly regularly. Do you always fly back to Vancouver for the night?"

"I fly back most of the time," he says. "Home to my wife." Almost subconsciously, he massages the clearly-new wedding band on his ring finger.

Ah, marriage. Always answerable to someone. No decision made without consultation. The cloying language of 'we.' Erased as a person to become a family unit.

"Do you fly to other cities besides Vancouver and Lake Templeton?"

"Not at this time."

"Are most of your flights for Lake Templeton City staff and council members?" I inquire. "What about leisure travelers?"

"There are *some* leisure travelers," Aditya acknowledges. "But not a lot. The City's been good to me. I started my airline in Nanaimo but Harbor Air owns that route. So, I came here."

"Would you like to expand at some point?"

"I'd like to go back to the big cities," Aditya says. "Nanaimo, Victoria, maybe even Kelowna. But I need more planes for that. And pilots."

"I'd like to return to Vancouver later tonight, if you have room for one more."

Aditya nods. "I've got just one person flying back tonight. It's a four-seater plane so there's lots of room."

I wonder how Aditya covers his costs. I glance at his shoes, my keen eyes picking up the distinctive Prada logo. A popular style among the downtown-dwelling executives I sometimes pal around with. Twelve hundred dollars, at least.

With my travel plans settled, I bid Aditya goodbye, promising to meet him back at the airport in six hours. It's time to hunt down Ms. Korinne Kendall, fitness-model-turned-author - and my next target.

CHAPTER 4

Friday, December 13, 2019

At the hotel, I throw my meager belongings in my overnight bag. I'm an expert at traveling light. People don't notice when you're wearing those nondescript black pants for the third day in a row. And my black boots effortlessly transition from fall to winter to early spring.

I had a frugal childhood plagued by scarcity. Every dollar was revered and knitted together for a rainy day. My mother insisted I only purchase black or brown shoes. We couldn't afford more than two pairs per child - and *'black and brown go with everything.'* My circumstances have changed, but the habit has stuck.

With a couple of hours to go before I meet Aditya at the airport, I put on another coffee pot. The motel brew is gritty and crumbly - but it packs a sucker punch. As my coffee heats and sputters, I open my laptop to search for Aditya Roshan.

I wade through a sea of them spread out all over the world. But there's no airline pilot who lives in Vancouver and owns Pacific Air. Aditya has no Facebook, LinkedIn, Instagram, or Twitter. Is Mr. Roshan a ghost?

The website for Pacific Air looks like it was created by a teenager for a class project. The '*About Us*' page contains a Vancouver address and a phone number, but no details about ownership and management.

There are no Google reviews. It makes sense given Aditya's dismal passenger volumes. The price tag of a Pacific Air flight is eye-popping when compared to the alternative - the ferry. The target market is limited to rushed business travelers and card-carrying members of the one percent. Or a nosy private detective with ulterior motives.

My frustration at Aditya's murky online presence is interrupted by the coffee maker announcing with a shrill beep that my brew is ready. As I pour my coffee, I scroll through my to-do list on my iPad. '*Research YWCA Gala 2009*' immediately jumps out.

I peruse the photo of the gala that I took at Sharon's office. It's likely that Sharon was honored for her courage and bravery in escaping the Nation of People cult. She must have given a speech. Maybe the YWCA has a video or a transcript.

I dial the YWCA Vancouver. A friendly voice picks up on the third ring. She confirms that Sharon was an award recipient in 2009. There's no recording or transcript of her speech but they do have photos in an unlisted page on their website. The employee offers to send me a link via email. Grateful, I give her my email address and hang up.

On my way to the airport, I stop at City Hall. Alena agrees to give me the airport CCTV footage but she isn't going to make it easy.

"It will take me a day or two. I don't have staff today. We are also preparing for Sharon's funeral so I am tied up with that."

"I'm heading back to Vancouver later today," I say. "Is there no way I can see the video right now?"

Is that relief I see on Alena's face? Her poker face slips, very briefly. Within seconds, she is back to her usual, neutral expression.

"Unfortunately not," Alena says. "Are you done with your investigation?"

"Not even close." I deflate her balloon. "I will be back in a day or two. Please have the video ready by then."

Alena nods.

"I'm flying back on Pacific Air with Aditya Roshan," I say. "Is he a good pilot?"

"Yes. That's why we gave him a contract."

"Why *did* you give him a contract?" I ask. "His airline is a one-man show, quite unknown. Surely there were other options."

Alena tightens her lips, clearly irked by my pointless line of questioning. "He was recommended by one of our investors."

With forty minutes to go until my flight, I find a spot at a local coffee shop and crack into Korinne's book. It's a riveting read, written in short snippets and sentences like rubber bullets. I flip through it quickly. Korinne has interviewed several cult escapees. But only one of them was thirty years old at the time and the sole survivor of her cult, which perished eight years prior.

Sharon's story is gripping. Her mother abandoned her shortly after they arrived at the remote commune in the Haida Gwaii Queen Charlotte Islands. She relinquished her daughter's hand without hesitation, as if under a trance. A confused Sharon was shuffled screaming and wailing into a wooden cage where she was kept for two weeks. Twice a day, a stone-faced woman would push a leaky gruel through a trapdoor, ignoring Sharon's dirty fingers that tried to grab at her ankles. This was Sharon's initiation. She was seven years old.

On the ninth day of her confinement, Sharon stopped crying. She drew inwards. At the two week mark, they took her out of the cage, washed her down with cold water, and gave her clean clothes. She was cleansed. Now, she was worthy.

Sharon joined a community of zombies, paralyzed by ideological rigidity. Haunted souls searching for something elusive. They wore simple clothing and grew their own food. No one talked about where they came from. They were there to be reborn.

The cult leader, Jefferson Wall, lived with them like a God among men. When he entered a room, everyone froze in rapt attention. His words were napalm, soothing and irresistible. Several hours every day were spent in prayer, meditating on the leader's sermons. As per the usual cult formula, he had his pick of girls of all ages at the commune.

Alcohol abuse was rampant. They drank moonshine they brewed themselves. Girls as young as eleven were force-fed the brew to dull their senses on nights they had to copulate with the leader. Being drunk was the only way to survive this life. But Sharon never partook, not even once. And no one pushed her.

Sharon escaped the fate of the other young women at the cult. She was never raped by the leader. Instead, she became his sidekick. He took a keen interest in her - groomed her like a daughter. Sometimes slipped her chocolates and let her read the news, which only he had access to.

Maybe it was because she was stronger than the others. The two weeks at the cage affected her differently. She didn't shrink into a sniveling mess. She lengthened, strengthened, and endured. She walked out with her eyes dry and her head held high. At seven years old.

Sharon said she was not privy to the mass suicide plan. I am skeptical. She was the only one at the commune that Jefferson Wall took into his confidence. Why would he have kept this from her?

Sharon said that the poison in her drink was diluted, not as potent as what others took. Maybe Jefferson Wall wanted her to continue his quest, to build a new flock, to carry on his legacy.

Something is niggling at me. Sharon said that she kept her senses during her cult imprisonment by refusing moonshine. She had traumatic associations with alcohol. After leaving the cult, she avoided parties where booze was flowing because alcohol triggered her post traumatic stress disorder.

Was Sharon a teetotaler?

I reach for my iPad in a daze. I see the email from YWCA, containing a link to a web address. I click on it and a mosaic of photos from the YWCA 2009 gala pops up on my screen.

There are photos of the head table from different angles. A couple of familiar faces jump out at me. There's a curvy woman in a bleached blonde pixie cut. It's Lona Mason, the MLA from Vancouver-Fraserview. There's Korinne Kendall, her leathery skin offset by a bright orange off-the-shoulder silk gown.

There are two bottles of wine at the center of the table. Everyone has a glass in front of them, filled with either red or white.

Everyone except for Sharon. Sharon only has a water glass.

I scour photos of the networking reception. In a tapestry of wine glasses, Sharon only holds a glass of water.

It's obvious. Sharon did not drink. Alcohol reminded her of her terrible past. At the compound, it culled the weak from the strong. She had learned to avoid it to survive. None of her colleagues at City Hall ever saw her drink.

So why was her blood alcohol level nearly three times the legal limit the night she died?

My flight back to Vancouver is calm. Aditya is a deft pilot and expertly navigates through the swirling winter air. I don't spill my water even once despite taking large gulps every ten minutes.

The plane is compact with a small cargo hold. The open cockpit has one pilot's seat, snug around Aditya's rangy frame. The passenger space is narrow with limited space to stretch your legs. A black grocery bag is tucked into a corner with a loose pile of plastic water bottles. Maybe to calm the passengers' nerves and soothe their dry throats in inclement weather.

A weather-beaten messenger bag is tucked under the pilot's seat. My feet are almost touching its frayed straps, as I am folded into the passenger seat right behind Aditya. My fellow passenger lists to the other side of the plane, letting out an unbidden snore every few minutes as his head tips back and his eyes drift shut. Several times, he visibly shakes himself awake. But as the plane straightens its wings and achieves cruising altitude, he descends into an unbroken slumber.

Maintaining my even, open-faced expression, I surreptitiously poke the messenger bag with my toe. Its flap shifts to reveal the edge of a cellphone. I shimmy my foot to gently guide the phone out of the bag. Pretending to lean down to grab my water bottle, I grasp the device, careful to maneuver it outside of Aditya's line of sight. A firm press on the home button and the device lights up. It's unlocked. I cannot believe my luck.

This uneventful flight just got a whole lot more interesting.

We arrive in Vancouver at just after eight p.m. The plane touches down on a secluded private airstrip. Swollen clouds are about to burst and empty their bellies. As we exit the plane, Aditya stands at the bottom of the metal stairs, a polite smile on his face, ready to bid us goodbye. He is the picture of solicitous customer service, a solo entrepreneur who wins hearts with a soft touch and a personalized approach. A solo entrepreneur with no online presence.

On a whim, I decide to follow him. When digital tools fail, it's time for some old-fashioned sleuthing.

I left my car at the airport parking lot in Lake Templeton. But any good PI has other spies on speed dial. I call my friend, Zed. He agrees to pick me up at the airport, no questions asked.

I wait for Zed inside the airport gate, keeping a surreptitious eye on Aditya through the window. It will take Aditya time to complete his post-arrival admin and technical logs and to park his plane and lock up. That's enough time for Zed to get here.

Sheets of rain pour down as if from an overhead shower. Fog is building up outside. Aditya is a small, shadowy figure, moving about the side of his plane. An aircraft marshal in a neon green jacket runs over to him. The two chat for a few minutes, then Aditya climbs back into his plane. The plane lights up and starts taxiing backward. Transfixed on the dark, shape shifting landscape, I lose track of time.

I know that Zed has arrived when he sneaks up and grabs my arm. I don't flinch.

"Good, you're here," I say, without shifting my gaze from the blob floating towards the exit. "He should be coming back any time now. He already parked the plane."

"Well, hello to you too," Zed says with a sniff.

I turn to look at him. Zed is a lanky, lantern-eyed young man in his late twenties with a buzz cut and silver half moon earrings glinting on his lobes. His left eyebrow is pierced with a barrel running through it, a laser pattern shaved through the light brown hair. Expressive blue eyes burn bright with intelligence and a naughty-schoolboy zest for life. Skinny jeans rest low on his hip bones, held up by a shiny leather belt. Gucci. Zed has expensive tastes.

I ran into him on a case several years ago. He was twenty-five but looked fifteen. Initially, I dismissed him as a child playing in adult clothing. But he surprised me.

Zed is witty and has an unusual way with people. While I am to-the-point and often gruff, Zed is a charmer. Although he can be a bit of a bumbling fool at times, he has an endearing quality about him. And he's unafraid to take risks. He's still finding his footing as a PI but he makes tens of thousands of dollars playing video games on YouTube.

I smile an obligatory smile. "Hello, Zed. Thank you for coming. Now let's go and wait for him in the car."

"You know what kind of car he drives?"

I look at him as if he has asked me whether the rain outside is actually snow. "Of course. I swiped his phone during the flight to have a quick look through his photos."

"Of course you did."

Zed drives a yellow Mini Cooper. I have told him many times he should consider replacing it with something forgettable like a black sedan, but he doesn't listen. The Mini Cooper reflects his personality and is easy to maneuver through tight spaces and between cars on a road chase.

I'm never going to lose a suspect because I'm stuck behind a school bus turning left, Zed says.

I scour the parking lot and see Aditya's Ford Escape SUV parked in the overnight parking section. Zed and I huddle in his Mini Cooper, which is hard to do given its size. Thankfully, the rain gushing from the star-less sky gives us natural cover.

Visibility is minimal. Not a bad thing for PIs on a stakeout. In most cases, we have a keener eye than our suspects. But Aditya is an airline pilot, and a damned good one. He could fly fighter planes if he chooses, with his steady hand and lake water calm nerves. But we have an advantage. Aditya doesn't know that we're waiting for him, crouched under the low ceiling of Zed's Mini Cooper, foot hovering over gas, ready to follow.

"So why are we following this man?" Zed asks. "And who is he?"

"He's connected to this new case I'm working - a murder in Lake Templeton."

"Is he a suspect?"

I consider the question. "Not exactly. But I'm at the stage where everyone is a suspect."

Zed rubs his hands together as if about to dig into a succulent tomahawk steak. "I love that stage. It's so full of possibility. Motive?"

"His airline has an exclusive contract with Lake Templeton - no other airlines can operate there," I say. "They're working on a big project to revitalize the waterfront, create better roads, more restaurants and amenities, a new resort, the whole bit. They want to make it a tourist mecca. This could mean big money for Aditya. He can hire more people, buy more planes, add new routes. The murder victim is suspected of embezzling money from this project."

"Worthy of a soap opera!" Zed shifts in his seat, pulling out a crumpled cigarette packet from his pants pocket.

I crinkle my nose as Zed flicks his lighter and a nuclear cloud of smoke fills the air.

"So you swiped the pilot's phone during the flight," Zed says. "What else did you find?"

"Photos of his wife and his home, stuff like that. I didn't have much time."

"Anything interesting?"

"His wife looked oddly familiar," I say. "But I can't put my finger on where I've seen her before."

We follow Aditya, hanging several car distances behind. It's Friday evening in Vancouver, after seven p.m. Traffic is light as we leave the airport but steadily builds as we approach the city. We drive through blinking yellow to red to green lights, tracking Aditya like trained bloodhounds. He appears to be making his way to downtown Vancouver.

His car crests Cambie Bridge, which connects the Vancouver mainland to the downtown peninsula. Rolling off the bridge, Aditya switches on his left turn signal. He gets off the ramp and starts moving towards the Yaletown marina.

Yaletown is a trendy community spotted with tall residential towers and older townhomes in odd shapes, guarding over buzzy artisanal restaurants with in-demand patios and long wait times. The urban sprawl looks out over the famed Vancouver seawall where, even in pouring rain, you find stalwart runners, dog walkers, and couples snuggling under large umbrellas.

"Does he live in Yaletown?" Zed asks.

"It didn't look that way from his photos," I say. "There was a big, fancy house. I was thinking West Vancouver or maybe Point Grey."

"Maybe he's here to see a friend." Zed takes a long drag of his cigarette and plumes out a stream of smoke. One arm hangs outside the open window of his car.

"Maybe. But he was going on and on about how he can't wait to get home to his wife."

Zed rolls his eyes. "Newlyweds?"

"You got it."

I wouldn't know anything about the glow of love that envelops bright-eyed hopefuls as they embark upon what they foolishly believe is happily ever after. The closest I've come to being married is cohabiting with a casual college boyfriend for three months to save rent. When he started pestering me about holding hands in public, I broke up with him and started charging to solve cases.

Through the spotty windshield, I see Aditya turning left into Cooperage Way, a small lane with access to underground parking for two residential towers. Nestled between the towers is Cooper's Park, a small green space with a few benches and a children's play area with a see-saw, a slide, and monkey bars. Alongside the road, there are three spots for street parking, one of them empty. Aditya parallel parks with ease in a fluid motion, lining his wheels up perfectly with the sidewalk. The car lights turn off.

"There's no place to park." Zed's voice is a furious whisper. "We can't go into underground parking. What do we do?"

"You wait here." I unbuckle my seatbelt. "I'm going to follow him."

"Oh no, you're not!" Zed exclaims, swiftly unbuckling his own belt. "*I'm* going to follow him. Switch with me. He knows what you look like. But he hasn't seen me."

Zed is right. I roll over to the driver's side as he slips out of the car, silent and stealthy like a shadow merging into a moving body as it turns a corner. He's made for this work. There are few people I've met after fifteen years in the business that I trust as much as Zed.

I peer through the window. Aditya is pacing on the wet grass of Cooper's Park, ear glued to his phone. He balances an umbrella over his head with one hand. His movements are nervous and jittery. He's waiting for someone.

And then, a new figure appears, slipping out of the lit foyer of one of the apartment buildings. He's far and it's wet so all I see is that it's a tall man with a loping gait, wearing glasses. He walks towards Aditya with casual confidence, making no effort to hide.

It's going down! Whatever '*it*' is. But where the hell is Zed?

Aditya and the man start talking, heads together. While Aditya paces in place, the other man appears relaxed. I gulp down air electrified with possibility.

Is it a friend? If it is, why does Aditya seem so anxious? And why are they meeting in the pouring rain in a dark corner of a semi-public park?

Aditya is reaching into his pocket. The other man reaches into his. They shake hands. Something is exchanged. My eyebrows shoot up like a drop tower in an amusement park.

A drug deal?

Suddenly, a third figure bumps into them, sideswiping like an errant golf club. It's another man, smaller than Aditya and the stranger. It's Zed.

Aditya and the stranger jump back, startled. Zed breaks out in exaggerated, apologetic gestures, reaches out to touch Aditya's arm, brushes across his jacket pocket.

What is he doing? I sink deeper into my seat. *Please don't get us caught, Zed.*

The next few minutes tick by like drops of sand in an hourglass. And then, Zed appears. I blink and he's sitting in the passenger seat, murmuring, first softly then with increasing urgency.

"Drive, drive, drive!"

Without another word, I drive. I don't look back to see what Aditya is doing or whether he is following us. We are on the Cambie bridge heading out of downtown when Zed turns to me and grins. "So you wouldn't believe what happened."

I look at him. "Try me."

Zed reaches into his pocket, pulls out something, and holds it up between two fingers. It's a small plastic baggie, half filled with crystalline white powder. "Looks like cocaine but can be something else. MDMA, GHB, PCP. Something fun for me to partake in tonight."

"Give me that!" I swipe at it like a cat batting at a furball.

"Not a chance," Zed says. "I can tell you what it is tomorrow morning."

"How nice of you."

"Well, what else are you going to do with it?" Zed says. "Have it sent in for testing? You know this isn't admissible in any court of law. My methods aren't exactly 'officially approved.'"

"You better believe I will have it sent in for testing!" I look at Zed as if he is an unruly child with his hand stuck in the cookie jar.

"I thought you might say that," Zed says in a matter-of-fact tone. He opens up a fist to reveal another baggie in his palm. "That's why I grabbed a couple!"

I chuckle. "I suppose you've earned it after making yourself available on short notice tonight. I won't bother reminding you that you have no idea what's in that powder and whether or not it can kill you."

Zed smiles, broadly. "I love surprises."

I shake my head and wonder how Zed has kept himself alive for twenty-eight years. We crawl through traffic, every light popped to red by Saturday night partygoers pealing in enthusiasm, taking their time swaying across pedestrian crossings, while drivers look on in annoyance.

"Did you get a look at the other guy?" I ask.

"Yeah, a little bit." An exaggerated shudder. "Big ugly neck tattoo. Short blonde hair, standing up in ends. It was dark so I didn't see his face clearly. Don't put me in front of a sketch artist!"

"You did pretty good."

"Who are you calling?" Zed opens the baggie and touches the tip of his tongue to the corrugated opening.

"Sergeant Keller." One hand on the wheel, my other flickers over the glowing screen on my lap. "Keep an eye out for cops, please. If I get busted for distracted driving, they'll see the drugs and then, we'll *really* be in trouble."

Sergeant Keller steps away from dinner with his family to talk to me. I fill him in on the events of the day, holding back the information about Zed's stolen goods.

"When are you getting Sharon's tox screen back?" I ask, knowing one wasn't ordered. "I have a feeling you will find cocaine or some designer drug in her system. That would explain everything, Sergeant! Sharon didn't drink - it's how she survived the cult. Someone drugged her before they pumped her full of alcohol!"

"I can talk to the coroner about a tox screen. It can take up to a week…"

"Do it, please. And until we get the results, we can't rule this an accident."

Alena won't be pleased. I get perverse pleasure at the thought.

Sergeant Keller agrees and I hang up.

My thoughts are racing, bumping into each other like go-karts.

Did Aditya slip Sharon the drugs during the flight? Or was someone else involved? If Sharon ingested the drugs on the plane, the airport CCTV footage will show her tottering out, maybe aided by someone, or even being carried. If Sergio took her home from the airport, he would've known something wasn't right. And who was the man that Aditya met at Cooper's Park?

Sharon did not drink and nothing in my investigations hinted that she took drugs. Not to mention she was taking Ativan. The mysterious white powder, whatever it is, must have hit her like a cement drum. A drugged Sharon would have been easy to push off the dock. There was no railing to break her fall. A practiced swimmer, she was incapacitated to the point where she couldn't flap her arms and legs to save herself as her lungs filled with water.

If Aditya is our culprit, his most likely motive is the Lake Templeton revitalization project. The project has the potential to transform the forgettable town into a tourism magnet. A luxury five-star resort overlooking the water, gleaming bump-free roads that grip your tires, a refreshed waterfront with a renovated pier, freshly potted plants in a cornucopia of colors in newly built nature spaces, a new art gallery and aquarium, sailing and snorkeling adventures, new restaurants, and so much more.

New leisure travelers will flock to the town. So will business executives on retreats with company expense accounts. A fresh new market for Aditya and his overpriced four-seater private flights. He could even launch aerial tours of Lake Templeton. Charge at least two hundred dollars for twenty minutes in the air. Target foreign vacationers who wouldn't realize they're being fleeced.

Aditya is relying on the Lake Templeton revitalization project to supercharge his business. And Sharon's theft had the potential to bring it to a halt.

But what purpose did the murder serve? The money was gone. If Aditya's objective was to get it back, he should've kept Sharon alive to interrogate, blackmail, or strongarm her.

Maybe Aditya did not want to kill Sharon when he gave her his black-market drugs. Maybe they were meant to be a truth serum, to get Sharon to talk. But then, how did Sharon end up dead? What went wrong?

Unless...

Maybe Sharon did not steal the money at all. Maybe Aditya stole it. And framed Sharon. And she found out, so he killed her.

Zed interrupts my reverie by snapping two fingers in front of my face. "Are you alive? You're driving fine but I'm not sure."

I look at Zed as if seeing him for the first time. "I must get my hands on Aditya's company financials. I need to know how deep underwater he is."

"I can help you break into his office tomorrow," Zed says eagerly.

Another thought hits me. "If Aditya only purchased the drugs to poison Sharon, what the hell was he doing here tonight picking up more? He must be dealing drugs to pad his wallet."

"Maybe Sharon found out he was dealing drugs and threatened to tell," Zed says. "This wife he was gushing about - maybe she didn't know and the pilot guy wanted to make sure she never found out."

"That's a good thought," I say. "It could be as simple as that. Maybe this has nothing to do with the Lake Templeton revitalization project." I drum my fingers on the steering wheel, waiting for the light to turn green. "The CCTV footage from the airport will make things clearer. It will tell me whether Sharon ingested the drugs on the plane."

"When do you get access to that?"

"Soon," I say. "Should we go to your place?" Zed lives in Richmond, a twenty-minute drive from Vancouver, on a third-floor apartment close to a subway station. "I'm staying with you tonight to chaperone your drug taking."

CHAPTER 5

Saturday, December 14, 2019

It's a hazy Vancouver morning and I am ready to hunt down Korinne Kendall at her favourite coffee shop. I wait outside Figaro, five minutes before it opens at eight a.m. With the overcast weather, there's barely anyone around, besides the odd restaurateur straightening chairs, getting ready for opening.

I already grabbed my coffee at Starbucks. I sip at the sharp brew - extra dark. It warms my chest and starts to awaken the tired nerves around my eyes.

It was a long night. Zed's trip kept me awake for most of it. He was still in bed when I left this morning, passed out flat on his back, mouth open. We now know the white powder definitely isn't cocaine. But I won't get the lab report until later today or tomorrow.

After an initial period of rabbit-like euphoria, Zed settled into a serene, floaty calm. The happy-as-a-clam smile never left his face. *Like walking barefoot on a sparkly rainbow*, he said. At one point, he could hear the owls singing on his family farm.

I am certain Sharon took the drugs unknowingly. She grew up in a pressure cooker. She didn't survive the cult by letting people talk her into things she had to avoid to stay alive.

My thoughts are interrupted by the arrival of Korinne Kendall, ombre hair pulled into a neat ponytail. She is dressed in head-to-toe Lululemon, the snug fabric bandaging firm calves, sinewy arms, and cat-like proportions. Her puppy is as pristine white as newly unwrapped bedsheets. She must have a standing reservation at the doggy day spa. The dog yaps softly at Korinne's heels, bouncing up and down in perfectly behaved enthusiasm.

As Korinne disappears into the coffee shop, I take one last swig from my lukewarm Starbucks cup and reach for my door handle. It's showtime.

I enter the low-lit coffee shop. Korinne is at the counter, grinning her toothy smile, tapping her credit card on the machine. Her dog pulls at its leash as it sniffs at the heels of the only other patron, engrossed in a book. Korinne slides her credit card into an invisible pocket in her windbreaker, and pulls out an iPhone. She punches in her pin code and my keen eyes quickly capture it and imprint it on my brain.

I make my way to her. "Hello, Korinne. Ms. Korinne Kendall?"

She looks at me, startled. My dark brown eyes collide with her lighter orbs. Her eyebrows rise but her forehead moves only slightly - a pretty good Botox job, no doubt. Her lean face splits into an automatic, polite smile that indents her cheeks and exposes unnaturally white veneers.

"Yes... Do I know you?"

Maybe she thinks I'm a fan.

"No," I say. "But I know you. I read your book last night - the one about the cults."

Her guarded smile relaxes slightly. "Oh yes, that was the first book I wrote. What did you think? Did you enjoy it?"

"It was a fascinating read!" I say. "I blew through the whole thing in one night. What inspired you to write it?"

Korinne places one hand across her chest and tilts her head thoughtfully, opening up into an answer she has probably practiced in the mirror dozens of times. "I've always been interested in the subject. I had the privilege to meet a few incredibly brave survivors that opened up to me and trusted me enough to share their story. I was so moved by these stories, I simply had to share them with the world."

"And one of these cult survivors was Ms. Sharon Reese of Lake Templeton."

Korinne looks at me as if I have flicked her across her smooth forehead. She recovers quickly. "Unfortunately, I cannot share the names of my sources." She glances at the barista who is foaming her coffee mug. "Well then, it was nice chatting with you but I must be on my way."

"Are you aware that Ms. Sharon Reese was killed earlier this week?"

Korinne rocks back on her heels. Genuine surprise floods her face. "What are you talking about? And who are you, really?"

"Oh, I apologize - I did not introduce myself." I stick out my hand. "My name is Fati Rizvi. I'm a private investigator hired by the police to find out who killed Sharon."

Okay, so it's a small fib. The police didn't hire me as much as begrudgingly allowed me to insert myself into the investigation. But I have a feeling that Korinne won't talk to me unless she could place me in a more official capacity.

Korinne takes my hand as if in a dream. I meet her loose, fumbled grip. Her fingernails are short and filed into rounded squares. Apropos for someone who clacks away on a keyboard all day. They're painted fuchsia, the lacquer freshly applied and chip-free.

"Sharon is dead?" Korinne's voice is a weak, uncertain whisper. She clears her throat, clearly trying to compose herself. "What happened?"

"Why don't we sit down? Can I grab your coffee for you?"

Korinne nods, sinking into the nearest chair. I go to the counter to grab Korinne's latte and return to find her sitting, deflated. On her Botoxed face, her anguish looks like mild annoyance.

"What happened?" she asks again, as I take a seat opposite her, pulling out my iPad.

"Her body was found washed up on the shore. She drowned."

"Drowned? Sharon is a fantastic swimmer!"

"She was intoxicated when she fell," I share. "The alcohol blunted her senses - that's why she couldn't save herself."

"Intoxicated?" Korinne stares at me in bafflement. "Are we talking about the same person? Sharon does not drink!"

"I'm aware." So my hunch was correct. "What do you think could have happened?"

"I - I don't know," Korinne draws a heavy breath.

"How did you know Sharon?"

Korinne takes a small sip from her coffee, a bead pearling on her bottom lip. "I met her at the YWCA gala ten years ago. She moved to Lake Templeton on my recommendation."

"You lived at Lake Templeton? How long ago was that?"

"I've owned a vacation home there for ten years now," Korinne says. "It's great when I'm working on a book and need privacy."

"So you met Sharon in 2009 and the two of you became close," I say. "But she only moved to Lake Templeton in 2016, seven years after you first met. Why did it take her so long?"

"She needed a job," Korinne says, as if stating the obvious. "When the Treasurer position came up with the City, I immediately called Sharon. I knew it would be a great fit for her. Happy coincidence - Sharon already knew the mayor, Alena Krutova. From some volunteer work she did for BC Children's Hospital. This was right around the time Alena was elected and started building her team. It all came together beautifully."

"What were Sharon's qualifications for this role?"

"I wouldn't think she was the *most* qualified candidate for the role," Korinne says. "But she *was* the only one willing to move to Lake Templeton. Sharon took some night classes in Accounting and Finance after she left the cult. She enjoyed numbers. Black and white with one right answer, she said."

"Do you know why Sharon never married or had children?"

Korinne gives me an admonishing look, as if I am a grounded child asking to go to a birthday party. "It's because of her past. The cult. She never learned how to form healthy relationships, the poor thing."

"Do you know what will happen with Sharon's home and other assets?" I say. "There's no one to inherit them."

Korinne takes a deep breath. "She had a will, I believe. She said she wanted it all to go to charity. Sharon *really* wanted to give back."

"Why did she agree to give you an exclusive for your book?" I say. "Sharon never gave interviews before. How did you convince her?"

"She was ready to talk," Korinne says. "We connected. She trusted me. And I promised her anonymity."

"But you weren't even a published author at the time," I remind her. "This was your first book."

Frustration creeps into Korinne's voice. "Yes, but I was *ready* to write a book. I told Sharon that. I didn't know what topic. But after we spoke, I knew."

"Can you think of anyone who wanted to hurt Sharon?"

"No!" Korinne says immediately. "I can't believe it. I really can't."

"So you think her death was an accident?"

"I don't know!" Korinne throws up her hands, nearly knocking her coffee off the table. Instinct kicking in, I grab the cup to prevent spillage.

"I'm sorry about that." Korinne folds her hands back on her lap. She is clearly struggling to maintain her composure.

I ignore her mini outburst and it seems to put her at ease. "When was the last time you talked to Sharon?"

"It's been weeks," Korinne says. "We talked about grabbing lunch next time she came to Vancouver."

"She was in Vancouver the day she was murdered."

Korinne looks surprised. "That's odd. We always met when she came to Vancouver. At least for coffee if not lunch."

"Did Sharon mention anything to you about the Lake Templeton revitalization project?"

"Yes she did, she was quite excited about it," Korinne says. "She was pitching to a lot of prominent investors. Sharon was kind of an introvert but she was really enjoying raising money for this project."

"Why is that?" I ask. "A fundraising role seems like an odd choice for an introvert."

"Yes," Korinne agrees. "I think Sharon was living in her shell for so long that this was a nice change for her. She was discovering new skills she didn't even know she had."

Like a butterfly unfurling its wings for the first time.

"Did she mention the names of any of these prominent investors?"

Korinne considers my question. "Well - she *did* ask me for referrals through my network. My fiancé is a... he has his own business. He knows people. I connected her to him. I think he made a few introductions."

"How long have you and your fiancé been engaged?" I ask, glancing down at her ring finger, which sports a weighty cushion-cut rock. At least four carats.

"Not that it's any of your business but we're long haulers. We may never get married."

Sensing her closing off, I change tack. "Do you know who your fiancé introduced to Sharon?"

"Oh gosh - the only person I can think of is Lona Mason," Korinne says. "And that's just because we move in the same circles."

"Lona Mason? The MLA from Vancouver Fraserview?"

This is the second time that name has come up. Lona is the same legislative assembly member who was reacting to Alena's Twitter posts promoting the Lake Templeton revitalization project.

"You know her?"

"Well, I'm a voter. I've heard of her. Did she invest in the project?"

"I don't know," Korinne says. "You'll have to ask her. But knowing Lona, she's always on the hunt for a good place to park her money. She's a shrewd investor. Very smart woman."

I pull out my iPad and jot down Lona's name, carefully, in clean block letters. "How much do you know about the progress of this project?"

"Not too much."

"What was your overall impression of Sharon? Was she an honest and forthright person?"

Korinne looks puzzled. "Yes, of course. Well, she was a reserved person, of course. Didn't share too much about her private life with anyone. I mean, she opened up to *me*. But with other people...I don't know. She mostly kept to herself. Only shared what she wanted to share. I think she enjoyed being alone."

"Do you know if she was dating anyone?"

"No," Korinne says, in a dubious tone, as if she finds the idea implausible. "If she was, she never mentioned it."

"Would it surprise you if she were?"

"Well - yes!" Korinne says. "Sharon had no interest in romance. I don't even know if she liked men. Although she gave no indication of liking women, either, I suppose. I always thought she had an attachment disorder of some kind. Not surprising, given her cult background."

No one in Sharon's orbit had any inkling of her mysterious relationship with Sergio. As hard as I try, I can't visualize them together either. I superimpose his bullpen of a house with Sharon's spotless living quarters. His bubbly chatter with her composed calm. What did they have in common? They couldn't be more different.

"What did she do for fun?" I ask.

"She enjoyed the outdoors," Korinne says. "She was a runner. Always training for the next marathon."

"And did she run alone?"

"Mostly," Korinne says. "Although last time I met her, she mentioned she started running with some guy at the office - in the marketing department, I think."

Sergio. Maybe those early morning runs sparked the flame between them that grew into a clandestine relationship.

"Her time in the cult was understandably quite stressful. Do you know of any psychological issues she struggled with as a result?" I am curious whether Korinne knows anything about Sharon's Ativan prescription.

"She had anxiety," Korinne says. "But can you really blame her? If any of us experienced what she did..."

"I read your book," I say. "Abuse and brainwashing, days without food - it's scary stuff. Is there anything she shared with you about her time in the cult that isn't in your book?"

Korinne shakes her head. "I stand by the integrity of my narrative. I told the story exactly the way Sharon wanted it to be told."

"Since you knew Sharon so well, you must know that she was being investigated for embezzling money from the Lake Templeton revitalization project."

I can't help myself. Oh well - I will happily face Alena's wrath later for my flapping lips.

Korinne looks at me blankly. "What are you talking about?"

"The Lake Templeton mayor suspects that Sharon was stealing money from the project."

"Nonsense," Korinne says dismissively. "Alena is out of her mind."

"So you know Alena?"

"Everyone knows Alena. I've owned property there for ten years."

"Why do you think Alena suspects Sharon of embezzling money?"

"She probably stole it herself," Korinne says. "And now she's trying to shift the blame."

"Why do you think that?"

"Because I don't trust her," Korinne says. "She hasn't exactly been transparent with the residents on the status of the project. She only shares what she wants to share. She hides as much as she can get away with."

"Thank you for your time." I click my iPad closed and slide it into my bag. "I may reach out to you again if I have more questions. Can I get your phone number? That may be easier than trying to hunt you down on your morning run."

Korinne recites it automatically. As I slip out the door and start walking towards my car, I look back and see her sitting there, motionless, like a stone statue, staring out the window, a faraway look in her eyes. Her dog is nipping at her heels, emitting an increasingly insistent bark but she ignores it, lost in thought.

That afternoon, I run down my list of pending tasks. Lona Mason dangles like a hangnail. Despite several calls to her office, I am unable to book a meeting. I would set up camp at her office but her assistant assured me that Lona is out of town.

It's not surprising that Lona is hard to pin down. She's visibly a very busy woman. She flashes across my screen a little too often in various media appearances. Always a bold opinion to share, never hesitating to weigh in on a contentious issue. But unfailingly committed to her blueblood, old Canadian values of staunch conservatism. Just the right amount of sass without too much controversy.

There are knots to untangle with Aditya and his drug deal. I also need to meet his wife and learn more about their life. But it's more pressing to return to Lake Templeton before Alena destroys the airport CCTV footage.

I can kill two birds with one stone by hitching a ride back with Aditya. In the dead of winter, Lake Templeton is a ghost town. Odds are I will be the only passenger on the flight, which means we can have a nice, intimate chat. It will cost me eight times as much as the ferry but it's worth it.

I'm really racking up the bills on this case. Thankfully, my last one paid quite well. That one was for the money. This one is just for me. I feel like the jet-setting idle rich. Quite a feat for a Muslim girl from a working-class immigrant family in Abbotsford.

Aditya takes my call in his usual easy tone. I breathe a sigh of relief, reassured that he doesn't suspect I was following him and saw his drug deal go down. He tells me he plans to fly to Lake Templeton in the morning - eight a.m. sharp. I will be ready.

Sunday, December 15, 2019

The next morning, I arrive at the airport, feeling buoyant, fresh cup of Starbucks Venti dark roast in hand, wearing a freshly pressed button-down. My shoulder-length hair is freshly-washed, static ends clouding around my head. I must find time for a haircut as soon as this case is over.

Aditya smiles when he sees me, a disarming twist of the lips that transforms his face. "Hello, Fati."

Why is he being so friendly? A great night spent in his wife's arms - or something more?

"Hello, Aditya." I return his smile with gusto. "How was your evening?"

"Great," he says. "My wife was thrilled to have me home for a whole day."

"Did you get married recently?" I ask casually.

He nods. "Yes, I did. Her name is Kim."

I settle into my corner of Aditya's four-seater plane. We loiter on the runway for some time as Aditya shoots multiple glances at his watch, clearly waiting for someone. Thankfully, that person doesn't arrive. Five minutes past the scheduled flight time, Aditya shuts the door, grumbles something to the air traffic controller on the garbled radio, and prepares for flight.

"How did you and Kim meet?" I ask, as the plane straightens its wings into the propelling wind.

"A friend introduced us," Aditya says.

"Were you dating for a long time before you got engaged?"

"Thankfully, no." Aditya chuckles. "We both knew right away we were meant to be together. I proposed after six months of dating."

Time for a gently angled curveball. "Did you grow up in Vancouver, Aditya?"

"No, I did not." Aditya's smile vacillates to a glower. "As a visible minority yourself, I'm surprised you would ask me such a question."

Whoa! That sounds like a sore spot.

"I didn't mean it like that," I say, in a pacifying tone. "Just making conversation." It's time to ease up on the interrogation. I look out the window with a half-smile, ignoring Aditya.

As I expected, after several minutes, Aditya speaks up. People cannot help but fill uncomfortable silences. It's basic human psychology. It never fails.

"I'm sorry," he says. "Force of habit. My wife is white. She has some fancy friends that have never accepted me - let's be honest, they never will."

"I hope you don't think of me as 'fancy'," I say easily. "I'm wearing the same pants you dropped me off in."

Aditya laughs. "I didn't notice."

"I *was* born here," I share. "But my family wasn't exactly part of high society. My parents are immigrants from Pakistan. They came here in the eighties. My mother was pregnant with me at the time. She barely spoke English. My father was a successful banker in Karachi but couldn't even get a job as a teller here. And so, he worked as a cashier at the supermarket for many years."

"Your story reminds me of so many others I've heard," Aditya says. "Vancouver wasn't great for immigrants forty years ago."

"No, it wasn't," I agree. "And my parents are Muslims. They didn't fit in with the Hindu and Sikh communities, either. But they found their place eventually. We Rizvi's are a scrappy bunch."

"Things have changed today," Aditya says. "I have lots of Muslim friends. We are all one and the same - as far as the *goras* are concerned anyway."

So now we are bantering in our native language. By referring to white people as *goras*, Aditya has put us in the same camp. We are part of the same brotherhood. It's us versus them. Good. He's exactly where I want him.

"There must be a lot of *goras* in your circle - with your wife, I mean."

"Yes," he says, noncommittal.

"So you emigrated here from India?"

"Yes, I did," Aditya says. "Fifteen years ago."

"What brought you here?"

"School. I enrolled in an MBA program."

"Which MBA program did you take?"

"The University of British Columbia Sauder program."

Jackpot. The Dean at UBC is a good friend of mine. He would have information on Aditya Roshan. Aditya's classmates would remember him. I make a mental note.

"Did you always want to be a pilot?"

"I did my pilot training in India," Aditya says. "After I finished my engineering degree. But I always wanted to own my own airline so I took the MBA program to learn business."

"You should be very proud of what you've accomplished in Canada."

"Yes, I am," Aditya says. "It wasn't easy. It takes a lot of money to start an airline. My parents always said - I love to choose the hard path."

"It's a big undertaking, I'm sure!" I say. "I hope you had *some* help."

"Yes, it was tough. My parents lent me some money. But I couldn't have done it without my generous investor..." Aditya cuts off abruptly, maybe realizing he's revealed too much.

Now is not the time to probe the identity of this 'generous investor.' I add the tidbit to my mental note on Aditya, feeling crabby that I cannot open my iPad to write it down.

"Most of us have help to get to where we are," I say. "I did too."

Aditya's shoulders visibly relax. He sounds relieved at the opening I have given him to change the topic. "Did you always want to be a detective?"

"Oh yes," I say. "It started with reading detective stories when I was a child. At one point, I wanted to marry Sherlock Holmes! My parents thought I was crazy. They insisted I go to school to get a degree in something practical. They wanted me to get a stable job with a pension."

Aditya chuckles, nods knowingly. "Why not go into the police?"

"I did - for some time," I admit. "I studied Criminal Justice in college and then took Masters electives in Forensic Investigation. I was a beat cop for three years - even made junior detective. But I didn't like the restrictions and the policies and the admin and the bureaucracy - all that crap."

"Good, secure income though."

"Secure - yes," I agree. "Good - most definitely not! I make way more doing private investigations."

"It must have been hard in the beginning," Aditya says, commiserating. "It's like running your own business, isn't it?"

"Yes," I say. "We business owners never know where our next dollar is coming from, do we?"

"You're right." Aditya's voice is heavy. "Sometimes I think...it must be nice to get a guaranteed salary, paid vacation, dental benefits. But then I think...the whole point of life is to build something that's your own. Isn't it?"

I smile. "Tell my parents that! Thankfully, my brother and sister chose more traditional career paths which keeps the heat off me - somewhat."

"That's the thing about Indian families," Aditya says. "There's too much pressure. It's like our lives don't belong to us."

"So you have a big family?" I ask. "Brothers and sisters?"

"Three sisters."

"So you're the only son." I shake my head. "That's a special kind of pressure in our culture."

"It's just the way it is." Aditya's voice is clipped. "Nothing you or I can do to change it."

I've hit a nerve. I take my foot off the gas pedal with an empathetic nod.

"Who is paying you for the Lake Templeton case?" Aditya asks.

I am taken aback by his boldness. Who is interrogating whom now? But sometimes, a suspect's questions are more telling than their answers. It's obvious that money swims close to the surface of Aditya's mind. I flash back to the thought I had yesterday. How is he keeping his airline afloat? Are money worries at the root of his ebbing and flowing stress and hair-trigger temper?

I briefly mull over my response, and then decide to be honest. If he finds out I lied to him, I will lose his trust.

"No one," I say. "The Sergeant asked me to take it on pro-bono." Okay - so I don't have to be *completely* honest.

"You can afford to do that?"

"I live simply," I say. "I don't have any expensive habits."

"Must be nice."

My eyes dart to Aditya's designer shoes. Is he playing a part to impress his wife's 'fancy' friends? Is that why he's dealing drugs for extra cash?

"A lot of people living alone in this town." I deftly shift topic. "Alena, the mayor. Sergio. Sharon, of course."

"Most people come to live here because they like to be alone," Aditya says. "It's a great place to cut off from the world."

"Or maybe they're coming here to hide."

"Are you single?" Aditya asks abruptly.

I don't miss a beat. "Yes."

"Then you should look at buying property in Lake Templeton," Aditya says flippantly.

"Maybe." I am unsure where he is going with this conversation.

"Being single has its own charm," Aditya says with a smile. "You answer to no one and you don't have to make your bed when you don't feel like it."

"Do you miss it?" I ask. "Being single?"

Is there a thread of regret undergirding his marital joy?

Aditya shakes his head, vigorously. "No, of course not. I love being married. And my wife is great. I travel a lot for work and she's very understanding."

A reasonable arrangement or the precursor for separate lives?

"Have you found anything so far?" Aditya says. "About the case, I mean."

"I'm working on it," I say lightly. "Still trying to track Sharon's whereabouts after the time you dropped her off at the airport."

Aditya nods in understanding. I grab the opening he's given me.

"I know you don't know where Sharon went after you dropped her off on Wednesday," I say carefully. "But do you know where she *usually* went? You flew her back and forth regularly. Did someone usually pick her up?"

"Sergio at the office," Aditya answers. "They were friends. He came to get her once or twice."

"How well do you know Sergio?"

"Not well," Aditya says. "He works at the office, that's all I know. Sharon liked him."

"You mentioned you don't serve alcohol on your flights," I say. "But it looks like you do provide bottled water service. Can I grab one?"

I point to the black grocery bag resting in a corner in the passenger seating area. A couple of plastic water bottles peek through its opening.

A cloud descends over Aditya's face. Small veins pulsate on the side of his clenched neck.

"Those aren't for the passengers." Aditya's voice is a bark. "Those are mine. Please don't take those."

That sudden mood swing again. A pendulum going crazy. What is going on with Aditya Roshan?

CHAPTER 6

Sunday, December 15, 2019

We descend into clear skies at Lake Templeton. Although I'm the only passenger, Aditya stands at the bottom of the stairs, a one-man welcome committee, hands clasped in front. I walk down the stairs, duffel bag over one shoulder, laptop bag on the other.

Aditya takes his routines quite seriously. The hands-on, family-style approach is part of the charm of the quaint mom-and-pop shop, Pacific Air. You don't get free drinks on board but you get to shake the owner's hand.

My Mazda sits sentinel at the airport where I left it. Besides the frost on the windows, it looks untouched. I scrape the crystalline particles off my windshield before sliding in. I sit inside, arms folded in the frozen tundra of the interior while the heat cranks up and slowly seeps from the vents. The gurgling sound of the engine reminds me that my service is several months overdue.

One of these days, I will give in and buy a better car. A few weeks ago, my sister, Ayesha, dragged me to a BMW showroom. I was admiring the high-shine exteriors and plush cabins until my eyes fell on the price tags. I couldn't get out of there fast enough.

Some lessons from childhood stay attached to us, hidden from sight, like stubborn barnacles under a saltwater pier. My parents taught me that cars are transportation - nothing more. They are not a status symbol. Dependability trumps titanium rims. Fuel efficiency beats heated steering wheels. You need a car that won't break down in the middle of the highway. Everything else is luxury. And therefore, unnecessary.

Ayesha drives a BMW X7 - a seven-seater with an eye-popping six-figure price tag. She rationalizes it. She has worked hard and earned her indulgences. The vehicle is part of her brand as a senior executive. She has a child and needs more space. I always tell her to get over her guilt and own her wants, no matter how ludicrous our parents think they are.

It's nine a.m. on Sunday morning. City Hall is closed but Alena asked me to meet her there.

Alena is impeccably dressed in light gray slacks and a cream-colored blouse. Smoky eye pencil illustrates piercing eyes. Never in jeans and a tee-shirt, even on Sunday.

"I have the CCTV footage you asked for," Alena says curtly. No smile or word of welcome.

"Good," I say. "I appreciate it. Hey - I have another question for you. About the money you believe Sharon stole. Was it taken in a lump sum or in a series of smaller transactions?"

Alena raises her eyebrows. "In a series of small transactions, I believe. Why?"

"That makes sense," I say. "An extra zero here and there is easy to bury. A big number withdrawn all at once is harder to hide."

Alena nods.

"What do you think happened to the money?" I ask. "I asked the police to do a discreet inquiry into Sharon's bank accounts. They found nothing unusual."

Alena looks at me like a bug she's too disgusted to squash. "She wouldn't have put the money in her bank account. She'd get caught. She was too smart for that."

Just a garden variety scofflaw living a hermit's life.

"The video, please." I hold out my hand.

"I can't let you take it offsite," Alena says. "I have arranged a viewing room for you."

The dankest, crummiest corner of City Hall, undoubtedly.

I smile broadly. "You're a gem - thank you."

Ten minutes later, I am sitting in the stock room, shivering and rubbing my arms. The heating appears to be switched off but the cargo-box computer in front of me works just fine. Alena has pre-loaded the video on the screen. I hit 'play.'

There was a rainstorm that night, so the video quality isn't great. At least it's in color. I am glad the City found a few extra dollars in their budget for that.

Sharon approaches the airport, a large umbrella shielding her from the pelleting droplets. Her stride is firm and steady; not like someone walloped with a healthy dose of anesthetic. She is carrying a large camel leather purse and a plastic water bottle. Her fawn-colored jacket is open in the front to reveal her outfit - a dark gray skirt and royal blue blouse - the same clothes her body was found in, waterlogged and motionless on the beach. She is alone.

Something is nagging at me but I can't quite grasp it. What is it? What am I missing?

Sharon moves closer to the airport gate. Someone opens the door and steps out. A flash of red hair, a gangly shuffle of the feet - it's Sergio. He's wearing jeans and a polo shirt. He takes one hand out of his pocket and reaches for Sharon. Pulls her into a hug.

So he met Sharon at the airport. Just like he said.

Their embrace is intimate and easy. Like two people that are very comfortable in each other's presence. Consistent with a relationship that blossomed from a friendship.

They break apart and linger. I can tell they are talking. Their body language indicates that the topic is light. Chatting about the weather. Small talk about Sharon's trip. Nothing confrontational, like the theft of a half a million dollars from City coffers.

How could Sergio maintain this easy demeanor with Sharon when he knew she was being investigated for fraud? Pretend to be her friend, share her bed, while plotting to bring her down, possibly send her to prison?

Sergio puts his arm around Sharon's waist and steers her inside the airport. They disappear from view.

I load the second video. It's from the interior overhead camera in the airport seating area. I forward through the dead time until Sharon and Sergio walk in.

They are still talking, looking at each other. Sharon appears subdued. Sergio is nodding, his face angled away from the camera and towards Sharon. A few seconds later, they pass out the front door towards the parking lot. The video splinters off.

Alena told me there are only two CCTV cameras at the airport: one at the tarmac and the other inside the seating area. There was one at the front entrance near the parking lot, but it recently blinked out and hasn't been fixed yet.

Tapping my feet, I switch back to the first video. Something is still gnawing at me. What is it?

I start the video. Sharon approaches the airport, firm and confident in her stride, one hand grasping an umbrella. Her other hand, holding a plastic water bottle, rests on a slouchy camel leather purse hanging from her shoulder, with a dark gray sweater folded on top of it. It's the same purse that was found at her house.

And then it hits me. The answer is right in front of my face. Sharon's umbrella - large and white with colored stripes. The same umbrella I saw in her office at City Hall. And then, my eyes shift to her fawn-colored jacket. It looks like the one that was hanging behind her office door.

My instinct was right. Sharon took the umbrella and jacket with her to Vancouver. So how did they end up back in her office the morning her body was found? Who took them there? Was it Sharon herself? Did she stop by City Hall on her way home from the airport?

And what about that dark gray sweater folded over her purse? She must have been wearing it when she got on the plane in Vancouver. Maybe she took it off during the flight. That sweater wasn't in Sharon's office but I have a vague feeling I've seen it somewhere before. Maybe in her closet at her lodge? I can't recall.

There must be a CCTV camera at City Hall. I have to get my hands on the footage. Sergio told me that he took Sharon straight home from the airport. Was he lying?

There is a pep in my step when I walk into Alena's office to let her know I am done viewing the airport CCTV footage. But I need to examine Sharon's office again.

"I don't know what you think you're going to find," Alena bristles. "We've shown you everything. I don't know why you can't accept that this was an accident."

"If it was an accident, it's a little too convenient, don't you think?" I rebut, refusing to back down.

"I don't know what you mean." Alena's face is stolid.

"An accidental drowning at a time when Sharon was suspected of embezzling money from a project where lots of high-profile people invested millions of dollars?"

"There's no connection between the embezzlement and Sharon's death," Alena snaps. "Why don't you understand - Sharon's death helps no one. Actually, it's made our lives very difficult. We need the money back. And we have no idea where it is."

I won't probe further. For now.

"I'd also like to view the CCTV footage from City Hall," I say. "When can I get access to it?"

Alena turns up her nose. "That camera has been broken for weeks."

I fold my arms across my chest, frustration roiling. When I speak, my voice is clipped. "Lots of broken CCTV cameras here at Lake Templeton. The City's financial position looks healthy, judging from the financials I saw in Sharon's office. So why haven't the cameras been fixed?"

"As you are aware, I have other priorities at the moment," Alena says coldly. "I will get to it."

"I meant to ask you," I say. "I didn't see any City paperwork when I searched Sharon's lodge. Did she ever take work home with her?"

"Never," Alena says. "City files are highly confidential. We don't allow our employees to work from home."

"But wouldn't Sharon take some documents or files with her when she flew to Vancouver for investor presentations?"

"Sure..." Alena searches my face, maybe wondering where I'm going with this.

"I see." I smile. "So explain to me what happened to the City files that Sharon took with her to Vancouver. We didn't find them in her purse or anywhere else at her lodge. The only logical explanation is that she came to City Hall to drop off these files *before* she went home that night. And Sergio is lying. Now tell me - when can I get that CCTV footage?"

Sharon's office is exactly how I left it last time. Her umbrella and jacket are behind the door, linchpins hiding in plain sight. I log into Sharon's computer and get a nasty surprise. Her profile has been deactivated and her files swept clean.

Outraged, I march towards Alena's office. The door is ajar and Alena is on the phone, her head turned away from me, talking to someone softly. I do not recognize the words. The angular, throaty dialect sounds like Russian.

Alena turns towards me, sensing my presence. Her face freezes mid-expression.

She speaks into the phone in English, "I will call you back," before resting the slim, black receiver in its place.

Turns to me with a thunderous expression. "Can you please not barge into my office unannounced?"

"City business?" I ask.

Alena floats to her feet like steam rising from a grate. Even in anger, her movements are elegant, coordinated, almost ethereal.

"What do you want?" Her silver-gray orbs laser at me.

"Why has Sharon's profile been deleted?" I demand.

"I didn't know it had been," Alena says. "But I'm not surprised. We automatically delete employee profiles after they have left City Hall. Within three days."

"It didn't occur to you that just this once, during a police investigation, it would make sense to leave the profile active?"

"If the police thought it was important, they should have told us."

She will never accept responsibility. I wonder if Alena has ever felt remorse or apologized for anything in her life.

"What happens to Sharon's digital files?"

"Her personal files get deleted. Whatever she has on the City's shared server will remain."

"And can I get access to the City's server?"

"You can make a request under the Freedom of Information Act," Alena says. "But it will most likely be denied. Most of the City's files are confidential."

Great. Another roadblock. "You know I can get a warrant, don't you?"

I have no power to get warrants. But Alena doesn't know that - hopefully.

She is unperturbed. "You would have to if you want to access the City's server. There's nothing I can do about that."

"Police will have to come to Lake Templeton again. I got the sense you wanted to avoid that." I try a different hook, at a different angle.

"Look, Ms. Rizvi, I'm not sure what kind of evidence you have so far," Alena says. "From what I hear, it's not enough to get a warrant to access sensitive City files that have nothing to do with your investigation."

From what she's heard? What *has* she heard? And more importantly, from whom? Marla, the office gossip? I am in her playground. Alena has eyes everywhere. And she owns everyone.

I open my mouth to shoot back an acrid response and then promptly shut it, backing down, taking the path of pragmatism. Trying to obtain a warrant would be a fruitless, time-consuming exercise - not one I would bother with. And Alena knows that. As much as it irks me, I will let this one go.

"Fine. You win," I say. "I will go and review the hard copy files in Sharon's credenza again. Hopefully, those have not been destroyed."

"Most certainly not," Alena says. "Take all the time you need."

With a nod, I turn back towards Sharon's office.

I am relieved to see that Sharon's filing cabinet appears untouched. I dive into the treasure chest.

Many investigators balk at paperwork, preferring to spend their time in the field. But paper trails contain clues. You find the hidden path and follow it. And are rewarded every step of the way with a new puzzle piece to take on your journey.

I rifle through Sharon's credenza. Color-coded, alphabetized manila folders hang. Is there a declined permit buried in here that caused murderous sour grapes? Was it a contract gone sideways or a large fine she levied that caused someone to go berserk?

I pull out a folder titled 'Receipts.' It contains printouts of itemized expense claims going back a couple of years. Sharon was charging a lot for travel. Flights back and forth to Vancouver - $235 for a roundtrip each time with Pacific Air. Lower than what Aditya charged me for the two flights I took with him. But he is the exclusive travel concierge for the City of Lake Templeton. He has to give them a healthy discount.

Still, it must have irked Sharon every time she got on the plane instead of taking the ferry. A love of luxury wasn't one of her shortcomings. She could have slept on dirt with a brick for a pillow.

There are invoices stamped 'Paid' for design work and architectural drawings for the new Lake Templeton resort. Interesting. Why is the City covering these bills? The rights to the resort were sold to a developer.

And then, something catches my eye and pulls me in like a fishing rod reeling in its prey. It's an invoice from Manulife Insurance stamped 'Paid.' A credit card statement is stapled to the top left. The payment is for premiums for key person life insurance policies taken out on the City executive staff. Each person is insured for one million dollars.

Why does a government department need to insure their staff? They're not hard to replace. Mayor is an elected position. The government will not stop functioning if Alena Krutova gets hit by a bus. I wonder who authorized this. And why?

Could this be a motive for murder? The life insurance payout would more than cover the money Sharon purportedly stole. But the insurance company would not pay until the case is closed. Is this why Alena is so annoyed every time I show up at her door with a new offbeat idea? She wants the case closed - immediately.

As I wrap up and exit Sharon's office, I see a few of the City staff gathered around Marla's table. Sergio is one of them. I peruse their jeans and sweatshirts. No one appears to be dressed for work. Given it's Sunday, I'm not surprised.

I move closer to hear their conversation.

"So we will meet at ten a.m. sharp then?"

"Yes. It's so sad. I hear there's no family - at all."

"Why would there be? Her mother cut off everyone when she left. And Sharon never bothered to call anyone after she escaped."

"She was seven when she left. She probably didn't even remember anyone."

"No one wanted her or cared about her. If they did, they would have called her. Her rescue was front page news."

"I heard that they did but Sharon rebuffed them."

"I've ordered flowers and booked the funeral service. Everyone - don't forget to sign the card. And please give me your fifty dollars."

I approach the group.

"If you don't mind, I'd love to contribute towards the funeral arrangements," I say, reaching into my shoulder bag to pull out my wallet.

"Oh hello, Fati," Sergio says, smiling. "I didn't know you were back."

"Nice to see you, Sergio," I say. "It's wonderful what you guys are doing - organizing a funeral for your colleague."

"Well, someone has to do it," Marla speaks up, eyes wide. She stands at the center of the knot of people, a small but mighty hub directing the spokes. Her curly brown hair cloud around her head, haloing with flyaways, air dried after her morning shower in the winter air blasting through open car windows on her drive over.

"So no family came to claim her?" I ask, although I know the answer.

Marla shakes her head vigorously. "No... Sharon had no one. Except for us." She gestures to the people gathered around her. "We canceled vacations for this. I know she's dead but... we still want to be there for her."

"That must have cost a lot."

"Well yes," Marla says. "The funeral home, flowers, urn, it all adds up."

"If there's no family or next of kin, what happens to her lodge and other assets?"

"Well, *we* don't know," one of the other employees jumps in. It's a bespectacled forty-ish gentleman with a crew cut.

"I heard that she had a will," Marla says with the gleeful gravity of someone sharing a saucy secret. "She's donating everything to some charity in Maple Ridge."

"Really?" I ask. "Which charity?"

Marla shrugs. "I don't know."

"I have to head out now," I tell the group, placing three folded up twenty-dollar bills on the table. "Please keep the change. See you tomorrow at the funeral."

"Did you know Sharon?" Marla peers at me curiously.

"I'm learning more about her every day," I say. With a smile and a nod, I walk out.

Sergeant Keller told me that the coroner has completed the tox screen but the body hasn't been released yet. The service is proceeding anyway. The cremation will happen later - quietly and efficiently - and the ashes dispersed over Lake Templeton. Just as Sharon stipulated in her will and last testament.

Sharon must have money socked away somewhere. More than a little if she stole from Lake Templeton. I have to find out who is handling her estate. I need to learn which mysterious charity in Maple Ridge she willed her earthly possessions to.

Alena must be fixated on that like military radar. If there's one thing Alena wants, it's to get her hands on Sharon's money. Milk her for everything she can to get her precious project off the ground. And I have a feeling she will do whatever it takes to make that happen.

When the front door is barred shut with a barking dog guarding it, I sneak in through the back door. In this spirit, I decide to pay a secret visit to Alena's home. I found her address in Sharon's files.

It's a few minutes past noon. Alena is at the office so now is the perfect time. But first - my ritualistic coffee and croissant to shore up my energy. The coffee shop at the Lakeside Inn will do. They know me by name now. I am always quick to make friends with the person pouring my coffee. Some call it self-serving. I prefer to think of myself as resourceful.

The Lakeside Inn 'coffee shop' is more of a coffee counter carved into a corner of the lobby opposite the reception desk, flanked by four bar stools. When I arrive, all are empty. The display case contains several croissants and a couple of Danishes. The bored barista is scrubbing down a back counter with one hand while scrolling on her phone with the other. She breaks into a welcoming smile when she sees me.

I find a seat and order the largest cup of coffee and a chocolate croissant. As the server microwaves my croissant, the smell wafts towards me, awakening my stomach. Nibbling on the stale dessert, I recall Alena's mumbled phone conversation at her office.

Unfortunately, I can't speak Russian. Not yet. I boast native fluency in English and French. I can hold my own in a conversation in Hindi or Urdu, and stumble my way through Punjabi. I have been hacking away at Spanish on and off for the past two years. It was only during a case which landed me in Mexico that I realized how good I have gotten. I picked up Mandarin eight months ago and it's been my Achilles heel so far. I need to find a meaty case in Chinatown to throw myself into the linguistic deep end.

As I sip my coffee, I dial George. He lives in my speed dial top ten.

He picks up on the fourth ring. "You again?"

I'm not offended. George and I are tight - we have been friends for years. He'll never say it but George admires my bulldog perseverance.

"Me again," I say pleasantly. "There's something else I want you to find out more about. A company called Pacific Air."

"Are you getting paid for this case?"

I chuckle. "If you must know, no, I am not."

"That's too bad. I was going to ask for a cut."

"And one of these days, I will give it to you."

"Promises, promises."

"There's more to life than money," I say. "If there's anyone who has given you more interesting cases than me, I'd like to meet them."

I shovel the rest of my rapidly cooling croissant in my mouth and wash it down with coffee. There's no time to waste. With a broad smile aimed at the bored barista, I get up, grab my jacket from the adjoining bar stool and head out.

Alena's home is not too far from the Lakeside Inn. Given the size of Lake Templeton, most people live within a home run's distance from each other.

It's a beautiful day. The sun brightens the clear sky, spreading its tentacles through the cold winter air. I am disappointed. When you're sneaking into someone's house, a rain-drenched, cloud-cloaked day offers cover. There's less chance of sun-seeking neighbors catching you in the act.

I drive along the beach-hugging Island Highway that winds through grassy plains dense with groves of trees. Alena's home faces the lake, like many in Lake Templeton.

It's painted a cream color with modern decorative black turrets rising out the sides. The moist air laden with lake water hasn't yet faded its luster. A small promenade encircles the house, redolent of tree-lined walkways in rural Europe. Perfectly pruned lavender bushes provide solace to tired eyes.

I circle the block once and then park two houses down, under the shade of a large tree.

The back gate isn't barricaded, which is unsurprising. This is Vancouver Island, not Mexico City. The side borders of the property are lined with neatly trimmed cedar trees. Their dense, knotty thicket provides the perfect cover for me to scan for CCTV cameras before I walk up to the door.

When breaking into houses, you can't guarantee that someone won't see you. The trick is to make sure that any passerby that glances your way suspects nothing out of the ordinary. I'm wearing a woolen cap, jeans, and a nondescript black winter jacket. Nothing to distinguish me. Nothing to stick in anyone's mind.

I loiter behind the cedars, darting my eyes, this way, that way, and then in a three-sixty-degree scan. Spotting no one, and surprisingly, no CCTV cameras, I straighten my back and stride to the door as if I were Alena's sister visiting from abroad.

The swish of the wind blocks the sound of my footsteps. Unlike at Sergio's home, there are no fallen leaves. Clearly, Alena is paying someone to maintain the premises. Her unblemished hands have never touched a rake.

There is no car in the driveway. Perfect.

The back door is locked, as expected, but it's nothing I can't handle. I work quickly and the lock gives way easily in my hands.

The interior walls are painted soft white and arch into high ceilings with designer pot lights. No scrapes or stains mar the surface. The kitchen is neat with sparkling stoves that look like they've never been used. In the living room, a light gray sofa and loveseat face a small flatscreen TV mounted on a wall. Large picture windows look out into the front lawn and the vivid blue water.

Angled to the picture window sits a small cabinet. On top of it, a marble sculpture and a large abstract vase. They look like ornaments purchased at a high-end home furnishings store. No personality, just aesthetic. Stairs in a twisted spiral with a floating black railing lead to the second floor.

There's a doorway at the end of the hall, cracked open. I see a table lamp resting on an office table. And the edge of a laptop. That's where the payload is. But first, the low hanging fruit. A quick scan through cabinet drawers.

I pull open the top drawer - towels. Neatly folded bath towels, hand towels, kitchen towels. Different sizes but all clean, unblemished white. I feel around and under, careful not to disturb their alignment. Alena must never know that foreign hands touched her stuff and violated her space. At least not until I had enough to hang her.

Nothing here. I move to the next drawer. A folded-up blanket and a pair of camel leather gloves and winter hat tucked. I move to the next two drawers - nothing.

I am advancing towards the study when I hear something. A clatter. It's coming from upstairs.

My body freezes. My canine ears turn up, blocking out all my senses but sound.

Something thuds to the floor, the sound dulled around the edges by the wooden flooring. And then - footsteps. Dread rises in me.

Who is it?

CHAPTER 7

Sunday, December 15, 2019

Thoughts race through my brain but my body is frozen, nearly breathless.

Alena is the only known occupant of the house on Spencer St.

Is it last night's hookup? Alena wouldn't sully her reputation by bringing a flappy-lipped townsman home. And even if she did, she wouldn't leave him alone in her house. That would require a lot of trust for someone so untrusting. Maybe it's a friend crashing in her guest room or a family member visiting from Russia. That's not unusual. I also grew up with a revolving door of relatives from Pakistan rotating through our guest room.

The footsteps are advancing left - towards the staircase.

Crap!

Whoever it is, they're coming down. In seconds, they will be at the top of the stairs. And then a few steps and voila - eye level with the sprawling living room where I stand - a juvenile delinquent with my hand in the cookie jar.

My body awakens from its trance. Instinct takes over. In this soulless museum-like home, there are no cozy nooks to make myself disappear. The back door is too far and the path towards it crosses ground zero, the spiral staircase that is about to blow my cover. The study is unseen territory, a potential landmine. The only option is the front door, looking out on the garden which opens up into mountain views and blue water.

I slide towards the door like a mako shark on high alert. I push down the lock and the door swings open, all movement and no sound as if freshly greased on the hinges. I slip out and push the door shut. I cower behind it, stuck between the two picture windows, yawning open like wide-awake eyes, on either side of the front door.

I can't move. I hope Alena's mysterious guest doesn't decide to take in some sun on the front lawn. I crouch, ear pressed to the door, quiet as a jewel thief sneaking up behind a security guard. Footsteps are now descending the stairs.

The front door features a hammered silver mail slot. My dexterous fingers find it, grab its edge and push up the flap. It moves up dutifully, and I bend down, bringing my eyes level with the small opening.

A man. Disheveled and gray-haired. Wearing a housecoat loosely wrapped around his paunchy waist. His feet drag in black-and-white striped shower slides. A five o'clock shadow topped with an overgrown buzz cut completes the look.

Who is this man? Is he the reason Alena didn't accompany Sharon to the investor meetings in Vancouver? Is it because of him Alena didn't host her birthday party at her home, a beachfront palace designed for entertaining? Or is he an intruder? But an intruder wouldn't lounge around so comfortably, moving at the pace of a seal caught in quicksand. *I'm* an intruder - we move fast.

The man shuffles about in the living room, his movements sludgy, as if he has just woken up after a ten-hour slumber. He looks this way and that as if trying to figure out where to go.

Please don't come to the front. Please don't come to the front. The last thing I need is for the police to be called to arrest me for trespassing. Alena would hire the most vicious attorney to skewer me in court.

Another five seconds heavy with tension, then the man clearly realizes that the kitchen is where the coffee is kept - which he obviously needs. He turns around and heads towards it, receding from my view.

Relief floods me. But there's no time to waste. The man may come back.

I turn around, looking at the front lawn for the first time. It's a good-sized space, bordered with a four-foot hedge. A gap in the front leads to a set of stairs that descend down to the beach. A cobblestoned pathway starts at the front door and cuts through the lawn to the stairs. Can't have Alena's three-hundred-dollar flip flops muddied on the wet grass as she goes for a spiritually cleansing walk on the beach.

A deck is carved into one corner of the lawn. A vinyl-covered barbeque grill rests under its awning. Hibernating for the winter. In front of it, rattan patio furniture - a loveseat and two chairs. Light gray, of course, with darker gray cushions.

I try to imagine Alena flipping burgers with her sweaty hair pulled back under a baseball cap, wearing a ribbed tank top and denim shorts and a stained apron with "Number One Chef" emblazoned on it. I can't.

The patio furniture is arranged around a small propane fire pit. A heavy-duty slate tabletop rests on it, nestling the burning area covered in lava rocks.

I picture Alena serving filet mignon on crystal plates while her guests - dressed in fine silks and pressed linen pants - sip champagne in cut glass tumblers. Fall-in-the-Hamptons style.

I glance back at the house. It's silent. The woeful-looking man is nowhere in sight.

I make my way to the picnic area. Run my hand over the fabric of the patio chair - it's slightly damp from the rain. I pick up a lava rock from the fire pit and turn it over in my hands. It's cold.

And that's when I see it.

A rolled-up soot-gray sweater buried under the pockmarked rocks.

I pull it out, bring it closer to my face, smell it. No whiff of smoke or ash, although it does smell grimy. It must have been placed here recently.

It's a women's sweater, size small. It doesn't belong to Alena. It's too dark. Too homely. Too forgettable.

Also, It's from Gap. In Alena's mind, the Gap is probably the same as the Salvation Army thrift store.

The sweater belongs to Sharon.

It's the sweater she was carrying in the CCTV footage from the airport. Hours before she died.

I lay it on the fire pit and run my hands over its ribbed surface. And there it is - what I was hoping for. A long, dark hair, hiding in the weave.

What is Sharon's sweater doing in Alena's fire pit?

Heat rises in my throat. It's a familiar sensation. One that I crave. It's the next, harder level in the video game. It's the bigger boulder on the hiking trail. You're getting closer but you're not at the finish line. Not yet.

The finish line is disappointing. Anticlimactic. At the finish line, the adventure ends and it's time to move on.

I consider taking the sweater with me and handing it to the Sergeant. Forensics can run a DNA test - that's the only way to know for sure whether it belonged to Sharon.

But I pause. I obtained the sweater illegally. The Sergeant might salute me, then hit me with a breaking and entering charge. Not to mention, Alena will know I was here.

I'll put the sweater back where I found it. But I'm taking the hair with me. The Sergeant and I will have an off-the-books chat. Maybe we could finagle an under-the-radar DNA test. If the hair matches Sharon's DNA, it would give the police ammunition to investigate Alena further.

I take the hair and carefully place it into a palm-sized plastic envelope that I pull out of my wallet. Yes, I carry several of those around - just in case. I take a few photos of the sweater before rolling it up and shoving it back into the fire pit. I place the lava rocks on top of it.

I feel a driving need to go back inside Alena's house, to look through her stuff. Tomorrow. During Sharon's funeral. All of City Hall will attend.

As I am walking across Alena's lawn, towards the stairs that lead to the beach, I throw one last glance back at the house.

And freeze.

The stranger is watching me. Through the drawn blinds of the front picture windows. His intense gray eyes piercing and inscrutable. Still as a stone statue. Expressionless.

My pulse quickens. I tighten my muscles resisting the urge to take flight. Slow down my breathing, taking a few quick gulps of air. I don't see a gun in the stranger's hand. Or a phone, fingers poised to dial 911.

Tentatively, I raise one hand, twirl my fingers. Force a smile. Hope that he thinks I'm a friendly neighbour or a friend passing through.

Then, I start backing away. Turn around. One foot in front of the other, my best imitation of a normal pace. Ears peeled for the cock of a rifle behind me.

I dial Zed as I walk down the front steps of Alena's house. I will need him to serve up a platter of distraction. The stranger has seen me, knows what I look like. Will he rat on me to Alena?

Zed can be a creative conversationalist. He can pull the man out of the house long enough for me to do my thing. I am efficient and I work fast. A quick search through the contents hidden behind drawers, cabinets, and locked doors. A clean, no-paper-trail break-and-ransack through Alena's laptop. I need thirty minutes tops.

The cherry on top? Zed can find out the identity of the stranger. Extract information in his friendly, roundabout way. Sometimes, tact gets you further than my direct, hard-charging style.

On the beach, I start sprinting lightly, towards my car.

One thing that's baffling me - why doesn't Alena have CCTV cameras at her home? Maybe the stranger inside is her watchdog. But in that case, why did he let me get away?

After leaving Alena's home, I head to Sergio's. He's still within my circle of suspicion. I don't fully buy his explanation of an innocent, doe-eyed relationship with Sharon that no one knew about.

Sergio's street is quiet. Tall trees sing in the breeze. The neighbouring houses are snoozing, the only signs of life the rustle of squirrels as they scamper from bush to bush. I slow down as I pull up to Sergio's house. And see the flash of bright blue in his driveway. His car is here. He's home. I press down on my accelerator and my car rolls on. I will return another time.

I call George as I am stepping into my hotel room. "I think it's time to go to a phase two on Alena Krutova."

"Great," George says in a resigned voice.

"I don't know exactly what she's mixed up in but it's something," I say. "Misuse of taxpayer funds, maybe. I know you said there are no lawsuits, no parking tickets, no arrests or warrants, no nothing. But she won't have any of that - she's too smart. What I need is stuff that the authorities haven't found yet."

George sighs, pauses. I wait.

"It's going to cost you," he finally says.

At this point, I don't care. My bank account is healthy, always has been. When you're born into a lower middle class immigrant family, you're taught to always have three months' salary on hand in cash. Due to the volatile nature of my work, I usually keep nine months' worth.

"I found a man in her house today," I say. "I need to know who it is. If you can find out more about her family in Russia, her history before she came to Canada..."

As for me, I need to return to Alena's house, peel back the wallpaper, and uncover the squirming worms underneath. I am on the cusp of something. I can feel it.

Monday, December 16, 2019

At Sharon's service, Alena is the perfectly composed mourner. No tears, only calculated despair. She looks at me and nods briefly, acknowledging my presence. No accusation. No cold fury. My tension dissolves in relief. It doesn't appear that she knows I broke into her house yesterday.

It's a blustery day. The service is held at the only funeral home in town, built into a grassy knell off the main Island Highway. The sounds of children playing waft from a neighbouring athletic field. Over thirty people are in attendance - mostly employees from City Hall and a few unfamiliar faces.

There are heartfelt tributes to Sharon, but not many words are said. Sharon was dependable and a team player. She was friendly, cordial, and reliable. Platitudes. No one really knew Sharon. Not even Sergio, her lover, who is mingling with his colleagues as if at an office party. Not even Korinne, who stands head bowed, in a knee-length black woollen dress that looks pulled from the closet of Coco Chanel herself.

The townspeople don't wallow. Once the eulogies are over, they laugh and talk, nibbling on the baked goods and veggie platter that were ordered for the occasion.

My phone buzzes. Zed is here. It's time for round two of my covert operation on Alena Krutova.

We drive to Alena's house, muscles tight in anticipation. Like with many cases before, Zed is now in it. He's invested. He wants to untangle this thread as badly as I do.

"Remember - you're from the local Boys and Girls club, collecting money for the new playground," I say. "Engage him in conversation. Once I trigger the shock sensor on my car, the alarm will go off. Tell him you need his help with your car - bring him out and away from the house. And that's when I will run in. Through the neighbour's hedge. It's very important that he not see me — he knows what I look like. You draw him out and I slide in - got it?"

"Yes," Zed agrees. "What's your plan once you're inside?"

"It depends on how much time I have," I say. "I'll try to get into her computer first."

"What if there's a password? Are you ready?"

"Yes." I pat my jacket pocket, feeling the reassuring presence of my USB stick. "As long as she's using a Windows computer, I'm all good. I've got my password recovery program ready."

"Got it." Zed salutes like a soldier accepting an order from a military sergeant.

The town square recedes in my rear-view mirror like mist from a cooling coffee cup. We weave through boxy city blocks, lined with slumbering houses and naked tree branches standing sharply, erect against the flat, hard light of the daytime sky.

At Alena's house, I wait in the car, parked under the same shady tree that gave me cover yesterday. It sways in the breeze, dropping a sprinkle of leaves on my car, like a bridal party tossing rose petals on a newly married couple.

Zed lopes over to Alena's house, across the promenade, and to the back door. He straightens his shoulders and takes a deep breath before lifting his hand and rapping loudly with his knuckle. And waits.

My fingers clutch the steering wheel as I lean over it to get a closer look through the windshield awash with a curtain of rain.

Ten seconds go by. Zed knocks again. Stands back. Shifts from one foot to the other. There is no answer. Another five seconds and I can see Zed getting impatient as he lifts his hand one more time.

Where is the disheveled stranger? Is he gone? Was he only a figment of my overactive imagination?

One final knock, a shake of his head, then Zed gives up. He turns around and starts walking back. I slide out, soundless in the aggressive patter of the rain.

"Either he's not home or he's sound asleep," Zed says as he approaches me. He looks disappointed - like an understudy at a play that never gets his shot at a curtain call. "This is good news for you. You can break in and break things at your leisure."

"Perfect," I say. "You coming?"

Zed's face lights up. "Of course! Lead the way."

"I need you to be my lookout in case he comes back."

"I was afraid you'd make me stand guard in the car."

"Well, that's not a bad idea now that you mention it…"

"You already said yes!" Zed is skipping ahead.

I follow him with a smile. Cases are more fun to solve with the right sidekick.

Zed and I are inside Alena's house. The blinds are open. Spotty dark clouds have metastasized into swollen globs crowding the sky. Rain arrives, sudden and ferocious. It batters the lakefront into a black and white landscape, melting and shifting with the trailing water. The lake laps softly outside. Inside, the muted hum of the latent heating system. Other than that, the house is silent.

Is the stranger home, sprawled on the bed, body like molasses but mind as sharp as a fresh nail?

"You stand guard at the staircase," I whisper to Zed, positioning him underneath the slats of the floating spiral. "I'm going to the study."

I advance through the living room, stepping softly around anything that might crack or pop. It's a good thing I had the chance to stake out the place yesterday. I know exactly where to go. I dart across the living room and into the study, built into the west corner of the home.

Inside, a glossy white writing desk rests on silver wrought iron legs. The ribbed leather office chair is light gray, just like the one in Alena's office at City Hall. A half bookcase stands behind, punctuated with abstract marble vases, one in each corner. A painting hangs on the back wall - vivid and washed-out blues and greens spackled on white canvas, dissected with a smear of corrugated silver. It's the most color that I have seen in Alena's house so far.

And on the desk, a laptop. A gleaming platinum Microsoft Surface Pro. I approach it like a virgin bride on her wedding day. My fingers flick over the touchpad. The homepage springs to life. No password needed. I stare in disbelief.

For all her bravado, Alena is pretty average when it comes to her internet security. It makes her seem almost human. Or is it her god complex? Does she really believe her fortress by the water is invincible? That no one would dare try to breach it?

I click into the 'My Documents' folder, and the 'Photos' sub-folder. And then, another subfolder titled 'Family Photos.'

Jackpot. I enter Alena's digital front door.

I open the first photo. An older woman who looks remarkably like Alena is holding a young child. Must be her mother with a nephew or niece. I click the next one. A sea of pale blondes grinning into the camera. And the next - smiling faces gathered around a cake. Someone's birthday.

Ten photos in, Alena makes an appearance. She looks younger - softer, not yet hardened by life and expectations. The smile glimmers on her face like Christmas lights.

The next photo... I do a double take. Two blondes together, smiling into a camera. Two very familiar blondes.

What?

I rub my eyes. No, I am not dreaming. Alena hasn't arrived and hit me over the head with her vase.

It's a twin. Alena has a twin.

Same blonde hair and pale skin. The only difference - Alena's twin wears her hair in blunt bangs.

I look up the photo properties - 2008. Eleven years ago.

Where is Alena's twin? Is she still in Russia? Why are there no recent photos of her?

An unbelievable idea germinates in my brain. Maybe Alena isn't Alena at all. Maybe it's an evil twin. I shake my head. I need to stop watching B horror movies on my days off.

My heart racing, I flip through more photos. And the second bludgeon hits.

There's a man in some of the photos. A man I've seen before. Very recently. It's the man upstairs, currently living at Alena's place! The man who may be asleep above my head, stirring from his siesta any minute now. Who is he?

There are several photos of him standing next to Alena, his arm around her, a craggy smile on his face. Alena looks almost happy in these photos. With both casting mischievous smiles into the camera, I see the resemblance. He has the same deep set, mystical gray eyes that Alena does.

Alena's brother. Has to be!

I reach into my shoulder bag for my USB drive. As the photos are downloading, I look up Alena's hidden files.

And there - under that blinking cursor, I find a series of grainy videos, shot on a camcorder. The picture wavers, as if bouncing on an inflatable boat in a bathtub. As if the camcorder was held in a sweaty, slippery hand.

A group of people sitting in a circle on metal chairs. They are wearing simple clothing that looks homespun, and identical sandals. Some hold small paperbacks. Others have their palms together, eyes closed, as if in a trance. A man stands in the middle, gesturing with his hands, shoulders squared in a power pose. He is the leader, bestowing commandments and giving directions.

My pulse quickens. Could it be...?

The leader is turned away from the camera. I can see the back of his head. There's something about the fading hairline, the sunspot that marks the balding crest. It looks like Jefferson Walls, former cult leader of the Nation of People. Sharon's erstwhile mentor.

The air feels thick and I gulp down a breath, my mouth dry.

Where did Alena find these videos?

I click the next video. Blurry gray and white appear on the screen. It's a box-like room. Bare bones. Austere. Evokes prison or a mental institution. A single bed sits in one corner - a metallic frame and deflated mattress covered with a white sheet. There is no pillow. A shelf-like structure stands in the other corner. No drawers. Its open compartments contain folded up fabric - probably clothing, maybe bedsheets. Up above, a square window watches over, covered with fine steel netting.

A young girl sits on a foldable chair next to the shelf. Head down, dark hair loose, tumbling wildly over sunken shoulders. I cannot see her face but, from her stature, she looks to be twelve or thirteen years old. She is wearing a loose tunic that goes down to her shins. Bare feet twitch, in an involuntary movement. Dark spots mar her skinny limbs.

Are those bruises? It's hard to be sure, due to the picture quality.

A young woman stands over the girl, berating her. She wears a robe over her tunic. Her feet are in sandals and her hair is pulled back behind her ears into a high bun. She is clearly in a position of authority.

I watch, on the edge of my seat, as the woman raises her hand and smacks the girl - hard - across her head. The young girl crumples as her head rocks forward, tangled hair shifting. Her shoulders shudder in a soundless cry.

The woman, stiff as a headmistress at a boarding school, is unmoved. She raises her hand, hits the girl again, harder this time, and the victim tilts to the side, off the chair, and collapses to the floor.

And then the young woman, the aggressor, turns around and starts walking in the direction of the camera. I can see her face - all of it. And then the picture freezes and blinks off.

It's Sharon.

A younger Sharon. A harsher Sharon. But undeniably Sharon.

Inside the mausoleum-like walls of the Nation of People cult, Sharon wasn't the victim. She was the aggressor. She had no need for moonshine to dull her senses because she held the stick. She did not die with the rest of the cult adherents because she probably spiked the punch herself.

And Alena found out about it. Started blackmailing her. Sharon wouldn't have wanted this to get out. It would have decimated her 'victim' image. Raised unwanted questions. Exposed the lies she told. Even led to criminal charges. Maybe this video was Alena's ace-in-the-hole to force Sharon to return the money she stole.

After leaving the cult, Sharon did charity work for the prevention of violence against women and children. She volunteered at BC Children's Hospital. Was it to make up for her behavior in the cult? Was she trying to atone for the violence she inflicted on young children for the sake of saving herself? Grappling with a guilt slowly consuming her, bite-by-bite.

I am about to press play on the next video when a frantic Zed appears. He waves his arms in front of my face. I look up.

"We need to get out of here - now," Zed whispers, his voice pitching higher than he intended which causes him to clap a hand over his mouth.

I shake my head in annoyance, hold up one hand to hold him at bay. "I'm not leaving," I whisper back. "There's too much good stuff here."

"You don't understand!" Zed grabs my arm and pulls me up, and starts dragging me away.

I grunt. It's always befuddled me how much stronger Zed is than he appears.

And that's when I hear the beep of a car lock outside. Oh crap!

Engulfed with sudden urgency, caught with my pants down, I instinctively turn back to the laptop and press down hard on the power button until the screen goes black. I pull out my USB stick, and hold on to it like a life raft, as I scurry out behind Zed, bumping into him and tripping over his feet.

We run out the front door and spill into Alena's lawn just as the back door in the kitchen clicks open.

Rain immediately drenches me from head to toe as I lie on all fours on Alena's lawn. I can hear Zed breathing hard next to me. Two danger junkies flushed from their fix.

We are safe. Or are we?

"Was that Alena?" My voice is a ragged whisper, nearly drowned out by the whiplash of rain.

Zed nods, his face white. Dark red splotches blossom on his cheeks. "Sure looked like it from the photos you showed me online."

"Was she alone?"

"I think so," Zed says, rising up slowly. "I saw her in her car as she was pulling into the driveway."

"Did she see you?"

"I don't know," Zed says. "But let's get out of here before we find out."

Zed is right. Even if Alena didn't see us, all it would take is one look out the front picture windows. Two figures dressed in black, sprawled across the lawn. I promised Sergeant Keller I wouldn't embarrass him.

Zed starts to stand. I grab his legs, yanking him back down. He stumbles, falls, curses loudly, and then slaps a hand across his mouth remembering that we are spies still on duty.

"What the hell are you doing?" he barks at me, in a low voice.

"The blinds are open," I say, as if stating the obvious. "We have to be careful. She can see us."

Zed nods and sinks back down. We crawl on all fours across the wet grass, like soldiers traversing a trench, our elbows sinking into soft mud.

On my left, I see the patio furniture arranged around the fire pit. And the sweater hiding inside it. I feel an irresistible urge to see it again, to confirm that it's still there. Like an obsessive compulsive with money hidden in a pillowcase.

"Where are you going?" Zed grabs my foot as I turn left instead of going straight.

"I need to show you the sweater I found yesterday!"

I move resolutely towards the fire pit, grab its edge, pull myself up.

"You are crazy, you know that?" But Zed is right behind me.

We straighten up together and face the fire pit. The lava rocks are darker, inked by the rain. I start picking up the rocks with both hands, moving them aside, here and there, first carefully and then rapidly, until my fingers are covered in black skid marks.

It's not there. The sweater is gone.

"Do you have a sixth sense?" Zed says in wonder. "It's not there, is it?"

"She moved it." I am stunned. My body feels heavy as if a baby grizzly has attached itself to my back. "The man in her house – he saw me yesterday. He must have told her."

"Come on, we need to get out of here," Zed says, in an appeasing tone, as he takes my hand. Giving in, I nod, squeeze Zed's hand, and turn around.

And come face-to-face with Alena's piercing gaze.

CHAPTER 8

Monday, December 16, 2019

Alena is at her front door, under the awning, dry as dehydrated fruit, arms folded across her chest. Her laser gray eyes burn through my retinas, imprinting her victory on my brain.

"Did you find what you were looking for, Ms. Rizvi?" she says. No sharpness, no accusation. Just an amiable question, a friendly chat between friends.

Zed and I are frozen in place, set in stone, unable to speak. I feel like an inmate breaking out of jail caught in the floodlights of the guard's tower. In the jaws of calamity.

"Please leave my property now, before I call the police and have you arrested," Alena says.

I find my voice and the words rush out of me as if through a bursting dam. "Why *don't* you, Alena? Why *don't* you call the police? Wait - don't answer that. We both know the answer to that question."

"I don't know what you're talking about." Alena's expression doesn't change. "You're trespassing on my property. I'm certain you don't have a warrant. Because you're not police. Despite all your time in the academy."

I feel a flush of unreasonable anger.

"I found the sweater, Alena," I blurt out. "I found the sweater and you know about it because you've gotten rid of it."

"I don't know what you're talking about," Alena says. "But I'm asking you again. Get off my property before I call the police."

"Sharon's sweater - in your fire pit!"

"Why would Sharon's sweater be in my fire pit?" Alena says, as if talking to a five-year-old.

"That's what I want to know!"

"Even if such a sweater existed, anyone could have put it there," Alena says. "My front lawn is accessible to anyone. *You're* here - and I certainly didn't invite you."

"She's right, Fati." It's Zed's voice. I forgot he was there. "Let's go."

I briefly consider revealing to Alena what I found on her laptop. But I hold back. Why give her an opportunity to get rid of the videos? It's time to downshift, accept defeat, and move on. It's the only way to live to fight another day. But I can't resist a parting shot.

"You won't get away with it forever, Alena," I say. "Whatever you've done, you'll get caught. Eventually, they all do."

"Your investigations in my town are complete." Alena's voice is hard. "I don't want to see you back here. If I do, I'll tell the Sergeant you broke into my home. And as you know from your time on the police force, that's the end of any *evidence* you think you have gathered."

"I'm leaving - for now." I start backing away.

"Goodbye, Ms. Rizvi," Alena says with a spiteful smile. She does not acknowledge Zed. "It was nice to know you."

Without another look, Alena slips back inside her house. Zed and I walk away.

We drive down Island Highway in silence, the only sound the creak of my overworked windshield wipers.

Zed shifts restlessly, scrolls through his phone, looks at me eyebrows raised in question. He can be tactful when the occasion calls for it. But he can never stay silent for long. He breaks when I drive past the Lakeside Inn without slowing down.

"Okay, so since you clearly don't want to go back to the motel, pack up, and get the hell out of this hick town, let's chat. All is not lost."

"Of course I'm not leaving," I snap. "This is just a temporary setback."

"That's right," Zed says encouragingly. "A temporary setback. You *had* to walk away. If she called the police, we would be done. So what do you want to do now?"

I sigh. "I was hoping to break into Sergio's house but I can't take the chance anymore."

"Next time," Zed says placatingly.

"I need a break from this case," I say, making a decision. "There's an awesome steakhouse in Nanaimo."

Zed grins. "Perfect."

Several hours later, after working my way through an eight-ounce ribeye, I am feeling better.

Zed chose the shrimp and lobster combo. "You're paying," he said, as he dug in.

We polish off our bottle of pinot noir - one glass for me and four for Zed. As we walk back to my car, Zed prattles on about someone called Brad - a new boyfriend, maybe. I am barely listening.

The knots of this case are burrowing and tightening in my brain. After fifteen years of detective work, I am not in the habit of being bested. And Alena bested me. How did I let that happen?

We are driving back to Lake Templeton when something strikes me. "Alena had a birthday party the night Sharon died! Her staff from City Hall was there. People must have taken photos and posted on social media."

"So the break from the case is over then?" Zed looks mildly miffed at my interruption of his glowing descriptions of Brad's quads.

"I need to trace Sharon's whereabouts the night she died," I say, as if Zed hasn't spoken. "I have proof that Sergio picked her up at the airport. But did she go straight home after that?"

Zed pulls out his phone. "Is it time to do a thread count?"

A thread count is my proprietary process where I list all open threads in a case to find connections between them.

"I feel that Sharon may have gone to City Hall from the airport," I say. "The jacket and umbrella she was wearing in the CCTV footage - I found them in her office. But Sergio said he took her straight home."

"That's the cute redhead with the Instagram, right? Maybe he lied."

On our way back to Lakeside Inn, I stop at a Chapters bookstore and pick up a poster board, sticky notes, and markers. Back at the motel, I lean the poster board against the wall, get down on my knees, and write out 'Sharon' in all caps in the middle.

Zed is perched at the window, blowing plumes of smoke through the open vent. The wind swirls them around and spits them back, which Zed doesn't seem to mind. The clean air is slowly becoming diluted with the grassy smell of marijuana.

"Can you please put that out and help me?" I say in annoyance. "I need you alert and my eyes are burning!"

Zed rolls his eyes as he crushes the half-smoked blunt into the ashtray he holds in his other hand. He saunters over to me.

"Okay, okay, Jesus, I thought you said you wanted to take a night off."

"I said I wanted to take a break," I correct him. "You know I never take a whole night off."

"You should try smoking," Zed grumbles. "It will calm you down."

"Who says I want to be calm?" I snap. "I'm trying to solve a case."

Zed sits down beside me, cross-legged. We face the empty poster board that holds the promise of a story untold.

"The likeliest motives for the murder are the embezzlement and the Lake Templeton revitalization project," I say.

I write these out in capital letters on the poster board, branching out under Sharon's name.

"Tell me why you think the revitalization project is connected to Sharon's murder," Zed says.

"There's so much that's off about this project," I say. "Why is the City making payments for the new resort that was licensed to a developer? Why did they have a life insurance policy on Sharon? It reeks of corruption - and corruption is a pretty big motive for murder."

"Where does the embezzlement fit in?"

"I'm not convinced that Sharon *did* embezzle," I say. "Alena says she did. But this embezzlement charge might be a gigantic farce to throw suspicion on someone who is no longer here to defend herself."

I write down Alena's name in capital letters on the poster board with a question mark next to it.

"Could be, for sure," Zed says. "But why would Alena derail her own project by stealing the money and blaming Sharon? You said her reputation and re-election depend on it."

"I don't know," I admit.

"We've talked enough about the mayor," Zed declares. "Let's discuss the airline pilot."

I write down Aditya's name next to Alena's on the poster board.

"Something seemed off when I first met him," I say. "He was unshaven and he looked restless. I wonder why he looked that way - Stress? Guilt?"

"Could be," Zed says. "Or maybe he was distressed because one of his frequent fliers died."

"It's not just that," I say. "He has an erratic temperament. Super friendly one moment, biting your head off the next, upset about some innocuous comment. He went crazy when I asked if I could take a water bottle from his plane."

"How about his socials?"

"He doesn't have any," I say. "No Facebook, Instagram, Twitter, none of it. Last time I flew with him, he let it slip that he went to business school at UBC. So I find it odd that he has no LinkedIn page either. I know from my friend, Leon, the Dean at the career center - creating a LinkedIn profile is MBA training 101."

"Yeah - maybe today it is," Zed says. "Maybe it wasn't back when your airline pilot went to school. What year was it anyway?"

"Good point," I agree. "And I don't know. But I'm sure Leon can look him up. Aditya also mentioned a mysterious benefactor who helped him start Pacific Air."

"Don't forget his wife," Zed says. "We don't know if she knows about her husband's illegal side business."

"Oh yes." I nod. "Kim Roshan. Maybe she's Pacific Air's wealthy investor. Or someone in her circle. I get the sense she comes from money."

"She has to if they live in West Van. Those houses start at three million. And you said the airline is in trouble."

"I have a feeling the long-term viability of Pacific Air hinges upon this project getting off the ground," I say. "There's not many people flying in and out of Lake Templeton. There's only so many times Aditya can take the City Hall executive team back and forth. I asked George to dig up his last tax filing. It will tell us if he's making losses and how big they are."

"Can the police run phone record searches for your key suspects?"

"There's not enough cause," I say. "I have a phone tracing contact, as you know. But she's expensive and I'm not getting paid for this case. And it's not exactly legal."

Zed tilts his head towards the posted board. "Why is the redhead not on there? You said he took Sharon home from the airport. Last person to see her alive."

"Sergio Alvarez, Marketing Manager at City Hall," I say, contemplating. I scribble his name next to Alena's and Aditya's on my poster board. "He says he was in a secret relationship with the victim. I can't think of a motive for him, though."

"Lover's spat?"

"Could be, I guess," I say. "Also, Sergio is Alena's protégé. The two could be in cahoots."

"Anyone else?"

"Not a suspect," I say. "But I'm curious about Korinne Kendall, the writer. She was close with Sharon. She was at the service this morning. I wanted to talk to her but she got there late and I had to leave early. I memorized her pin code when I first met her in Vancouver. I just need an opportunity to swipe her phone."

I recall Korinne's mournful face. It seemed too contrived, as if she was a stage actress putting on a performance.

"She's probably gone back to Vancouver now," Zed says. "Why would anyone stay in this crummy town longer than they need to?"

"There's something else that's bothering me." I rest my chin on interlaced fingers. "Sharon always met up with Korinne when she traveled to Vancouver. So why not last time?"

"You said her investor meetings didn't go well," Zed says. "Maybe she didn't feel like socializing."

"Yeah, but she would've called up Korinne *before* she left Lake Templeton - to book a time."

"Good point," Zed says, thoughtfully. "Do you know which investors she was meeting with?"

I shake my head in frustration. "Alena won't give me that information. There was no meeting agenda in Sharon's files. And the City deleted her work profile before I could get into her email and calendar."

"Assuming it was the mayor's doing," Zed says. "What a snake. So should we break into City Hall?"

"Do you *want* to spend the night in jail?" I say. "We both know Alena did us a solid when she let us walk away earlier. Although it wasn't out of the goodness of her heart."

"Of course not," Zed mutters. "She doesn't have a heart. Only scales and a forked tongue."

"I know one name that's maybe on that investor list," I say. "Lona Mason - the MLA for Vancouver-Fraserview. I've been trying to set up a meeting with her but she's supposedly out of town."

"Busy woman. I see her on the news all the time."

"I can't fully rule out Sharon's cult connection, either." I am already on to my next thought. "Her past is shrouded in mystery. We now know she wasn't just an innocent victim of the cult."

Zed and I toss around options and trade ideas until late in the night. We look through social media photos of every employee connected to Alena and Sharon at City Hall. There are photos from Alena's birthday party but none that feature Sharon or Sergio. No glimpse of Alena's brother, the man currently living in her house. Either he arrived after her birthday or he was hiding at home while the festivities raged on at the dimly-lit French bistro, one of a handful of high-end restaurants in Lake Templeton.

Later that night, I lie in bed, struggling to fall asleep. Five days of chaos, disruption, and distraction. For a pro bono case no one asked me to take on. Volunteer work was discouraged at my house while I was growing up. The purpose of work is to earn money - so you could buy a house and build a healthy savings account. Foregoing a salary to follow your heart is a mistake only stupid people make.

So why am I doing this? Is it to get justice for Sharon? The reality is, I don't do this work for altruistic reasons. The truth is - once I seize upon something, I struggle to let go. It becomes a quest. A hunt. I'm a starving predator that will perish if it doesn't catch its prey.

It's no way to live, my mom always says. But she never understood me.

Tuesday, December 17, 2019

It's half past ten when I awaken from an uneasy sleep. I roll out of bed, grimacing at the rank smell of my hair as I peel away the few matted strands that are stuck on my cheek. I need to wash it at some point.

Maybe, I should buzz it all off like Zed. He says he does it for the craft. A buzzed head makes it super easy to slip in and out of different wigs. Zed takes his disguises very seriously.

Zed is sprawled across the floor in an awkward, twisted position, a small trickle of drool dried into a thin droplet on his open mouth. I kick his shin softly as I skip over him to make my way to my laptop.

"Rise and shine," I yell. Zed doesn't stir.

My laptop is waiting for me like a bullied child waiting for their mother after kindergarten. It blinks awake at my touch. I navigate to my emails.

No response yet from my friend Leon, the Dean at the business school. He promised to send me a dossier on Aditya Roshan, Class of 2004, as a bright-eyed, bushy-tailed, eager-beaver international student.

I maintain a very clean email inbox - no useless subscriptions - thanks to a ruthless spam detection software. The email from Korinne Kendall rises up immediately, demanding my attention. Oh right. I signed up for her email list when I was scouring her website the other day.

I open the email, wondering when she had time to craft it, given she was in Lake Templeton for Sharon's service yesterday. Maybe she has an assistant who writes her emails for her. I don't know if Korinne is financially successful as an author but, judging from her former media notoriety and the size of her engagement ring, Ms. Korinne Kendall isn't hurting for money.

In her email, Korinne talks about what she's reading these days - her 'soul food.' She describes a recent trip to Spain with her fiancé. She plugs the sparkling five star resort she stayed at - for a kickback, no doubt. She teases her upcoming project, a new book.

A dramatic retelling of a true story. An exposé on a small town with dark and devastating secrets. A small town which is the site of a shocking murder. A small town called Trout Lake, BC (*name changed for privacy reasons*).

Am I reading that right? Trout Lake, BC?

Korinne is writing about Lake Templeton. About Sharon's murder.

Korinne acted like she knew nothing. She couldn't even take a guess at a possible suspect and motive. And now she's writing a book about it?

It's a wonder she fizzled out on TV. She could've won an Oscar for the performance she gave when we met at Figaro. She fooled even a skeptic like me.

I pick up my phone and dial Korinne's number. No answer. Of course. I leave a message asking her to call me right back.

My mind is racing. I feel restless and I haven't even had my first cup of coffee yet. A walk might freshen me up. Too many late nights spent in the dark dungeon of my thoughts.

I put on a mug of coffee and while waiting for it to brew, I shake Zed again - hard. Is he alive? He consumed copious amounts of wine and marijuana last night.

A few minutes later, my coffee is ready. I pour it into a takeaway mug. It's time for more drastic methods to wake up my sleeping sidekick. I walk into the bathroom and fill a glass with the coldest water I can draw from the tap. I walk over to Zed and pour the water on his face.

He jostles awake with a violent cry, a jack-in-the-box. A jerky splice in an old film. He shakes his head like a dog after a swim, rubs his eyes in confusion.

"Good morning, Zed," I say. "You've had enough sleep. We have work to do."

As Zed is sputtering awake, George calls me.

"I found out the ownership structure of Pacific Air."

"And?" My body tightens in anticipation.

"Just as you suspected," George says, and I can hear him smiling. "Aditya Roshan owns 49% of the shares. The rest - 51% controlling share - is registered under the name of Lona Mason."

Sergeant Keller calls me later that morning.

"The tox screen came back," he says. "You were right. We found PCP in her system."

PCP - a designer drug that falls into the dissociative category. It produces feelings of detachment and creates a dream-like state in the user. A bit like Zed's behavior the night he test drove the powder he stole from Aditya.

"Sergeant - are you absolutely sure that the cause of death was drowning?" I ask. "I'm perplexed that someone like Sharon - someone who never drank or took drugs - could be so completely toasted on PCP and alcohol, and not die of toxic drug interactions. Not to mention, she had a prescription for Ativan, an anti-anxiety medication. What am I missing here?"

"I get what you're saying," the Sergeant says. "The coroner feels that the alcohol was ingested not too long before she went overboard. In other words - if she hadn't drowned, she would've likely died of overdose."

"How are you feeling about the accident theory now?"

"Technically, it doesn't disprove it," Sergeant Keller says. "She was heavily under the influence. She could've fallen overboard."

"But why would she go out on the dock at eleven at night? Wearing heels?"

"Maybe she heard something or went to get something."

"Or maybe she was drawn out by someone," I say. "Also, your team didn't find anything on the dock besides the rope securing her boat."

"It could have gone overboard with her," Sergeant Keller suggests.

"But why was she drugged and drunk in the first place? Sharon didn't drink *or* do drugs."

"I'm not closing the case, Fati," the Sergeant says. "I agree with you - there are unanswered questions here."

"Well, good."

"I've ordered her phone history," Sergeant Keller says. "It will tell us more about her whereabouts in the hours leading up to her death."

"Perfect. It's about time."

"Also, the DNA test came back on that sweater you found in Mayor Krutova's fire pit," Sergeant Keller says. "That hair belongs to Sharon Reese. But Fati, it doesn't prove anything. Sharon and Alena worked together. Maybe Sharon left the sweater at Alena's place."

"Alena never invited her staff to her home," I say. "And Sharon was carrying the same sweater in the CCTV footage from the airport. When she returned home to Lake Templeton the night she died. The last known footage of her alive, I should remind you."

"I know, Fati," Sergeant Keller says. "But *you* know too. Unless you can find more to incriminate Mayor Krutova, or something damning comes up in the phone records, my hands are tied."

It's late afternoon and Zed and I are having lunch at the Lakeside Inn pub. He has finally stopped pouting about my cold water trick from the morning. I had to buy him a burger and beer to make it up to him. We've decided to return to Vancouver later today. Changing my environment might give me a fresh perspective on the conundrum of Sharon's death.

This case is becoming more expensive every day. I console myself by thinking of what a big coup it would be once the killer is unmasked. A gold star on my resume. All the referrals I get will pay for it. Maybe.

I am popping the last of my fries into my mouth when my friend Leon, the Dean at the business school, calls.

"That's odd," I say to Zed. "He was going to email me a dossier. God - I hope he hasn't suddenly grown a conscience about sharing private information on alumni."

Zed crosses one set of fingers as he reaches for his beer with the other, finishing off the brew with one swig.

"Hello, Leon," I say into the phone. "Please tell me you're still sending me the file on Aditya Roshan."

"I would if one existed," Leon says. "You're not going out with this guy, are you?"

Leon and I went to college together. He knew me when I was twenty and an outspoken force majeure at the undergraduate Department of Criminal Justice. He always thought I would go to law school and was bitterly disappointed when I enrolled in the police academy.

Bloody waste of talent, he said. I always thought that Leon was a little in love with me. I tease his wife about it now, when I visit them at their penthouse overlooking the sweeping sands of Kitsilano beach.

"Of course not," I say. "He's not my type. Why do you ask?"

"The guy is a ghost," Leon shares. "He never graduated with an MBA."

"You're kidding."

"Afraid not," Leon says. "There was an Aditya Roshan enrolled in the Class of 2004. But he only attended for a semester before failing out."

"And his classmates? Someone's got to remember him."

"I called a few people I know from that class," Leon says. "No one remembers him. For the short time he was there, he didn't socialize much. I can send you the class profile book in case you spot a familiar face. What's this guy done anyway?"

"He's mixed up in a murder I'm investigating."

"Whoa boy," Leon says. "Good luck to you. Aditya Roshan seems like one shady character, especially as he lied to you about finishing his MBA."

"Do you have a current address for him?"

"Nope," Leon says. "When someone fails out, we don't keep track of them."

I hang up the phone and fill Zed in.

"Why would he tell you he came here for his MBA if he never finished?" Zed is incredulous. "Did he not think you'd find out?"

I shrug. "Most people don't think that far ahead. I asked him what brought him to Vancouver and he answered - it's instinct, really."

What else is Aditya Roshan hiding?

Back at the motel, I inform the disappointed proprietor that I am checking out. Steady guests that pre-pay for multiple nights are clearly a rarity in wintertime Lake Templeton.

"Oh, I thought you might stay for Christmas," she says without irony.

I cast a glance at the worn-out decorations in the motel lobby. A five-foot plastic Christmas tree in the corner with fading lights, capped with a single, star-shaped ornament. A wreath on the door that looks stapled together and is starting to unravel.

I smile at the proprietor. "No. My family is expecting me."

How she must see me - an obsessive, lonely woman in her mid-thirties with strands of salt and pepper popping up like stubborn whack-a-moles on her hairline. Primitive clothes that run the range from gray to black to blacker, with the occasional tan thrown in. Nothing memorable, no distinguishing features. No ring on her finger, no diamonds dotting her earlobes, no makeup to make her pretty - and, unsurprisingly, no man to keep her company.

Maybe I can convince her that Zed is my boy toy.

I take Zed's hand as we walk towards the hotel elevator to go down to parking. My other hand rests on my shoulder bag that contains everything I packed for this trip. In contrast, Zed is dragging a knee-high hard-case roller bag that would barely fit into a plane's overhead cabin. He always brings a bookcase to a mountain trek.

Our elevator arrives and, as I turn to wave a final goodbye to the proprietor, I plant a full-mouthed kiss on a startled Zed's lips.

"What the hell was that for?" Zed exclaims, shaking me off as we step into the elevator.

"Just a little message for little miss-know-it-all over there," I say with a cryptic smile. "You owe me - after making me listen to your constant jabber about Brad. Are you spending Christmas with him this year?"

Zed looks at me in surprise. "I didn't think you were listening."

"Of course I was listening," I say with mock outrage. "Give me some credit. I think of things besides the case, you know."

"So you don't think it's a problem that Brad is married?"

Okay - I totally missed that one.

"Of course I don't care," I say airily. "You do you. All I worry about is the detrimental effect on your mental health from dating another married man. Have you forgotten what happened last time?"

Zed rolls his eyes, mouth pursing in a pout. How could he forget being handcuffed by the police for creating a disturbance and destroying property? Being dragged away while kicking his heels and screaming loudly enough to wake up the whole neighbourhood? But who can blame his former paramour's husband for calling the cops? By the time they arrived, Zed had pulled out all the flowers in his front lawn by their roots.

It's a two-hour drive to the Nanaimo ferry terminal. The morning's rain has stopped. The sun is struggling against heavy cloud cover, desperately wanting to shine but only able to poke a finger or two through the downy cumulus blankets.

Zed tentatively asks if he can smoke and I shoot him down. Last time I allowed that, it took me weeks to get the stench out of my car. As I drive, I let my mind wander. It skates past thought after thought, grasping and letting go at will.

And then Zed speaks, matter-of-fact, piercing through my meandering thought train, stopping it in its tracks.

"I think Aditya's wife is having an affair."

CHAPTER 9

Tuesday, December 17, 2019

"What are you talking about?" I ask, floored at Zed's unexpected revelation.

"While you've been lost in god knows what world, I've been researching," Zed says, clearly proud of himself. "I don't know how we did this job before social media."

"I don't know either," I murmur. "It took a lot longer to solve cases before everyone and their mother had a Facebook profile. Tell me what you found."

"I started with Kim Roshan's Facebook - quite a social butterfly. A very ladies-who-lunch type but, get this, she's also some kind of lifestyle-slash-fitness influencer. You know the type - doesn't need to work but thinks she can make a few quick bucks from sponsored posts on Instagram."

"Tell me more." My fingers tighten over the steering wheel in anticipation.

An extra-marital affair. Is this the stressor keeping Aditya up at night, causing him to neglect his appearance?

"Her maiden name is Cromwell," Zed says. "She still goes by Kim Cromwell on her website, Instagram, and Twitter. Probably has to do with personal branding. She's Kim Roshan on Facebook."

"Chip off a block of money?"

"Oh yeah." Zed nods. "Lots of it. The Cromwells are involved in a shipping and transportation empire that controls a big chunk of the Vancouver port."

A prosperous family with old money clout. Aditya hit the jackpot.

"Are there photos of Aditya on her profile?"

"Oh yeah," Zed says. "Wedding photos, too. From this past summer. Big white wedding, expensive flowers, silk tablecloth, the whole bit."

"What makes you think she's cheating on Aditya?"

"A comment on one of their wedding photos," Zed says. "It has thirty-two likes. I'm surprised Kim didn't delete it. But then, she probably hasn't seen it. There are dozens of comments on all her photos. Mrs. Kim Roshan, formerly Cromwell, is a popular girl."

"How much stock can we put in a Facebook comment?" I say. "It may be a jilted lover or jealous frenemy."

"Could be," Zed agrees. "But where there's smoke, there's usually hot, hot fire."

"Who made the comment?"

"I can't tell. Looks like it's a dummy profile. No photos."

Is Aditya's drug dealing the spiteful revenge of a cowed husband? He felt sidelined and judged in his wife's blue chip, white-bread world. Maybe this was his backlash.

Zed and I arrive at the ferry terminal twenty minutes earlier than expected. I must have been zipping down the highway fast. I roll my car into the vehicle line-up and put it into 'park.' Turning to Zed, I snatch his phone from his hand, ignoring his protest.

Kim Roshan - the woman of the hour. Zed wasn't joking about her internet presence. She's expressive and incandescent in photos, the opposite of her husband. There's so much of her - photos, videos, even GIFs - as if she wants the whole world to know all of her. Again, I feel a stab of recognition. A vague feeling of familiarity as if I have seen her somewhere before.

Kim is a brunette with a square jaw, almond shaped eyes and a small mouth that smiles big. She has a stocky build that she keeps in shape through religious exercise. Her broad shoulders are firm and slope into well-defined arms. Wispy, layered bangs soften the sharp angles of her face.

Kim posts on social media throughout the day. There are photos of her meals - *I eat all the colors of the rainbow.* There are photos of the Vancouver skyline with fiery sunsets bleeding into majestic mountains and pouring into crystalline ocean. There are videos of Kim's workout routines which she cycles through with a performative energy - as if their purpose is not to improve her health but to project an image.

Her website is an explosion of color and energy. Her 'About Me' page is a descriptive sonnet about passion and purpose with no reference to any hard qualifications she has to teach fitness and nutrition.

Her 'Services' page lists group workout packages (including pole dancing and belly dancing workouts), one-on-one training, nutritional consulting. And life coaching - to help you heal after trauma.

Except that Ms. Kim Roshan won't know trauma if it walked up to her and shook her hand. Judging by appearances, Kim has an easy life. Privileged upbringing, trust fund, skiing in Aspen, vacations glamping through Europe, no devastating accidents, both parents still alive, happily married. If there is trauma in Kim's past, it's well-hidden.

Aditya could spend the rest of his life jet setting from the couch to the hot tub to a hammock on the patio while sipping Dom Perignon and getting daily massages. Given his wife's net worth, he isn't struggling to pay the bills.

If Pacific Air is struggling, why doesn't he use his wife's money to lift it off the ground (pun intended)? Is it a misplaced sense of pride? Manly bravado that he wears the pants, and so, has to take care of the bills?

I navigate to the 'Events' page on Kim's website. Something catches my attention.

THE LAKE TEMPLETON MURDERS

"I guess I'm going to a '*healing circle*,'" I say to Zed, barely able to keep the disgust from my voice. "Kim hosts them every week at the yacht club."

Zed raises his eyebrows. "And anyone can attend?"

"With a small registration fee, yes," I say. "And by small, I mean one hundred dollars."

Zed chuckles, shakes his head. "And when is this healing circle?"

"Tomorrow."

"And there's a spot available at the last minute?"

"Did you not hear me? It's one hundred dollars for a healing circle. I won't be surprised if I'm the only one there."

The cars in front of me are starting to move. I turn on my ignition, put my car into 'drive.' I'm going home.

My apartment is an ice box when I return to it that evening. I hang up my jacket and crank up the heat.

My condo is located on a hilly bluff on Broadway and Ash Street. It's an older building with rental restrictions, which means all the units are owner-occupied with an older millennial and Gen-X population. That's just the way I like it. Loud parties with kegs, shooter flights, and revolving doors of overnight guests aren't my thing.

I sit on my recliner on the wraparound terrace with a glass of pinot noir - poured into a water glass because I always shatter thin-stemmed wine glasses. The glittering lights of Vancouver shimmer and ululate like a sea of gemstones on the black cashmere shawl of night.

The wine warms my blood and slows my incessant thought sprint and without realizing it, I doze off. My thoughts dislocate from the confounding mess of this case. The noise of the neighborhood fades into a comforting hum as it reaches my twelfth-floor apartment, lulling me to the world of dreams.

Wednesday, December 18, 2019

I sleep for a good six hours before I am woken up by a muscle screaming in my back, reminding me that I am not Dorothy in the world of Oz but a thirty-five-year-old woman entering the second half of her life.

I drag myself inside - to bed - and collapse for another four hours before my shrilling phone jars me awake.

I pick it up, hold it close to my face, reminding myself for the tenth time to go to the optometrist to have my eyes checked out. I am also a woman who will need reading glasses not too many years from now.

It's Sergeant Keller. I accept the call, put it on speaker.

"Hello, Sergeant," I mumble.

"Where are you, Fati?" Sergeant Keller says. "Are you still on the Island?"

"No - I left yesterday." I sit up, yawn, rub my eyes, push my sticky hair away from my forehead. I must wash it before I head to the yacht club. Otherwise, they will mistake me for a vagrant and refuse to let me in.

"I was talking with the Super yesterday," Sergeant Keller says. "Filling him in on the Sharon Reese case. He feels - and I agree - given recent revelations, we can't have an unpaid PI run point on this."

Suddenly, I am wide awake. "What do you mean?"

"This is looking more and more like foul play."

"I told you from Day One this was murder," I remind him. "You're the one who refused to believe it."

"Well, I believe it now," Sergeant Keller says. "You've done good work, Fati."

"So why are you firing me?"

"Firing you?" Sergeant Keller seems taken aback. "I'm not firing you. I'm giving you help."

"What?" My brain feels fuzzy. I need coffee.

"I made a request to the Police Department a week ago for extra resources," Sergeant Keller says. "But then you came and I didn't push it. I expected to close this as an accident or suicide. But now it's looking like a homicide and homicides have to be solved by the police."

"I told you it's murder," I remind the Sergeant again, in an accusatory tone. "We've worked together enough times for you to know I'm rarely wrong about stuff like this, Sergeant. In fact, you're the one who taught me. Told me I had a gift. Encouraged me to pursue policing. I thought you trusted me."

"I do trust you," Sergeant Keller says, in a placating tone. "Effective immediately, we're assigning a Detective to this case. Singh. But he has three other cases he's working on. So, we'll keep you on as a civilian consultant and pay you a small stipend, plus expenses."

"Well, that's great news," I say petulantly. "But I'm not babysitting a Detective. Happy to report back to him but I work alone. That's why I left the force, remember?"

"He may be okay with that," Sergeant Keller says. "As long as you do things above board and report back to him regularly."

"What's he like, this Detective Singh?"

"A solid police officer," Sergeant Keller says. "Dependable, reliable, efficient on the field. A little curt when you first meet him, but he has a near perfect solve rate."

"Sounds like my kind of guy."

"This is a good thing, Fati," Sergeant Keller says. "You can do more with police resources. No one refuses to talk to you when you flash a badge."

That may be true but they rarely tell the truth.

The police's intrusion isn't a surprise. I knew this where the case was heading. The men and women in blue are too eager to steal my thunder. I don't have a badge. I'm easy to shove behind the curtain.

I think about how Alena would react if I show up to Lake Templeton with a police cruiser in tow. She must have destroyed all evidence against her by now. She would relish the chance to air the dirty laundry of my methods for the police. This could be bad. Very bad.

"What's the name of this detective? Singh, you said?" I pop open my iPad. It scans my retina and lets me in.

"Talvir Singh."

I write it down in block letters. I need to handle Detective Talvir Singh very carefully.

"I'm assuming I can claim expenses I've already incurred in this case?" I say, thinking of the hundred dollars - plus GST - charge for Kim's healing circle. Not to mention the flights back and forth on Pacific Air.

"As long as Talvir approves them."

Great. Well, for better or for worse, I have a boss now. There are rules. I will have to be on my best behavior for the remainder of this case - within reason. In my experience, no case is ever solved by following the rules.

I spend thirty minutes soaking in the shower - a rare indulgence.

What do you wear to a healing circle? My meager wardrobe offers limited options. And a reminder that my last laundry day was three weeks ago.

Something calming and pastel, maybe. A floral scarf or flowing robes, perhaps. Are beads optional or mandatory? I settle on jeans and a tee-shirt topped with a zip-up hoodie.

I make my customary stopover at Starbucks on my way to the yacht club. I sip my Venti dark roast as I drive, steeling myself for an eye-roll of an hour.

What do you do in a healing circle? I should've done more research before offering myself up to be emotionally sliced and diced.

The yacht club lets me in when I present my electronic receipt for the event. I guide my aging Mazda 3 into the lot and park it in a corner, away from the disapproving gaze of the Range Rovers and Teslas.

The yacht club is a long, rectangular, gray-tiled building with dark turrets and white trim, a symbol of status from colonial times. The front lawn is clipped neatly, as if every blade of grass has been properly measured. Its rich green is bordered by a cornucopia of winter flowers. Hedges are shaped in beautiful domes. It must take a string quartet of gardeners to maintain.

A hammered gold sign at the entrance warns - 'Members Only.' I raise a middle finger at it in childish defiance.

The interior offers sloping ceilings in polished wood paneling and a tiled floor that looks freshly mopped. It's eerily quiet inside. I realize why when my cell phone shrills and I reach for it automatically, only to be interrupted by a man in a three-piece suit who scurries over in admonishment. He points to a sign by the front entrance: '*Please turn off the ringer on your cell phone.*'

Great. They really want to take you back to the turn of the twentieth century. I suppose it's part of the authentic experience. It harkens back to a time when the blue-chip old-money families of Vancouver were secure in the knowledge that the nouveau riche upstarts - and heaven forbid, the unwashed masses, were kept far away from their exclusive spaces.

The sign also outlines a dress code. Oh, so there's a uniform too? How stiff upper lipped of them. Uniforms make it easy to organize people under labels. They effortlessly separate those that are here to serve from those that are here to *be* served.

I ask the flustered, suited man for directions. He ushers me in the direction of a private room, a carpeted, ocean-facing space with wooden pillars flanking full-length picture windows rising high into the ceiling. An army of sailboats is docked outside, sitting calmly on the flat, silver-gray water. The North Shore mountains tease from the distance, opening up into vivid blue sky brushed with slate gray and white clouds and little pockets of sun, still fighting to push through the gaseous thickets.

"Quite a view, isn't it?" A chipper voice speaks beside me. Distracted from the visual bounty of nature, I turn to the speaker.

I've never met Kim before but after perusing her social media, I feel that I know her.

"Yes, it is," I say. "I never get tired of it. It's very - healing."

Kim nods rapidly. Her every gesture bubbles with enthusiasm, punctuated with her wide-eyed, big-mouthed smile. Her dark hair is pulled back in a ponytail. She looks like an excitable puppy, friendly and oozing with affection for every stranger.

She sticks out her hand to greet me. "My name is Kim. Welcome, and thank you for coming. Is this your first time attending a healing circle?"

I take her hand. "Nice to meet you. My name is Fati. And yes, this is my first healing circle."

"So what brought you here today, Fati?" Kim starts walking, and I fall into step beside her. She is wearing pressed khaki chino pants with a loose-fitting emerald silk blouse. She looks like an off-duty power broker on vacation.

"Curiosity, I guess," I murmur, feeling terribly underdressed in my tee-shirt and jeans.

There are five other people in the room, four women and a lone man. I size them up. There is an easy familiarity between them. They've been here before. They know each other well.

And here I am - the new face. Object of their unbridled curiosity. They probably don't get a lot of newbies here. Maybe the price point is meant to discourage new converts.

As I am introducing myself, a woman walks in. With her head down, I can't fully see her face. She's slightly heavyset with a blonde pixie cut. Feathered bangs cover her narrow forehead and fall over her eyebrows. She probably trims them every couple of weeks. She is wearing jeans and a cream-colored tunic that covers her hips. She is distracted, one hand in her Burberry bucket bag. As she comes closer, I realize that she is surreptitiously checking emails on a carefully hidden cell phone. Naughty, naughty.

"Oh good, Lona is here," someone says. "We can get started now."

Lona? My pulse quickens as she approaches, switches off her phone, lifts her head.

It's Lona Mason, the MLA from Vancouver-Fraserview. The politician whose name has come up several times in my investigation. A mysterious investor of the Lake Templeton revitalization project. The lifeline keeping Pacific Air alive. The woman whose office I have been calling for days - only to be barred and barricaded by an officious gatekeeper. My dashed hopes awaken, re-energized.

Lona is in her early forties. A smattering of sunspots dots her face, partly concealed with a light layer of foundation. Her skin appears translucent, well-hydrated, the skin of someone who takes her hot yoga classes and acupuncture seriously. When she smiles, dimples appear like craters, and soft crow's feet treadmill the corners of her eyes.

Kim lights up at the sight of Lona, like a blooming bud spreading its petals. They lock arms. It's obvious they are close. Did Kim engineer Lona's investment into her husband's company, Pacific Air?

I wonder why Lona wasn't in any of Kim's social media photos. An over-sharer like Kim would have written effusive posts about her dear friend, a woman on the Premier's speed dial, according to political chatter. But Kim is very well-connected herself, with a heavy-duty family name that wields economy-moving clout.

I hang back as hugs are exchanged. Lona and I shake hands. I introduce myself as an 'investigator.' deliberately glossing over the type of work that I do. I need to watch my step, move cautiously. If Lona and Kim get their backs up, they will shut down. Fortress themselves behind a medieval moat.

We sit down on the plush chairs, arranged in a circle. Kim calls the meeting to order by putting her hands together and bringing them close to her heart. Her fingernails are well-manicured with subtle French tips. On her ring finger, a simple eternity band, encircled in high-shine diamonds.

Thankfully, there are no candles or chanting. Instead, Kim thanks everyone for bringing their whole selves and opening up to sharing. She talks about healing and nurturing your tender inner child; empty words adapted from a mealy-mouthed self-help tome. I observe each person in the circle.

Their faces are rapt; they are clearly hooked on the linguistic drug that Kim is dispensing through the lilting cadence of her soothing voice.

I glance down at the glass of fruit-infused water that Kim handed to me before starting. Has she mixed in the hallucinatory drug her husband is hawking? How else could she get these people to hang on her every word, as if she were a messiah?

It's time to share the source of our trauma. Someone talks about losing a close friend to a disfiguring car accident. Another shares a story of a sexual assault.

It's my turn. Everyone is looking at me expectantly. *You've heard our ugly stories, it's time to share yours.*

I wrack my brain. I had a loving, though simple upbringing. I wasn't a popular girl in school but I was well-liked. Being a loner was my choice, not one imposed on me by a lack of attention. Both my parents are still alive, although my relationship with my mother has always been strained. Neither of my siblings is a drug addict. I've never been married or gone through a traumatic breakup, and I drive relatively carefully, even when I'm distracted and speeding. It's a gift.

"I would rather wait," I say, with false hesitancy. "It's my first time here. I don't think I'm comfortable baring myself yet."

Borrowing some of Kim's language yields the result I was hoping for. She nods sympathetically.

"We understand. It can take time to shake off the walls we have been taught to erect around us from childhood." She gestures to the group. "And you don't know us yet. But I hope you will let us in. This is a circle of trust. We are all here because we're not afraid to be vulnerable."

Sure, I can be vulnerable. I just need a little more time to make something up.

It's Lona's turn. What will she pull out of her closet of pain and sin? Nothing too incendiary, I'm sure. She's a public figure. An MLA, with a stated desire to run for parliament. I have no doubt she has a carefully crafted story that would pass political muster. Present her as authentic, while avoiding the scarring brush of human weakness.

"I still think about my son," Lona says. "All the time."

That's a strange comment. Lona has a ten-year-old son and an eight-year-old daughter. They appear on her website and in her official photos. She speaks of them proudly as the glue that holds her together, particularly after her divorce. As far as I know, they live with her and her ex-husband has visitation rights.

"Doesn't your son live with you?" I blurt out.

The members of the circle of trust swivel their heads to look at me in rebuke. Kim's disapproving eyes rest on me, a departure from her smiling visage.

"We don't interrupt someone when they're talking," she admonishes, softening her words with a half-smile, acknowledging that this is my first time in the sacred circle of sharing.

"I'm not talking about Timmy, my younger son," Lona says. "I'm talking about my firstborn, the one I gave up. I regret it every day."

The son she gave up? She must have shared this morsel publicly in the past.

"I was a teen mother," Lona says. "When I got pregnant, my family was worried I would ruin my life. They convinced me to put the baby up for adoption."

"Why not get an abortion?" I ask.

Lona looks at me sharply. "It goes against my personal beliefs," she says tightly.

Spoken like a true conservative. Lona's political leanings are not a secret. Coming from a moneyed oil family in Alberta, the power structures in her life have always leaned right.

On stage, Lona is a vocal advocate for adoption, lobbying to simplify our unwieldy laws to make it easier for good families to adopt. She openly praises adoptive parents and encourages those that struggle with infertility to look at adoption as a viable option. Now that I know her history, it makes sense.

I can't help but compare Lona to Sharon. Both went through trauma early in life. But chose to handle it very differently. Sharon withdrew into herself; shunned everyone around her. Lona created a dollhouse over a crater. A seemingly normal life. A picture-perfect family, well-behaved kids, deep friendships, an enviable career in public service.

Was family the answer? Lona's buttressed her. Sharon's had betrayed her.

"Do you know where your child is?" I ask, ignoring the put-off looks from the rest of the circle.

"No," Lona says. "I've spoken about him publicly but I respect his timing. He will come look for me when it's right for him. I cannot overstep his adoptive parents' rights by initiating contact."

Something about the way her lips tighten and her brows furrow makes me suspect she is lying. If Lona was a teenage mother, her son is older than nineteen, past the age of majority, a legal adult. And with her connections, it's hard to believe that Lona wouldn't have made the effort, at least discreetly, to locate him. Whether or not she made contact is another matter.

Lona's story is interesting, but I'm not sure if it has any bearing on my case. I let go of my invasive line of questioning. Reproductive decisions and maternal instincts are hardly an area of interest for me.

The circle members look relieved when I stop talking. They bid Lona peace, healing, and good tidings. And it's my turn again. After how involved I got in another's problems, I can't get away with failing to share my own.

I open my mouth and say the first words that come to mind. "I can't have children. That's why I'm single at thirty-five."

Knowing looks dawn around the room. Here's an explanation for all my questions for Lona. Humans are so predictable. That's why people like me stay in business - and make a pretty good living from time to time.

The healing circle wraps shortly after. It took a little more than an hour. I still can't figure out where my hundred dollars went. The things I could have bought with that money - five mystery novels by Harlen Coben, a new sweater I've been eyeing at Brooks Brothers, a Rosetta Stone course to kickstart my Russian, a bottle of perfectly aged Gevrey Chambertin Pinot Noir. Sheriff Keller and the new entrant, Detective Talvir Singh, better pay me back for this waste of time.

I remind myself why I came in the first place. I came to talk to Kim - and got the unexpected gift of Lona Mason. I cannot leave without cracking the surface of these two women, huddled together in conversation, laughing and touching each other's arms.

They look up when I approach, an almost imperceptible guardrail descending over their faces.

"Thank you for coming," Kim says, the perfect hostess. "It was so nice to meet you."

"It was a pleasure to meet you too," I say. "Actually, I came here for a reason. I was curious about you, Kim."

Kim raises her eyebrows. "Oh? I don't think we've met before, have we?"

"No, we have not," I say. "But I know your husband."

"I see," Kim says. "He's never mentioned you to me."

I suppose I'm not important enough for Aditya to discuss with his wife. But what else do they have in common? What do they talk about when they're alone? Maybe he reads her sixteenth century love sonnets like a misty-eyed Romeo.

"He wouldn't have," I say. "We're not friends."

"Then?"

"He's flown me several times to Lake Templeton in the past week. I talked to him about a murder that took place there. A Sharon Reese. Do you know her?"

There is no hint of recognition on Kim's face.

CHAPTER 10

Wednesday, December 18, 2019

Kim looks befuddled at my question. She shakes her head. No, she doesn't know Sharon Reese.

Lona speaks up. "Sharon Reese - she works for the City, doesn't she? Lake Templeton."

"That's correct," I pounce on her words. "So you know her? I know you met at the YWCA Gala ten years ago. You gave her an award. I saw the photos."

"I wouldn't say I *know* her, but I've met her," Lona says. "I'm an investor in a project there - me personally. Not the government."

"The Lake Templeton revitalization project?"

"Yes, that's what I think they're calling it," Lona says. She turns to Kim. "It's a big project to completely transform the town by 2023. They're putting up a resort, upgrades to the civil infrastructure, internet connectivity, amenities. It's a public private partnership."

"Surely, your husband mentioned this to you," I say to Kim.

"Yes, I'm aware of the project," Kim says, hesitantly. "I don't know too many details though."

"Why did you invest in the Lake Templeton revitalization project?" I ask Lona.

"The same reason anyone invests in anything," Lona says. "To get a return."

"Are the investors involved in decision making?" I say. "Or are they silent partners, only putting up the money and expecting dividends once the project is completed?"

"We're not involved in decision making but we get periodic updates from the Lake Templeton team," Lona says. "That's the way it usually works with these projects."

"And you trust the City government to get this project off the ground?"

"I trust them to oversee it," Lona says. "But we're getting an independent general contractor and project monitor."

"And these people have already been hired?"

"It's in process, as per the last update Mayor Krutova gave us," Lona says. "A few weeks ago."

"I see."

The general contractor and project monitor haven't been hired, but payments to vendors have already started. I'm no expert in construction projects but that sounds odd.

"Sharon has been murdered?" Lona says, suddenly understanding what I said. "Oh my goodness. When? Why?"

"A week ago," I say. "As for the why... that's what I'm here to find out."

"Are you working with the police?" Kim says. "Is that why you came here today?"

"Yes," I admit.

Kim looks pained, let down, maybe realizing her healing circles don't have mass appeal, after all.

"Why did you want to talk to Kim?" Lona says. "What does she have to do with it?"

Lona is bold and outspoken, and packs a commanding persona. She seems protective of Kim, a woman seven or eight years younger than her. A mama bear, ready to step into the hunter's line of fire while shuffling her cub behind her.

"I believe in pursuing every lead, no matter how small," I say. I turn to Kim. "Your husband, Aditya, flew Sharon back to Lake Templeton the night she was killed."

"You think my husband killed Sharon just because he flew her home?" Kim is incredulous. "He regularly flies the City Hall staff. That's his job."

I decide not to share about Aditya's drug dealing. I don't want to raise the alarm yet. Leaving Aditya in the dark will allow me to trail him stealthily a little longer. See if he makes a mistake.

"As I said, I'm talking to anyone I can," I say. I turn to Lona. "And that's why I've been trying to get a hold of you,

Ms. Mason. I called your office several times over the last few days to try and book a meeting."

"You can book a meeting with me anytime you want," Lona says. "Any voter can."

How generous.

"That's good to know," I say. "Because your office was giving me the runaround."

"My schedule gets booked weeks in advance," Lona says. "But if you told them you were with the police, they'd let you in right away."

Sure, they would. Except I'm not with the police. And I want to avoid bringing in my official babysitter, Detective Talvir Singh, for as long as I can.

"Well, since you're here, why don't you ask me what you need to know?" Lona offers.

I eye Lona curiously. She is being quite helpful.

"I wanted to know about your involvement with the Lake Templeton revitalization project," I say. "You've already confirmed that you're an investor. I think the project may have something to do with Sharon's death."

Now I've gone and done it. I've let an investor know there's a bug in the soup of the Lake Templeton revitalization project. I can visualize Alena breathing fire, cutting me to shards with her eyes.

"What do you mean?" Lona says. "You think someone connected with the project killed her?"

"Can you tell me who else has invested in the project?" I ask, avoiding her question.

"It's not my place to share that," Lona says. "You'll have to ask Mayor Krutova."

Do all roads lead back to Alena? Round and round in circles and always back to her. Alena, the immovable brick wall. Has she coached everyone to parrot her party line?

"How well do you know Alena?" I ask, tamping back my frustration.

"Not too well," Lona says. "I first met her when she worked at BC Children's Hospital - in Vancouver. She told me about her political ambitions. I encouraged her. God knows we need more women in politics. I was surprised when she went to Lake Templeton. I thought she had a good chance of rising up the ranks here in Vancouver."

We chat for a few more minutes. Nothing is shared that I don't already know. I bid the women goodbye and make my way to the exit.

Kim is a lost puppy who yaps all day for show and Lona is a protector. A woman in charge who takes no bullshit from anyone. They seem like the kind of friends who call each other at midnight when they can't sleep because they've fought with their spouses. Lona probably had the if-you-hurt-her-I-will-kill-you talk with Aditya when he married Kim.

Sitting in my car, I turn over different thoughts like patterned rocks at the beach. Where do I go from here?

I press the 'start' button and my car sputters to life. Waits for the flood of acceleration. A few seconds later, I switch it off and lean back. I stormed the front door and found no one home. It's time to try the back door. And so, I wait.

Fifteen minutes later, Kim comes out, looking preoccupied. I sink deeper in my seat. Thankfully, my Mazda is invisible - that's why I drive it. Designer wheels dot the yacht club parking lot. In a flock of peacocks, who will notice the gray rat lurking in the corner?

Kim stands at the yacht club entrance. She pulls her loose-fitting camel leather jacket closer to her. She reaches into one pocket, takes out a palm-sized packet, shakes out a cigarette and raises it to her lips.

A nasty habit for someone who flouts an aspirational healthy lifestyle all over social media.

A few minutes go by with Kim taking long, guiltless drags, blowing out plumes that rest like tired workers on the cold air. And then, a familiar figure emerges from the front door. It's Lona. She glances at the cellphone she holds in one hand, tosses it into the yawning mouth of her Burberry bag, and approaches Kim. She smiles, touches Kim's arm, grasps her wrist that holds the cigarette, shakes her head, as if disapprovingly. A loved one reminding another that their filthy habits lead to an early grave.

They lock arms. Kim tosses her cigarette away dutifully. They start walking, in lockstep with one another, strangely coordinated as if they've walked this path together for years. Two gazelles on a journey.

I watch, transfixed. They approach a car - a white Mercedes Benz SUV that looks like it would be just as comfortable on rugged mountain terrain as it is on the freshly paved parking lot of a modern metropolitan castle. Kim raises her hand, activates her key, and the car beeps into attendance.

The two women pause, chat imperceptibly. Lona starts to turn towards what must be her car - a larger Cadillac Escalade in high-shine black, parked right beside Kim's SUV. Even their cars cannot live without one another.

Kim holds firm on Lona's arm, unable or unwilling to let go, pulls her towards her, pushes her slightly towards the passenger side door of her Mercedes SUV. Lona obliges, gets in, while Kim walks around to the driver's side.

I turn on my engine ready to follow, cursing when it barks awake, the sound impossibly loud. I wait, foot poised over the accelerator.

The Mercedes SUV does not move. It doesn't even turn on. I lean over the passenger's seat of my car, trying to get a better look.

Kim's head is turned away from me, towards Lona. I see a sliver of her moving mouth. They are talking. God, what I wouldn't give to be a fly stuck to that window.

My foot hovers over my accelerator, presses down slightly, and my car rolls forward. Just a few more inches...

And then I see it. And slam on the brakes. My car croaks in protest, jerks to a stop.

They are kissing. Deep, full-throated kissing. Not a peck between friends. It's foreplay, the kind that leads to the seats pushed back, windows steamed, and a cop arriving at your window.

Kim is having an affair with Lona.

"So you followed them *where?*"

I grip my phone hard. It's the third time he has asked me the same question. Is Detective Talvir Singh deliberately being obtuse or does his brain work slower than a snail on a cross country trek?

I was flying high after returning from the Vancouver Yacht Club. But a few minutes on the phone with Detective Talvir Singh, and I have whiplash from the nosedive.

"A healing circle," I repeat - again. "And I didn't follow them. I paid for a ticket." I enunciate each word, realize that I sound condescending and stop myself with some effort.

There's no point in antagonizing him. This is a man with the power to kick me off the case, no explanation needed. I take a deep breath and lean against my kitchen table. I gaze at the calming blue of the sky outside my window to cool my internal thermometer.

"Why are you wasting time chasing blind leads? What evidence do you have to link Kim Roshan or Lona Mason to this case?"

"As I said, Kim Roshan is Aditya Roshan's wife, the airline pilot who…"

"I know who she is." Detective Singh cuts me off sharply. "And I don't see how her extramarital affair is any of our business. We are a police department, not *People* magazine."

"It's our business because her husband is connected to our case!"

"You've already told me about the supposed evidence on Aditya Roshan, which you obtained illegally," Detective Singh says. "You know I can't do anything with it in court."

"You don't have to take it to court yet," I say in exasperation. "Just let me work this case in my own way. I'll bring you more, I promise you."

"So I should let you - a civilian - run around pissing off God knows how many people, putting everyone on edge with your roughhousing."

I grit my teeth. I am not a ten-year-old in a playground.

"Look, Detective Singh," I say tightly. "I think you haven't worked with a PI before. If you ask Sergeant Keller, he can share more about how I work…"

"No, I haven't worked with a PI before because I've never had a problem solving my own cases." Detective Singh's voice is laced with disdain, possibly directed at Sergeant Keller.

"I'm sure you haven't." I adopt a conciliatory tone. "I'm sure you're a great detective. But I also know you have two other murders on the go - one of them a gang execution, possibly linked to the Surrey 6."

He should know I have connections at the police department too.

"What do you know about that?" Detective Singh barks.

"I know you have enough on your plate," I say soothingly, raging inside.

"Have you tracked down the stolen money?" Detective Singh's clipped words challenge my competence.

"No," I say. "Mayor Krutova's independent audit isn't yet complete. But I'm not sure I believe Sharon Reese stole the money. She had no need for it. She lived a simple life."

"We dug up her bank details - no suspicious transactions," Detective Singh says gruffly.

"I'm trying to find out more about her will," I say. "I talked to the folks at City Hall. They said there's no next of kin and most of the money is going to a charity in Maple Ridge. Doesn't sound like someone who'd steal money from the City."

"I got those details from the executor," Detective Singh says begrudgingly, forced by an invisible puppeteer to share information with a lowly PI. "There's just under a hundred and fifty thousand dollars. And thirty-five thousand in equity in her lodge. The charity in Maple Ridge is an orphanage called the Thriving Mind Society."

Thriving Mind Society. I reach for my iPad across my kitchen table, flip it open, jot the name down in capital letters.

"Swing by the RCMP office on Wesbrook Mall tomorrow so we can chat in person," Detective Singh says. "And I'm not

paying for that kitty cocktail party or whatever you attended."
He hangs up.

Ass. There goes my hundred dollars. Plus GST.

The evening is rising in Vancouver, darkness advancing
up the fading blue sky, smothering it. I pour a glass of pinot
noir and walk barefoot across my cold hardwood floor to the
balcony.

Lona Mason. What could she have to do with Sharon's
death? She's an investor in the Lake Templeton revitalization
project. She's also an investor in Aditya's airline, Pacific Air.
And she's having an affair with his wife. Lona must know
Aditya is struggling. Was she putting pressure on him to
return her money? Is that why he started dealing drugs?

It's not just Aditya and Kim Roshan that connect Lona to
this case. Lona knew Sharon, the victim. Presented her with
an award at the YWCA gala in 2009. When Sharon was a
newly minted cult escapee, the enigma of the hour.

I pull out my phone to look at the photo of the gala from
Sharon's office. Four women and three men standing around
Sharon like carefully arranged chess pieces.

And then I spot something I missed before. Another
familiar face. A face I didn't recognize before because it was
foreign to me.

It's Kim.

She stands next to Lona, tucked into her shoulder like
a loving spouse. She's wearing a flowy, pale blue gown

that looks like it was pulled off a fashion model walking the runway. A fuzzy purse that looks like a pom-pom, no bigger than your palm, hangs off a shoulder from a thin gold-link chain.

So that's why Kim looked so familiar! Does her relationship with Lona go back that far?

Heart pumping, I navigate to the link the helpful YWCA employee sent me. I scroll through the photos from the event.

Sharon in her black gown, enigmatic smile tinged with I-don't-know-what-I'm-doing-here hesitation. Korinne Kendall with her fake bake, muscled cleavage, and bowling ball veneers.

And there she is - Kim. Hiding in plain sight. Always next to Lona - their chairs drawn close together, knees colliding. Fingers brushing as they reach for their wine glasses. Shared-secret smiles.

A wedding band encircles Lona's ring finger. She was married at the time. A few months postpartum after giving birth to her son, Timmy.

Was Lona sleeping with Kim while pregnant with her husband's child? And how did she hide it for years during her relentless climb up the political flagpole?

Kim - so innocent and blameless on the surface. A young woman, only twenty-five. A best friend to share girlish confidences with during a sex-free sleepover. A best friend with cleavage that won't quit. Cleavage on full display like a luxury car in a showroom as she leans towards Lona, one hand grazing her arm while the other saddles an iPhone...

An iPhone! Kim must have dozens of photos of the YWCA gala, maybe even videos. A woman with her affinity for self promotion doesn't leave any opportunity untapped.

Forgetting my glass of wine, I eagerly dive into Kim's world through the screen. Scroll, scroll, scroll on her Instagram. The years whir by like a microfilm racing backwards.

And there it is - May 2009.

As I expected, there are photos. Dozens of them. Various angles of Kim in her silky blue gown that moves this way and that even in pictures. As if she is standing over an air vent.

And then, I find what I am looking for - a video. I feel like a formerly infertile woman holding a positive pregnancy test in her hand.

It's a dimly lit recording of Sharon accepting her award. It's taken from a low angle close to the stage, from Kim's vantage point at the head table. The sound is crystal clear and, even from a distance of years, I can tell the audience is hanging on Sharon's every word.

Sharon does not have any notes. She holds her award, cradles it. She looks out on the audience as if looking through them. She speaks about the maelstrom of the cult but does not offer too many details. She talks about what happened after she left, alone and friendless, shellshocked at being confronted with a world that felt alien. Time passed slowly during her entrapment but the world whizzed by without her. Technologies changed. The sun rose and the moon sank, again and again in a repetitive blur of transformation, bringing new trends, phasing out old ones. Sharon felt overwhelmed, as if she were an ossified pharaoh brought back to life in the twenty-first century.

There were people who helped her. A foster home sheltered her, gave her room and board in exchange for taking care of the kids. A foster home called Thriving Mind Society, located in the suburb of Maple Ridge, an hour's drive from Vancouver.

Thriving Mind Society. The same charity that Sharon willed her fortune to. Now I know why.

I fall into bed early, to conserve my energy for the long drive to Maple Ridge tomorrow. But I can't sleep. I lie in the dark, my eyes bat-like, counting the grains in my corrugated ceiling.

Why did Kim lie about not knowing Sharon? She sat next to her at the YWCA gala, took a video of her accepting her award, posted it online with a cloying barrage of hashtags and heart emojis. And yet, she was utterly blank when I confronted her with the dead woman's name.

Does she have the memory of a hummingbird? Or is she a closeted psychopath?

My gut tells me that Kim is simply oblivious. She must meet hundreds of people at the multiple events she attends every week. The YWCA Gala was ten years ago.

I don't trust Kim but she's not my target. Between her lover, Lona, and her husband, Aditya, Kim is a vibrant-winged butterfly caught in a hornet's nest. Whether or not she's secretly feral remains to be seen. But I will find out eventually.

Thursday, December 19, 2019

The day dawns clear and bright. My feet hit the floor ten seconds after my alarm goes off. I am filled with the purpose that only comes with a fresh lead. I change into black chino pants and a pullover, twisting my hair into a bun.

I consider giving Detective Singh a heads-up on where I'm headed but quickly dismiss the thought. When dealing with the police, asking for forgiveness is better than asking for permission.

I hit the road at just after nine a.m., picking up my coffee at a Starbucks on a roadside strip mall. Traffic is spotty. I barrel down the highway. The road roars beside me. Every few minutes, a daredevil whips past, edging over my comfortable 120 km per hour, as if readying their whimpering vehicle for a rocket launch.

I half listen to the radio. Lost cat. Young boy perished in a house fire. A local woman releasing her first book about daily acts of courage performed by regular people. Nothing about a woman who met her end in the small town of Lake Templeton on the coast of Vancouver Island. A woman whose murder remains unsolved. A week after her death, the media has forgotten about Sharon. But they will remember. I will remind them.

I arrive at the Thriving Mind Society after ten o'clock. It's a red brick building nestled in a residential neighborhood, tucked out of sight of a townhouse sprawl. Can't offend the sensibilities of the blueblood, meat-and-potatoes families that populate the area.

Trees guard the entrance which emerges from a petal-strewn walkway, courtesy of an explosion of flower pots placed lovingly along its outline. Off to the side is a children's playground with slides, monkey bars, and see-saws in a mutiny of colors. A gaggle of children are running around, watched by two young women in workout wear, chatting with each other, turning their heads every minute or so to make sure the kids are still breathing.

As I enter through the front door, peace descends over me. A hint of lavender hangs in the air, lulling the senses into a blood-warming feeling of security. Christmas decorations hang from the low ceiling. A gargantuan tree in the corner is festooned with ribbons, streamers, lights, and enough ornaments to empty out the local Home Depot.

A silver-haired disco ball of a woman appears at my side as if out of nowhere. Flashy earrings dangle from stretched lobes. Her blouse screams at me in clashing neons.

"Can I help you?" she says. "Are you looking to foster a child?"

Heaven forbid. Anyone that gives me a child should be charged with criminal negligence.

"Maybe," I say. "Can I look around?"

"Of course!" The woman throws out her arms in an expansive gesture, as if attempting to embrace the universe. Metallic bracelets peal, punctuating her point. "We are a place of fun and adventure and possibility."

She must have been an entertainer on a carnival cruise in a previous life. I don't have the heart to tell her I can't stand children.

I smile weakly and sidle away, hoping she leaves me alone. The woman hangs back but I can feel her eyes on me.

The interior walls of the Thriving Mind Society are painted in pastel colors, each a different tone, as if to signify the individuality of each child that walks through its doors.

I wander over to the festive seating area, furnished with plush fabric couches in bright yellows and greens. A vase with fresh flowers sits on a side table. The wall overlooking the couches is covered with an irregularly arranged patchwork of photos and plaques.

A plaque embossed in gold contains a dedication to the major donors of the Thriving Mind Society. I skim the names, my eyes screeching to a halt when I encounter a familiar one - Lona Mason.

Lona Mason, a benefactor of the Thriving Mind Society.

I stare in disbelief. Another link between Lona and Sharon. New spiderwebs of connections are erupting.

I look closer at the photos. Groups of children dating back to the 1990s. I scan the dates, searching for 2003, the year that Sharon's cult imploded and she found herself homeless and friendless.

And there it is. Sharon, standing behind the kids alongside the employees and social workers, wearing jeans and a navy blouse.

I hope she wasn't smacking the kids around like she did at the Nation of People cult.

My eyes shift to the others in the photo. There is a young woman standing behind the children, with Sharon. Long, limp blonde hair pushed behind her ears reveal a weak jaw and closely-set eyes. The girl is portly with a dimpled chin. I'm sure I've seen her somewhere before.

I squint, lean closer, and a tidal wave knocks me back on my heels. It's Lona Mason.

What is Lona doing in this mildewy photo with Sharon at the Thriving Mind Society foster home? And why didn't she tell me her connection with Sharon goes that deep?

The photo is sixteen years old. Lona has since invested in nips and tucks, and a decent hairdresser and dermatologist.

I take a photo with my cell phone and turn away, scanning the area for the chippy receptionist. As if sensing my need, she pops up behind me like a whack-a-mole.

"Can I help you with something?" Again, that broad, painted-on smile.

"Is there someone I can talk to about a woman who stayed here in 2003, sixteen years ago?"

The receptionist raises her eyebrows, taken aback by my question. "Oh. I don't know. I wasn't here back then. Why do you want to know?"

I come clean. "I'm a private investigator looking into a murder. It's a young girl that stayed here back in 2003 - took care of the kids, I think. Can I get a list of the people who worked here at that time?"

"I'm afraid I'm not at liberty to share that information."

"Who is? Who's in charge here?" I struggle to keep the impatience from my voice.

"That would be our headmistress, but she's not here today."

"When will she be here?"

"Maybe in a few days. She's on vacation. But she can't help you, either. This is a foster home. We take the privacy of our residents and staff very seriously."

Damn it. I will need Detective Talvir Singh to pave the way for this one. I say a curt goodbye and head back to my car.

Next stop - Royal Canadian Mounted Police, Wesbrook Mall detachment. It's time Detective Talvir Singh looked me in the eye and saw what I am made of.

CHAPTER 11

Thursday, December 19, 2019

At the RCMP office at Wesbrook Mall, I come face-to-face with a nasty surprise. After waiting for twenty minutes in an uncomfortable plastic chair at the entrance, on the wrong side of the barred front door, I am ushered in by a bored-looking administrator who sniffs at me disapprovingly. She peruses my jeans and hoodie, my lack of uniform, and makes a judgment about my place in the pecking order. I'm not important enough to waste a smile on.

Inside the station, I wait for another five minutes, resisting the urge to pace. And then, he appears.

A Greek god of a man with mystic hazel eyes, the physique of a Michelangelo statue, rugged golden skin, a firm stride. Tall and bearded, a black turban with clean lines perfectly wrapped around his head. Capping off the glower that darkens his brow. A cowboy getting ready for a duel.

Who is he? I wonder as I make a conscious effort to pick my jaw off the floor. This can't possibly be Detective Singh. No way.

And then he's standing right in front of me, frowning at me. Arms folded across his expansive chest. No hand outstretched for a customary handshake.

"You must be Fati," he says in a clipped tone. "I'm Detective Talvir Singh."

I stare. Open my mouth and no words come out. I can feel my face getting warm, and then hot enough to fry an egg on.

I nod and then croak out a "Hi".

He turns on his heel, motions for me to follow him with a flick of his hand. I walk behind him on rubbery legs. My eyes glued to the shifting muscles in his back as he glides, a fashion model walking down the runway.

What kind of cop is this? Is this the secret of his near perfect solve rate? Otherworldly good looks that turn criminals' brains to putty? What has Sheriff Keller gotten me into?

"You want to bang the detective on your case?" Zed's voice drips with disbelief.

"No, I don't!" I say, immediately realizing I'm lying. I sink into my living room couch.

"Are you going to wait until the case is over to make your move?"

"I'm not *going* to make a move. He was just - surprisingly attractive, that's all."

"You spend far too much time alone," Zed says. "Do you want to end up like Sharon Reese? So alone there's no one to claim your property when you die?"

"Don't be ridiculous," I snap. "I'm not alone. I have enough family to fight over my assets, thank you."

"When was the last time you got some sweet, sweet loving?"

"I don't remember," I say honestly. "There was that hunky neighbour on a case I worked some time ago..."

"The murder by golf cart case? That was almost nine months ago."

Zed is right. Oh my God...

"Why didn't you tell me you slept with that neighbour?" Zed is saying. "He was hot. Did you at least wait until the case was over?"

"Of course," I say. "I'm a professional. I would never do anything to jeopardize my case."

"So then, you *will* make your move on Detective Dreamy once the case is over?"

"Absolutely not," I say, resolutely. "It was a moment of weakness, that's all. He was such a gruff bastard on the phone, I was expecting him to look like an ogre. I was caught off guard, that's all. You know I have a thing for bearded, broad-shouldered men in turbans."

"Don't forget his hazel eyes…"

"It doesn't matter what color his eyes are," I say. "He's my boss. Not to mention, he's married."

"So?" Zed asks, bored.

"You know I don't like drama. *I* would never dig up his spouse's flower pots in a jealous rage."

"Why do you bring that up again and again?" Zed says, pouting. "It was an isolated incident. A lapse of judgment. I fell hard for that ass. Won't happen again. It *hasn't* happened again."

I bite my tongue. I know Zed doesn't like to be reminded of a not-too-long-ago incident with a married ex-boyfriend. The night he told Zed he was breaking things off to work on his marriage, Zed showed up on his lawn after consuming a chemical cocktail and a few too many shots. Started digging up his husband's carefully tended flower pots. Police were called. Zed spent the night in jail. And woke up the next morning humiliated with a hangover that lasted for days.

"That's why I don't do relationships," I say. "The last thing I need is some scorned wife showing up with a steak knife to kill me in my sleep."

"You sure he's *happily* married?" Zed says. "You must've snooped online."

"He's separated…"

"So what's the problem then?" Zed demands to know.

"He's trying to work things out with his wife," I say. "They're going to counseling. That means it's not over. Also, he has kids. You know I don't like kids."

"You seem awfully invested for someone who doesn't like drama."

Zed is right. I need to quiet the rapidly turning gears in my brain. Even if he was single, Detective Talvir Singh would be firmly off limits. He's my de facto boss. He's holding the reins of my case. I need to stay in my lane. This is a powder keg that can get me kicked off the good books of the police force forever.

But even if Detective Singh was single, we are hardly well-matched. The man drives me up the wall, and I do the same to him. I'm creative and big-picture, a little haphazard. I flout rules and mock procedure. Detective Singh is linear and methodical and respects the hierarchy.

"So what does his wife look like?" Zed asks. "Beautiful?"

"She wears makeup," I say. "And irons her shirts. And blow-dries her hair. Need I say more?"

"Nope," Zed says, merrily. "You look like a hole in the wall next to her. Got it."

"Not to mention, she can cook. I bet she doesn't feed her man croissants and microwaved pizza for dinner."

"But can she solve cases?"

"Nah," I say. "But he doesn't need a woman who can solve cases. He's pretty good at doing that himself - or so he said."

"Yeah, but you're fun," Zed says. "You break locks and hack computers. You'll keep him on edge. Bet his wife can't stay up all night doing a thread count. It's brain stuff. It's sexy."

I finish the call, still unsettled from my encounter with the mesmerizing Detective Talvir Singh. It was a total failure. I clumsily meandered through a weak explanation for why I wanted him to accompany me to the Thriving Mind Society. As expected, he refused.

"You have no evidence against Lona Mason and I have no time". As brusque and irritated as he was over the phone.

Not one to give up, I try another tack. A more direct confrontation with Lona herself. I call her office, taking her suggestion to bypass her gatekeeper by fibbing that I am with the police.

"I need to see her today," I say, in a tone that leaves no room for argument.

It works. I am in.

Later that afternoon, I am seated in Lona's office. It's a bright, airy room that smells like spring, bookended with tasteful planters in boisterous shades of green.

Lona sits behind her desk, legs folded and shoulders back in a power pose. Her flawless skin shines with health and just the right amount of no-makeup makeup. A glimmering gold locket pokes through the lapel of a perfectly-pressed silk button-down shirt. One hand fans out on her desk as if marking her territory, her fingernails filed in perfect squares and topped with streak-free nude-toned polish.

I flash back to the photo I saw at the Thriving Mind Society. What a long way she has come since then.

"I didn't expect to see you again so soon," Lona says. Her voice is matter-of-fact, uninflected, subtly commanding me to get to the point - immediately.

"I went to the Thriving Mind Society today," I say, watching her carefully. "As you can imagine, I was quite surprised when I saw the photos and plaque on the wall. Why didn't you tell me the truth about how long you've known Sharon?"

Lona looks at me with a neutral expression, weighing her words. A few seconds later, she leans forward and intersperses her hands. "It's a part of my past. I don't speak of it often."

A part of her past. And yet, there she is on the wall, front and center in embossed gold.

"Tell me about it," I say.

"I'm adopted," Lona says. "I spent a good part of my early life at the Thriving Mind Society foster home. I was barely twenty when I gave my child away…" Lona pauses, draws a deep, unsteady breath, lets it out. "I struggled through a dark period in my life. It took me years to get better. I left Calgary, moved back to Vancouver, and started volunteering at the Thriving Mind society. I did that for years. Going back to the home that raised me, helping care for the kids - it was cathartic."

"And that's where you first met Sharon," I state.

I'm not surprised Lona is cagey about her past. Blood diluted by adoption, a teen pregnancy, foster homes - very unsavory in the upturned-nose, aristocratic circles she dwells in.

"Yes," Lona says. "We lost touch over the years. But when she came to me and asked me to invest in the Lake Templeton revitalization project, I couldn't say no."

"Why did you lie?"

"Look - I'm devastated about Sharon's passing," Lona says. "But I don't want to get mixed up in this business. I have a career - a family - to think of."

Don't they all! I toy with the idea of revealing what I know about her affair with Kim but instinct holds me back. It's not time to play that card yet.

"You and Kim seem quite close," I say instead. "How long have you known each other?"

Lona raises one hand, flicks her fingers. "Forever. She's a lovely woman."

"Who do you think is responsible for Sharon's death?"

"I don't know," Lona says. "I didn't lie about that."

"Did you know that Sharon was embezzling money from the Lake Templeton revitalization project?" I detonate the bomb and wait for the carnage.

Lona stares at me, utterly still. "What?"

"So you didn't know," I say. "I'm not surprised. Alena has been trying to keep it under wraps."

Lona's face tightens. She laces her hands together, shoulders strained. "I have no comment on the matter at this time."

I can feel Lona retreating into her political poker face. I will not get anything further out of her. I thank Lona for her time and find my way to the door.

When I get home, I call George. "Did you get a hold of Aditya Roshan's company financials?"

"Yes, I did," George says. "I was just about to call you."

"And?"

"Just as you suspected, he's bleeding money," George says. "He hasn't paid taxes in five years, not even once since he started the company. Too many accumulated losses. I'm emailing you the statements."

"I feel for the guy - no wonder he's on edge," I say. "Cheating wife, struggling business, side hustle pushing drugs, pressure from all sides."

My laptop announces the arrival of George's email.

"How's the search on Alena Krutova coming along?" I ask, as I scroll to my inbox.

"I've uncovered some odd things but I'm still trying to figure out what it means," George says. "That's why I haven't called you."

"Tell me."

"I was following a lead on Alena's tax history," George says. "She's paying very little. You'd think she's working a minimum-wage cashier job. I reached out to one of my sources at the revenue agency. She's been making large transfers to a family trust to reduce her tax burden. The sole beneficiary of the trust is a 'Katya Krutova.' Maybe a family member of hers?"

I search Facebook for Katya Krutova. After a handful of profiles, one grabs my throat and stops my breath.

It's Alena.

Or a woman who looks an awful lot like Alena. Her twin sister, Katya Krutova.

I saw her in the family photos on Alena's computer. She seems to have disappeared from Alena's life ten years ago - around the time Alena came to Canada. If the two are estranged, how is Alena using her as a tax shield?

Katya's profile photo is from 2008. No new photos have been uploaded since then. Wearing a tank dress, she is leaning over a printed fabric sofa. Her blonde hair is thick, like bunched up straw. Blunt bangs cover her brows, crowding against steely silver-gray eyes that glimmer like the surface of a lake on a moonlit night.

Where is Katya Krutova? Is she still in Russia?

Words tumble out of my mouth. "Katya is Alena's twin sister. I bet she's either unemployed or working five hours a week as a lunchroom monitor, or something. She must be in the lowest tax bracket."

"Alena can lower her taxes significantly by transferring the bulk of her income to her sister by way of a loan to the family trust," George says thoughtfully. "Charge her a one percent interest rate with no repayment. If Katya has no income, she won't be hit by a big tax bill, either."

Maybe this is the reason Alena left Vancouver to pursue her lust for power in a small town. Running for mayor in Vancouver would have exposed her ugly underbelly of lies. It's easier to fly under the radar in a town of five thousand people. You can wear your crown and make your speeches and ignore the fact that there's only a handful of people watching.

"Mind-blowing," I say breathlessly. "We're on the right track. I can feel it in my bones. Find out what you can about Katya Krutova."

"I'm on it," George says. "This case of yours is becoming weirder and weirder."

This feels like a watershed moment. Maybe Sharon's murder has nothing to do with the Lake Templeton revitalization project. Maybe it has to do with an underhanded mayor with secrets that run as deep as the city's sewers. Maybe Sharon was killed because she found out the truth about Alena. And Alena silenced her to stop her from blowing the lid.

Friday, December 20, 2019

George calls me at ten a.m. I scramble awake from a disturbed slumber.

In the thick of a case, sleep plays hide and seek. It eludes me when I am desperate to shut my brain off and then hits me out of nowhere when I'm on the cusp of a discovery. I have no idea what time my brain powered off last night.

"Katya Krutova died in 2009," George says, without preamble. "Breast cancer."

"In Russia?"

"You got it."

The pieces are starting to fall into place. "So no death record in Canada. There's one thing I don't understand. How could Katya Krutova be the beneficiary of a local family trust if she was never in Canada?"

"That's the interesting part," George says. "Katya Krutova *was* in Canada. She went to college here, and worked for a number of years. She became a permanent resident."

"A permanent resident card has to be renewed every five years. If Katya Krutova died ten years ago, how is she…?" I trail off.

Dumb question. Alena has been renewing her sister's PR card. They have the same face, after all. And the authorities don't track fingerprints.

"So Alena was in Russia when Katya was here in Canada?" I ask.

"That's right," George says. "I found some details on Alena's life in Russia. She was quite prominent on the social scene. Wore pearls and silks and drank apple martinis. Dated some high-powered men - her last relationship was with a tycoon with links to the KGB."

"So Katya Krutova is settled in Canada and her sister, Alena, is in Russia living the high life," I say. "Katya gets diagnosed with a terminal illness and returns to Russia to die. That's when her sister Alena, who never wanted to immigrate to Canada before, decides to come here to take her place?"

"Alena left Russia shortly after Katya's death," George says. "Around the time she broke up with the KGB guy. Maybe losing her sister and her boyfriend at the same time was too much for her and she wanted to escape."

And replicate her fancy life in Russia here in Canada. Maybe Alena's the one siphoning money off the City treasury. A misplaced zero here, a balloon payment there, infrequent enough to bypass even a trained auditor's eye. Those Jimmy Choo shoes and Armani slacks don't pay for themselves. And Sharon, City Treasurer with a scandalous past, was the perfect patsy to pin everything on.

"Maybe Alena is afraid she'll die young too," I say. "Breast cancer is genetic. The chances of Alena getting it are quite high."

"So she's committing fraud because she could die tomorrow?" George says dubiously. "Not live long enough to face charges?"

When he puts it like that, it sounds ridiculous. But Lake Templeton's shiftless mayor wouldn't be the first person to throw caution to the winds when faced with the grim reality of their own mortality.

"What are you going to do?" George asks. "I can have someone drop an anonymous tip to the CRA. Or do you want to take public credit?"

I'm sure the Canada Revenue Agency would find this very interesting. But...

"I'm going to keep this close to my chest for now," I say. "I'm not ready to pop Alena's balloon. I've got my sights set on something bigger and better."

"Bigger and better than tax fraud by a public servant?"

"Murder," I say, a smile of anticipation bubbling to my lips.

Alena must have a homing radar - most pestilent insects do. A few hours after my chat with George, she calls me.

I'm embroiled in a solo whiteboard session at my home office. Dry erase markers are scattered on the floor. I sit cross-legged in a spiderweb of theories, fingers resting on burning temples, overheated with a barrage of thoughts.

"You told Lona about the embezzlement," Alena snaps at me. "I will sue you."

Guilty as charged. I remember Lona's clenched face when I dropped the accusation yesterday. She must have called Alena to read her the riot act at keeping this a secret.

"This is a police investigation, Ms. Krutova," I say in a friendly tone. "Do I need to remind you that someone - your staff member - has died?"

"I don't care," Alena snarls. Her composure crumbles as angry words spill from her mouth like drone strikes. "If this project goes south, I will hold you responsible. I shared classified information with you in confidence. I thought a private investigator with your supposed experience would understand the importance of discretion."

"I'm not employed by you, Alena," I say. "I'm working for the police. It's my responsibility to..."

Alena cuts me off, in no mood to hear me out. "I informed you I was handling it. I begged you to be discreet. But you couldn't help yourself. This was vicious. And it was personal. You will pay for it."

"If you wanted me to cooperate with you, you shouldn't have told so many lies," I shoot back.

"I *did not* lie," comes the flaming response. "If I withheld information, it was for the sake of the project."

"You see - I think you're lying to me about suspecting Sharon for the embezzlement," I say. "The woman had no need for a half a million dollars. What did she do with the money? Eat it?"

"That's what I was trying to find out!" Alena's fury is like a storm, advancing with every word, on a quest to obliterate all.

"I'm not sure I understand why you're so angry," I say. "As you said, you've done all the right things. You discovered that an employee was stealing and you launched an investigation. Surely your investors will understand. They were going to find out about the embezzlement at some point. This is hardly your fault."

I bite my lip to keep the sarcasm at bay. I toy with the idea of opening my cards on what I know about Alena's tax fraud. But I hold back. The prospect of actually seeing her face when her sandcastle turns to dust is too tempting.

"No, they most certainly *do not!*" Alena's voice is a sharpened lance. "The police stormed my office this morning. Lake Templeton is being investigated for fraud. I put night and day into getting this project off the ground. And then *you* showed up. And it's all gone to *shit!*"

The expletive spits out of Alena like a regurgitated bitter almond. It sounds shocking - scandalous - coming from her.

I rise to my feet in a daze. "The police are at Lake Templeton?" I say, my voice tinny.

My carelessly spoken words had unintended consequences. I was twisting Lona like a pepper grinder for the sake of the truth. I never meant to shatter glass and slice my own hands in the process.

"They raided City Hall. They've seized everything!" Alena shouts. "The project has been suspended. It's stopped. All of it."

My legs feel rubbery as I rabbit over to my coat closet, reaching for my shoulder bag with one shaky hand while the other fights to keep the phone glued to my ear. I can feel the case slipping from my hands like drying sand.

Alena's animus aside, a raid is serious business. The police will swat me away like an irritating fly. They will bulldoze everything and scatter my evidence like toys in a tantrum-throwing child's playhouse. I must get to Lake Templeton - immediately.

"Look - I will try to fix this, okay?" I say to Alena in a conciliatory tone. The irony doesn't escape me that I am cajoling a suspect with a false promise that I will glue their house of cards back together. "I'm going to grab the first ferry over to Lake Templeton."

"If you really want to help me, you will take that ferry - and jump off when it hits deep water," Alena says spitefully. "I told you I never wanted to see you back in Lake Templeton again and I meant it." She hangs up.

If I took threats seriously, I would never solve a case. I pack my overnight bag in under ten minutes. Two tee-shirts, a pair of jeans, toothbrush, iPad, iPhone. Chargers shoved in a side pocket.

I dial Detective Singh as I careen down the highway to the ferry terminal. Five rings and then voicemail. I cancel the call and dial again. And again. No answer.

Either Detective Singh is ignoring my calls or he is at Lake Templeton already, knee deep in an alphabet soup of budgets and contracts. Or maybe he's stopped on the side of the road somewhere, gun drawn, eyes on a suspect, tailing a gang member.

I arrive at the ferry terminal with ten minutes to go until the 2:30 p.m. sailing. During the two-hour journey, I pace the halls, restless, wandering up and down the stairs to the deck, downing coffee after coffee. I try Detective Singh again and now I am sure he's avoiding me.

It's quarter past six when I sail into Lake Templeton, road burn on my tires and, miraculously, no speeding tickets. Despite Alena's threats, there's no police barricade stopping me from entering. But the mayor no longer has the power to stall me.

The proprietress at the Lakeside Inn welcomes me with a knowing smile.

I can hear her phantom voice inside my head: *I knew you would be back. And I also know that little gay kid is not your boyfriend. And you're crazy if you think that sexy detective has any interest in you.'*

I blink back to reality. The proprietress is asking for my credit card.

"Just keep it on file," I say, handing it to her. "Then you won't need to ask for it next time I'm checking in."

I have a feeling this case is far from over.

Evening rolls in rapidly. Detective Talvir Singh is still missing in action. Zed is tied up in an illicit liaison with his married lover, Brad. *Brad's wife is having surgery so she's gone all night*, Zed texts me.

Alena refuses to take my calls; she's excised me from her life as neatly as a zit. She's probably on her seventh apple martini by now. Lona never gave me her cell number and her office is closed. I receive no response to my three voicemails asking to speak to her right away. Korinne Kendall continues to ignore me, although I can recite her voicemail message by heart now.

A PI's life can be lonely. But I wouldn't have it any other way. I fondly recall the first case I ever solved. The mystery of a missing diamond ring, belonging to a Masters' student who had just accepted a premature marriage proposal from her twenty-two-year-old Theta Chi hookup-turned-boyfriend. As compensation, she gave me a two-hundred-dollar gift card for the Fairmont Hotel spa, and told all her friends about me. That was the birth of my business. Although I think the pair broke up long before they could make it down the aisle.

Later that night, head ringing from the fruitless dials, I pop out for a bite. A freeze-dried, flash-fried burger washed down with sugary soda will keep my body fueled as my mind maps out the mess of Sharon Reese's murder.

Darkness muffles the town in the foggy night. My Mazda ricochets through the wind on the Island Highway, the lake a silent spectator behind the whispering trees.

It's Friday night, not yet ten p.m., but downtown Lake Templeton is a ghost town. Shops have shuttered and cars have buttoned up in their driveways for the night. Wreaths on doors and street lamps linked with ropes of pale lights remind me that Christmas is five days away.

At City Hall, there's no crime scene tape. No scowling officer patrolling the entrance. No padlock on the door. Nothing to indicate that anything's different.

I drive back to the Lakeside Inn, enjoying the quiet. It feels like the deceiving stillness before a ferocious storm.

Saturday, December 21, 2019

The ringing phone awakens me at ten past nine. It's Detective Singh. Finally.

"Fati, are you in Lake Templeton?" he says, getting right down to business.

"Yes, I am," I say, eagerly. "I arrived last night."

"Good," he says. "Get down to Pebble Beach right away. I'm here already."

No explanation for why he ghosted me yesterday. No information on what is happening at Pebble Beach. True to form for Detective Talvir Singh.

I get ready in a hurry. Last night's clothes still cling to my skin through splotches of gluey sweat. I rip them off in disgust and step into the shower, gasping as the cold pellets assail me in an icy gunfire.

There's no time to wait for the water to heat up in these crummy old pipes. And I can't go to Pebble Beach smelling of last night's beef patty and cheddar cheese. Not when Detective Singh will be there, smelling like a snack and looking like a GQ model. By the time I slide into my car, I've put more effort into my appearance than I've made in job interviews.

Pebble Beach is under ten minutes from the Lakeside Inn. It's a rocky shelf of land that hugs the lapping tongue of Lake Templeton. A small grassy area is covered with picnic tables and logs for lovers and Instagrammers alike. A grove of trees creates a privacy screen, separating the area from the highway.

I'm parking my car on the dirt shoulder off the side of the road when I realize that I forgot to grab a coffee. I step out of my car in a huff. But my frivolous worries evaporate when I see the flashing police cruiser and the small crowd gathered on the beach.

As I approach the crowd, I notice a pair of feet, encased in runners, resting sideways on the wet grass. Jeans-clad legs extend from the feet. As I get closer, a comatose body emerges, lying bedraggled and motionless. Topped with a shock of damp red hair that conceals a face turned away from me on a pallid neck, marred with dark smudges. Fingermarks, applied with brutal force, as if the perpetrator was pressing down on a dried-out ink pad.

My legs like spaghetti, I hobble over, unable to believe my eyes. Ferocious whispers bubble around me, some civilians, others police officers. I can't see the dead body's face but I know who it is.

It's Sergio.

Sergio is dead. Strangled and thrown, washed up on the beach just like his paramour, Sharon Reese.

"Was he one of your suspects?"

I blink at Detective Singh as I consider the question. "Not really," I finally say.

The dilapidated back room at City Hall smells faintly of mildew, even after we open the windows. The closest police station is the Sergeant's office at Otter Lake but we can't leave Lake Templeton, not yet.

The coroner is on site at Pebble Beach and Sergio's body is being photographed and prepared for transport. In the meantime, I'm the one in the hot seat.

Me, the rogue private investigator who failed to prevent a second death.

Our eyes meet. I have a feeling Detective Singh is mentally pistol-whipping me while I am mentally undressing him. Even in a crisis, his sex appeal does not have a dimmer switch.

Detective Singh sighs, rubs his forehead, looks up, and looks me in the eye. His expression is somber. I sense a job-in-jeopardy conversation coming and steel myself.

"You've been on this case for ten days," Detective Singh says. "Who do you think killed Sergio Alvarez?"

CHAPTER 12

Friday, Dec 20, 2019

Who killed Sergio Alvarez?

I shuffle my mental filing cabinet like a pack of cards. I am stymied. Whatever I say will be like picking a random card from a deck and crossing my fingers for an ace of spades. I need time to think.

"It could be the same person who killed Sharon Reese," I tell Detective Singh, cringing at my own response.

"And that would be?" He glowers at me.

"Alena Krutova remains my top suspect, Detective," I say with a little more confidence.

Detective Singh laces his hands together, knuckles white with the effort. "And what's the motive for the mayor of Lake Templeton to murder her right-hand man?"

"I think it has to do with the embezzlement... or the various other frauds Alena was involved in."

"So you think both Sharon and Sergio found out that Alena was committing fraud, and so she killed them both?"

"It's a possibility," I say. "I suspect Alena stole the money and framed Sharon."

Detective Singh rubs his forehead like a weary schoolteacher dealing with an unruly child. "If Alena Krutova was your prime suspect, why the irrelevant tangent involving Lona Mason?"

"She has too many connections to the case," I say. "It can't be coincidental. She knew the murder victim ten years ago from the Thriving Mind Society foster home. She invested in the Lake Templeton revitalization project. She was the sole investor in Pacific Air, the company started by Aditya Roshan, the pilot who flew Sharon home the night she died. This same pilot is the likely source of the drugs that Sharon took the night she died. Not to mention, Lona is having a secret affair with this same pilot's wife."

"Aditya has a bigger motive for Sharon's murder than Lona does."

"I know," I say. "But what's his motive to kill Sergio? Do we have a cause of death yet?"

"He was strangled," Detective Singh says flatly. "With some force."

"So you think it was a man who killed him?"

"Or a very strong woman. I don't think Mayor Krutova fits the bill."

"What about time of death?"

"Last night," Detective Singh says. "Between midnight and three a.m."

"Who found the body?"

"A woman walking her dog called it in," Detective Singh says. He rises to his feet, starts walking towards the door.

I get up, gather my shoulder bag, and start to follow him.

"Why don't you take a break?" Detective Singh says coldly, without turning around to look at me. "I'll call you when I need you."

And he walks out, the door swinging shut behind him, inches from my face. I stare, crestfallen.

I've been booted from the club. All I can do is look longingly through the barred window while the bus rolls on without me.

I drive back to the Lakeside Inn with my tail between my legs. Failure liquifies my bones. I want to sink into a puddle of self-pity and pinot noir.

I am staring at the exorbitant prices on the Lakeside Inn room service menu when my phone rings. It's Lona Mason.

"I need your help, Fati," Lona says. "You're a private investigator, right? I want to hire you to find someone."

"And who would that be?" Maybe a new case is just what I need to take my mind off Sergio's murder.

"It's my son, Caleb," Lona says quietly, as if measuring each word.

"Now would this be your elder son, the one you gave away? The same one you've never tried to search for?" I speak in a matter-of-fact tone, without irony. I know her younger son is called Timothy.

"I wasn't entirely honest with you," Lona says. "You're right. It *is* my elder son, Caleb, who's missing."

"What makes you think he's missing?"

"He's been kidnapped," Lona says with a sigh. She sounds incredibly composed for someone whose son has been nabbed. "I got a call this afternoon. They want a hundred thousand dollars to release him."

"I see," I say. "And is there a reason you're calling me and not the police?"

"I don't want to involve the police. I worry for Caleb's safety."

"And your own, no doubt," I say, caustically. "If the police find out, it'll be headline news tomorrow. And you don't want that. That won't jive with your official party line about respecting adoptive parents."

"I'm not proud of how I've handled this situation," Lona says. "If you had children, you'd understand." She stops, realizing what she's said. As far as she knows, I'm traumatically barren. "I'm sorry," she says. "I shouldn't have said that."

"It's all right," I say, easily. "I'll help you. It'll cost you, though - five hundred dollars an hour plus expenses."

"It's a deal," Lona readily agrees.

I've lowballed her. I should've quoted at least seven fifty.

"I need his full name and phone number," I say. "I'm assuming the call you received was from a private number?"

"That's right."

"And is there a reason you won't just pay the hundred thousand dollars and get your son back?" I say. "That sounds like chump change for you."

"Because there's no guarantee I'll *get* him back."

"How many people know that Caleb is your son?"

A short pause. Then Lona says, "My ex-husband...And my best friend, Kim."

"Does *Caleb* know?" I ask. "Have you ever approached him or have you been stalking him at a distance?"

If Lona is offended, she doesn't say so. "No, he doesn't know," is all she says.

"Why are you so invested in the child that you gave away?" I ask. "You have two other children. They live with you. Why not direct your energies there?"

Silence. I wait as Lona mulls over a tactical response to my audacious question. When she speaks, her voice is tight.

"You don't stop loving a child when you have more. I love all my children equally."

I don't doubt it. During her divorce, Lona vigorously pursued primary custody of her two young children. Railroaded by her considerably greater energy and resources, her ex-husband finally gave in.

Grateful to have a new puzzle to solve in a bleak afternoon. I set my sights on Caleb Bateman, Lona's twenty-two-year-old son.

Caleb is a singer-songwriter and a bit of a degenerate, judging from his social media posts. Flagrant drug use is a defining feature of his online brand. He never went to college or worked a traditional job, but most people who want to work traditional jobs don't get neck tattoos.

I wonder what Caleb's life would have been like had Lona not given him up. Would he have flourished in the love and acceptance of a powerful family? Probably not, since Lona's family saw Caleb as an inconvenience. They had big plans for their daughter. Caleb was a transitory bump.

I call my phone tracing source and give them Caleb's number. That's the first line of inquiry in a missing person's case. Eliminate the obvious. Maybe Caleb does know about his wealthy birth mother, and is hiding somewhere, trying to extort money through a fake kidnapping phone call.

That afternoon, I head out for a bite. It's nearly three p.m. and the sun is starting to ebb to seek cover from the wintry air. The weather is turning. Flurries are expected overnight.

Driving back to the hotel, I feel an irresistible pull towards Pebble Beach, where Sergio's body was found. I find myself back there, on the dirt road, in the same spot where I parked this morning. When I was blissfully unaware that I was being positioned on the chopping board.

The police have cleared out and the body has been taken away. Muddy boot prints mar the patchy grass, remnants of the morning's events. I blink and can see Sergio's reposed body, like an apparition floating like dark spots behind tired eyes.

My fingers itch to call Detective Singh. Ah, screw it.

I take a deep breath and dial, fully expecting to make my case to his voicemail inbox.

He picks up on the second ring.

"I thought I asked you to take a break," he says, his voice strained. No greeting, just as expected.

"I respect that," I concede. "But I wanted to explain myself. I was a little flustered when we spoke this morning and I don't think I fully explained the evidence I've found."

I was flustered, all right. Like a tongue-tied schoolgirl with a crush.

"Go on," he says.

I tell Detective Singh about Alena using her late sister, Katya, as a tax shield. I come clean about Sharon's sweater buried in her fire pit. I share the tidbit about the key person life insurance, and the one-million-dollar payout that will be coming to the City. I describe the videos I found on Alena's computer from Sharon's cult days. I flesh out Aditya as a suspect, expound upon his possible motive. His airline is in dire straits and Sharon's purported theft was threatening the only thing that could rescue it - the Lake Templeton revitalization project.

"Have you found out whether Sergio was killed at the beach or dumped there?" I ask, timidly, testing the waters.

A few seconds of silence. I wait with bated breath.

"He was killed at the beach, at around twelve-thirty a.m."

"Any witnesses?"

"Some reports of a gray Honda Civic in the area but we don't have a plate number."

"Forensics at the crime scene?"

"Medical examiner found some DNA. There were skin fragments under Sergio's fingernails."

"Have you already searched Sergio's house?"

"I'm on my way over there right now," Detective Singh says. He pauses.

I wait, silently pleading for an invitation.

Finally, Detective Singh takes pity on me and says, "Do you want to join me, Fati?"

Do I? About as much as a drug addict wants their next hit. I agree hurriedly, tripping over my words, afraid that Detective Singh will change his mind. I turn my car around sharply with the speed of a gymnast performing a pole vault, a road-burning three-sixty degree turn that practically splits my tires.

I'm on my way to Sergio's house. Caleb Bateman slips from my mind like morning fog in the rising sun.

Sergio's house hibernates, squeezed in the warm hug of the thicket of trees that surround it. They're evergreens so they hold on to their leaves, even in winter, until the whistling wind snatches them away and showers them on the lawn. Despite Sergio's gallant efforts with the rake, his driveway is again covered in shrubs and branches.

I pull up behind Sergio's car, parked in its usual spot in the driveway, the mud cracked and crusting on its back tires, windows streaked with messy wet tracks made when rain intermingled with dust. The killer must have picked him up and driven him to Pebble Beach.

Detective Singh's police cruiser is parked neatly angled to the side of the road. As I approach the house, I see a shattered window in the front.

I haven't seen young children living in the neighbourhood. Most houses in Sergio's vicinity belong to empty-nester retirees and snowbirds. Was this an accident or something more sinister? Did someone smash Sergio's window?

At the foot of Sergio's porch stands his city recycling box. It's filled to the brim with plastic containers and folded up cardboard boxes, as if Sergio had just finished cleaning and decluttering. I move closer for a better look. An empty bottle of Tito's vodka, several Amazon boxes, soup cans, and yogurt containers. A box for a Blackmagic Design pro camera that costs almost thirteen thousand dollars. A black rectangular tube that housed a Chanel snowboard.

How much was the City paying Sergio?

The front door is open. I resist the urge to slide off my shoes before entering. Do I need to respect the sacred spaces left behind by the dead?

Detective Singh is standing in the living room, his spine ramrod straight, supporting the ropy muscles flaring in his back, constrained by his cotton shirt. He is turned away from me and his arms are folded, looking down at something on the living room floor. As I move closer, he turns to me.

"His car is still in the driveway," I say, stating the obvious.

Detective Singh nods absently.

The living room seems neater. The knickknacks previously strewn haphazardly have been swept up and kept away. The throw pillows on the sofas are placed to the sides. Photos have been removed. The yellowing macrame placemats on the dining table are gone, and the table wiped down. The house looks organized, as if staged for sale.

I look down at what Detective Singh was eyeing when I walked in.

Luggage. Two Samsonite hard-shelled mini-suitcases in dusty blue, waiting patiently for their owner, unaware that he is never coming back. Next to the suitcases sits a gray messenger bag in a rough water-resistant fabric.

"Sergio was running away!" I blurt out.

Detective Singh nods grimly. He holds out his hand. "I found a passport in his bag and a printout of a one-way ticket to Lima, Peru."

"I don't understand." My voice fades. My thoughts are in disarray. "Maybe he was just taking a trip." It sounds ridiculous and I know it, even as the words escape my lips.

"The timing is very convenient," Detective Singh says, sounding like an adult explaining to a child that there's no Santa Claus. "And if he intended to come back, why a one-way ticket?"

The wheels start turning in my brain.

"Sergio didn't run when Sharon's body was found. Something that happened recently caused him to panic... The police raid at City Hall! Maybe Sergio was involved in the embezzlement and he ran because he knew he would be found out."

The expensive purchase, the high-flying lifestyle, splashed out on Instagram. It all makes sense.

"Yes," Detective Singh says.

It clicks into place. "Someone must have found out about his plans, and resorted to murder to stop him."

A scuffle. Two desperate men, both vying to get out on top. Pushing and shoving. A disabling knee to the groin. A lion-like roar and furious, vein-popped hands finding the soft spot on Sergio's neck. And then - oblivion. The killer running away but leaving skin fragments behind underneath Sergio's fingernails.

"We're running Sergio's phone records," Detective Singh says. "Forensics is on their way. You and I should look around before they get here."

"Maybe he and Sharon stole the money together," I say thoughtfully, my mind whirring. "They were involved in a romantic relationship. Maybe they planned to run away together."

"But Sharon ended up dead," Detective Singh says, considering my theory.

Detective Singh and I look at each other in unspoken agreement, and split up. He moves towards the bedroom and I make my way to the kitchen. It's time to roll up our sleeves.

The police find the money later that day, in a bank account at an unsuspecting credit union.

Smart idea. Credit unions aren't subject to the stringent regulations banks have to comply with. All Sergio had to do was charm a lonely banking advisor, flash a smile that accentuated his full mouth and glass-shard cheekbones, and get her to buy into a dubious explanation for the origin of funds.

An inheritance from an uncle - Alberto Alvarez. The same uncle who is listed as the sole owner of a design firm contracted by Lake Templeton for the revitalization project. A design firm that received a series of payments from the City over the past three months, ostensibly for completed work. But Alberto Alvarez died over a year ago. He's the one who left Sergio his cottage in Lake Templeton.

My research into Alberto Alvarez reveals that he immigrated to Canada from Peru twenty-three years ago. Worked a solid nine-to-five job at a manufacturing company. Lost his wife and daughter in a car accident. Shellacked by life, he became a hermit. Quit his job, sold his house in Vancouver, bought property in Lake Templeton, and lived off a meager income selling homegrown crops to the local grocery.

Too bad his nephew, Sergio, did not inherit his green thumb.

The deceit must go deeper than Sergio. Sharon must have been involved. How could she not be? She was Lake Templeton's Treasurer. She would've had to sign off on the payments.

Maybe Sharon was innocent and only recently discovered the theft. Did she deliberately bomb her latest investor pitch? Not wanting to lead unsuspecting investors to slaughter?

I put in a request, with police support, for signing authorities on Lake Templeton's bank accounts at the Royal Bank of Canada. I need to find out whether Sergio had the authority to make payments to his dead uncle's fake design firm without Sharon's concurrence.

Maybe Sergeant Keller is right. Having the police's blessing is like wind at my back, opening up my sails.

The cards are opening on Sergio Alvarez and it's not pretty. I was so distracted by my obsession with Alena that I missed the goblin standing on her shoulder, grinning at me.

That afternoon, we ransack Sergio's home, opening every dusty cabinet and lifting up every piece of furniture. The police confiscate his laptop, found in the messenger bag perched at the foot of his living room sofa.

I return to the Lakeside Inn, spent. That evening, I pick through Sergio's online brand. His social media profiles reflect the world as seen through his eyes. He was a talented photographer - his scenic snapshots of Lake Templeton are good enough to be printed on coffee table books. Maybe Sergio's digital mecca contains clues about why he stole the money. It had to be more than his love for designer snowboards. I click my way through page after page, filing, collating, discarding.

The shrill scream of my phone snaps me out of my virtual dreamscape and back to reality. It's my phone tracing contact.

Caleb Bateman. Of course. I forgot about him. Even though he's the one paying my bills.

"We found Caleb Bateman," my contact says. "Either he's hiding out or he was taken by the dumbest kidnappers in the world that allowed him to keep his phone."

Well, that was easy. "Where is he?"

"Whistler - at the Fairmont Chateau. I thought the kid was a struggling musician."

"Musician, yes. Struggling...clearly not."

How can Caleb afford the Fairmont Chateau Whistler? Rooms in the December peak season run up to eight hundred dollars a night. This is a twenty-two-year-old, skating through life playing half-hearted gigs to spotty crowds in nameless bars. He probably earns just enough to sustain his chain-vaping habit. His parents, salt-of-the-earth working class folk that barely crack the middle class, are probably paying his rent.

Unless… Was Lona lying to me? She has done it before - with a straight face and a steady hand. Is she the one bankrolling Caleb's indulgent lifestyle?

Maybe Caleb is not working because he doesn't need to. Maybe he knows that the gravy train, fueled by a mother's guilty tears, will never stop running.

"Is it possible that the kidnappers dumped him somewhere, took his phone, and went vacationing to Whistler?" I ask.

"It's possible, but doubtful," she says. "The first thing kidnappers do is switch off or destroy their victim's phone. Everyone's watched CSI. They know the police can trace a phone."

I consider driving to Whistler to catch Caleb in the act, and quickly abandon the idea. I have no time for that, even though at five hundred dollars an hour, it would be the easiest twenty-five hundred dollars I've made all month.

A chess master doesn't walk away when their queen is poised to storm the castle. Lake Templeton is holding me down, as if the roots of the majestic Vancouver Island cedar trees are wrapped around my ankles, holding me in place. I will find paying work later.

"Can you find out how long Caleb has been in Whistler?" I ask. "And where he was yesterday and the day before."

If Caleb has been in Whistler for a few days, he's definitely extorting Lona for money. She only got the ransom call this morning.

Assured of an answer in the next hour, I wait. I am enjoying a cold dinner of nacho chips from the motel vending machine when my phone tracing contact calls me back.

"He was at a small town in Vancouver Island last night - Lake Templeton, it's called. Do you know it?"

A chip crumbles in my hand and my mouth drops open. What was Caleb Bateman doing in Lake Templeton last night? Could he have anything to do with Sergio's murder? And if so, why? The question caterwauls louder and louder, echoing off the inner walls of my skull.

Did Caleb know Sergio?

There's a quick and dirty way to find out. I navigate to Sergio's Facebook page and search for Caleb Bateman. They *are* friends. I search Instagram. Bingo. Sergio and Caleb are connected on social media.

But that doesn't answer the question - *how* did they know each other?

The only link between the two is Lona. Lona is an investor in Sergio's employer's most mission-critical project. And she is Caleb's birth mother.

My hand hovers over my phone, debating whether to call Lona. She can go collect her wayward son and discipline him for extorting her. I can collect my five hundred dollars plus GST and satisfy my financial planner that I wasn't productively unemployed this month.

But I decide to hold off. Given Caleb's possible involvement in Sergio's murder, I have to walk a careful line. Lona may be an elected official but she is a mother first. I have a feeling she would rather burn her political career to the ground than abrogate her responsibility to her son a second time. But there's another reason I stop short of calling Lona to tell her what I found. It's my childish desire to punish her for lying to me about her son.

Lona can suffer for a little while longer. She's earned it.

That evening, Detective Singh calls me. "I will be at the Sergeant's office at Otter Lake tomorrow. Examining Sergio's phone records."

"I'll be there," I say immediately, recognizing that this is Detective Singh's way of inviting me over.

"Good," Detective Singh says in a clipped tone. Short pause. And then, "I asked a couple of guys on the force about you. You've done good work for us over the years. Earned a reputation."

A grin splits my face so deeply that my ears hurt. I'm glad Detective Singh can't see me. Holding my triumph in check, I say, "Thank you."

Silence at the other end. The niceties are over.

"What about Sergio's laptop?" I say. "Did the tech find anything?"

"Emails Sergio sent to his mother recently," Detective Singh says. "Turns out he had a gambling problem and racked up quite a bit of debt."

Sunday, December 22, 2019

I awaken with a pep in my step. Maybe it's because the funhouse mirrors shielding the culprits are about to topple over, exposing guilty faces. Or maybe it's because I get to see the hunky Detective Singh, this time under more auspicious circumstances.

I spend a long twenty minutes in the shower. I wash my hair and subject it to a sixty-second blast of the hair dryer on high heat. By the time I am pulling on my jeans and a clean polo shirt, the coffee pot is foaming and sputtering, demanding attention.

I make the forty-five-minute journey to Otter Lake in thirty-two minutes. If a roadstop cop pulled me over, I could shamelessly name-drop Detective Talvir Singh, dreamboat and criminal hunter extraordinaire.

Otter Lake is a thriving metropolis compared to Lake Templeton. More amenities, more restaurants, more to do for more people. The mayor is business savvy, anchoring winter with an annual music festival which has developed a cult following in the indie rock community. Ragged posters announcing the festival line-up are stuck to lamp posts around town. The date of the festival is in bold red type: *Friday, Dec 20, 2019.*

Two days ago. No wonder Lake Templeton was an empty ghost town on Friday night. Everyone probably fled to Otter Lake. The Lake Templeton City Hall staff was looking forward to the festival all month.

I drive through tree-lined roadways, festive with the gold and green of Christmas decorations. They remind me that I need to call my mother back. As we approach Christmas, the spotty reminders are coming daily.

'Family dinner on Dec 25 - DO NOT FORGET.'

That depends, mom. Will I solve this case in four days? I want to come home as badly as you want me to. We are on the same side here. For a change.

Over the years, my mother has accepted that she will not enjoy the same close relationship with me that she has with my younger sister, Ayesha. But on special occasions like Christmas - and Eid, of course - she digs in her heels.

It's not that I don't want to see my family. It's that my mother doesn't understand that my love life, or lack thereof, is not a suitable topic for dinner table conversation.

Ayesha also bugs me about it sometimes. But playfully, knowing she could be slapped upside the head - just like when we were kids and she snooped through my drawers. She hoped to find candy and naughty magazines. Instead, she found crossword puzzles and Sidney Sheldon contraband novels. No wonder she thought I was odd. And cool. She always treated me with a starry-eyed reverence.

The Royal Canadian Mounted Police detachment at Otter Lake is a noisy box of footsteps, clicking keys, and phone conversations. I have barely said hello to Sergeant Keller when Detective Singh appears, slim-hipped and broad-shouldered, his dark blue shirt painted on to his body. His gun holster rides his hip as if surfing a wave.

"Detective Singh!" I say, feeling my face warming as my gaze captures his, after lingering a little too long on his sculpted physique.

He beckons me with a flick of his wrist towards a makeshift office a few doors down from Sergeant Keller. I follow like a faithful man's-best-friend, tongue practically lolling out my mouth. I do not like the person I become in the company of this beautiful man.

We settle into his office. Detective Singh gets right to the point.

Sergio owed two hundred thousand dollars to loan sharks for his escapades at the illegal craps tables. Threatening messages accompanying official-looking invoices were found at his house. I recall the shattered window on Sergio's front porch. A subtle message from the mob.

248

The initial swipe from Lake Templeton's accounts was likely a desperate attempt by a man caught in untenable circumstances. But once he realized how easy it was, greed gripped him and loosened his hand.

"Did anything in his emails indicate whether Sharon or Alena knew about his crimes?" I ask.

"No," Detective Singh says. "But they won't have left a paper trail. Why send emails when you can pop into the next office to chat."

"Do you think he always intended to run? After paying off his debtors, Sergio could buy a mansion in Peru and an army of bodyguards. He could charter a helicopter, build an underground bunker. He could've lived like a king."

Instead, he ended up strangled on a strip of rocky land that could barely be called a beach. Angry hands permanently stamped on his milky skin, the bruises a necklace around his swollen neck. A life lived on the edge snuffed out like a matchstick in a tornado. A sad, but inevitable end.

CHAPTER 13

Sunday, December 22, 2019

Detective Singh and I spend the next half hour poring over Sergio's phone records. He and Sharon talked every couple of days. There's a handful of phone calls between him and Alena. Several calls through a calling card company to his family in Lima, Peru. And a number for a talent agent in Toronto whose claim to fame is igniting pop singer careers.

Sergio was a singer? Nothing on his social media pointed to that.

There's another familiar phone number in Sergio's phone records. Caleb Bateman. They talked several times in the past couple of weeks.

"This number belongs to Caleb Bateman," I say, pointing to it on the page. "His mother hired me to find him yesterday. She thought he'd been kidnapped. Got a ransom call. I think he's extorting her for money - I tracked him down to the Fairmont Chateau Whistler."

Detective Singh looks at me intently, nods, scribbles something on his notepad. "I'll have one of our officers track him down."

"What about Sergio's whereabouts the night of his death?"

"Based on phone location records, he left home just after midnight and drove to the woods near Pebble Beach. His phone was switched off there. It hasn't been found. The killer must have destroyed it or dumped it in the ocean."

"The same thing was done to Sharon Reese's phone," I say. "I'm sensing a pattern."

"It could be the same person," Detective Singh agrees.

"How about the night of Sharon's death?" I ask. "Where was Sergio's phone that night?"

"Sergio was with Sharon that night," Detective Singh says. "But he admitted as much when you confronted him about the hair in the drain - good catch on that. It's embarrassing that the police department missed that."

I preen under his praise. "Thank you, Detective."

"Here's what's interesting," Detective Singh says. "Sergio told you he picked up Sharon at the airport and took her home?"

I nod.

"That was a lie," Detective Singh says. "They went to City Hall first. And *then*, he took her home."

"What?"

"We dug up the CCTV footage from City Hall."

"CCTV footage?" I exclaim. "Alena told me the CCTV at City Hall hasn't worked for months!"

"She lied."

My insides curdle. Alena must be so proud that she fooled me. "Can I see the footage?" I ask.

Detective Singh folds his hands across the table, a crooked smile splitting crossbow lips. "Of course."

The viewing room at Otter Lake is warmer and more comfortable than the one Alena made up for me at Lake Templeton City Hall.

Grainy footage springs to life on the log-like laptop. The CCTV camera guards the front entrance of City Hall. I clench my fists in my lap, tilting forward, back tense. The gray pixelated picture runs through the time stamp, second by interminable second.

Sharon and Sergio walk in at 6:44 p.m. Sharon holds her umbrella in one hand. In the other, a plastic water bottle. Her large camel leather purse hangs from one shoulder.

Sergio walks beside her, head down, shuffling his feet. He stretches one hand towards Sharon, and tries to take her arm. Sharon doesn't respond to his gesture. They look like insurrectionists after a crushing defeat.

Did they have a fight in the car on the way? Their body language is very different from what I observed in the airport CCTV footage. The easy camaraderie is gone.

They approach the front entrance of City Hall, faces set, and disappear inside. There's no one else around. The building would have emptied out at four-thirty p.m. when the light leaked out of the sky.

I flip to the video of when they departed, over an hour later, at 8:17 p.m. Their chemistry has shifted again. Sergio's gait is choppy and his body looks tense. His steps are short and hurried at the same time, burdened by the weight of Sharon, leaning heavily into him. Her head lolls to the side, and her dark hair spills over Sergio's shoulder. One hand is placed loosely on Sergio's back, inches upwards as if reaching for something, and then falls back down, dragging against Sergio's jacket. Her feet wobble as she places one foot in front of the other like a child learning to walk.

I rewind the video and watch it again. And again.

A dour-faced, wits-about-her Sharon entered City Hall in a foul mood. Over an hour later, she walked out, barely standing, unable to walk without assistance, her body unraveling like an old sweater.

She must have ingested the PCP at City Hall!

But how? And who gave it to her? Was it Sergio? He's the only one in the CCTV footage.

Something else about the picture seems off, misplaced somehow. I rewind and hit 'play,' and the video sprouts back to life.

Then it hits me. Sharon's arms are bare as she walks out, turning to prune in the whipping wind and spitting rain.

Where is her jacket? And her umbrella?

A picture is starting to emerge. Sharon, tidy by nature, walks into her office, taking off her jacket and hanging it on the back of her door. She closes her umbrella, tightens the strap around it, and tucks it behind the door. She unlocks her credenza, puts files in their proper place, and locks back up. When it's time to leave, she's no longer in control of her senses.

She probably didn't feel the cold wind blistering her overheated skin. The drug was burrowing into her bloodstream, turning her brain to putty. Sergio, clearly agitated, couldn't be bothered to cover her up before he dragged her to the parking lot. But if he gave Sharon the drug, her wellbeing was the furthest thing from his mind. As Sergio and Sharon hang left towards the parking lot, I notice that he is holding her purse in one hand. How chivalrous of him.

Even if Sergio gave Sharon the drug, the source had to be Aditya Roshan. Sergio wasn't a party parrot, despite his social media affiliation with gratuitous drug user, Caleb Bateman.

Another question burns my brain. Why did Alena withhold this footage? She must know what happened that night, even if she wasn't involved. Why is she protecting Sergio? Is she trying to protect her protégé, Sergio, by tossing Sharon to the wolves? Dead women can't defend themselves, after all. Or is it because she always knew

Sergio stole the money and was using this footage to blackmail him into giving it back?

Monday, December 23, 2019

I awaken from a shaky sleep. Sunlight is piercing through the pillowy white curtains of my room at the Lakeside Inn. So much for the weather prediction.

As I prepare my coffee, I contemplate last night. Enclosed in tight quarters with Detective Singh. Cracking through the foundations of this mystery. A forgettable dinner of Hakka noodles from the hole-in-the-wall Chinese takeout place.

Detective Singh is a good cop, salt-of-the-earth, whip-smart, perspicacious. Sure, he's impatient and can be curt, but so what? The quicker you solve a problem, the sooner you can move on to the next one. Isn't that my approach as well?

I sit at the scratched hotel desk with my coffee and run down my list of tasks.

Korinne Kendall still hasn't called me back. I call her again and leave another message. I am now certain that she is ignoring me. She isn't on vacation. Her Instagram is a photo reel of Vancouver living, walks on the beach, her dog posing against the familiar skyline.

As for Alena? I haven't heard from her since our last tense exchange. I know the police have grilled her. She's not talking.

Hunkered down in her postcard-worthy home by the beach, building a wall of lawyers around her with the money she's been siphoning off taxpayers. I wonder if her brother is still with her, a shoulder to cry on.

The police are building a case against Alena. The books are opening and they have stories to tell. Alena won't be able to escape consequences for much longer.

With no other pressing tasks, I call my mother, steeling myself for a tongue lashing. She doesn't disappoint. She reminds me that Christmas is in two days. If I fail to show up, she will not talk to me again, no matter how tightly I'm clutching the tail between my legs.

"I promise I'll try, mom," I say. "This case…"

"I don't care about your case," my mother snaps. "There's always a case. Every year. You can take one day off to spend with family. Aren't your killers taking the day off to be with their families?"

"It doesn't work that way, mom." I sigh. My mother treats my work like playacting in a video game. No wonder our relationship has always been stilted.

"Ayesha is Vice President at the Bank of Montreal. She has a two-year-old. She comes every year - her work is very busy too. She's in line to be the next Regional Vice President. They've sent her to Toronto twice this year!"

Ayesha is the feather in my mother's cap. My thirty-two-year-old sister, the youngest VP at the Bank of Montreal, who also found a good Muslim boy and birthed a perfectly behaved grandchild. I've often wondered what irks my mother more - my career choice or my refusal to fulfill my reproductive duty.

"And Mubin - he travels all the time. Deloitte sent him to Singapore for two months this year! But he's still coming home for Christmas. He's bringing Stephanie. I think he will propose this year." The deflation in my mother's voice is barely perceptible but it's there.

Mubin is my younger brother, Ayesha's twin. Stephanie is his girlfriend - white, blonde, Protestant, and doesn't speak a word of Urdu even after dating Mubin for four years. But Mubin himself barely speaks Urdu. My grandmother could pry a few mumbled words out of him but she passed away last year.

Ayesha and Mubin are close - in their twin way. It's telepathy, a language unspoken, a bond like underground power lines. Did Alena have a bond like that with her twin sister, Katya? One that survived the distance between continents?

"I'm assuming it's just you - again this year?" My mother's voice is heavy with ill-concealed disappointment.

I wonder how my mother would react if I show up with a hazel-eyed man in a sharply-folded turban, light-skinned enough to be ethnically ambiguous but darker than Stephanie. Will she be happy I found someone or distraught that it's the wrong kind of someone?

"Yes, mother," I say sarcastically. "No man again this year."

"You don't have much time left, you know," my mother says. "To have children. I don't understand why you don't take this seriously. There is a boy you should consider meeting… you know Auntie Nargis who lives next door? Her nephew is a pilot! I think the two of you will get along. He works odd hours too. Divorced, of course, but at your age, what do you expect…"

"I'm not interested in Auntie Nargis's nephew, mom," I say, trying to stay patient. Or in pilots.

"It's very hard to find boys that can tolerate your strange lifestyle," my mother says. "I wish you had gone to law school…"

Of course, she has to dredge that up again. It doesn't matter that the life I'm living now transcends my boldest expectations. I may be single - but I'm happy. And I make a damn good living. That's the dream, isn't it?

Maybe I should go home for Christmas. It will shut my mother up at least until Family Day in February.

I cut off my mother's complaints, promising to consider her proposition. She grumbles but finally drops the emotional blackmail, perhaps knowing it bounces off me like a tennis ball off the hard ground.

That afternoon, I put on a clean pair of jeans and a collared shirt for an excursion to the Royal Bank branch in Lake Templeton. I pull my hair into a bun, tight enough to give me a mini facelift. Absent a badge, I have to look as official as possible when I waltz in to view the signing authorities on the City's bank accounts.

I tried to cajole them to send me an email instead. But the bank manager insisted I come in. They need to look into the whites of my eyes before they breach their privacy walls. Maybe take a photo for their file. Make sure I'm a real person and not a bot.

I am ushered into a small enclave with embossed glass walls. The manager, a middle-aged man, puts a manila folder on the table, with care as if it were a newborn baby. He hovers over me, hands clasped in front, as I flip open the file. Like a royal paperwork protection officer. My eyes skip over the legalese and settle on the bullseye - names and signatures of signing authorities.

Two familiar names rise up. Alena Krutova and Sharon Reese. Any one to sign.

Both Alena and Sharon had the authority to sign off on payments alone. Only one scribble is needed to release taxpayer and investor funds into the wild. No additional oversight, no second set of eyes.

I drop my head into one hand, massage my forehead. Sergio is not a signing authority. So how did he make those payments to Alberto Alvarez's fake design firm? Was Sharon his accomplice? Was she involved in the theft, after all?

I am back at the Lakeside Inn, pacing the halls, when Detective Singh calls.

"We tracked Caleb Bateman to the Fairmont Chateau Whistler."

"And?"

"He admits to a casual friendship with Sergio Alvarez. But says he wasn't at Lake Templeton the night of his murder."

"Oh."

"He's lying," Detective Singh says. "We tracked his phone location. He *was* in Lake Templeton that night. Left town in the early hours of morning."

I know this already. But it's wise to keep my methods and sources under wraps when it comes to the salaried men in blue.

"There's more," Detective Singh says. "His phone pinged a cell tower close to Pebble Beach just after midnight. He was in the area at the same time that Sergio Alvarez was killed."

My heart is singing. I hold back a pirouette and a hallelujah with some difficulty.

"Here's what's interesting," Detective Singh says. "There's no ferry to Vancouver in the middle of the night - the last sailing is at eight p.m. No scheduled flights either."

"What time did he leave the Island?" I say, dumbfounded. I didn't ask my source to dig that far.

"Two-thirty a.m.," Detective Singh says. "We tracked flight plans and aerial radar. After Sergio Alvarez's murder,

Caleb Bateman left the Island on a private flight. With an airline called Pacific Air."

I sink to the floor, collapsing on crossed legs, head ringing.

I should've known Aditya Roshan was mixed up in this mess. After all, it was his pill that incapacitated Sharon.

"The next step is to dig into Caleb's phone records," Detective Singh says. "Do you want to meet me in Otter Lake?"

The 'yes' rushes out of me, fast and furious, as if afraid of missing the last train home. I have a date with Detective Dreamy. For crime solvers, poring over phone records is like a hand-in-hand walk in a flowery park.

At the RCMP detachment in Otter Lake, a man is seated in the waiting area. I recognize him right away.

It's Alena's brother, the one staying at her house. He is freshly shaven, and looks more put-together in jeans and a pullover sweater. One ankle rests on his knee, rocking restlessly. Now that he is washed and de-puffed, the resemblance to Alena is stark. His silver-gray eyes case the room, settle on me.

Flustered, I brush past him and slip inside the belly of the station, hightailing it to Detective Singh's makeshift office.

He is out of uniform, dressed in a crisp white shirt, gray pants, and a black turban sculpted against his strong forehead. When he walks into a room, his rumpled, sleep-deprived colleagues must shrink in shame. The box-like room can barely contain his splendor. He's like light shining through dusty glass stinging my eyes. He looks up as I enter.

"That's Alena Krutova's brother out there," I say, in a stage whisper, before I catch myself and clear my throat to a normal voice.

"Yes - Nicholai Krutov," Detective Singh confirms. "He's here about his sister."

"What about her?"

"We brought her in this morning."

"Alena has been arrested?" It seems too good to be true.

"We're getting there," Detective Singh says. "We found irregularities in Lake Templeton's finances. Payments made to unaccredited companies. And we're looking into her taxes. Thanks to your great tip."

The noose is tightening. "And her brother?"

"Recently divorced, visiting his sister from Russia."

A tight-knit clan, the Krutovs. Family photos sent over WhatsApp. Visiting each other abroad, staying in one another's homes. As normal as can be. If you ignore the identity theft and tax evasion.

"How long has he been in town?" I ask.

"Two and a half weeks."

So Nicholai Krutov arrived in Canada before Sharon's murder. Maybe that's why Alena didn't go to the investor meetings in Vancouver. To avoid leaving her suicidally depressed sibling alone for too long, drowning in tears and vodka. That's almost human of her. Although she had no qualms about driving to City Hall every day, leaving Nicholai to wallow at home, asleep for most of the morning, maybe sitting on the deck barefoot, freeze-baking in the winter sun.

I wonder if Nicholai Krutov knows about his sister's nefarious activities. I'm also curious whether Detective Singh can empathize with a dejected man seeking company in the wake of a devastating divorce.

"Does he know about his sister's illegal activities?" I ask.

"We found no evidence of that."

I sink down into a seat across from Detective Singh. While Nicholai Krutov is in the station, I must be very careful. He cannot see me. With no CCTV cameras in attendance, it's my word against his if he blabs about me puttering about on Alena's lawn. But still. I don't want to cast a doubt, make a splash about my unconventional methods.

For some reason, Alena is silent about my break-in. Maybe it's because she has no proof. Or maybe she's simply lying low, staying quiet, and refraining from doing anything that might make the police's job easy. There's no point in her complaining about a PI's illegal evidence gathering when we have plenty of legally gathered evidence to hang her.

"Are those Caleb Bateman's call records?"

Detective Singh pushes the pile of paper towards me. It's covered in neat lines of dates and times with corresponding letters and figures. Highlighted rows jump off the page.

Detective Singh is organized and detail-oriented. His linear approach is a nice complement to my scattershot, shoot-for-the-moon style. Maybe we will work more cases together. To my surprise, it's a pleasing thought.

"We found an interesting phone number in Caleb's call records."

"Yes?" I wait, breathless.

"It belongs to Lona Mason, MLA for Vancouver-Fraserview."

A frisson goes up and down my spine. "Oh really? Did she call him often?"

"A few times a week."

Lona's sandcastle is collapsing inwards. It's time to tell Detective Singh the whole truth.

"She's Caleb Bateman's birth mother," I say. "She's the one who hired me to track him down."

"I see."

"She got a call from an unlisted number yesterday, demanding ransom," I say. "She didn't want to go to the police so she hired me to make some discreet inquiries." Something occurs to me. "Did she speak to him the night of Sergio's murder?"

"Doesn't look like it."

My face falls. "Oh."

"But there's an unlisted number Caleb talked to several times that night."

"And?"

"It was purchased with a credit card belonging to a 'Kim Cromwell.'"

"Kim Roshan," I say, breathless. "Aditya Roshan's wife. And Lona Mason's lover."

I wonder why Kim Roshan is still Kim Cromwell at the bank. Maybe she hasn't gotten around to changing her records in the six months since her wedding. Or maybe she's keeping her financial life separate so she can make a clean break when the time comes.

"Do you want to talk to Kim?" Detective Singh says. "I'm going to Aditya Roshan's place to question him. You could come with me and talk to his wife."

I practically rub my hands together in glee. I get to talk to Kim Roshan. Alone. With the police's blessing.

"Be careful," Detective Singh says. "We don't want to spook her. We have no real evidence against her and the family has connections. I don't want her to lawyer up."

I reassure Detective Singh that I will use the most dulcet tones in my vocal toolbelt when talking to Kim.

I picture Detective Singh and I on the ferry together. Two colleagues on the same side in a game of cops and robbers. Dependent on each other. Trading ideas on the deck as the wind teases the air around us, pushing us closer together, the softly lapping water creating the perfect ambiance for a kiss.

I feel Detective Singh's questioning eyes boring a hole into me. Shame buckles me over.

What is wrong with me? I need a cold shower. Or a good lay with a random I picked up at a bar. It's been a while since I've had a crush. It's inconvenient, annoying, and unprofessional.

"If we leave now, we can grab the noon ferry to Vancouver," Detective Singh is saying, impatience creeping into his voice. "How soon can you be ready to leave?"

"Now," I say dutifully, squelching my fanciful thoughts. "I just need to make a quick call."

I step outside the station to call Lona. She's probably waiting by the phone like a military wife. I have her cell number now so I bypass her snooty receptionist. Lona picks up on the first ring.

"I found your son," I say abruptly.

"Oh, thank God," Lona says, words gushing with relief. "Is he okay?"

"Oh yes," I say. "More than okay. He's hiding - at the Fairmont Chateau Whistler. Or *was* hiding, anyway. I'm sure the police will be picking him up any minute now."

"Hiding?" Lona sounds confused. "What do you mean *'hiding?'* The kidnappers must have taken him to Whistler."

"There *are* no kidnappers, Lona," I say bluntly. "Kidnappers don't take their victims to luxe ski resorts. The extortion call you got came from one of Caleb's friends."

"Caleb doesn't know I'm his mother," Lona says, quietly. "How would he know to call me?"

"Oh, give it up already," I say, dismissively. "Did it not occur to you that the police would run Caleb's phone records and find your number?"

A short pause. Then Lona says, tightly, "I didn't call the police. I called you." She sounds like a teakettle about to boil over.

"Good. You're not denying it. Now tell me why you've been pretending to have no contact with your son."

"I want to respect Caleb's privacy," Lona says. "His parents don't know he's in touch with me."

"He's twenty-two," I say in exasperation. "At this point, I doubt his parents care."

"You and I have very different opinions on boundaries," Lona says coldly, in a tone of finality.

"That's probably true," I agree. "In any case, there's no kidnapping. Caleb's trying to swindle you. Sorry your son's a crook. This ends our professional engagement. I'll send you an invoice in a few days. It will be less than a thousand dollars. And you're welcome."

"Hold on a minute," Lona says. "You said Caleb is being picked up by the police. Why?"

"I'm not at liberty to share that information," I say. "It has to do with an active case."

"You think I can't place one call to the police chief and find out?" Lona's voice is tense.

"Why don't you do that then?"

I'm deliberately provoking Lona but there's a reason. Cornered people make mistakes. When you pull someone to the edge of the cliff, truth tumbles out.

A click, and then the dial tone. Lona has hung up on me. I chuckle as I slide my phone into my pocket.

When Lona finds out that her son, Caleb, is a suspect in a murder, she will descend from her rarefied air in a private helicopter, and tear through Lake Templeton, knocking over everyone who stands in her path. It will be a sight to see.

The ferry moves sluggishly across the water. We sit in the cacophonous cafeteria, squeezed into narrow wooden seats. I can practically feel Detective Singh's breath on my face. Or maybe that's just my overactive imagination.

An ocean rages inside me as I meet his hazel eyes. Electricity crackles between us, but it's not sexual tension. It's the snap-crackle-pop of a case about to crack. We're on the edge of the plane under a skydiver's toes just before freefall.

The steam from our coffee cups mists the air. He likes his black, just like I do. It's lunchtime, but neither of us is in the mood to eat. The shuffling feet and jovial chatter around us is white noise in our bubble. The water is turbulent today and every few minutes, my stomach sways to the side, along with the boat.

A festive mood hangs in the air. Christmas carols peal from the overhead speakers. Most ferry passengers are headed home for the holidays. Family, hearty meals, eggnog, fuzzy slippers.

I glance at my watch. Another forty-five minutes to go until we reach the heartland. Detective Singh is getting restless as well; he starts scrolling through his phone.

"They're matching Caleb against the fingerprints at Sergio's house and the DNA on the body," Detective Singh says.

"Beautiful," I say with a contented smile. The evidence is mounting against Caleb Bateman. I take a sip of my tepid coffee. "An early birthday present for me."

"And when is your birthday?"

I laugh. "I wasn't dropping a hint, I swear. It's the day after Christmas. Yes, I know - Boxing Day baby. Thank God it gets lost in the hoopla of post-Christmas binge shopping. I've never cared much about my birthday."

"Do you celebrate?"

"Usually with my head buried in a case."

"No friends and family?"

I shrug. "My mom hasn't even broached the topic of a birthday dinner. She's still trying to get me to come home for Christmas."

"And are you going to go?"

"I don't know," I answer honestly. "I might. I'll decide tomorrow."

"It's okay to take an evening off."

"Are *you* going to take the evening off?"

"No," Detective Singh says shortly. After a few seconds of silence, he continues, "My wife has the kids so, no, I don't have plans for Christmas."

So he's not spending Christmas with his estranged wife and children. Maybe the rupture in his relationship goes deeper than I thought. It looks like reconciliation efforts aren't going well. My heart lifts. I should feel guilty about being unreasonably happy at the sad state of Detective Singh's marriage. But I don't.

"You and your wife aren't together?" I ask, doe-eyed.

"We're separated," Detective Singh says.

Always the abridged version with Detective Singh. His expression doesn't change. But I see the weariness on his face. It's the look of a man who has been hammering the same nail for hours, and is finally ready to admit it won't go in.

After a few seconds, he continues, "The pressures of the job are hard on a marriage."

I know. That's one of the reasons I'm single. When you're hunting criminals, the macabre spectre of death always hangs around you. Not very romantic. Or conducive to long-term plans.

"You've never been married?" Detective Singh asks.

"No, I have not," I say. "As you said, work hours. Also - I like my freedom. I don't like being beholden to anyone."

"Smart idea," Detective Singh says.

I toss him a cheeky smile and say, timidly. "Maybe you should've married someone in the force."

"Maybe," Detective Singh says. "But we can't help who we fall in love with."

No, we can't. But the real question is - is he *still* in love? Or is his relationship with his wife curdled milk, left out for too long, stuck like mucus to the milk carton?

I am contemplating this, rattling words around in my brain to pry further when his phone rings. He raises one finger at me, asking me to pause. I watch him as he listens, brow furrowed in attention, mouth like a slash, shoulders tightening and then releasing.

He hangs up and turns back to me. His hazel eyes are glittering, light brown flecks skipping over dark irises.

"What happened?" I ask, fingers gripping the edge of the table.

"We got a hit on Caleb Bateman," Detective Singh says. "He matched the prints we found at Sergio's house."

CHAPTER 14

Monday, December 23, 2019

Kim and Aditya live in a majestic hilltop house, walled off from the main road, in Vancouver's tony Point Grey neighbourhood. A small slope curves down to the black-marbled entrance. Shining ten-foot picture windows welcome visitors to an *Architectural Digest* interior. Freshly painted beige walls remind me of froth on a cappuccino. The flowering trees adorning the front lawn have been carefully chosen to evoke a tropical oasis in an urban center. You can hear the muted splash of the ocean in the distance, beneath the backdrop of snow-streaked mountains and blue sky.

I wonder if Kim and Aditya bought this house together. Aditya's income could qualify for a mortgage on the garage, but not much more. Kim's family could have purchased this for her in cash, as a wedding present.

"At least ten million dollars, probably fifteen," I murmur to Detective Singh.

"You know real estate?"

"A case," I say. "Three years ago. Right here on Marine Drive. Ugly business."

Detective Singh nods. He is starting to understand that everything I know, every experience I've had, can be traced back to a case I worked.

Kim is confused to see us. Her eyes widen when we tell her we're investigating Sergio's death and want to talk to her husband. She tells us he is at his office. He left early in the morning before Kim woke up. Detective Singh takes the address and leaves for Aditya's office, leaving me there to talk to Kim.

Kim invites me into her spacious living room. I kick off my shoes and walk across the polished cedarwood floor. It emanates a comforting heat, like a massage therapist's hands. The center rug is densely knotted sheep's wool. I can feel its softness through my socks. I sit down on a cushioned sofa. It's bright blue pops against the beige walls.

An eight-foot-tall Christmas tree stands in one corner, white leaves dipped in gold, decorated with crystal ornaments. A sash of brilliant lights is draped around it. An angel watches over it, dressed in silken robes, wings raised, like an eagle about to take flight.

"Do you suspect my husband in this murder?" Kim asks, after I decline her cursory offer of a coffee or tea.

I artfully evade her question. "We just want to talk to him. He flew the suspect out of Lake Templeton the night of the murder."

Just like he flew our first murder victim, Sharon Reese, *back to* Lake Templeton the night she died. Coincidence? Hardly.

"Aditya flies a lot of people," Kim says, in a skeptical tone. "That's his job."

"Sure," I say. "But this was a private, chartered flight."

"Someone at Lake Templeton must have asked him," Kim claims. "That's the only client he does charters for."

"Do you know who?"

"No, why would I?" Kim looks genuinely perplexed.

"I know that you and Lona Mason are having an affair," I say, casually.

The color drains from Kim's face. She braids her arms together, as if catching a chill through her cashmere cardigan. Red spots flower on her cheeks, tendril across her face. A vein jumps in her neck, blood gushing through it.

"How long has it been going on?" I ask, in the same light tone.

"I…," Kim sputters. "I don't…"

"There's no point denying it," I say. "I saw the two of you at the yacht club after the healing circle."

"Please don't tell Aditya about this." Kim's voice is a choked whisper. "He doesn't know."

"But it's been going on long before you and Aditya met," I say, stating a fact.

Kim ducks her head. Her layered bangs swing down, a curtain concealing her face. "Yes. It has."

"So why marry Aditya?"

"I didn't want to," Kim admits, hands contorting in her lap. Her wedding band catches the light, like a centerpiece at a museum. She touches it, twists it, avoiding my eyes. "But Lona insisted."

"So Lona introduced the two of you?"

"Yes," Kim says. "Lona invested in Aditya's company. I was with her one day when he came by. I guess he fell in love with me, or something." She takes a deep breath, raises a shaking hand to push her dark brown bangs off her brow.

"But you don't love him back?"

Kim struggles to find words, looks up, gazes into the distance. "I do love him," she finally says. "But not in the way that he loves me."

"Does he know that? Did that make him angry? Did he ever scream at you? Or worse?"

Kim earnest brown eyes snap at me, as if released from a rubber band. The suggestion seems more shocking to her than her husband possibly being a murderer.

"No." The word drops from her mouth like a rock. "No - never. Aditya is a gentle person. He would never."

"If he's so great, why are you deceiving him with this sham marriage?" Sometimes, the best way to trap a bull is to run around it in circles.

"Lona wanted me to!" Kim is starting to get agitated. Good.

"But why?" I probe.

"It's the only way we could be together." Kim shifts uneasily in her seat. "People were starting to suspect there was something between us. Lona was married at the time. She thought if I married too, the talk would die down."

So Lona desperately wanted to keep her relationship with Kim a secret. If outed, her affair would force her down a politically perilous road. Much of her conservative base frowns upon same-sex relationships. And staunchly believes in the sanctity of marriage. Rumors of an extramarital affair with a woman would have ruined her.

I recall the anonymous comment on Kim's Facebook profile. Someone knew about the clandestine affair. They wanted to reveal it. Wanted the filth to fly but didn't want to be splashed by it. Could it be Lona's ex-husband?

"But Lona divorced her husband - around the time you and Aditya got married."

"Yes," Kim says, hesitantly. "The thing is… her husband, well, he found us one day and threatened to tell. She paid him off, of course - that was part of their divorce settlement. Made him sign a non-disclosure agreement."

"But Lona didn't want the divorce."

"No." Kim winces as if I've pressed down on a healing wound. "She wanted to stay married. She has two children. She didn't want their lives disrupted. She's very protective of them. Especially after…"

"Especially after she abandoned her first child, Caleb Bateman," I interject.

Astounded, Kim stares at me, opens her mouth, then closes it again.

"That's right," I say. "I know about Caleb Bateman. In fact, he's our top suspect in Sergio Alvarez's murder."

"No," Kim whispers, shellshocked. "It can't be. That would destroy Lona."

"Did Lona's relationship with Caleb cause friction in her marriage?"

Kim nods, reluctantly. "Lona's ex never understood why Caleb was so important to her. He thought it took away from her love for their two children. But he was wrong. Lona is the most devoted mother ever. That's why she fought so hard for custody."

"Primary custody must have cost her," I say. "Her ex must've wanted the payoff more than he wanted their kids."

Kim's face scrunches and her brow darkens. It's clear she isn't a fan of Lona's ex-husband. "He was always a greedy man."

Lona's ex knew she was secretly in touch with her firstborn, Caleb. He was aware of her trysts with her lover, Kim. He could have ruined Lona. But he didn't. He zipped up, buttoned down, signed a non-disclosure agreement, and exited center stage.

Was it for money? For the sake of his kids? Or his own sanity, smothered under the weight of Lona's power and reach?

"Now tell me why you talked to Caleb three times on the night of Sergio's murder."

Kim stares at me. Reaches up to her temples, starts massaging them like a child confronted with the news that Santa isn't real. "I don't know what you're talking about. I've never spoken to Caleb. I *want* to. But Lona wouldn't let me."

"Do you need Lona's permission to make *all* your decisions in life?"

"I'd like you to leave now," Kim says in a small voice. She rises to her feet.

Gladly. My work here is done. I pick up my shoulder bag.

"It was nice to see you again, Kim," I say, my voice friendly, like a casual acquaintance you bump into on the street. "But don't go anywhere. I may come back if I have more questions."

I leave Kim there, hugging herself by her bespoke designer sofa. Have I given her new trauma to exploit for her next healing circle? A negative emotion she can talk about on Instagram?

As I walk out of the estate, I remember that my car is still at Lake Templeton and my ride, Detective Singh, is off turning Aditya Roshan over on a barbecue spit.

Oh well - it's a lovely day for a walk on the beach.

Ten minutes later, I am on Kits beach, loose hair blowing around my shoulders, bare feet sinking into the wet sand.

The blinding brilliance of the sun cuts through the winter air, like a hot knife through butter. My nose and the tips of my ears are reddening, turning numb. I feel euphoric, like a shaken cola bottle. There's something about cornering a suspect. Especially one that rests under the velvet overhang of money and authority.

I glance at my watch. Twelve minutes since I left Kim's home. Why hasn't she called me yet? I continue my stroll. Every few seconds, an ice bath of water rolls over my blanched toes, jolting me out of my thoughts.

Another three minutes and my phone rings. I accept the call with a smile. "Hello, Lona."

"Hello, Fati," she says, coldly. "I just spoke with my friend, Kim Roshan."

"Friend?" I say playfully. "Give it up, Lona. I know she's your lover."

"What you saw... it's nothing like that," Lona says, carefully.

"Oh really?" I say. "It's *exactly* like that. There's no point denying. Your *friend*, Kim, admitted to everything."

Silence at the other end. I picture Lona, sitting with my words, absorbing them, reflecting, in her expressionless politician style. You can throw rocks at Lona and she won't budge. The storm brewing inside will find another outlet - when you least expect it.

"Kim told me that Aditya doesn't know his wife is sleeping with her best friend." I double down, elbowing into Lona's silence.

"I have no comment on this matter," Lona finally says.

"Why am I not surprised?" I say. "Let me tell you, Lona, secrets have a way of rising to the top, no matter how deeply they're buried."

"Is that a threat?"

"A warning," I say in a friendly tone. "We're questioning Aditya too. Things like this don't stay hidden for too long."

No response from Lona.

"It was a masterful strategy," I say. "I have to give you that. You found the perfect patsy. Poor Aditya. It was too good to be true. A white savior investor with deep pockets shows up to rescue his struggling airline. Not only that, she brings him a perfect woman way out of his league who takes his breath away. An arranged marriage out of a Disney movie. And then - bam! Reality hits. The genie in the bottle was actually *Jafar*. You really did a number on him."

"Kim tells me that my son, Caleb, is a suspect in this murder."

"Oh yes," I say. Popping her balloon like a schoolyard bully.

"And the police are aware that Caleb is my son?" Lona says, in the same matter-of-fact tone.

"We have the full kit and caboodle of evidence against him," I say, evading her question, toying with her. "But then you know that, right? After all, *you're* the one he called after he murdered Sergio. Smart idea buying that unlisted SIM with Kim's credit card. She's got her head so far in the clouds, she probably didn't even notice. Was that your in-case-of-emergency number for Caleb?"

"I don't know what you're talking about," Lona says, tightly.

I ignore her. "*You're* the one who arranged for Aditya Roshan to get Caleb the hell out of Lake Templeton. *You're* the one who arranged the suite at the Fairmont Chateau Whistler, to hide him away. Created this elaborate ruse of a kidnapping that was so shoddily put together no cop in the world would have believed you. And that's why you called me. An amateur PI, you thought. You thought you could fool me. Well, *you thought wrong*."

"You have no evidence to support this elaborate theory," Lona says, evenly.

"Maybe not," I say. "But we have evidence against Caleb. And after a few hours in police custody, he *will* crack. Then what will you do?"

"Your evidence against Caleb is circumstantial," Lona says. "My lawyers are already on it. He will be out in the next half hour."

"There's also Aditya," I say. "Are you going to pay for fancy lawyers for him too? *He* can't afford it. I have a feeling that big, fancy house on Marine Drive is in Kim's name."

"You're making some wild accusations - all unsubstantiated."

"Using big words doesn't change anything, Lona," I say. "Also - I'm curious. Did you have any idea about the extent of the fraud with the Lake Templeton revitalization project? The City making payments for a resort that was already licensed out. Insurance policies on key executives - one of them Sharon Reese, our murder victim. I find it strange that someone in your position would have had no idea about any of this."

"Goodbye, Fati." Lona hangs up.

I chuckle as I slide my phone into my pocket. Call all the fancy lawyers that you want, Miss Lona Mason. They can't save you. You can't bicker your way out of this one.

As I key my location into my Uber app, I ponder - How did Lona convince Kim to keep their relationship a secret for so long? And to enact the charade of marriage with Aditya? And why?

A picture is starting to emerge as I put the puzzle pieces together. Lona, a woman from a traditional family, couldn't shake her roots. The law told her it was okay to be with a woman but she couldn't reconcile the idea in her brain. She worried that a marital breakup involving another woman would alienate her voters.

If she urged Kim to marry another woman for cover, Kim would be outed as a lesbian. She and Lona attend events arm-in-arm, giggling together in dark corners. It would have raised too many eyebrows. There's also the risk that Kim falls in love with the decoy whose bed she's sharing.

No, Lona couldn't have that. Aditya was a helpless puppy dog Kim needed to take out for a walk once in a while. He was someone Lona could keep in his rightful place under her thumb.

Lona is divorced now. Her coupling with Kim would hardly cause a flaming scandal. Same-sex relationships are no longer radical, even amongst conservatives. Kim could quietly punt Aditya and a few months later, she and Lona could make an under-the-radar debut as a pair. No one needs to know the timeline. Lona's career ambitions don't have to be derailed.

I think about Aditya, mired in this mess. At first, Lona must have seemed like a haloed angel descending from the sky. A flush of money for his dehydrated business. An exclusive contract with an underdog city moon-bound to tourism mecca. A beautiful wife with connections and clout that personified the Canadian dream. Aditya must have felt he's found the magic lamp. Blissfully unaware of the poison that lined its walls.

Detective Singh returns my call that evening. I'm in stitches to find out about his interview with Aditya Roshan.

"Did he tell you who hired him to fly out Caleb Bateman that night?"

"He said it was booked through Pacific Air's online booking system," Detective Singh says.

"Clearly a made-up story," I say, grimly. "He wouldn't accept an anonymous booking for two-thirty a.m."

"He said his business is struggling, so he's taking any booking he can get," Detective Singh says.

I don't buy it. It was Lona. Lona asked him to fly Caleb out after Sergio's murder. But how do I prove it?

Tuesday, December 24, 2019

Christmas Eve dawns bright. At ten a.m., a loud banging on my door jars me awake. I push my hair out of my face and look down at the dark wine stain bleeding into my bedsheet.

Great. I fell asleep with my half-drunk glass of pinot noir again.

I drag my feet off the bed. The floor feels like a block of ice, raising the tiny hairs on my legs into drawn arrows.

I fling open the door to find Zed, hand raised to knock again, a Starbucks coffee tray in one hand loaded with two cups of Venti and three muffins in different flavors.

"What are you doing here?" I groan. "How did you get in?"

Zed grins, elbowing his way inside, and says in a chipper voice, "I have my ways."

"So much for twenty-four-hour security," I grumble. "That's why I bought this place. I'm nervous now. Too many people who want to kill me!"

"Not me," Zed says, merrily, waltzing in with a flourish. "I'm here to *save* you - you look like death. And I brought coffee."

I shut the door behind him with a sigh. "That better be a dark roast."

"Venti dark roast - black," Zed says. "Yes, I know how you like your coffee." Zed places the precious package on my kitchen table. "Sorry - they were all out of chocolate croissants."

He pulls out a chair and plops down, crossing his jeans-clad legs. Undone laces spill over his leather-top sneakers.

"Oh, you're staying for breakfast then," I say through a face that feels swollen. I drop into a chair across from Zed.

"You never returned my last call." Zed peels the paper off a blueberry muffin with the precision of a surgeon making an incision.

"You took over a day to return mine!" I exclaim. "If you want to be a part of my cases, you need to pick up the phone when I call you - right away!"

"I know," Zed says, a flash of guilt crossing his face, which quickly disappears as he sinks his teeth into a doughy muffin. "I was busy with Brad. But that's over now. His wife found out. And Brad decided it's more important to be a good little Mormon than play around with his gay side."

Religion. Always demanding we kill our legitimate desires to be soldiers in God's army.

I take a long, welcome draw of my coffee. "You sure know how to pick 'em."

"Me? How about you? Have you bedded Detective Dreamy yet?"

"Do I look like a femme fatale that breaks up marriages?"

Zed takes a delicate sip of his coffee as he crosses his legs. "Based on what you told me, this marriage is already pretty broken up."

I take another pull from my coffee cup, my brain rapidly rejuvenating. "So no Christmas Eve with Brad then? What are you going to do? You're still estranged from your family, from what I remember."

"They're jerks," Zed says with a sniff. "And yes - I'm all alone on Christmas Eve. Which is why I was thinking the two of us can do something. Not to mention - it's your birthday in a couple of days! You thought I forgot, didn't you?"

"I was hoping you did." I find the idea of birthday celebrations abhorrent. "I'm sure I'll be back on the Island by then."

"Then I'll be on that ferry *with* you," Zed says, with a wave of his hand. "Who knows - I might actually get some action there."

"Don't bet on it," I say. "Lake Templeton isn't exactly teeming with hot gay nightspots."

"I'm sure I'll be fine," Zed says. "You know my theory. There's a little bit of gay in everyone. Even your Detective Dreamy."

"That would be way hotter than imagining him with his perfect child psychologist wife."

I think back to my conversation with Detective Singh on the ferry. He is not spending Christmas with his family. Is it a portent that his marriage is on its last sputtering breath?

It doesn't matter. My only interest in Detective Singh is to solve this case. And if I keep reminding myself, one day I might believe it.

After breakfast, Zed and I settle behind my computer. He pulls up a dining room chair, sets it beside me, and perches on it. A brand-new double barrel piercing splits his right eyebrow. The flesh around it looks tender, as if newly mangled. That's a page from Zed's breakup playbook. He always changes his look after bidding adios to a partner.

I am grateful for his presence. He has a gift for pulling me back to reality when I go too far down a blind alley and find myself trapped.

"So what's on the docket today?" Zed asks as he polishes off my half-eaten muffin, having already downed two whole ones. Emotional eating is Zed's cure-all for breakup doldrums. "Catch me up."

"We now know that Sergio is the one who embezzled from the City, not Sharon," I recount. "But Sharon may have been involved. Sergio had no authority to sign off on payments for the City. Sharon did. And she and Sergio were a couple."

Zed listens intently, like the neighbourhood gossip soaking in details of the latest scandal.

"I think Caleb murdered Sergio," I continue. "But I don't know why. And I still don't know who killed Sharon. I can't connect Caleb to her at all."

"How did Caleb know Sergio?" Zed asks.

"That's what I need to find out," I say. "They're connected on social media - but how did they meet?"

"Let me guess," Zed says. "Caleb isn't talking."

I shake my head in frustration. "It doesn't help that Lona Mason has descended like a mama bear - reassuring him she'll get him out of this."

"And she'll throw the pilot under the bus to do it."

"Absolutely," I say. "I'm convinced Caleb called her the night of the murder and she promptly sent Aditya to rescue him. Lona has leverage over Aditya. She's an investor in his company. She can pull the rug out from under him if she wanted."

"Aditya's wife also has money."

"Kim Roshan belongs to Lona Mason too."

"That's right, poor bastard," Zed says, commiserating with Aditya.

We enter through the magic gates of the web with a clear goal - find out why Caleb killed Sergio. Caleb and Sergio became friends on Instagram in 2013 and on Facebook two months later. Both 'liked' the pages for the 'Commodore Ballroom,' 'Burnaby Skate Park,' and 'X Factor.'

Curious about the last one, I click to their page. It's a talent agency, with bold claims of launching unknown singers into stratospheric success.

My intuition taps me on my shoulder. I'm missing something. The last few days are a blur. Where have I heard of X Factor before?

And then it clicks into place.

"Sergio's phone records," I say, turning to face Zed. "There were phone calls between him and an agent who works at X Factor!"

"Caleb Bateman is a wannabe singer too!" Zed says, rubbing his hands together. "It's perfect. Let's call that agent!"

I am already reaching for my phone. Namedropping the police has benefits. A few minutes later, I'm speaking with the agent. He confirms that he was talking with Sergio Alvarez about optioning some of his music.

"Has Sergio been singing for a while?" I ask. "There's nothing about it on his social media. I'm sure you'll agree that's highly unusual - especially for his generation."

"Oh yeah, I thought that was interesting too," the agent says. "Sergio told me he used to sing but took a different direction some years ago. He decided to return to it recently and asked to be referred to me. He had great demo tapes so

I was interested - we hadn't finalized a deal yet. I'm sorry to hear what happened to him."

"Did he mention why he stopped singing?"

"No, he did not," the agent says. "I'm not interested in my clients' personal history as long as they can sing."

"And Sergio can sing?" I ask, slightly dubious. Photography, snowboarding, singing - Sergio, a man of many talents. All scuppered because of an inconvenient gambling addiction.

"Oh yeah... I can send you his demo tapes if you'd like."

"That would be great," I say. "One last thing - you mentioned Sergio came to you through a referral. Who referred him?"

"Oh... it was through one of our patrons. She's a well-known MLA. Her name is Lona Mason."

Later, Zed and I sit cross-legged on my shag rug, bent over my laptop as if about to watch a hotly anticipated Marvel movie.

The agent sent over five audition tapes, two audios and three videos. Zed and I go straight for the videos, impatient with anticipation.

The first is a homespun video of a young Sergio, sitting behind a keyboard. He looks nervous as if the eyes of the world are on him. His cheeks are flushed and he giggles, clears his throat. Then he opens his mouth and his fingers start flying across his instrument, and my jaw drops in astonishment. The agent was not being charitable. Sergio *is* - was - good.

"Did you find a keyboard at his house when you searched it?" Zed whispers, eyes glued to the screen.

"No," I say. "But Sergio was running away. Maybe he got rid of the keyboard."

"Maybe he sold it on Facebook Marketplace," Zed suggests.

"Good point," I say. "Let's check Facebook for any listings he made in the days leading up to his death."

"Play the next one, please." Zed's voice is a command. I comply.

The second video is on a stage and there are other people there. Sergio is standing behind a mike, affixed to a tall, skinny stand. He doesn't have a keyboard but there's a full string quartet behind him.

He is wearing a concert tee-shirt and distressed jeans. Rich red waves of hair surf his forehead. He looks like a man who puts minimal effort into his appearance because his voice is all he needs to soar. A faceless man asks Sergio what he will sing today. Sergio smiles a shaky smile, mumbles out wobbly words, takes a deep breath, and launches into song. As his torrid voice surges, it transforms him from a shuffling, underconfident youth to a musical messiah, floating above the crowd, enrapturing them.

Zed and I watch, awed. Sergio was poised to have a blockbuster singing career. His voice was stirring, like a sensory caress. What happened to curtail his nascent ambitions?

"Wow, he's good," Zed says, starting to clap, perhaps without even realizing it. "I wonder why he stopped singing."

"I wonder too," I say, thoughtfully. "And why was Lona Mason, who seems to be at the center of it all, the one to push him back into the ring?"

"Maybe he asked her," Zed says. "He knew her from the Lake Templeton project, didn't he? Maybe he knew she was a patron at this agency and asked for a favor."

"Sure," I say. "But would Lona have been receptive to the request?"

Sergio was a little folksy, a bumbling boy-next-door. Lona is cultured and put-together and cavorts in the upper echelon of society. Would she have helped him, used her connections, opened doors, out of the goodness of her heart?

Maybe it was a political ploy. Maybe she intended to parade Sergio around as her success story, a product of her selfless drive to support her community.

"It's a singing competition of some kind," Zed says. "Look at the banner behind Sergio. Vocal Heroes 2015."

"Let's find out everything we can about that show," I say. "Who competed, who won, who the judges were, where it took place, was there prize money, everything."

"I'm on it," Zed says. He starts swiping rapidly on his phone.

"I'll help." I click out of the video clip and open up a web browser.

It takes us only a few minutes to arrive at the pinnacle of discovery. We get there together, like two coordinated lovers in climax. We look up from our screens at the same time. Nothing further needs to be said.

We now have the missing link between Sergio and Caleb. Both competed in the Vocal Heroes singing competition in 2015.

CHAPTER 15

Tuesday, December 24, 2019

"I don't understand how Sergio did not win this competition," I say. "How could Caleb beat him? He's a god-awful singer - all scratch and angst."

Zed and I stand on my balcony, me in the quest for fresh air, Zed in the quest for a mild high laced with nicotine. He holds his phone loosely in one hand, cigarette hooked between two fingers.

In the distance, people are walking their dogs. Water taxis skim across the surface of the calm waters of False Creek. Gritty joggers in unseasonal shorts and tee-shirts huff and puff down the seawall.

"Ugh, yes. I saw his awful Instagram videos." Zed breaks out into an exaggerated shudder which he caps off with a long pull of his joint.

"Maybe Lona paid off the judges to get Caleb the big prize," I say.

Maybe getting Caleb a win at the singing competition was Lona's way of shoehorning into his life. That would mean Lona has been tracking Caleb for at least four years. Hanging in the sidelines. Appearing to let go on the surface, with hidden rug burn from holding on in secret.

No wonder family rights is her capstone political issue. But why not be open about her relationship with Caleb? Why not embrace him in full view of her constituents? Why not be authentic about the regrets she holds deep in her belly, where she nurtured Caleb? Why not share her personal story to empower other conflicted teen mothers? Lona's public posturing is political theater, nothing more.

"Do you think she has the pull to grease enough palms to win her son a hundred-thousand-dollar payday?" Zed says.

"I won't be surprised," I say. "She's spent her entire career shaking the right hands and kissing the right babies."

"What do you think Caleb did with the money?" Zed says. "Maybe that's how he's living large with no apparent income."

"A hundred thousand dollars wouldn't last so long," I say. "I'm sure Lona is bankrolling him. We're talking about someone with a two hundred dollar a day coke habit."

"Maybe losing this competition was the catalyst to make Sergio give up singing," Zed posits.

I contemplate this. It's a possibility. Maybe it embittered Sergio, made him think his talent wasn't enough, that good guys never win. Maybe he vowed that he too would play dirty, stack the deck in his favor by manipulating cards out of sight. After all, playing by the rules got him nowhere. He had to bear the humiliation of losing to Caleb. Someone who rose through the cream like a dead bug to float on top. Just because he had the right connections.

"Could be," I say. "But why go back to it now?"

"Maybe Lona was trying to make up for tampering with the competition by getting Sergio a record deal."

"Four years later?" I say, dubiously.

"Do you think Sergio recently found out Lona tampered with the competition all those years ago?" Zed says. "Maybe he was blackmailing her. And that's why she made the referral to the agent at X Factor."

"Could be, but it still doesn't give us a reason for why Caleb killed Sergio," I say. "Even if Sergio blew the lid on the singing competition fraud, it hardly impacts Caleb now. It's Vocal Heroes, not American Idol. It's not even enough motive for Lona to want him dead. I mean - if Sergio reveals everything, Lona could just deny it. Who would believe Sergio over Lona?"

Zed nods, thoughtfully, tosses his cigarette in a dried-out flower pot on my balcony, and cracks his knuckles. He turns on his phone, pulls up Facebook Marketplace, starts scrolling through the posts. Used wedding dress. Designer shoes. Portable heater. Accounting services. Christmas decorations. One post after another flashing by. He sees something and pauses.

"So Sergio posted a bunch of stuff on Facebook marketplace," Zed says. "Looks way underpriced. Maybe for a quick sale."

"When?" I ask, eagerly.

"Friday afternoon, same day he was killed."

I reach for Zed's phone, snatching it from his palm before he has a chance to protest. Quick scan through Sergio's listings. Designer snowboard and shoes. Photo lighting equipment. Keyboard.

Sergio was decluttering. Offloading large items that evidenced his lavish lifestyle created from stolen taxpayer funds. Things that would hinder a quick getaway. He wanted to generate some fast cash that he can stuff in his pockets as he slipped away, back to Peru, a wraith.

Zed shuffles his feet, crosses his arm, looks out into the distance. "There's something that's been bothering me about Caleb Bateman," he says, uncertainly. "I keep thinking I've seen him somewhere before."

I open my mouth and my phone rings. It's Detective Singh. I hold up a finger at Zed before retreating inside my apartment to take the call.

"You will not believe what I've found," I say, feeling like a kid coming home with a straight A report card.

"Do you have a TV?" Detective Singh asks.

"Huh?"

"If you don't have a TV, go to YouTube," Detective Singh says. "Check out what's on Global BC right now."

I turn to my laptop, open up the local news website, and navigate to their live feed. A press conference. Two women stand behind a podium, surrounded by raised mikes.

It's Lona - and Kim.

Lona is wearing a light gray suit jacket over a luxe white tee-shirt from an athleisure line. She speaks confidently into the camera with just the right amount of gravitas. Her words hit me like pellets as they pour out of her.

"Caleb Bateman, the young man arrested in connection with the recent murder at Lake Templeton... he is my son. I am his birth mother..."

"Caleb is innocent... I will do everything in my power to prove it to the police...and to all of you..."

"I'm grateful for everyone who has been there for me during this difficult time... my best friend, Kim Cromwell, we are in love."

"What the hell is going on?" Zed's voice drops on me like a boulder.

I whip my head to look at him. "It's a pre-emptive strike. She's coming out with all of it - before I can use it to hurt her."

"She just said that Kim is separated from her husband and they are now dating!" Zed sounds incredulous.

"It's not a new relationship! And Aditya never emotionally abused Kim!" I shout. "She's lying."

Detective Singh is still on the phone and trying to talk. I look down at the lit-up device on my lap and pick it up.

"We have Aditya Roshan at the station," Detective Singh says. "Get down here fast."

"Be right there," I say, and hang up.

Aditya Roshan, bitter, broken, and desolate, betrayed by his wife. His world shattered one day before Christmas. The hairline fractures I saw the first day I met him must be gaping ruptures now, the cries of the earth about to be ripped open by a mammoth earthquake. I have a feeling he will be the one to crack this case wide open.

I sit across from Aditya Roshan in a rickety chair that squeaks every time I move. His shoulders are slumped and his head is down. I expected to see white hot fury, defiance. But all I see is a man clobbered by life. Sitting inside the windowless walls of police confinement.

I wonder why Aditya is here, willing to share secrets. Lona's press conference was a great defense strategy. Aditya wants to copy it. And lash out at Kim and Lona in the process.

Private investigators aren't allowed to question persons of interest. Sometimes, we get the privilege to watch from behind one-way glass as the fruits of our hard work are claimed by accredited individuals with a badge. But this time - due to Detective Singh's largesse - I am inside.

"Did you know your wife was gay before you married her?" I ask.

My words twist like a poisoned knife. Aditya grimaces.

"No, I didn't," he says, his voice bitter. "If I had known, do you think I would've married her?"

"I know you're dealing drugs, Aditya," I tell him in a level voice, looking him in the eye. "It was your PCP that caused Sharon's death."

Aditya raises shaky hands, beading with sweat, to his temples, grinds them into his skin as if kneading dough.

"Why?" I ask.

Aditya doesn't respond.

I press on. "Why did you give Sharon the drugs, Aditya? Was it because she found out that Sergio was embezzling from the Lake Templeton revitalization project and you wanted to silence her?"

Aditya looks at me and takes a deep breath. When he speaks, his voice is firm and final. "I did not kill Sharon."

I probe further. "But you know who did?"

Aditya looks away, curls his hands into loose fists as if gathering strength. His face is weary, corrugated with lines that have popped up from nowhere to party.

"Sergio never had good intentions," he says. "He was a grifter and a thief who wanted it easy in life. His generation - they never want to work. They want it all for free."

"You didn't answer my question."

"Sharon told me that Sergio was stealing money from Lake Templeton," Aditya admits. "The night I flew her back from the investor meetings in Vancouver."

THE LAKE TEMPLETON MURDERS

"How did she find out?"

"Reviewing bank statements," Aditya says. "Sharon was smart. After leaving the cult, she took night classes in Accounting and Finance. She took her role as City Treasurer very seriously."

"Did she confront Sergio that night? And he killed her?"

Aditya drops his head into his hands, digs the pads of his fingers into his temples.

"I don't know," he mumbles. He looks up at me. His eyes are bloodshot. "She told me she was going to talk to him. She thought it could be a mistake. She trusted him."

"And she was going to wait until they were home?" I say. "They looked perfectly normal in the CCTV footage from the airport."

Aditya nods. "She wasn't going to threaten him. I don't know what provoked him to kill her!"

"So he *did* kill her?"

Aditya shakes his head. "I don't know. Who else?"

"Was Sergio using Sharon's user ID at the bank?" I ask. "To make the fraudulent payments?"

Sharon's bank profile was used in the theft. But how difficult would it have been for Sergio to steal her password? They were sleeping together. He must have used intimate moments to breach her defenses. A drawer left carelessly unlocked, a private scribble on a piece of paper on her desk. As long as Sharon was in the dark about Sergio's embezzlement, he could pin things on her behind her back. When she found out the truth, she became a hindrance.

"I don't know," Aditya says.

"Was Sergio a violent person?"

"I don't know," Aditya parrots again. "I didn't have much contact with him."

"Why did you protect him?" I challenge Aditya. "Why not tell me all this when I first talked to you?"

Aditya's shoulders slump. "I didn't want to get involved."

"But you knew Sharon took your PCP," I say. "Weren't you worried it would be traced back to you?"

"You told me that Sharon was drunk," Aditya says. "I didn't know PCP was found in her body."

"Why did you give it to her?"

"I didn't!" The words spring from Aditya's lips. "She must have taken it by accident."

"Do you leave your drugs lying around for people to take by accident?" I say sharply.

And then, something strikes me. My mind runs a mental replay of the past few days, zooms in on a moment, and freeze frames there.

"The water bottles in your plane," I say, as it comes into focus. "I saw Sharon carrying one off the plane. They were laced with PCP, weren't they? That's why you didn't want me to take one."

"She must have taken a bottle when I wasn't looking. I wasn't paying attention."

I visualize Sharon gripped with a cocktail of emotions - fury, confusion, righteousness, hurt, her blood warming, throat raw, as she spilled her guts to Aditya. Her eyes falling to the mundane grocery bag filled with water bottles. Why else were they there if not for the passengers to take? Grabbing one, a tense Aditya hanging on her every word, oblivious to the movement of her hands.

Did she unscrew the bottle and take a sip? Surely, Aditya would have noticed if she had. Maybe she forgot about the bottle as soon as she grabbed it, placed it absently on her lap. Took it with her off the plane. It was just a plastic water bottle. Like billions polluting our planet. How could Aditya know it was PCP-laced water from his own stash?

Maybe Sharon started sipping it at City Hall, when she confronted Sergio about the embezzlement. Her mouth dry, her throat scratchy, pregnant with the thorny words that would destroy the only meaningful relationship in her life.

"Why did you start dealing drugs, Aditya?" My tone is direct, demanding.

"Why does *anyone* start dealing drugs?" Aditya says. "Money. Why else? I saw how that kid was living. Large and in charge, not a care in the world. Just moved a few pills here and there and never had to work a day in his life. I thought I could do it too. Help out my business."

"What kid?" I ask, my voice insistent. "Who is your supplier?"

Aditya shakes his head, wearily. A storm of indecision crosses his face, hovers.

I press further. "Look, Aditya, you came here because you were ready to tell the truth. Lona and Kim didn't care about you when they callously went and did that press conference. Lied about you abusing your wife. When all you've given her is love. It was cruel. You came here to retaliate. So tell us what you know."

The door clicks open. It's Detective Singh. He looks at me gravely and nods in a single tilt of his chin. It's time to wrap it up and join him outside. Reluctantly, I comply, leaving Aditya to wallow in his grief.

"Did he give you anything?" Detective Singh asks.

"He was just starting to open up," I say, with some irritation. "Why the interruption?"

"We have to let him go," Detective Singh says. "Lawyer's here. They're going to close him up like a clam. Unless you've uncovered enough to arrest him."

"No, I haven't," I admit. I frown. "Who called a lawyer? He's not exactly crowing about his rights in there." I point my thumb at the one-way glass that reveals Aditya Roshan, limp in his chair like a wet dishrag.

"His wife, Kim," Detective Singh says.

An expletive escapes my lips. I should've expected this. Aditya Roshan knows too much. Lona isn't going to let her banished golden goose make scurrilous claims about her, even after it's been shunned.

We watch, helplessly, as a confused Aditya Roshan is ushered out by a dark-suited, no-nonsense man. I've seen him before - on TV and in *Business in Vancouver*, the premium business publication in BC. He's one of the best and boldest criminal lawyers in town.

"What next?" I ask, tapping my feet in impatience. "What about Caleb Bateman? Is he back in custody after his fingerprints were found at Sergio's home?"

Detective Singh nods. "Yes - but he's not talking. And we don't have the DNA results yet."

A silencing order from Lona. Caleb knows which side his bread is buttered. The fingerprints in Sergio's house can be explained away. The DNA found on Sergio's body is the real linchpin. I mentally berate the forensics department for dragging their heels. I have no doubt Detective Singh is pulling every string he can to expedite the results.

"Can I talk to Caleb?" I ask, pushing my luck.

Detective Singh shakes his head. "Not this time, Fati. If Caleb's team finds out I let an unlicensed PI talk to him, they'll scream bloody murder."

Detective Singh is right. I accept defeat. I will handle things my own way. Thankfully, I have a newly single sidekick to help me along my journey.

Wednesday, December 25, 2019

It's Christmas Day and I resign myself to a couple of hours in the company of my family. My parents have lived in the same house in Abbotsford since they immigrated to Canada over thirty-five years ago. The kitchen was remodeled seven years ago after Ayesha's repeated nagging. The rest of the house remains the same, a relic from the past. A magic portal into my childhood.

I park on the sloping driveway behind the four cars already crammed in at awkward angles. One of them looks brand new - a white Porsche Cayenne SUV.

Ayesha is moving up in the world again. I am proud of my sister, even though we don't have much in common. I always knew she was destined for big things. When I was floundering, tormented at the thought of inevitable admission into law school, fighting panic at the pre-ordained boredom of my future life, Ayesha remained laser focused. She achieved every goal she set, met every milestone, accumulated awards, check mark after check mark.

I knock on the front door of my parents' house. Excited chatter drifts outside, intermingled with the clanging of pots. One more knock and I grab the handle and push open the door. It's unlocked.

In their early years of being Canadian, my parents dismissed Christmas as white people's tradition. But when the twins were born, their thinking evolved. Today, the house groans under the weight of gaudy, crinkly decorations. All picked out at the dollar store.

The plastic tree in the corner has seen better days. Its branches are chafed from being dragged across the floor and shoved into and out of a box year after year. The red and gold packages under the tree remind me that I forgot to pick up presents for my family. Oh well. Digital gift cards always serve me well.

Despite her threats, my mother seems surprised to see me. Her salt and pepper hair is swept up into a high bun. Earlier this year, she turned sixty, and decided it was the appropriate time to stop soaking her hair in henna and to accept aging gracefully with her head held high. She was miffed when I reminded her that women her age powerlift, run marathons, and wear red lips and short dresses. My mother prefers demure makeup, having long retired the bold colors as a young woman's indulgences. Her taut skin is starting to line. The mole that rides high above her papery lips is fraying with peach fuzz.

She is dressed in a high-neck beaded silk top that covers her arms and extends past her hips. High-shine stretchy black pants complete the look. This is as far as my mother will go to embrace the culture and garb of her adoptive country. In the thirty-five plus years she has been here, she's never once acquiesced to wearing a dress. Anything that exposes limbs - the most scandalous parts of a woman's body - is firmly off limits.

Ayesha bounces over to give me a hug. Her son, Azeem, is tucked over one slim hip. Her satin, A-line floral dress looks like it came off a rack at Holt Renfrew, Vancouver's luxury retail giant. Red lipstick pops under contoured cheeks. As her arms wrap around me, I am enveloped in a cloud of perfume.

My brother's girlfriend, Stephanie, sparkles in a sleeveless, flouncy emerald green cocktail dress. Her sun-kissed dirty blonde hair is piled up on her crown in a messy bun. Jewelry is minimal, maybe to show off the new rock on her finger, catching light from all directions. Congratulations are in order.

I am underdressed in my pullover and jeans. At least I wore some color. And put on concealer and cover-up. I had to - my family could have pitched a tent under my dark circles. My freshly washed hair curls in its customary waves over my shoulders.

My father and Mubin are in the living room, holding soda cans, pretending it's beer. No pinot noir in this Muslim household. Knowing Mubin, he probably cracked open a fresh bottle of aged Macallan before he drove to my parents' house.

We sit down to a roast chicken dinner. Despite all the years in Canada, my parents' palette never accustomed to the salty taste of turkey.

We start with a heartfelt toast to the newly engaged couple. Stephanie is officially part of our family now. My mom teasingly reminds her that she better start learning Urdu. Mubin rolls his eyes.

The conversation moves to Ayesha and her new car and upcoming promotion. I am curious about why Ayesha is here alone - where is her husband, Mubashir? But no one mentions it.

I see the strain in Ayesha's eyes that she has valiantly attempted to cover up with crystalline eyeshadow. It looks like my sister isn't immune to the pressure a woman's thriving career can put on a relationship. She did all the right things - education, marriage, procreation, career. But balance is elusive. When one thing is ratcheting up, something else must come down.

We are finishing our salad when Zed starts texting me. My phone vibrates in my pants' pocket, screaming silently, kneading into my quad. I surreptitiously slip it out to glance at it.

"You home? I'm bored. Can I come over?"

"Where are you? Don't tell me you went to your parents for dinner."

"Can we break in somewhere, please? I'm bored!"

Shaking my head, I move to turn my phone off, knowing there's a long litany of messages still to come. But a new email notification catches my eye. I have half the world on my blocked list, so every new message carries weight.

I open my inbox. It's an email from Korinne Kendall.

"That's enough, Fatima!" The sharp voice belongs to my mother. I cringe. No one else calls me by my full name. "No phones at the table. Thirty-five years and you still haven't learned."

"Sorry, mom." I rise, folding up my napkin in one fluid motion and setting it down on my chair. "This is important."

"Let me guess," my mother says in resignation. "Your latest case."

"You got it," I say cheerfully.

"*Ya Allah*, I'm just waiting for the day she leaves in the middle of dinner because she got a message from a nice boy."

I've already slipped away. My mother's laments are as familiar to me as my scowling face in the mirror in the morning. I make my way to the living room as I open up the email from Korinne Kendall. She still hasn't responded to any of my voicemail messages.

The email starts off with an effusive '*Happy Holidays! And Merry Christmas - if you celebrate.*' There is an excerpt from her upcoming book, 'The Murders at Trout Lake.'

I skim through it. Nothing earth-shattering. There's promise of more. But I will have to wait for her book to be released to find out.

I wonder whether Alena knows about Korinne's upcoming book. If not for her current travails, she would be getting her lawyers ready. No one soils the good name of Lake Templeton, even if they call it Trout Lake instead.

Ting! Another message from Zed. *"Fine - you're busy. At least give me something to do."*

I call him.

"Thank God," he says. "Where are you? I'm going crazy. It's all Christmas carols everywhere. Even the bar is full of family types. Yuck."

"I'm with my family," I say. "But I've got something for us to do tomorrow if you're interested."

"Of course I'm interested! Give me, give me."

"We're going to break into Korinne Kendall's phone," I say. "She just sent an email to her mailing list. She's signing books tomorrow at Chapters downtown. We need to come up with a plan for you to distract her so I can swipe her phone."

"This is the best Christmas gift," Zed says.

I hang up and make my way back to the dinner table. Plates are laden with roast chicken with a side of masala potatoes. Ayesha smiles at me as I enter. My mother glowers. I slide back into my seat.

A PI's life can be lonely. I disappoint many people. I'm unreliable to the ones that I love. But it's a compromise I made years ago. In the pursuit of a case, nothing else matters. Not until the killer is behind bars, awaiting trial. And in the murders of Sharon Reese and Sergio Alvarez, it's about to happen very soon.

Thursday, December 26, 2019

It's Boxing Day and Zed and I are at the Chapters bookstore in downtown Vancouver. It's in the corner nook of a boxy building that covers an entire block on Vancouver's trendy Robson Street. The walls are made entirely of soaring panes of latticed glass. The streets are flooded with tributaries of people slinging colorful shopping bags, rubbing shoulders as they share the narrow sidewalks. There's exuberance in the air, a break from the haunting sameness of winter.

It's also my thirty-fifth birthday. As usual, I switched my phone off to avoid the annoying barrage of text messages and phone calls. Each well-wisher will get a carefully worded, copy and pasted text message by the end of the day, thanking them for their solicitousness. As for my family? I was turning twenty-five when they finally believed I had no interest in parties, cakes, or gifts.

Korinne Kendall is scheduled to appear at an author book signing and Boxing Day sale. Surrounded by her fans, their adulation feeding her ego, Korinne will be easily distractible. In the hubbub of people clamoring for her attention, she may become careless with valuables, like her phone that unlocks the keys to her life.

There is a throng of people inside, buzzing around tables laid out in a scattershot arrangement. Korinne's table is in a far corner. I melt away behind a knot of taller men. Korinne must not see me.

She is dressed in a bright red collared shirt, top button undone to show off bronzed collar bones. A silver locket glimmers against her artificially darkened skin. Her ombre hair is blown out in voluminous waves that counterbalance her slight frame like a large dollop of whipped cream on a too-small sundae. Her attention-seeking engagement ring overwhelms her slim hands, flashing its presence across the room.

Our plan is simple. We will scope out the set-up from a distance, honing in on the location of Korinne's cell phone. Zed will use his charm to pull Korinne away from it. I will then sneak up to the table, swipe her phone, search through it, and replace it before she notices.

We shuffle along the periphery of the book signing buffet, lost among the multiple bobbing heads. Sliding behind a floor-length banner, we see Korinne chatting with a group of people. Her beatific smile, clearly constructed at a dentist's office, is on full display, carved into her animated face.

She is holding her cell phone in her hand.

CHAPTER 16

Thursday, December 26, 2019

Zed elbows me hard. "She's holding her cell phone in her hand!" he furiously whispers. "What are we going to do? How will you steal it?"

"We're going to make her put it down, of course," I say as I navigate to my contacts and dial Korinne's number.

It rings. A second later, Korinne glances at her phone and her face clouds over. She hits what must be the 'Decline' button because the ringing dies in my ear, replaced by her voicemail message that, by now, I can recite in my sleep. I dial again.

Korinne looks sharply at her phone as if it were a mosquito that just bit her. Her smile wavers as she hits 'Decline' again, looks at her adoring fans in apology. She starts talking, apologizing, and holds up one finger. She turns around and reaches for her handbag that sits in a chair behind her, previously hidden from sight. She slides her cell phone into her handbag.

"You're a genius," Zed says, awestruck.

"It's showtime." I give Zed a decisive nudge towards Korinne and her table.

Zed scampers over, needing no further encouragement. I watch as he maneuvers through the crowd and towards Korinne, head held high in confidence. He slides through the people crowding against Korinne's table with the ease of a snake. Approaches her, engages her in conversation, reaches out to touch her arm as naturally as if he were a childhood friend. He leans in close, makes a comment, and they laugh. Zed is oblivious to the scowls of the other fans as he slowly steers Korinne away from the desk and towards the glass windows that run parallel to the leaf-strewn street.

Korinne's face is turned away from her author table. I move quickly, skating the edges of the crowd. Her fans have started to disperse, distracted by other authors, their bright banners like red to a bull.

As I near Korinne's table, I slow down, casually inching my way towards the chair - and Korine's handbag. My keen eye took a snapshot of exactly where she tucked away her phone and so, it takes only one deft movement for me to secure the device. The cold metal safe in my hands, I slink away, disappearing behind the staircase that leads to the second floor.

I have to work fast before Zed's spell is broken and Korinne remembers there are more fans clamoring for her. I punch in Korinne's passcode that I secured to memory that morning from my iPad notes.

I'm in.

I have broken into dozens of phones over the course of my PI career. When time is tight, photos and videos offer the biggest payload. I would love to look through her emails but there's no time for that. I fish out the nub-sized removable storage from my pocket. It's small but mighty, and will download the entirety of Korinne's photos and videos in a matter of minutes.

As I wait for the device to do its work, I keep a close eye on Korinne and Zed. They are still talking but Korinne's vibrant smile is starting to slip. Sensing this, Zed touches her arm again, leans in, mouth moving in animated words that incite another chuckle from Korinne.

I glance at the phone - 64% complete. Just a little while longer.

Another minute goes by. Korinne glances back at her table, looking distracted.

I shrink deeper into the shadows behind the staircase. Korinne raises one arm at Zed in an apologetic gesture, shakes her head as she takes a sideways step towards her table.

I glance at the phone again - 89% complete. So close.

Zed grasps Korinne's silk-clad arm, nodding effusively. He will let her go but not until he's thanked her for everything he can think of - her inspirational books, her graciousness in abandoning her family to amuse her fans on a statutory holiday, her blowout, her makeup, her manicure - all of it.

A soft vibration in my palm tells me that the download is 99% complete with another 5 seconds to go. Meanwhile, Korinne finally disengages herself from Zed and starts walking back to her table.

Five, four, three, two, one... A soundless beep and the download is complete.

I pull out the storage device from Korinne's phone. And freeze. Smack dab in Korinne's eye-line. If I budge from under the stairs, Korinne will see me. What to do?

I could use my softball throwing arm to pitch her phone back into her purse. I played for the Abbotsford Fireballs for eight years. But I'm rusty. Maybe I could ditch her phone on another table. She'll think she either left it there by mistake or someone stole it.

As I am debating, reprieve arrives. A fan intercepts Korinne halfway back to her table. He is holding one of her books. Korinne stops, turns towards him.

I move - fast, fluid, and silent. I slide the phone back into her bag, turn around, and start walking, along the periphery and towards the exit, without looking back.

Zed is waiting for me. He looks at me expectantly. I raise one thumb up. His face breaks into a smile as bright as summer sunlight. I continue walking, past Zed, and he falls into lockstep behind me. It's time for a well-deserved viewing party.

Later, Zed and I huddle on my living room shag rug, flipping through the photos and videos we nabbed from Korinne's phone. I've seen most of them before on Instagram. Studio-quality professional author photos. Snapshots of Korinne and her fiancé on vacation, her dog clutched like a baby in her skinny arms.

Most of her videos are forwarded clips that make the rounds in messaging apps among friends. Meme videos on a writer's life. Provocative clips from *The Tonight Show* and other shock TV.

And then, we find the Kohinoor diamond in the bed of garbage. A video that stops us in our tracks. There are two familiar faces in the frozen frame - Sergio and Sharon.

The video is filmed inside Sharon's office at City Hall. Sergio and Sharon are arguing. She is standing, leaning against her desk, back stiff and unbending, face inscrutable. Sergio hovers in front of her, gesturing wildly with his hands, face twisted in panic.

The audio recording is faint and crinkly as if the speakers were pressed against something. Sharon is reprimanding Sergio, asking him why he stole money from Lake Templeton. She tells him she has proof and demands a reason why she shouldn't go to the authorities. Sergio is pleading, sweating like a wet dog, his polo shirt sticking to the wet droplets beading on his neck. He tells her he's sorry - again and again. He was desperate and didn't know what to do.

'Please don't go to the police,' he says. *'Just give me two weeks. I will give back everything, I swear to you.'*

"I feel like we need popcorn." Zed's voice is like a shout in an exam room and I jump, jolted. I turn towards him and see his mouth drop open. He silently points a finger back at the screen.

A new figure has entered the camera's vision. A familiar figure. My chest tightens. It's Aditya.

Aditya places a hand on Sergio's shoulder like a parental figure. He looks at Sharon and starts talking in a measured tone, like a mediator. Sergio made a mistake, he says. As a loyal City Hall employee, he deserves a second chance. He asks Sharon to reconsider going to the police and to accept Sergio's request to give him two weeks to return the money.

Sharon remains motionless, arms bracing her body, hands cupping elbows, like a displeased schoolmistress. She tilts her head to one side, as if considering. Behind her poker face, torment and indecision roil. Finally, she says, in a clipped tone, that she will think about it. Takes another gulp from her half empty water bottle. Sits down at her desk, robotic. Sergio's pleas continue.

Several minutes later, Sharon starts wavering. She rises to her feet, swoons, falls back down. *I'm not feeling well*, she says in a wobbly voice. Sergio and Aditya stare at her. Sergio grabs her by the waist, starts murmuring something to her. Sharon sinks against him, then suddenly jerks apart, maybe remembering he is no longer the Sergio she knows and trusts. She rocks on her feet, starts to glide, grabs the edge of the table for balance. Aditya steps in, voice tight, tells Sergio he better take her home immediately. Sergio nods rapidly, as if grateful to be given direction. He leads Sharon away from the table. She allows it, and starts walking with Sergio, gingerly. The trio disappears from view.

The video cuts off.

Zed and I stay still for several seconds, staring at the frozen video, turning it over in our minds, trying to make sense of it.

"Why was the airline pilot siding with the thief?" Zed says, puzzled.

"Self-interest," I say. "He knew if Sharon went to the authorities, the Lake Templeton revitalization project would be toast. An investigation would be done. Criminal charges would be laid. The investors could pull their money. Once the public loses trust, it would be very hard to get the project back up and running."

"And Aditya couldn't have that because his airline was relying on the increased revenues from the project to stay afloat." Zed sounds like someone hit with an epiphany.

"You got it," I say. "Aditya was there that night. He had a motive to kill Sharon. He's been lying all along."

"But there was someone else there too," Zed says. "The person who filmed the video."

"You're right," I say. "We need to find out who that person was."

"Korinne Kendall?" Zed theorizes. "You found the video on her phone."

"No, I don't think so," I say. "Korinne was in Vancouver that night at a networking event. Someone sent her that video. I need to find out who and why."

"I'm thinking it was the mayor," Zed says.

"That's my guess too," I say. "She knew all along that Sergio was the real thief. She was falsely accusing Sharon. While twisting the knife in Sergio to return the money."

"It fits," Zed says. "Maybe she was threatening Sergio behind closed doors. Give the money back in two weeks or I will crush you. If Sergio came through, she could avoid involving the police."

"Yes," I say, thoughtfully. "Involving the police would have blown the lid on her various frauds."

"But why did she give this video to Korinne Kendall?" Zed asks, bewildered.

"That's a very good question," I say. "We will find out. But first - I need to talk to Aditya Roshan again."

Zed rubs his hands together. "Are we going to tail him?"

I look at him and smile. "It's my Christmas gift to you."

Friday, December 27, 2019

When Kim and Aditya separated, three days ago, he moved into a fourth-floor condo in a low-rise, wood-frame building in Kitsilano. Quite a downgrade from his previous living arrangements.

Today, Aditya leaves home at eight-fifteen p.m. Zed and I are outside, parked two blocks away, behind a Ford F-150 truck.

As his car pulls away from the curb, we follow.

Aditya turns his car into the beach-hugging Point Grey Road and starts driving at a comfortable 40 km an hour, winding up the hilly pathway.

"Where do you think he's going?" Zed asks.

"His wife's house."

"A reconciliation?" Zed says, dubiously.

"I don't think a reconciliation is in the cards," I say. "Kim was in love with Lona long before Aditya appeared on the scene."

As I predicted, Aditya leads us to his estranged wife's house. Zed and I wait until Aditya exits his car and we hear the beep of the automated lock. As he is walking away, we park behind him, and watch.

Aditya walks up to the front door of Kim's byzantine fortress, head ducked, tilting to the left and then sharply turning right.

"He's evading the CCTV camera," I say. "He'll try to disable it once he gets inside. He's breaking in."

The house is guarded by a digital lock with a keypad entry panel. Aditya sidles up to it. His fingers move deftly across the pad. He knows the passcode. Clearly, Kim did not feel the need to change it once Aditya left. She probably never imagined that her ex, a morose lapdog stricken by love, would dare break into her home.

There is a soft beep, a flash of green, and a click. Aditya waits, punches more numbers on the touchscreen. He is disabling the CCTV camera. Another beep and he stands back, shoulders relaxing. He strolls up to the main gate, pushes it open, and walks in.

I grab Zed's arm. "Let's give him ten minutes, then we're going in. I hope he doesn't lock the gate behind him."

We slide out of the car and start moving toward the house. The gate is unlocked and we walk in. The front lawn slopes down, bisected by its pebbled walkway and explosion of multi-hued flowers. Our soft-soled shoes make no sound as we tread, ears attuned to every sound. The front door is ajar. A soft wash of pale light haloes its edges.

I take the lead, Zed following closely behind. I lean against the door, nudging it with my shoulder. It moves a few inches. We walk in.

The living room yawns in front of us, scattered and off-kilter with sofa cushions pulled out and tossed on the floor. The rug is half folded over. The drawers underneath the TV table are pulled out, tongues of fabric lolling from some of them. Books are scattered on the floor - knocked over from their perch above the television with one determined hand.

"He's ransacked the place!" Zed whispers breathlessly.

I raise one finger and press it against his lips, shooting him a sharp glance.

Kim wants to excise Aditya from her life but, judging from the condition of the living room, he won't go easily. A shame. They seemed so postcard perfect. A successful interracial couple that could be used for a Citizenship & Immigration Canada propaganda piece.

We move deeper into the kitchen. Cabinets are open and drawers have been pulled out.

"He's searching for something," Zed whispers, unable to stay quiet.

The kitchen narrows into an elongated hallway which leads to the backyard. Sounds of scraping and rustling emanate from that direction. Zed and I move in unison, slowly, cautiously.

We find Aditya in a small study at the end of the hall. On his knees, he's rifling through the bottom drawer of a bookcase that stretches all the way to the ceiling.

"Aditya," I say, my voice sounding like a bomb dropping on a sleeping village. "What are you looking for?"

Aditya jerks back as if shot. The stack of paper drops from his hands, fans out into his lap and on to the marble floor. He whips his head back to see Zed and I standing there, towering over him, in our black garb, like commandos storming a drug operation.

"What... What are you doing here?" Aditya sputters. "Did you follow me?"

"Yes, we did," I say. "Why don't you tell us what you're looking for?"

"This is *my* house!" Aditya snaps, rising to his feet.

"Not anymore," Zed says. "We know your wife kicked you out. Actually, the whole world knows your wife kicked you out!"

I reach for my phone. "I can call Kim right now."

Aditya's face crumples. He reaches up, digs his fingers into his temples, leans against the glass topped desk, nearly knocking over the ring light that sits on top of it.

"She's holding me hostage," Aditya says, his voice defeated. "She wants a divorce and she's blackmailing me for it."

"That doesn't sound like Kim," I say.

Aditya throws up his hands. "It's *not* Kim. Lona is the one who wants to destroy me."

"Why don't you just give her the divorce?" I ask.

"I love her!" Aditya says helplessly.

"But she doesn't love you," I say. "She can't. So why hang on?"

"I fought my family to marry Kim," Aditya says. "I broke off my engagement to the girl they chose for me. I disgraced my parents in their community. Kim and I haven't even been married a year. What will people say when they find out?"

His verbal salvo tapers off with a grunt, as if the words were physically painful to expel.

So it's not love that drives him. It's ego. A sense of wounded pride, maybe. Aditya came to Canada as an immigrant with towering dreams. And then he failed out of business school. He started his own airline but couldn't turn a profit for five years. He married a wealthy, white woman, convinced it was his ticket to acceptance, only to be confronted by indifference and infidelity.

Did Aditya know about Kim's affair all along? Was he gritting his teeth and bearing it to preserve the image of a perfect couple? What is he angrier about - Kim's cheating or the fact that it's front-page news?

"Why do you care what people you barely know in India are gossiping about?" Zed demands.

But I understand. Kim's abandonment is the last punch in the gut for a doubled-over man. It's the final shred of his dignity and Aditya will keep his fist clenched around it until his knuckles fracture.

"I can't fail at this too," Aditya says.

"Look - I get it," I say. "You didn't finish the MBA, your airline is struggling, and your marriage is on the rocks. But you're choosing the wrong thing to save here. Kim doesn't love you - she can't. Why not focus on lifting your airline out of its troubles? Why not expand outside of Lake Templeton? Explore a new market? Or shut down the business, sell your airplane, pay Lona back with the proceeds, and start a new life?"

Aditya looks at me, his eyes tortured.

"Why are you so hooked on Kim, Aditya?" I ask, genuinely baffled. "She cheated on you and tossed you aside. She disrespected you - in public, in the media. Wash your hands of her. Start a new life. It's got to be better than this, here, what you're doing now. Have some self-respect, man."

"What does she have on you?" Zed asks, bringing us back to the matter at hand. "What are you looking for?"

"Her laptop," Aditya says, his voice hoarse. "She has a video."

"From the night of Sharon's death?" I say, quietly, the pieces clicking together in my mind.

Aditya looks up, his lips parting in surprise.

"We know you were there, Aditya," Zed says.

He can't deny it. "Yes."

"What happened?" I ask.

Aditya takes a deep breath, lowers himself into the leathery hug of the desk chair. He rubs his temples again, pushes his hair back over his head. His stature looks shrunk down, as if he were a blow-up doll deflated by the travails of life.

"I told you Sharon shared with me that she was going to confront Sergio about the embezzlement," Aditya says. "If the Lake Templeton project falls apart, I'll be left with nothing. I was scared."

"Scared enough to kill?" Zed says, raising his eyebrows.

"No! Of course not!" Aditya's voice is an outcry. "*I'm* not the one who stole the money. How would killing Sharon help me? It won't bring the money back."

"So Lona's taps have dried up?" I say. "She won't rescue your airline because she's trying to control you, to put pressure on you to divorce Kim?"

"Kim started distancing herself from me a few months after our wedding," Aditya says, a faraway look in his eyes. "At first, I didn't know what was going on. Then I saw her and Lona together. I read their text messages - and I knew."

"Did you confront Kim?" I ask.

"No," Aditya says, with a sigh. "I hoped she would stop. I wanted to give her time..."

And you didn't want to upset the apple cart of your perfect marriage.

"Who took the video in Sharon's office that night?" I ask.

Aditya stares at me. "You've seen the video? Where is it? Did Lona give it to you?"

"That's beside the point," I say. "If you come forward now and tell us what you know, the police will go easier on you."

"I followed Sergio and Sharon when they left the airport," Aditya says. "They went to City Hall. Sharon wanted to drop off her files. She never took work documents home."

"So Sharon and Sergio were at City Hall, arguing about Sergio's theft," I say. "You stepped in, trying to convince Sharon to give Sergio time to return the money. And then what happened? Did you go with them to Sharon's house?"

"No," Aditya says. "I went home."

"Why weren't you on the CCTV footage from City Hall?" I ask. "Sharon and Sergio were on the video but not you. Why?"

"I went in through the back," Aditya says. "There's no CCTV there. I didn't want Sharon and Sergio to know I followed them."

"Why were you protecting Sergio?" I am still confused. "You must have suspected Sergio when Sharon's body washed up on the shore."

"I didn't know *what* to think. I couldn't believe Sergio would hurt Sharon deliberately."

"Is that the only reason? Or is it also the fact that Sharon ingested *your* drugs that night. And Sergio knew about it."

Aditya says nothing.

"How did Lona get a hold of the video?" I ask.

"I found out about the video a few days after Sharon's death when Sergio told me Alena was blackmailing him with it," Aditya says. "Return the money now or she goes to the police."

"And Lona got it from Alena?" I ask.

"When Lona found out about the embezzlement, she called Alena," Aditya says. "I think Alena tried to bargain with her using the video."

I picture a stone-faced Lona sitting in her office after I broke the news about the embezzlement. Dialing Alena with her calm precision. Furious. Diamond cutting diamond. Alena begging her not to go to the police. Attempting to buy her silence with the explosive video. To buy time. Give her comfort that she was handling the situation. *I know who the thief is and I will recover the money in my own way.* After all, if the Lake Templeton revitalization project imploded, Lona stood to lose her investment too.

Lona took the video, Alena's peace offering. And then called the police anyway. Cold.

"If Alena was blackmailing Sergio with the video, he must have put the screws on you," I say to Aditya. "You're on the video. Did Sergio ask you for money?"

"He did," Aditya admits. "But he knew I didn't have any. And what could he do? He couldn't go to the police. His neck was on the line too."

I throw a curveball. "Why did you lie about having your MBA?"

Aditya looks taken aback. His face flushes with shame. Again, his fingers rise to his face, knead into his temples.

"I was embarrassed!" he says. "A failure like me with a woman like Kim."

"So you lied to make yourself more palatable to Kim's snobbish friends."

"Kim is a gem of a woman," Aditya says, voice filled with longing. "I was never good enough for her."

I'm not sure I believe him. Aditya *thinks* he loves Kim. But he loves the '*idea*' of her more than he loves the flesh and blood woman. He doesn't see her as a fallible human with annoying behaviors and character scars. He loves her as a concept of what is desirable.

"How did you manage to fail your MBA?" I ask. "You're clearly smart. An absolute master in the air. I've been on your plane. What happened?"

"I'm an engineer," Aditya says. "I can work with my hands. I can do math. The MBA... I thought it would be about problem solving. But it's not. It's not about one correct answer. It's about how you think to arrive at it. Made no sense to me." He looks me straight in the eye. "Are you going to tell Kim I was here?"

"I won't - as long as you come to the station with me right now and tell the police everything you know."

Aditya nods in resignation, rises to his feet.

"I should mention - you're going to face charges for dealing drugs," I remind Aditya gently. "I hope you know that."

Aditya's shoulders stiffen briefly, and then relax. A tentative nod.

"If you confess everything, Kim loses her hold on you," I say. "You can fleece her in divorce court. She's the one who cheated. You can get more than enough in the settlement to rescue your airline."

Aditya looks at me, dead serious. "I can't do that to Kim. I love her."

Zed and I give each other dubious looks, our thoughts mirroring. Love - what a load of crap.

CHAPTER 17

Friday, December 27, 2019

When I bring Aditya to the police station, Detective Singh's eyes fill with respect.

"This is a big break in the case, Fati," he says. "Well done."

"We are *so* close to cracking Sharon's murder," I say. "I've almost put all the pieces together. I just need to know what happened after Sergio took Sharon home. But all signs point to Sergio as the culprit. He's the one who pushed her off the dock."

Detective Singh nods. "And we like Caleb Bateman for Sergio's murder."

"Caleb will crack eventually, won't he?" I say. "How long has he been in police custody?"

"He's not in police custody anymore," Detective Singh says. "His mother - Lona Mason - got him out."

"Let me guess - our evidence is circumstantial."

Lona will hire the most vicious legal bloodhounds to save her son. She failed him once. She won't do it again. Caleb's fingerprints at Sergio's home. Phone calls between them. All of it can be explained away by the right lawyer.

"What about Caleb's phone location at Pebble Beach at twelve-thirty a.m. - *exactly* the time that Sergio was killed?"

"Caleb claims the kidnappers took his phone."

"So they're still sticking to that ridiculous story," I say. "But clearly, Caleb has his phone back, judging from his recent posts on Instagram."

"I petitioned for a court order to confiscate Caleb's phone but it hasn't come through."

"I'll get you Caleb's phone," I say. "Give me a few hours."

"Fati," Detective Singh says in a warning tone. "You know I can't use evidence gathered illegally."

I am unfazed. "But you *can* use evidence from anonymous sources. I know. This isn't my first rodeo."

Detective Singh is shaking his head, mouth set. He pauses, blows out a breath. "That video from Sharon Reese's office the night of her death…"

"I'll email it to you," I say. "From an anonymous email account."

Detective Singh looks at me, torn between his moral compass and his hunger for justice. I leave him there, without waiting for a response.

I'm doing him a favor. When this case is over, he can look at himself in the mirror, at peace that he did things the way they should be done - by the book.

As for me, I have other, more effective methods. That's why I left the police force. I couldn't stand being handcuffed by procedure. When you're a free agent, no one questions how you got the job done - as long as you get it done.

Zed is waiting for me outside the police station. My black Mazda sedan looks forlorn, sandwiched between a row of police cars.

I slide into the driver's seat. Zed looks up from a game of exploding fireballs, and grins. "So what are we doing now?"

"We need to find Caleb Bateman," I say. "And steal his phone."

"Another tail?"

"Not this time," I say, putting the car into drive. "I know exactly where he is. Thank you, Instagram."

Since Lona's press conference, Caleb is having a very public meltdown. A storm of social media posts, every hour on the dot, meth pipe hanging from his mouth, sitting in a cloud of smoke. Cryptic ramblings that barely make sense. Tonight, Caleb is at the Legends nightclub in Downtown Vancouver on Granville Street. He posted an *'over and out'* message a half hour ago telling his 'homies' where they can find him.

Zed and I arrive after ten p.m. We park in an underground lot a few blocks away. Granville Street at night is a cornucopia of debauchery. Drunk girls totter on heels and too-tight skirts, giggling and holding each other. The heavy smell of sweat mixed with marijuana mixed with alcohol hangs in the air like a toxic thundercloud. The sidewalk is sticky with spilled drinks and other substances you don't want to think about. Bedraggled bums cluster in dark corners, their life's possessions gathered at their feet in duffel bags. They panhandle, lighting their pipes, smoking their cigarettes, and shooting their heroin without apology.

The street is dotted with black-doored establishments that advertise their presence with glowing signs and glowering bouncers. At the most popular clubs, lines of partygoers stretch, smoking cigarettes while waiting for entry. Zed and I blend into the shadows, two travelers that don't quite belong, but don't stick out either.

This is Caleb's world. In contrast, the clean-cut Sergio snowboarded on weekends and went running every morning. They had nothing in common besides their desire to sing. And it was this commonality that led their worlds to collide so painfully.

At Legends, the thrum of the music wafting from behind heavy curtain and chain gives away the mayhem brewing inside. The roasting interior is awash in flashing lights. The smell of stale beer and rank sweat overpowers me. I choke back my gag reflex.

Caleb is not hard to find. He is huddled with other youths, all misty eyes and lost faces, in a chemical-induced otherworld. Caleb is swaying from one foot to the other, talking very fast.

Zed beelines for him, while I hang out at the bar area. I order a drink and wait, tapping my fingers against my glass of vodka tonic, trying to blend in.

It doesn't take long for Zed to swipe Caleb's phone. A bump and '*I'm sorry,*' then he's sucked back into the cacophonous babble of the room. He returns, prize in hand. Looks at me, nods. I take a final sip, pushing away the nearly full glass, and rise from the barstool.

The pulsation of the music fades as we walk at a brisk pace to the exit, shouldering through drunk people. Minutes later, we are out. Without looking back or breaking stride, we continue towards the parking lot.

At my car, Zed pulls out a hard black box from my trunk that houses his laptop and assorted cables and wires. He settles into the passenger seat as he sets up a makeshift tech station. The parking lot is picking up faint Wi-Fi signals from the restaurant next door and the apartment building above it, but we ignore them, porting directly into the personal hotspot on my phone.

Caleb is high tonight, like he is every night. When he reaches into his pocket and finds nothing, he will think he dropped his phone somewhere. And distract himself by ordering another vodka shot.

I wait, tense, as Zed works his magic. A few minutes later, we are in. Caleb's phone background is a photo of a stage, a mike affixed on a stand, lying sideways in front of a drum set. His version of dream visualization. Zed quickly disables Caleb's 'Find my Phone' app.

"What are we looking for?" Zed asks.

"Give it to me."

I thumb through recent calls. A few from Lona, several from the lawyer she hired to defend him, and some names I recognize as Caleb's wannabe bandmates. But I am more interested in his messages. I suspect Caleb and Sergio used a messaging app to communicate. I navigate to the familiar WhatsApp icon on the screen.

Sergio leaps off the screen immediately. But the chat window is empty. The messages have been deleted. Lona must have commanded Caleb to delete Sergio from his life. Caleb expunged their messages, but he isn't smart enough to remove Sergio's phone number altogether.

"Don't worry," Zed says. "I doubt Caleb is tech savvy enough to know that WhatsApp automatically backs up messages. All we need to do is uninstall and reinstall."

"Brilliant," I say, handing the phone back to Zed.

Five minutes later, messages appear magically, meaty lines of code on the chat window.

I check the night of Sergio's death. Nothing. That's odd. I flip backward in time in confusion. A montage of messages, a few days before Sergio's death, a week before. There are some casual one-liners, laced with hidden meaning. '*You nervous?*' Caleb says. '*All clear?*' he asks in another message. Sergio's response - a lone thumbs-up icon.

I go back further and arrive at the night of Sharon's death. The messages start at 9:26 p.m. A couple of missed calls, and then a message from Sergio: '*Can I call you? It's urgent.*' Three more missed calls. And then a response from Caleb: '*Yo - what's up? I'm out.*' Another missed call from Sergio, followed by a message: '*I'm with a girl. She's taken PCP. She's freaking out. What to do?*'

Zed and I jerk our heads up to look at each other. Our eyes crackle with excitement.

And then, Caleb's response: '*Just get her drunk. She'll forget about it in the morning.*' Sergio: '*She doesn't drink.*' Caleb: '*Mix it in apple juice. She won't remember.*'

"So it was Caleb." My voice is exultant as the pieces click into place. "Caleb is responsible for Sharon's death."

"What was he thinking?" Zed says with amazement. "What a ridiculous suggestion! Alcohol and PCP together are dangerous."

"Maybe he just wanted Sergio to leave him alone," I say. "Also, Caleb regularly mixes alcohol and drugs.

He probably doesn't realize other people's bodies aren't chemical factories."

Caleb didn't think he was setting off a chain reaction with his throwaway words. He didn't know that a woman, out of control, senseless, on the verge of kindling, would lose her life that night.

"When Sharon started tripping, Sergio called the only drug user he knew for advice - Caleb," I say. "And signed Sharon's death warrant in the process."

Once Caleb realized what had happened, did he panic? Did Sergio threaten Caleb, lay the blame on him for Sharon's death? Is that why Caleb killed Sergio?

Zed has moved on to Caleb's email, working with calculated efficiency, his hands steady, focused on the task at hand.

"I want to know if there are any emails between him and Lona and how far back they go," I say.

"He would've deleted them," Zed murmurs. "But no problem. Everything lives on the server forever. It will just take me a few extra minutes to get to it."

The first email from Lona is dated March 2013, two years before the Vocal Heroes singing contest. But there are more. We click through them, one by one. Most are one-liners. A meeting place arranged. A confirmation of money transferred. A high school graduation photo. A proclamation of '*so much pride.*'

Clearly, email was not the primary channel of communication between Lona and Caleb. But it tells us what we need to know. Lona's intrusion in her son's life started when he was only sixteen years old.

Saturday, December 28, 2019

The RCMP office at Wesbrook Mall is frenetic with activity, even though it's Saturday. I couldn't reach Detective Singh last night. Maybe he was tied up in sweet reconciliation with his wife.

I park my Mazda in its rightful place between the police cars. I walk through the front doors, head held high, past reception, sliding into the secured area behind a departing officer.

Detective Singh's office is located in a far corner, away from the chattering coffeepot talk, incessantly ringing phones, and beeping printers. His door is closed when I arrive but I see him moving inside, a shapeshifting white blob behind the privacy glass. I knock once, twice, hear an unintelligible command from inside, and walk in.

Detective Singh's office is surprisingly well-organized. If he accumulates paperwork, he does a great job of keeping it hidden. His desk is freshly wiped down and there is barely a speck of lint on his carpeted floor.

He waves me over and motions to the empty seat across from his desk. I comply, and launch into an animated description of what I found on Caleb's phone.

"So Alena Krutova was not involved in Sharon's death," Detective Singh says thoughtfully.

"It's looking that way, yes," I admit, begrudgingly. "Although I suspect she knew what happened. Who else could have taken that video?"

"I had our tech look at it," Detective Singh says. "We believe it was taken on a hidden camera installed inside Sharon's office."

"Huh." I sit back. It makes sense. "Alena suspected Sharon was embezzling. She wanted to catch her in the act…"

Without having to bring in the police and risk unveiling her own fraud. Alena wanted to resolve the matter on her own.

"Did the police find any recording devices when they searched Sharon's office the morning after her body was found?" I ask.

"No," Detective Singh says. "Alena must have removed the camera by the time we arrived."

"Is she talking?"

"No," Detective Singh says. "But we found the Lake Templeton revitalization project file. There's incriminating evidence in there. Alena was taking bribes in exchange for preferential treatment in the bidding process. And then there's her taxes. She will be indicted on fraud charges."

"And what about Caleb?" I ask. "When can we bring him in?"

"We can't. You know that. I can't do anything with the evidence you gathered last night." Frustration threads Detective Singh's voice as he rests his corded hands on taut thighs.

"I can talk to him on my own," I say. "Try to get him to confess."

"You can't do that," Detective Singh says, but his voice sounds canned, robotic. As if he's saying what he thinks he should say, but fully expects me to disobey. *Hopes* I will disobey. "If they suspect I sent you, it could jeopardize the case."

This is Detective Singh's way of telling me to take a stab at Caleb. But be careful. He's not condoning it and will deny culpability if a complaint arrives on his desk.

"Don't worry, Detective," I say with a smile. "You can trust me."

I corner Caleb exactly where I expected to find him after a night of hard partying - crashed on his couch in his dank apartment, in desperate need of a power wash.

Caleb lives in a third-floor apartment in a high-rise building on Cooper's Way in Vancouver's trendy Yaletown neighbourhood. As my car rolls into a parking spot next to the curb, I am hit with an echoing sense of déjà vu. I've been here before - less than two weeks ago. With Zed.

I swing my feet out of my car, staring in wonder at the familiar landscape. The grassy mini playground with slides and monkey bars. Yapping dogs in the distance. Two high rise towers standing side to side like raised arms.

This is where Aditya's drug deal went down.

A wild thought hits me. Is Caleb the man Aditya was meeting that rain-drenched night?

From where I was sitting, he was only a shadow. But Zed must have seen him when he crashed into them…

I pull out my phone and dial Zed. No answer. Impatient, I tap out a text message. Heart thudding with excitement, I lock my car and start walking to the condo tower on the right, as if in a dream. The same condo tower that man emerged from less than two weeks ago. The man who sold Aditya the PCP that killed Sharon. Caleb Bateman?

I pace outside the condo building until a resident appears, buzzes open the gate, and I walk in behind them. Once inside, I make my way to Caleb's apartment. After several heavy knocks, I hear a guttural grunt followed by the sludgy sound of feet squishing over scattered clothes and bumping into a hard item or two as they make their way to the door. And then, Caleb stands before me, hair still on end from last night's gel, face creased from whatever object he fell asleep on after lumbering home.

"Who are you?" Caleb barks. "What do you want?"

I smile. I'm your worst nightmare come to life, Mr. Bateman.

"I'm a private investigator. I'm here to talk to you about the deaths of Sergio Alvarez and Sharon Reese at Lake Templeton."

A thundercloud darkens Caleb's face. "I have nothing to say to you. I've already talked to the police."

I ease past Caleb into his apartment, sideswiping the rigid doorstop of his body.

"Oh believe me, you want to talk to me," I say. "And you don't want to do it in the hallway where anyone can hear."

Caleb stands there, dumbfounded. His apartment reeks and I instantly regret entering. I should have invited him out for a refreshing cup of coffee. But I'm here now and I'm not leaving until I conclude my business. I face Caleb, arms folded across my chest.

"I know that your birth mother, Lona Mason, told you to get out of town the night of Sergio Alvarez's death," I say flatly. "In fact, she's the one who arranged to fly you out of Lake Templeton in the early hours of morning. Isn't that right?"

Caleb's mouth gapes in confusion. His hands, placed defensively on his hips, shudder and slip.

"I also know that Sergio messaged you the night of Sharon Reese's death," I say. "You gave him the ill-advised suggestion to get Sharon drunk after she ingested PCP. This directly led to her death. The two of you thought you were so smart, using WhatsApp, thinking you could avoid detection, get away with murder…"

"Now hold on a second there." Caleb finds his voice. "I had nothing to do with Sharon Reese's death. I didn't even know her!"

His pupils are darkening into angry points. His body tenses in a fight or flight response.

"It doesn't matter whether you knew her," I say, not backing down. "You gave Sergio instructions to kill her! She would've overdosed even if she didn't pitch over the dock!"

"You have no evidence against me," Caleb says, as if reciting words he has been practicing with a drama coach.

He curls his fingers into fists, retreats deeper into the living room, the backs of his legs brushing against the hard edge of his futon.

"Want to bet on it?" I say. "I found your phone, Caleb. I saw your messages."

Caleb rubs his hands on his crumpled black jeans. The tattoos on the nubs of his fingers are oil slicks of sweat.

"The police need a warrant to search through my phone."

"I'm not the police," I say. "Just a concerned citizen."

I see Caleb's hands move, as if in slow motion. His jerky fingers scrabble to find something on the coffee table, seize an overflowing ashtray. He grabs it and charges at me.

Instinct kicks in and I move to the side, in one fluid motion, leaving one outstretched leg in place. Caleb is bigger than me but I'm faster than him. Not to mention, lucid and sharp of mind. His shins hit my outstretched lag, hard, and I wince, but hold my position, as he trips, goes flying, a cry escaping his lips. The ashtray escapes his fist, clatters to the ground.

Caleb slams into the wall, headfirst, his arms rising to cushion his blow a split second too late. He slides to the floor like a silk shirt off a hanger. Moaning, he buries his head in his hands and starts shaking it side to side, back and forth.

I stare in fascination. Is he crying? Hyperventilating? I can't tell.

My voice is calm when I speak, brushing flecks of ash off my pants. "So your plan is to kill me too, just like you killed Sergio? It won't help. I'm not the only one who knows about what you've done."

"I didn't kill anyone!" Caleb bursts out. Shakes his head furiously, from side to side.

"The evidence suggests otherwise," I state, refusing to take pity on him. "You're going to go away for a long time, Caleb. It's time to tell the truth."

Caleb looks up at me like a forlorn child. The anger has drained away, replaced by confusion. He blinks, looks at me as if for the first time, his eyes like pools of mud. Raises a hand to massage his forehead, where a red welt is starting to rise.

He takes a few deep breaths, rises slightly. I tense immediately, kick the ashtray out of his reach, my eyes casing the room for any other hard objects he could grab. I reach under the flap of my shoulder bag. My fingers find the cold metal of the bear spray I carry when I go to confront suspects.

But Caleb is preoccupied with something other than me. He crawls over to the coffee table, grabs a half-empty pack of cigarettes. He shakes one out and raises it to his lips, reaching into his pocket for a lighter.

"Tell me how you know Sergio," I command, after he's taken a long drag, my fingers still touching the hidden bear spray canister.

But the fight has left Caleb. The cigarette is calming him down. "I've known him for years. We met at a talent competition."

"Yes, Vocal Heroes, 2015," I say. "Your birth mother, Lona Mason, bribed you to a win."

Caleb doesn't seem to have heard me. "That night, Sergio called me because his girlfriend took PCP..."

"Why did he call *you*?"

"He knows I'm into drugs and stuff..."

"And Sergio wasn't?"

"No," Caleb says. "I don't think so."

"Why did you tell him to get her drunk?"

An anxious shrug. "I don't know! I didn't mean anything. I was high on crystal. I thought he was joking. I mean - who accidentally takes PCP?"

"So Sharon died because you were high - and joking."

Caleb's face creases like a still lake disturbed by a thrown pebble. "How was I to know what he'd do? It's not my fault!"

"You must've been mad at Sergio when you found out what happened," I say. "Worried that you would be blamed for his stupid decision. And so, you decided to kill him to avoid being found out."

"I did not kill Sergio!" Caleb's aggravated voice rises. "I've told you all so many times. I *did not* kill him!" He scrambles to his feet, wrings his hands together, pulls up his jeans, lit cigarette tumbling from his shaking hands to the carpeted floor. He swats at it with one foot, attempting to put it out. He winces as the burning end of the cigarette sizzles his sole. Then, he turns back to me, his eyes stormy.

By the time he lunges at me again, I'm ready with the bear spray, pointed straight at his eyes. I press down firmly on the nozzle, releasing a small cloud of spray high above and slightly to the left of Caleb's head. Just enough to deter him but not enough to incapacitate him.

Caleb shrieks as the droplets hit him, falls to the floor, his hands frantically rubbing his face, digging into his eyes.

"I'm sorry I had to do that," I say, calmly. "But if you take a few more minutes to answer my questions, I will leave you alone. How does that sound?"

Caleb says nothing, keeps rubbing his reddening face. I take his silence as acquiescence.

"Help me understand - why was your phone at Pebble Beach when he was killed?" I say. "And don't give me your bullshit story about the kidnapping."

"I lost my phone," Caleb says in a weak whimper.

Could it be true? Caleb is an oddball. He had no idea that his phone was compromised at the club last night. Could he be telling the truth about misplacing his phone the night of Sergio's murder?

"Why did the police find your fingerprints at Sergio's home?"

"I visited him sometimes. We were buddies."

"How long have you been friends?" I press further.

A weak shrug - or maybe it's a shudder. Caleb looks at me, his eyes running. "I mean, we've known each other for long... maybe four, five years... but we didn't talk or nothing. He came to a show a few months ago. Told me he was thinking of going back to music again."

I doubt that someone with Sergio's lilting voice would seek advice from a nepotism-fueled foghorn like Caleb Bateman. Sergio had an ulterior motive in tracking Caleb down. Did he know Lona was Caleb's birth mother?

"Did you tell Sergio that your mother, Lona Mason, helped you win the Vocal Heroes singing competition in 2015?"

Caleb's reddened face darkens further. His dark blonde stubble stands on end. He rubs his cheek with one hand, a harried, anxious gesture.

"I didn't think he'd care," Caleb says, a woe-is-me child trying to talk his way out of fingerpainting the wall. "It was *so much time* ago. I thought he moved on. He wasn't even singing no more!"

"Even if I believe you, that *still* doesn't explain what you were doing at Lake Templeton that night," I say. "We know Aditya flew you back to Vancouver at two-thirty a.m. that morning. We have you on video at the airport, getting on the plane."

"I had a gig…"

"Really? Where?" I raise my eyebrows. "I was in Lake Templeton that night. There were no musical concerts or live shows. It was a ghost town."

"Not at Lake Templeton," Caleb says. "At Otter Lake."

The winter concert at Otter Lake! The annual celebration of indie rock that emptied out Lake Templeton. Was Caleb's band on the roster?

"Okay, I will verify that," I say. "But why were you flying out of Lake Templeton? And in the middle of the night?"

"I wanted to come home…"

"So you called Lona," I say, shaking my head, skeptical at his weak explanation, convinced that he is still lying. "You think mommy is going to save your ass from the cops. But you're wrong. Lona may be an MLA but she's not above the law."

Caleb brows furrow as if confronting a thorny problem. It's clear that he will say nothing about Lona. I sense him closing up like a clam. But eventually, he will crack. And when he does, I will be waiting.

Caleb is sticking to his story, but the day brings a new breakthrough from another direction.

Aditya Roshan.

Detective Singh calls me as I'm driving to the station after grabbing a Fatburger on the go. "Aditya has confirmed that it was Sergio Alvarez that caused Sharon Reese's death."

I pull over to the side of the road sharply, earning angry honks behind me. "What do you mean - *caused her death?*" I ask. Drops of mayo splotch onto my passenger seat from my abandoned, half-eaten burger.

"It wasn't deliberate," Detective Singh says. "He didn't set out to kill her."

"Could Aditya be lying to save himself?"

"I don't think so."

"But Aditya was claiming he went home when Sharon and Sergio left City Hall."

"He lied," Detective Singh says. "We ran his phone records. He followed them back to Sharon's place. He was there when she died."

I recall Aditya churning with despair as he spit out lie after lie with a straight face. Hangdog face, so gutted as he digs his fingers into his temples, massaging away the world's worst migraine.

Of course he went to Sharon's place. When Aditya arrived at City Hall and found Sharon melting like a chemically-induced puddle in a science experiment, he panicked. What if she died? What if she ran to the police? The drugs in her system could be traced back to Aditya. It must have been an unhinged instinct, his mad dash to Sharon's place, bumper to bumper with Sergio's car. He had to get control of the situation.

But why lie to me about it? Despite his failure to complete the MBA program, Aditya has a sharp mind. Did he not anticipate that, at some point, the police could run his phone records?

"He says her death was an accident," Detective Singh is saying. "Sharon was panicking. She ran out on the dock. Sergio followed her. They scuffled. She fell."

"And neither Sergio nor Aditya thought of going after her, trying to save her."

"Aditya says he can't swim," Detective Singh says. "He never learned in India."

A man who traversed continents, wrestles planes out of the sky in inclement weather, and started his own airline, doesn't know how to swim. An engineer who can maneuver a four-thousand-pound plane in turbulence without breaking a sweat, failed out of business school. Sounds like Aditya.

As for Sergio... I picture him, seized with shock as Sharon's body pitched into the water, swallowed whole, the splash turning into a ripple. She was gone. Staring down at his hands. *What have I done?* And then the night whispering back, *you're free.* And Sergio's panic dissolving into relief. In the charcoal night, with no one around for miles, the splash of the lake smothering her cry, the moon blindfolded by clouds. There was no one to miss her. And no one who saw her leave - except Aditya. Sergio's partner in crime.

"Why didn't he call the police?" I say, refusing to let Aditya off the hook.

"He *will* face charges for this, Fati," Detective Singh says. "Obstruction of justice, concealing evidence…"

"What happened to Sharon's phone?"

"Sergio dumped it in the lake when Sharon went overboard," Detective Singh says. "But we can't confirm it. We don't have the resources to dredge the lake."

"So Aditya was there when Sergio gave Sharon alcohol," I say. "Mixed with apple juice from her own fridge. And Sharon was too high to know the difference."

"Yes."

"And Aditya encouraged it because if she woke up with a monster hangover the next morning, she wouldn't know she took PCP," I say. "She'd just think she got drunk."

What would have happened if Sharon had woken up the next morning? Realized she was forcibly intoxicated? Sergio probably didn't think that far ahead. And Aditya - he had to choose his poison. Sharon must not find out she took PCP.

Aditya could explain away the alcohol - pin it on Sergio. After all, Sharon was already mad at him. He was a liar and a thief who couldn't be trusted. Aditya was her confidante. Her listening ear. She would have taken his word over Sergio's.

"Probably right," Detective Singh says. "Although Aditya says he warned Sergio it wasn't a good idea."

"Believe me, Detective, Aditya Roshan is way more complicit than he wants us to think."

CHAPTER 18

Saturday, December 28, 2019

A murder case is like a cheap sweater. Once you find a loose thread, it can quickly unravel the whole thing.

Detective Singh and I are enjoying a quiet cup of coffee at a cafe by the station when the call comes in. The overworked technician in charge of rifling through Sergio's emails has found the canary in the coalmine. We grab lids for our coffee cups and hurry back.

Ten minutes later, we are in the windowless tech room that always smells like a Subway sandwich - the tech's lunch of choice. She is a slight young woman, no older than twenty-five years old, thin hair in a ponytail, and a face set in sleepy concentration.

Detective Singh and I lean over to better view her screen. I try to ignore the musky scent of his cologne that tickles me in unwelcome places.

"I found emails between Sergio and Lona Mason," the tech blurts out.

My ears perk up instantly. Lona Mason! Do we finally have a link that ties her to this mess?

"He tried to delete them, you see," the tech is saying. "But I was able to intercept them from the server."

'*You haven't answered my calls,*' Sergio says in one email. '*I know you are having an affair with a married woman. I have evidence. Do you want to see it?*'

I whip my head around to Detective Singh. The red-haired Lake Templeton Marketing Manager with his dog-ate-my-homework expression was a secret blackmailer.

"What evidence did he have?" Detective Singh asks the tech.

"That's in another email," she says.

She clicks to open several photo attachments. Lona and Kim embracing, melded together, hiding behind a translucent curtain in a window, heads together. Walking together, their fingers grazing, their intimacy palpable even in stills. The images appear to be taken from a long-range camera.

"Did Sergio take these photos?" I ask.

"I don't know," the tech says. "He threatened to release them if she didn't pay up."

"Did Lona respond to these emails?"

"Not that I can see."

"She wouldn't leave a paper trail," Detective Singh says. "A woman in her position has to be careful. She would have contacted him in other ways."

"But we didn't find any phone calls between Lona and Sergio," I say, frustration creeping into my voice.

Detective Singh smiles. "But we *did* find phone calls between Sergio and a private number paid for by Kim Cromwell. The same number we found in Caleb's call records."

This is it. Lona is caught in our snare. Satisfaction fills my body.

"I'm struggling to understand how a woman in her position could allow these photos to be taken," I say. "Surprisingly sloppy."

"Love makes you stupid, I guess," the wide-eyed tech offers in a knowing voice.

"How much money was Sergio asking for?"

"A half a million dollars."

"That's the same amount he stole from Lake Templeton," I say. "He must've used the money to settle his gambling debts and buy his fancy gizmos. Then Alena found the video from Sharon's office and started putting pressure on Sergio to return what he stole. If he doesn't, she goes to the police."

Detective Singh is nodding.

"And so, Sergio thought he would tap a source he knew was flush with cash - Lona," I say. "He had just found out she helped her son, Caleb, win that talent competition through questionable means."

"But that wasn't enough to sway her, so he followed her and took photos," Detective Singh says.

"Maybe," I say. "Or someone else shared the photos with him. A certain airline pilot who was sick of Lona and the control she had over his life. He couldn't expose her himself - she could kill his business. And so he took a circuitous route - through Sergio - to get back at her. Maybe he thought Lona would get spooked and leave Kim alone."

And when the police arrived, breathing fire, ready to rip apart Lake Templeton's books, Sergio attempted to erase the emails. They were evidence that he was a blackmailer. One more charge the police could nail him on.

Detective Singh nods, folding his arms across his chest. "It gives her a motive for Sergio's murder."

"And her son, Caleb, was her weapon of choice." My face splits into an exuberant smile. "Do we have enough to formally question Lona now?"

Detective Singh blows out a breath, drops his arms by his side. "Yes," he says. "But you're looking forward to this more than I am. She's an MLA. Do you know what happens when word gets out she was questioned in connection to a murder?"

"Shit's going to hit the fan," I say. "Media will blow up, keyboard warriors will come out on Facebook, half of them condemning her and the other half professing their undying love for her. Global BC will camp outside her house. It will be beautiful. I can hardly wait."

2

1

As Detective Singh and I walk out of the station, my feet spring off the sidewalk in zest. A clear sky borders a sunny day. Cloud cover has dissipated, like the murky shadows lifting off our case, revealing the truth of the night Sharon died.

I imagine her lurching out on the dock, scattered, gasping for fresh air. Sergio chasing her, grabbing at her. Even under the influence, Sharon was faster than him. Aditya watching from the shadows, letting the tableau play out. Sharon pitching over, mouth open in surprise, not realizing what happened, body smacking against the frigid water, submerging in it. Sergio watching with cold finality.

Sergio and Aditya, reluctant co-conspirators, neither reaching for their phones to call the police. Sergio's mental wheels starting to turn, his steady hand retrieving Sharon's phone, switching it off, tossing it into the ocean. He had the wherewithal to take a shower after, maybe to wash the night off of him - along with any memories of Sharon.

And then, the next morning, he went out for his customary run. Not wanting to break from routine. Was it because he didn't want to raise suspicion? Or did he simply not care that Sharon was dead? We will never know.

It was an ironic twist of fate that Sergio stumbled over Sharon's body. Had no choice but to call the police. His face bleached white in fear under his carrot-colored hair. Sharon wasn't gone forever, after all. She was back - like the ghost of the woman you've murdered knocking from under your bed.

We slide into a cop car. Detective Singh drives. I stare out the windshield, my thoughts hammering away inside my head, knock, knock, clues touching each other, intertwining fingers, and then embracing. Detective Singh is maneuvering the car around a slow-moving dump truck.

"You can always turn on your police lights and zip out of here," I suggest gently, knowing full well that skirting the rules is outside of Detective Singh's comfort zone. That's why he's the perfect foil for my wrecking-ball ways.

He glances at me in rebuke but doesn't say anything.

"Has anyone come to claim Sergio's home?" I say, changing the subject.

"His closest kin is his mother in Peru," Detective Singh says. "She's his beneficiary."

We arrive at Lona's office. Her assistant tells us that Lona did not come in today.

Did Caleb call her to throw a hissy fit about my visit? Maybe Lona is gathering her troops for an all-out war against me and the police department. Or maybe she's just getting her story straight.

Detective Singh and I wait for twenty minutes for Lona to show up. Phone calls to her cell go unanswered. Eventually, we abandon our efforts. But not before Detective Singh issues a stern warning to Lona's assistant.

We are getting a search warrant. If Lona doesn't come willingly to the police station, all bets are off. We will ransack her office and her home - and make no effort to conceal anything once the press gets wind of our efforts.

We drive away, out of steam. I suggest that we swing by Lona's house but Detective Singh demurs. He wants to give her an opportunity to come to us. No need to poke an angry bear with a stick.

With Sharon's murder solved, Sergio's still hangs over our heads like a bloated rain cloud. Without a confession from Caleb or Lona, all we have are theories. I suggest that we pause and regroup with coffee.

"I have other cases, you know," Detective Singh reminds me.

Of course he does. For the past few days, I have fallen under the spell of thinking I have this rugged, handsome man all to myself.

What other avenues are left while we wait for Lona? I need to take action. I cannot sit by my window like a romantic heroine from the 1940s waiting for her beloved to come home.

"I want to talk to Alena Krutova," I say. "Is she in custody at Otter Lake?"

Detective Singh looks at me. I meet his eyes but am unable to decipher their message.

"She is being formally indicted on a raft of charges," he says. "We're getting the paperwork together. But she will make bail. You want to go back there again?"

I smile. "She was my first suspect. I'm still a little attached to her."

Zed calls me that night.

"Where have you been, buddy?" I say.

"I got your text message," Zed says. "You said you wanted to ask me something about Caleb. And it got me thinking. Something's been bothering me for a few days. Something about Caleb."

"Oh yeah?" I hold my breath.

"I kept getting this feeling I've seen him somewhere before," Zed says. "And now I know where. I am ninety-nine percent sure Caleb Bateman was the guy we saw at Cooper's Park with the airline pilot."

I freeze in place. "Aditya's drug dealer?"

"Yeah, that's the one," Zed says. "Same guy - same neck tattoo and everything."

I sink to the floor, knocking over my glass of pinot noir on my shag rug.

"Caleb's not just a drug *user*. He's a drug *dealer*." My voice rises in excitement as the puzzle pieces click into place. "Aditya was buying drugs from Caleb. So when Caleb murdered Sergio, *of course* Aditya wanted to protect him and fly him out of Lake Templeton as fast as possible. Caleb could have blown the lid on Aditya's illegal activities."

"This case is giving me a headache," Zed says. "I've never seen such a carnival crew of dodgy characters."

"Zed - buddy, thank you! But I have to go." I click off the phone, immediately dialing Detective Singh to share the news.

Sunday, December 29, 2019

I arrive at the ferry terminal forty-five minutes before my boat sails for Nanaimo, beating the morning clock. A rare occurrence for me.

During my journey, Alena makes bail. She is being pilloried in the press. The news is filled with photos of the slim blonde hiding under her umbrella, jacket pulled up to her chin.

The police have cautioned her not to leave her home. So I know that's where I will find her. Calling ahead would have been pointless. Since her last acid-dripping phone call when the police stormed City Hall, it has been deep freeze from Alena's direction.

It's a blustery day on the water. The sun is poking its sharp fingers through the clouds but the icy winds keep beating it back. I sit on the deck and chug my rapidly cooling cup of coffee, letting the wind tease my hair and embrace me with its frigid limbs. I need to wake up.

My drive to Lake Templeton stretches into miles of nothingness. The year 2020 is about to dawn. I need to put this case to rest in the next three days, otherwise it will linger into the new year like a bad hangover.

I pass the sign welcoming visitors to Lake Templeton, and point my car in the direction of Alena's home. The town square is a relic from a past life, hushed in an endless moment of silence for the loss of life as they know it.

I pull my car up to Alena's house, its white turrets rising unaffected from the beachy ground. I wonder if her mysterious brother is still with her. Alena needs the morale booster of a friendly face now more than ever.

I park my car in front of the house. No more sneaking around. Alena's secrets are like meowing cats previously locked in a cellar that I let out to run around in the open.

I walk through the flowering promenade that flanks the house and to the back door. I knock - loudly, shattering the serene stillness.

As if in a blink, Alena is there. It's as if she were sitting on the edge of her pristine couch, waiting for a visitor to arrive to break up the monotony of the day. Her pin-straight hair is swept back into a neat ponytail. She is barefoot and wearing lounge pants with a loose merino wool sweater. Her face looks softer, more vulnerable without makeup, but her sharp gray eyes are like quicksand, sucking in everything around them.

She sees me and, for a split second, her eyebrows shoot up in horror - as if she's seen a ghost. And then, she settles into a haughty glower, anger darkening her brow.

"What are you doing here?" she snaps, her body stiff, one foot extending to the doorjamb to block my entry.

"I was hoping we could talk," I say, in a conciliatory tone.

"There's nothing to talk about." Alena's face remains frozen in mutiny.

I better come straight to the point.

"We found the video from Sharon's office at City Hall the night she died," I say, carefully watching Alena. "We know you took it. You suspected that Sharon stole money from Lake Templeton. And so, you installed a hidden camera in her office to watch her, gather evidence, and find out where the money went. But the morning after Sharon's death, when you found out what the camera had recorded, you realized that Sergio was the thief. But you didn't go to the police. You decided to blackmail Sergio instead."

Alena remains silent but her face slips a little, a crack behind the coat of paint.

"I sensed something between you and Sergio," I say. "When I was questioning him about his hair in Sharon's drain. You were so protective towards him. Even recommending him for mayor. That was a trick, wasn't it? You were extending the promise of a carrot while you had him in a noose."

"I was trying to recover the City's money," Alena says, coolly. "One can hardly blame me for that."

"And poor Sergio playing along, brown nosing, flattering you, calling you his mentor, attributing his success to you - all in the hope that you'd go easy on him."

Alena folds her arms across her chest but says nothing.

"And the irony is now the money is found and the project is dead anyway," I say. I point one finger at her. "Because of *you*, Alena. The investors are spooked. They're pulling their money. The project is delayed indefinitely. It *will* start up again, maybe years from now, but it will be a feather in the next mayor's cap."

Alena's mouth tightens, her eyes flashing. She knows I'm right.

"Why blame Sharon after you found out she was innocent?" I ask. "Although, it was easy to implicate her - she was the Treasurer. The only signatory on the City's bank accounts. Besides you, of course."

Alena doesn't flinch.

"Did you confront Sharon about the theft?" I say. "Before she died? See - I suspect that you did and that's when she started digging to find the real culprit. To clear her name. And it led her directly to Sergio."

"If Sharon had come to me with evidence against Sergio, I would have listened." Alena's voice is hard, defiant.

Maybe. But Sharon wanted to talk to Sergio first. Look him in the eye and get him to admit his guilt. And it became her undoing.

I deftly change topics. "Where did you get those cult videos?"

I can see Alena struggling to maintain her composure. Her cards are fully laid out face-up on the table. She wants to hold on to her poker face, even when the law is crawling on her like lice.

"Anything that you illegally gathered by breaking into my house is not admissible in a court of law."

Steadfast in her practiced party line. My evidence is invalid. It doesn't matter. But that ship has sailed. What the police have on her is more potent, more compelling. And all of it is admissible.

I bet Alena is kicking herself for skipping out on CCTV cameras for her fortress-like home. And not putting a password on her personal laptop. Not so impregnable after all, even in a sleepy town. Maybe Lake Templeton put a spell on her, clouded her head with a false sense of security. She never imagined her walls could be breached. Not in a town of five thousand people, all of whom worshipped her.

"I'm not looking for additional evidence against you," I say. "We have enough. I only want to understand - why?"

Alena's level expression conceals an internal battle. And then she makes a decision and says, "She had them on her computer."

"Who filmed the videos?"

Alena evades my question. "I saw her looking at them from time to time in the office. Usually when she was stressed."

To punish herself. To remind herself where she came from and what she had to atone for.

"Did anyone else know the truth about Sharon's crimes in the cult?"

Alena lifts one shoulder in her signature half shrug. "I don't know."

"I have a theory," I say. "Sharon knew you were greasing palms through this weird numbered company that drew on a construction loan for a project that hasn't even started. A loan that was secured by a government guarantee signed by the City of Lake Templeton. You compelled Sharon to look the other way, using her cult videos as leverage. That must have been very difficult for her."

No response, just that impeccable poker face. Alena could make a lot of money at the casino. Why did she resort to fraud to pad her bank account?

"You got rid of the revitalization project file when you found out Sharon was dead and the police were coming," I say. "But why not get rid of the other incriminating files with details of the Royal Bank loan, the insurance policies, and the rest of it?"

Alena folds her arms across her chest. "None of that is 'incriminating.' It's normal course of business."

"I think I know the answer," I say. "You simply didn't have enough time. Sharon's body washed up on shore. You were informed. The police came, asked lots of questions.

And then, I showed up. You didn't have time to go through Sharon's credenza and search for the smoking guns. So you did what you could, hoping you could explain away the rest."

Alena raises her chin in defiance. Again chooses silence.

"How did Sharon's sweater end up in your fire pit?"

Alena's sharp eyes slice at me.

"There's no point denying it," I say. "Don't worry, though. We know Sergio was responsible for Sharon's death."

"I didn't lie to you, Ms. Rizvi," Alena says. "I know nothing about that sweater. You found it in my fire pit because Sergio placed it there."

"Why would he do that?"

"To annoy me," Alena says coolly. "Apply pressure."

So Sergio took out his claws. He wasn't going to let the conniving Alena bulldoze him. Not without biting back.

Alena is right about the sweater. I already had my three-a.m. moment where a memory wrung from a dream jarred me awake. I first saw that gray sweater several days before I saw it in Alena's fire pit. I saw it on the very first day I arrived at Lake Templeton. In Sergio's living room. He took it with him, as a souvenir, or an insurance policy, after the lake slurped Sharon. When Alena slapped him with the City Hall video, he knew how to slap back.

I can't hold back a chortle. "I thought you and Sergio were so close when I first met you. Like brother and sister. Mentor and mentee. I could never have imagined…"

Alena's barricaded arms across her bony chest tell me she's not amused. A rising tornado brews in her eyes but her lips remain pursed. Silent.

"Why did you share the video from City Hall with Korinne Kendall?"

"I have no idea what you're talking about," Alena says. "I did no such thing."

"You didn't?"

"That woman is a snoop," Alena says. "She's not what she appears to be."

"Korinne doesn't have a high opinion of you, either."

Alena's face clenches but she doesn't refute my statement.

"One last thing," I say. "Was there *actually* an audit or was that a story too? The thing is, legitimate auditors would have found the embezzled money. But they would also have found everything you were trying to hide. So there are two likely scenarios - either there *was* no audit, or you hired one of your crooked cronies on City dime."

"Does it matter?" Alena says bitterly. "The case is with the crown now. They will do their own audit. And then you can satisfy yourself."

With a nod of farewell, I walk away. Satisfied. In the last fifteen minutes, I got more from Alena than I did in the past two weeks. She is still obstinate, but lighter somehow. Looser. At a place of uneasy peace where one arrives when they know there's nowhere else to run. It's a place of inevitability.

As I walk past the promenade, the wind ruffles my hair softly, reminding me of its presence. The lake slaps against the rocky beach. Calm marinates the air.

Alena will lie in the bed she has made. As for me, I have one more murder to solve.

Monday, December 30, 2019

I didn't want to give Alena the tacit satisfaction of being the only reason I came to Lake Templeton. And so, I decided to stay overnight. The Lakeside Inn was waiting for me like an unrequited lover. The proprietress thought she was doing me a favor by offering me the same room I've enjoyed on previous trips. I thanked her with a genuine smile, even though I am not a fan of routine.

In the morning, I head to the Lake Templeton City Hall. It's the lull between Christmas and New Year and people are wandering listlessly and working half-heartedly.

But this is not a typical year. There's fear in their eyes. The terrifying overhang of the audit hovers like a spaceship housing alien species. They're worried about their jobs. The office is strangely full. Holidays are canceled as employees lurk, on watch, ready to defend their employment with all they've got.

A few people recognize me and say hello. Some crack a smile. They aren't suspicious of me. I am a barely remembered apparition who briefly drifted through their halls. I make my way to Marla, the receptionist and office gossip.

Marla is eager to talk to me, looking for respite from the monotony of her work against the backdrop of recent dramatic events. I make small talk to ease the conversation, before bringing the discussion to Sergio.

Marla reassures me that everyone in the office is broken up over Sergio's death. And no one knows why anyone would want to hurt him.

"And yet, it happened," I remind her gently. "Who do you suspect?"

"An out-of-towner, for sure," Marla says. "But then..." She hesitates. "I kind of suspected that something was going on with Sergio."

"What do you mean?"

"He was *really* stressed out when the police came."

"Really?"

"Yes," Marla says. "I heard him on the phone with his mom, raising his voice. He was never that way with her. Called her every day."

"Did you hear what he was saying?"

Marla shakes her head. "He spoke in Spanish. I could tell something was off by his tone. And I saw him taking his photos and personal stuff with him. Honestly - I thought maybe he was getting fired."

"Interesting."

"Sergio is normally such a happy-go-lucky kind of guy," Marla is saying. "Not very serious. Friends with everyone. But since Sharon died - he's been withdrawn, kind of on edge. I didn't think much of it at the time. I mean, who wouldn't be upset if their girlfriend died?"

I look at Marla sharply. "So you knew that Sharon and Sergio were a thing?"

Marla flushes under my accusing gaze. "Yeah, I knew. You see, I saw them in the office sometimes. They stood a little too close. Never anything inappropriate, mind you. But I'm usually pretty good about picking up on stuff like that."

A nosy busybody, that's what you are Marla. Hovering everywhere, a chameleon that sees and hears everything.

"Why didn't you say anything when I first asked you about it?"

"Sergio told me to keep it quiet," Marla says. "I asked him about it once - I saw him and Sharon leaving work together. Sergio said Sharon would flip if everyone found out. She was very private, you see."

"And did you tell your boss, Alena, about this relationship?"

A flash of indignation. "Of course not!"

"Tell me one more thing, Marla," I say. "Since you're in the mood to share. What was the relationship *really* like between Alena and Sharon?"

Marla bristles at my indirect reprimand behind her cats-eye glasses. She pushes a lock of curly hair behind one ear. "Pleasant - at least until recently," she confesses. "In the past few months, there was a strain. We all felt it. But we didn't know why."

"And did you know that Sergio was embezzling money from the Lake Templeton revitalization project?"

"No," she sputters. "Absolutely not. I knew nothing about that."

"And what about Aditya Roshan, the airline pilot?" I say. "Did you suspect that he was mixed up in this?"

Marla shakes her head rapidly, then pauses, raises one hand to her freckled face, touches her cheek thoughtfully. "I always thought he was weird. You see, I know someone who knows someone who went to university with him. She was quite surprised when I told her Lake Templeton gave Aditya an exclusive contract. She said that guy was invisible. No personality. Never spoke in class. Quiet as a church mouse."

CHAPTER 19

Monday, December 30, 2019

I thank Marla for her time and make my way out of City Hall. I am sitting in my car, contemplating my next move when Detective Singh calls me.

"I've got news for you."

"Tell me," I say, my body tensing with anticipation.

"We have new information in the matter of Sergio Alvarez's death," Detective Singh says. "We got the results on the DNA we found on his body."

"And…"

"It belongs to Aditya Roshan."

"You're kidding." My heart drops into my stomach with a thud. Forgetting I am in my car, I sit up sharply, cracking my skull against the ceiling. I yell out an expletive and quickly swallow my words.

"Is he talking?" I ask through cotton balls clogging my throat.

Detective Singh draws a weary breath. "He will."

DNA evidence is undeniable. Gold standard. I foresee a plea deal in Aditya's future.

"Why didn't this come up in his phone records?" I am flabbergasted.

"It did," Detective Singh says, his voice quiet. "The Lake Templeton airport is close to Pebble Beach. He said he got there early, to prepare for his morning flight."

"So Aditya killed Sergio?"

"His skin fibers were found on Sergio's shirt, underneath his fingernails," Detective Singh says. "Chances are he's our killer."

I sit back, my mind racing. Aditya and Sergio were tied together because of Sharon's death. Their fates were linked. But neither trusted the other. When the police stormed City Hall, Sergio panicked. Did he twist the knife in Aditya, threatening to reveal all, unless Aditya paid him? Aditya's wife, Kim, was a cash cow. She was best friends with Lona Mason, whom Sergio was already blackmailing. And Sergio needed money to escape. Did he push Aditya over the edge?

"The warrant came through," Detective Singh says. "For Caleb's home and phone."

"When is it going down?"

"Today," Detective Singh says. "Take the four o'clock ferry. By the time you're home, I may have more to share."

I throw my car into drive and screech out, pointing it in the direction of the ferry terminal.

Back at the RCMP detachment on Wesbrook Mall, I wait on pins and needles. Detective Singh is still at the raid at Caleb Bateman's place. Meanwhile, Lona Mason arrives, legal team in tow. She looks at me as if she has never seen me before.

I am not bothered. She will crack like an aging egg soon enough. She still hasn't remitted my five hundred dollars plus expenses. I make a mental note to send her a reminder with a late payment fee of a hundred dollars.

Ten minutes after Lona's arrival, Detective Singh walks through the door, looking like a GQ model. The golden halo of his presence warms the air like a summer heat dome. I rub my damp palms on my thighs and rise to my feet, placing myself in his path.

He sees me, nods slightly, touches my arm, and steers me towards his office. I follow like a dog that has been waiting a week for its vacationing owner to come home.

Lona sits there, eyes like sonic beams, boring holes in us.

"When will you talk to Lona?" I whisper to Detective Singh. "Can I join?"

His eyes tell me to hold on a minute and I close my mouth. As we walk into his office, I restrain the urge to glance back at

Lona, perched on the edge of her seat, stiff as a jammed door handle. The door closes behind us.

Detective Singh turns around to face me. "We have to look through Caleb's phone before talking to Lona. We need evidence to make her talk."

That makes sense. I sink into the now-familiar chair across from Detective Singh's desk.

"Did you find anything at Caleb's apartment?"

Detective Singh shakes his head, but doesn't look disappointed. "As expected, they anticipated this and had the place scrubbed."

"How long for the tech to take apart Caleb's phone?"

Detective Singh punches at his keyboard, clearly distracted. "An hour or two, maybe. She's working on it right now."

I know Detective Singh has other cases. As should I, if I plan to pay my mortgage next month.

"You can go home if you'd like," Detective Singh says. "I'll call you."

Not a chance. I'm not leaving until this case is solved. I can taste the sweet nectar of victory oozing behind my lips. But I do need to burn off my nervous energy. A quick circuit outside should do the trick.

I pace outside the police station, wrapping my arms around myself to block the cold. I forgot my jacket inside and the sunless alcove is unforgiving in the winter air. At times like these, I wish I smoked. Zed would be puffing away at a nicotine stick to warm his blood. Or - since legalization - a spiff of marijuana, unafraid of the errant eyes of a passing cop.

I lose track of time in the cacophony of my thoughts. Eventually, Detective Singh summons me back inside and to the tech room. The seat that Lona occupied is empty.

Where did she go?

But soon, my thoughts are pulled into another direction.

"Our tech has uncovered something interesting," Detective Singh tells me, closing the door behind me. "Nora, over to you."

Nora, the tech, readily takes the verbal cue. "On the night of Sergio's murder, Caleb had a long stretch of digital dead time," she says. "He wasn't active online and wasn't responding to messages. It coincides with an hour before Sergio's death to the time that Caleb got on a private plane at Lake Templeton airport, bound for Vancouver."

"So?" I am unsure what to make of it. "That's not surprising, is it? He had other things on his mind with planning and committing a murder."

Yes, I know, Aditya was the one that did the actual deed. But surely, Caleb was involved somehow. An accomplice.

"Before that, his phone was at the Cliff Hotel in Otter Lake," Nora says, looking at me with her wide, cerulean eyes. "That's where Caleb was staying the night Sergio was killed."

"That's right," I say. "Caleb had a gig there. He was playing at the annual winter concert - the indie rock festival in Otter Lake. I cross checked the roster already. And verified from his Instagram photos."

"Based on cell signal data, Aditya picked Caleb up at the Cliff Hotel in Otter Lake just after eleven-thirty p.m. that night," Nora says. "I found deleted WhatsApp messages on Caleb's phone, coordinating a meeting."

WhatsApp - the app of choice for drug traffickers and other unscrupulous types trying to skate under the surface of police detection. How did I miss that connection? Why didn't I search for Aditya in Caleb's WhatsApp contacts when I had the chance?

I take a deep breath. Swallow my ego. Acknowledge my rookie mistake. "So, are we thinking that Caleb and Aditya worked together? Aditya picked up Caleb at the Cliff Hotel, they drove over to Sergio's house, took him to Pebble Beach, and killed him."

Caleb's fifteen minutes of fame at the Otter Lake winter rock festival were scheduled at nine-thirty p.m. I know from checking with organizers that the concert was designated drug-free. Strict checkpoints at the entrance precluded anyone from entering with suspicious packets. Caleb must have finished his gig and headed back to his hotel right away, ravenous for a toke. No sense in staying at a dry party when the real fun was waiting in his hotel room.

Detective Singh shakes his head. "It was a drug pickup. Caleb says he met Aditya at the hotel briefly, then went back to his room and crashed - until later that night when Aditya picked him up to fly him back to Vancouver."

"The CCTV footage from the Cliff Hotel should confirm whether Caleb is telling the truth."

Detective Singh smiles - a rare, brilliant turn of his angled mouth. "That's right."

"Wait till you see what I found!" Nora jumps in, voice eager. She looks triumphant as she clicks through the network of buttons on her keyboard, like a child wanting to show off a drawing to its parents.

Detective Singh and I stand behind her, looking at the computer screen.

A grayscale film appears on screen. Standard CCTV footage. A nondescript reception area. The Cliff Hotel. I shuffle my feet as Nora forwards through the first few seconds of footage. Then, a figure appears in the distance, with a distinctive loping gait. Nora presses play. It's Caleb Bateman.

He is walking in his typical exaggerated stride, like a peacock sashaying with its feathers on display. He looks relaxed; not like someone planning a murder. He comes closer. For a few seconds, his face is dead center of the camera, then he sidles out the front door, and out of view.

Nora clicks to a companion video which shows the outside front entrance of the hotel. A blink and Caleb is standing there, next to a gray Honda Civic. He reaches over, pulls open the passenger door, and gets in. The driver is a dark gray blob, face not visible. The car loiters for a few minutes.

"It's Aditya Roshan, isn't it?" I ask, through a constricted throat. "In the gray Honda Civic. It's the same car witnesses reported seeing in the area."

"You got it," Detective Singh says. "We ran the plate. It's a Budget rental Aditya picked up the night before."

The time stamp on the screen indicates that just under ten minutes has passed when the passenger door opens and Caleb steps out. He closes the door behind him and walks back inside the hotel. The car lights up and drives away, a phantom into the night.

I glance at Detective Singh sharply. Could it be? His eyes silently corroborate my thoughts.

"He went back to the hotel," I say, breathlessly. "He didn't go with Aditya."

Detective Singh points to the time stamp on the video. "That exact moment - phone records show Caleb's cellphone in the car with Aditya driving towards Sergio's house."

"He left his phone in the car," I state as it clicks into place.

Detective Singh nods. "Caleb never went to Sergio's house. He left his phone in Aditya's car by mistake. Aditya was the one who went to Sergio's house - and then took him to Pebble Beach. Aditya Roshan killed Sergio."

From there, things move fast. Faced with the evidence against him, Aditya crumbles.

DNA evidence cannot be denied. Microscopic fragments of skin on Sergio's shirt, shed by the killer while he strangled him. Bits under his fingernails as he scratched at Aditya's hands hooked around his neck. Little flecks of saliva dried on Sergio's face.

And finally, Lona starts talking.

"Yes, Sergio was blackmailing me," Lona admits. "He was threatening to reveal intimate details of my private life. All I did was ask Mr. Roshan to talk some sense into him."

"He was asking for half a million dollars," I state. "Did you consider paying him off?"

Lona's eyes flare but she maintains her cold composure. "I don't keep a half a million dollars in cash under my pillow. Investments would need to be unwound. I would have to notify my wealth advisor. They would ask questions."

"And Sergio wanted the funds that night because he was running away?" Detective Singh says.

Lona raises her hands, as if in a question. "I didn't know he was running away. He didn't mention that to me."

"Did you know Sergio was involved in Sharon Reese's death and Aditya was there?" I ask.

A flash of annoyance crosses Lona's powdered face. "No, of course not." She glances pointedly at her watch, reminding us that her time is precious.

"If you didn't know, why did you think Aditya was the right person to talk sense into Sergio?" I challenge her. "He's a bit unpredictable. I wouldn't hire him as a hostage negotiator."

Lona's bow-tipped mouth remains set in its solemn expression. "They knew each other. I got Aditya the contract with Lake Templeton. He has flown Sergio several times."

Weak. A non-answer. Lona saw the video from City Hall. She knew that Aditya and Sergio were reluctant co-conspirators, holding identical nooses in their hands, teetering on a shaky trapdoor.

"Why not call Alena, the mayor?" I ask. "Surely, Sergio's boss would have more sway over him than an airline pilot who sometimes flew him places."

Lona lifts up her glass of water and sloshes it from side to side. "As I told you, at that time, I didn't want my personal life to become a distraction from my commitment to my people."

"In other words, if you told Alena what was going on, you couldn't prevent it from getting out," I say. "Your secrets would no longer remain secrets."

Lona only raises her eyebrows in confirmation.

I tighten the screw. "There's also the fact that you knew Sergio was the culprit in the Lake Templeton embezzlement case. Alena sent you that video from City Hall. Why not use that to get Sergio under control? He gives up on blackmailing you and you don't share that video with police."

Lona interlaces her fingers together in her lap and straightens her back. The political poker face emerges, sets over her heart-shaped face like a masquerade mask.

When she speaks, her voice is firm and clear. "That video is evidence of a crime. As a public servant and a law-abiding citizen, it's outrageous for you to suggest I would conceal it."

"No – you decided to use it to blackmail Aditya instead – to force him to give your girlfriend a divorce."

"I always intended to give the video to the police," Lona says firmly.

That's right. Ultimately, her promises nothing. She took the video as Alena's peace offering then reneged on her promise, snitched on the fraud, and sent a storm of troopers to raid City Hall. She would've done the same to Aditya, used the video as leverage to get Aditya to acquiesce and then blown his cover to the police anyway.

"That night, Aditya must have called you in a panic," I say. "Told you what happened."

Not to mention, told Lona that he had Caleb's phone to assure her cooperation. Lona would've maintained her cold, calm calculation. Making quick decisions. Ordering Aditya to fly Caleb back immediately. Dispatching him to Whistler. Concocting a fraudulent kidnapping story planted on an eager, inexperienced private investigator. Or so she thought.

"I have nothing further to say on the subject," Lona says with finality.

What would she have done if Aditya hadn't killed Sergio? Would she have paid him off? I suppose I will never know. Lona is done talking. She has shared her story and she's sticking to it. I will have to accept that.

Detective Singh asks me to accompany him to the windowless, metal box where Aditya waits.

Aditya, our killer. Caleb is just the poor sod who got caught in his crosshairs. Head-in-the-clouds, chemical-dependent, almost scion of a dynastic family.

The only question left to answer - Why? Why did Aditya kill Sergio?

Aditya's face is weathered with the toils of life, crushed under the weight of bad decisions.

What happened to the man who was once moon-bound, heady with the promise of a new and better life in Canada?

He remained an outsider at business school. He failed out of the MBA program. He started his own business and continued to flounder. Life teased an upturn when he met a vibrant woman he loved. But she couldn't love him back. He became a lackey for a powerful woman. He saw dealing drugs as his path out, started a dangerous game with the long-lost son of his dominating patron. His terrible choice caused a woman's death. One after the other, the rocks kept flying at him, until finally, caught in the riptide of life - he snapped.

Was Sergio blackmailing Aditya too? Threatening to go to the police and implicate him in Sharon's death? Is that why he was pushed to an unimaginable act?

Maybe, in the dark of night, Aditya couldn't help but compare himself to other successful immigrants that came before him, with him, after him. Building profitable businesses, getting promoted, buying property, being respected. Maybe he looked at them, then looked in the mirror and saw himself lacking.

"What happened that night?" I ask.

"Lona asked me to handle it," Aditya says quietly, but doesn't meet my eyes. "I didn't mean to kill him."

"So why did you?" Detective Singh asks in a mild tone.

Aditya raises shaking hands to his eyes, grinds his thumbs into the creased nubs, his head bobbing from side to side as if he is subjecting himself to bruising mental lashes.

"He became too greedy," Aditya says, his voice faraway. "I tried to make him understand, asked him nicely to leave Lona alone, to skip town. He could have left."

"But he wanted more money," I state. "Did he spend all the money he stole from Lake Templeton?"

"I think so…" Aditya says, uncertainly. "He had debts. He needed to get the sharks off his back. Sergio had a gambling problem, you know. He was a regular at the underground craps tables."

"Did Lona ask you to kill him?" Detective Singh asks.

Aditya thinks about it for a few minutes, chews his mouth, as if considering his response.

"There's no reason to protect her, Aditya," I remind him. "You're going away for this, whether you implicate her or not. You may think you're protecting Kim, but don't forget - Kim betrayed you. She doesn't care about you."

A pained look crosses Aditya's face. "She told me to take care of it," Aditya says, repeating himself.

"Has she asked you to do that before?" I ask.

Aditya shakes his head. He looks like an old man, run ragged from breaking rocks all day.

"You said you didn't mean to kill him," Detective Singh says. "So how did Sergio end up dead?"

Aditya rubs his eyes again, his head sinking into his shoulders, carrying the weight of the world. "He started threatening me. About Sharon's death. He knew the drugs she took came from me."

"How did he know the drugs Sharon took came from you?"

"It's *my* fault," Aditya's self-flagellates. "When Sharon started...reacting, I *had* to tell Sergio. I didn't want her to die. We tried to get control of the situation. But after Sharon's death, Sergio used it against me. Instead of leaving Lona alone, he made it *my* problem to get money from her."

"And so you killed him," I state, with an air of finality.

Aditya's mouth wobbles.

"Why did you take him to Pebble Beach?" I ask. "Why not kill him at home?"

"That was his idea," Aditya says. "I went to his house, but he didn't want me to come in. He asked if we could go somewhere to talk."

I look at Detective Singh. Our eyes meet in shared understanding. Sergio did not want Aditya to know he was running away.

"Did you threaten Caleb once you realized his phone was left in your car?" I ask, ratcheting up the heat.

"No, I didn't!" Aditya's face darkens with resentment. "I don't threaten anyone! That's not who I am. I told her what happened, that's all."

Another look flashes between me and Detective Singh. His face is set in its usual inscrutable expression - but I can read it as clearly as a front seater can read the class blackboard. Concealing evidence of a murder - maybe Lona isn't as law-abiding as she would like us to think.

When it came to her son, her flesh-and-blood, her righteous quest for justice dissipated. She knew Caleb would look guilty. So she shielded Aditya, the real murderer, maybe hoping the case would go away on its own, banished to the unsolved files that line the backroom of the police department, emblems of failure they would like to forget.

I picture Aditya's phone call, close to one a.m. The phone shrills on Lona's bedside table. Was Kim with her? In bed, clad in silk nightshirts, sipping glasses of port, watching late night TV. Aditya frantic, in a daze, staring at his hands that had done the unthinkable. His speech erratic, words battered by the wind whistling over the lake. But Lona heard what she needed to hear. Her errand boy overstepped. Lost his head.

Her problem was solved, but a new one had been created. A bigger one. The man she had positioned under her thumb had shifted. He was seeing her own son behind her back, buying drugs from him to free himself from her.

She thought fast, issued a directive. *Fly Caleb out of Lake Templeton immediately*. Hid her son away. And the next day, she called me. Caleb had been kidnapped and she needed my help. If only her wayward son had listened and switched off his phone when she told him to.

I turn back to Aditya. "I'm curious - did it not occur to you that we could run your phone records? You said you met Sharon and Sergio at City Hall and then left. You were adamant that you did *not* follow them to Sharon's place. Why? Did you really think we would simply take your word for it? That we won't verify what you were telling us?"

The pained look on Aditya's face tells me everything I need to know. As naive as it sounds, he didn't think that far ahead.

"People who knew you - back at UBC...no one thought you were particularly impressive - or memorable - but no one imagined you were a killer either," I say. "What happened, Aditya?"

Aditya looks at me as if I have slapped him.

The door flies open. A constable stands at the doorway, shame-faced at interrupting us. Behind him a tall man in a dark suit, his face twisted in righteous anger.

"I'm so sorry to interrupt," the constable says. "This is Mr. Roshan's lawyer."

The man walks into the room, swallowing the air. "You had no right to question my client without a lawyer present," he tells us, brusque and no-nonsense. "Anything he said is inadmissible in a court of law."

I fold my arms across my chest, unperturbed. "We know the law too. Your 'client' waived his right to a lawyer. He wants to tell the truth."

The relief that films Aditya's eyes isn't from being rescued. It's from finally telling the truth. Coming out of hiding. When you hit rock bottom, you can start to rebuild. Aditya is exhausted from lying. He is ready to set down the load. And breathe. Fully. For the first time in a long while.

"It will take me ten minutes to prove he was coerced," the man says, lip curling. "Leave me alone with my client, please."

Detective Singh and I comply, knowing we are defeated. The dark-suited man sits firmly across from Aditya while the suspect looks on in confusion.

"Do you think he will walk back his confession?" I ask Detective Singh.

"Even if he does, we have enough to charge him," Detective Singh says.

"I'm smelling Lona Mason behind this," I say. "I've run into that lawyer before. He charges upwards of a thousand dollars an hour."

"Could be."

"But she's not protecting Aditya, she's protecting herself," I say. "Aditya knows too much. He can implicate her - and he just did."

I follow Detective Singh into his office like a caffeine-addict sleepwalking into their favorite coffee shop. I will miss this. But my work here is done.

"So what happens next?" I ask, wanting to prolong the conversation.

"We build a case," Detective Singh says. "And we go to court."

"Do you think Aditya will give us Lona in return for lesser charges?" I say. "We've got him on the hook for Caleb's murder, concealing evidence in Sharon's murder, *and* drug dealing."

"Could be."

I shuffle my feet, wracking my brain. It's time to bid goodbye, to walk out the door, to start hunting for my next case, but something - a disquieting feeling - leaves my feet rooted to the ground.

"Until next time, Fati," Detective Singh says. "I enjoyed working with you."

I smile. "Did I change your opinion about working with private investigators?"

Detective Singh chuckles and it's like a rainbow splitting a rainy day. "No. But I won't say no to working with *you* again."

"I'm not so sure about that, Detective." I take a deep breath and plunge in. "You see, I find you impossibly attractive. And that's distracting. There's a reason I am single. And it's not because I'm a raging introvert - although that's part of it."

Detective Singh looks at me, his face unreadable.

"And so, it's best for my own peace of mind if I avoid cases that involve you," I finish clumsily.

Detective Singh keeps looking at me, his expression even, saying nothing.

"I think you're a great detective," I continue, stumbling over my words. Disengaging from my body, floating to the ceiling, watching myself in horror. Unable to stop talking, rambling on. "It's just that - I don't like distractions. It took nineteen days for me to solve this case. That's disappointing. And the reason is that half the time, I was daydreaming about you, looking forward to seeing you again."

Detective Singh looks thoughtful, as if I am a particularly puzzling math problem. Folds his arms across his chest. Continues to say nothing.

I am glad. I don't need his derision or his pity. I only want him to know that if he doesn't hear from me again, there is a reason. A lame one. An embarrassing one. But a valid one nonetheless. I'm way past the point where I let embarrassment hold me back from blunt honesty. Especially with people that I respect.

"That's all I wanted to say." My voice tapers off.

I reach out a stiff hand for a farewell handshake. Detective Singh takes my hand in his firm grip and places his other on top of our clasp, as if in consolation. Miffed, I gently shake myself free. I meant it when I said I don't want pity. I'm not an old lady he helped cross the sidewalk.

I can feel Detective Singh's eyes on my back as I walk out of his office. I can't help but think - *Damn, I should have brushed my hair this morning, maybe ironed my shirt.* I shake off the thought.

The cop on my next case will be an unpleasant sloth. Or a gray-haired grandfather-type. Or a dim bulb who can't tell his nose from his ears. Or a woman. Anyone but Detective Singh with his fiery hazel eyes and his quiet intelligence hidden behind the hard-shell exterior. I have to protect my crime-solving firepower.

Maybe he and I are not that different, after all. With his clipped manner and penchant for silence, maybe he's protecting himself too.

CHAPTER 20

Monday, December 30, 2019

As I slide into my car, I take out my phone and navigate to my list of 'special friends.' They're fuss-free and commitment-phobic, just like me, always ready for a transactional, one-night arrangement. Zed was right. It's time to clean out my steam engine.

Romantic relationships have never served me well. And frequently, in my work, I am reminded of their deceiving nature.

One-night arrangements don't melt under your touch while dreaming of someone else. They don't babble about forever while carrying on behind closed doors with their best friend. They don't manipulate you by extending and viciously retracting a marriage certificate.

I work my way through small talk with the first guy who picks up, anxious to get to the point. I scroll through my text messages absently and see one from my mother. A birthday message - from four days ago. I never returned her phone call.

I wonder if my mother would still call me if she found out about my clandestine trysts.

But marriage doesn't guarantee happiness, either. Aditya Roshan's story is a cautionary tale. And then there's my sister, Ayesha. Eyes filled with sadness that she desperately tried to conceal with fifty-dollar liner.

I set a time with my friend-with-benefits. Drinks after dinner at my place at nine p.m. *Don't be late*, I remind him. As the adrenaline of the case leaks out of me, I will crash. Alone on my balcony with a glass of wine by midnight.

As I drive home, I make a mental note to shower. Return my mother's call. And call Ayesha. The case is over and I can pause being a detective. It's time to briefly become a human.

Tuesday, December 31, 2019

Early in the morning, my sister Ayesha calls me, as if I've conjured her with my thoughts. We meet at a coffee shop near Kitsilano Beach. '*Figaro,*' I said immediately when Ayesha asked where I wanted to go.

The case is over but Korinne Kendall still rankles me. The enigma I couldn't solve. Who gave her the video from City Hall that broke Sharon's murder case? Maybe I'll never know.

Shards of rain splice the air as the year 2019 thunders towards its conclusion. Gray clouds weep, as if in pain. I drive to Figaro, my tires hitting deep puddles every few minutes, splashing water as high as the windows. Good. At least I won't have to wash my car. That's one task off my burgeoning list.

The streets of Vancouver are ripe with anticipation. New Year's Eve is approaching. Soon, they will be filled with revellers, dressed in their finest, filling the local bars and restaurants, stocked up and ready to feed and juice them. Fireworks will fill the sky. Tipsy youngsters will spill into the streets, hooting and yelling, alerting the world that they are here, they are unstoppable, and determined to have their best year ever.

I plan to spend the day studying Mandarin. It's been weeks since I cracked a lesson. At some point tonight, Zed will start texting me. After he's had a few shots, sampled the wares at the gay bars on Davie Street, and thrown a tantrum or two. He'll come over and we'll ring in the new year on my balcony, sipping pinot noir out of coffee mugs, like civilized adults. He'll crash on my shag rug, and we'll awaken the next day, re-born and ready for our next case.

I park outside Figaro and walk in. Ayesha is already there, dressed in a pinstripe skirt suit, a polished executive on lunch break. Her hair, as black, wavy, and unmanageable as mine, is ironed straight. Mascara, pink-nude lipstick, a gentle swirl of peach blush. Her signature attire. Not a crack in her shell.

She welcomes me with a life-goes-on smile. I'm sure her colleagues don't suspect. Her team doesn't see it. But I do. Maybe it's because I'm a PI. Or maybe it's because I'm her sister. I've loved and protected her for thirty-two years, seen past her bravado, called her out on her bullshit.

We hug and I remind Ayesha to not work so hard. It's New Year's Eve, not a boardroom brawl. My words are hollow, even to me.

After nearly three weeks submerged in a case, I am worse for wear. Ayesha sees my dark circles and strained smile, new laugh lines planting their flags in my cheeks. She and I may be very different, but when it comes to our dogged ambition in our chosen life paths, we are the same.

"I'm sure you've already suspected but Mubashir and I are separated," Ayesha confides, as she sips her tall dark roast. Our taste in caffeinated beverages is another thing we have in common.

"I'm sorry to hear that," I say, and genuinely mean it.

I never liked Mubashir. He isn't good enough for my sister. He tells her what to order at restaurants. He texts her incessantly when she's traveling for work and broods for hours when she returns. When she was pregnant, he criticized her weight gain and bullied her into juice cleanse after juice cleanse. He's an ogre. My sister is well rid of him.

"I may have rushed into marrying him," Ayesha says.

I raise my eyebrows, resisting the urge.

"You don't have to say it," Ayesha says quickly, reading my mind. "You told me so, I know."

"I've only ever wanted you to be happy," I say. "And you said Mubashir made you happy."

"*You* didn't make things easy for me, you know!" Ayesha slaps my arm in a playful gesture. "If you got married when you were supposed to, there would've been less pressure on me."

I smile, take a sip of my coffee, and my sister's hand "I told you - don't trust Auntie Nargis. She started sending proposals when I was twenty! Fifteen years later, she still hasn't given up."

"I've always admired you, Fati," Ayesha says. "You deal with family pressure way better than I ever did. Mom wanted me to be a perfect daughter, a wife and mother. I didn't know how to say no, how not to go along."

"If you were the type of person to always 'go along,' you wouldn't be where you are today - youngest VP at Bank of Montreal. I'm proud of you, sis."

But I know what Ayesha means. Throughout our childhoods, she went with the flow. She dutifully prayed five times a day, kept her fasts during *Ramadan*, dated only a handful of suitable, mom-approved Muslim boys from the mosque, and settled on Mubashir when she was just twenty-five.

"You were right when you said I shouldn't change my name," Ayesha says. "Now, I will have to change it back. That will be so awkward at work."

I was bitterly disappointed when she did it. I couldn't understand how Ayesha, an outspoken feminist, could let herself be subsumed under the yoke of a domineering husband. Ditch the name she was born with that represents her roots, forms the bedrock of her identity.

"Ayesha Rizvi always suited you a lot better than Ayesha Mubashir," I say.

"I got married so young, most people don't know Ayesha Rizvi. They only know Ayesha Mubashir."

"Did *you* even know who you were before you got married?" I ask, gently.

Ayesha sighs, looks away and out the window as if transported to another place. "It never felt right changing my name when I got married. But I did it - because it was expected."

"Doing something just because it's expected is never a good idea," I say. "But you've come a long way since then, sis. You should be proud. You're leaving a marriage that isn't right for you. In our Muslim community, that's revolutionary. It won't make you popular, though. What does Mom think about all this?"

"She doesn't get it," Ayesha says. "She keeps asking if he beat me. As if that's the only reason for divorce."

"He doesn't have the nerve," I say, dismissively. "Mubashir is all hot air and blah blah and not much else."

I've never hid my feelings about Mubashir. Ayesha knows I don't like him. But we always avoided talking about him before.

"He didn't want me to take this new job," Ayesha says. "He wanted to try for another baby instead. But I don't want another. One is enough."

"Hey, I get it," I say. "As far as I'm concerned, even one is more work than it's worth."

I love my nephew. Ayesha knows that. But I won't be volunteering to babysit anytime soon.

Ayesha sighs and takes a long draw of her drink. "I wish I could be like you, Fati. You don't get affected by any man."

I hold back a chortle. If only Ayesha knew. It's not that I'm not affected. I'm only human, after all. It's that I don't let myself *stay* affected for too long. Men, love, romance, relationships - none of it is that interesting to me. Not as much as a juicy case, a real-life Rubik's cube, a puzzle to engage the mind. Humans in love are so predictable. I called Ayesha's separation and inevitable divorce years ago. I knew it wouldn't last.

In a moment of impulse, I confess to my sister. "There *is* one man I can't seem to stop thinking about," I say. "I'm quite mad at myself. The detective on the case I just wrapped up. Married. Well, separated - just like you."

Ayesha shifts forward in anticipation, her eyes lighting up. It has been a long time since I admitted to a crush.

"A detective," she says. "I'm not surprised. Sometimes I feel that's the only kind of man who can keep up with you! That and criminal masterminds, of course."

"Nothing's going to happen between us," I say, firmly. "It's silly. I just got caught up in the excitement of the case. It's over now. I'm not going to see him again."

Detective Singh has probably lost all respect for me since he found out about my closeted feelings for him.

"Until the next one…"

"I'm not going to work with him again," I say, resolute. "I told him so. Besides - remember, he's married."

"Separated," Ayesha corrects me, flatly. "Let's be honest. Once you open the door to separation, it's very hard to find your way back."

"So you're sure that you and Mubashir…"

Ayesha looks at me and there is acceptance in her eyes. And a keen self-knowledge. "Yes," she says. "I don't see how we can find our way back to each other. But who knows? All I know is, for now, I need to be on my own."

A divorce would cause an uproar in my family. In our community. The downpour will be torrential. Ayesha will need every ounce of her strength to withstand the onslaught. But I can see from her implacable expression that she's ready. She has thought things through.

"You and Azeem."

My nephew is only two. He adores his mother. Despite her long nights at the office. Despite her quarterly work trips to Toronto. Despite the missed games and the bedtime stories read over the phone.

"Yes, me and Azeem," Ayesha says.

Her voice is grave. A flicker of pain on her face. She's acutely aware that her son no longer fully belongs to her. She will share custody with Mubashir. And she will do it with dignity, even as her soul kicks and screams inside.

"How is the new job?" I ask, trying to divert Ayesha's attention to happier topics.

She taps her fingertips on her coffee cup, thoughtfully. "It's good."

"Am I picking up a twinge of hesitation?"

"No, it's not that," Ayesha says. "It's just that… I've been offered to join a private company. Blue Wave Capital. It's a meaty opportunity, lots of growth. But it's a small firm."

"Are you considering it?" I ask. "You just started your new role at BMO."

Ayesha sighs. Indecision skips across her face. "I'm thinking about it. It will be a fresh start all round. It will be easier to go back to my maiden name if I'm at a new firm."

Ayesha's voice is resigned. But there's also a glimmer of hope - for a new life. My sister is moving on from her marriage, her domineering husband, and the suboptimal life decision she made in marrying him.

Ayesha, the perfect child. The daughter who can do no wrong. The foil for my failures. The pressure she must have been under to keep up with the expectations laden on her. Her share and mine. I feel a stab of guilt that I haven't been there for her the way I should have been.

In that moment, I make a decision. Ayesha and I will spend more time together. This weekend, we will have dinner. My inner voice reminds me that I've made that resolve before. And it only lasts until the next shiny case crosses my path and ensnares me with its tantalizing scent. I sweep the thought away.

Family is important. But complicated. Isn't it family that caused the downfall of every unsavory character in my recent case? Alena impersonating her dead sister. Lona torn with guilt over abandoning her firstborn son. And Aditya living in fear of disappointing his parents in India.

I should be glad my family is normal. Emotional blackmail from a disapproving mother, a brother's frowned-upon marriage to a white woman, a sister's divorce from a traditional husband. All pretty humdrum compared to my cast of characters from Lake Templeton.

I smile at Ayesha and reach forward to cover her hand with mine. "We should spend time together more often, sis," I say. "Let's have dinner this weekend."

Ayesha smiles back and nods. Outside, the sun pierces through the gray clouds. The rain has stopped. Sunshine is emerging like new life. A new beginning.

Detective Singh calls me that afternoon. I am at home, on my balcony, laptop on and headphones in, reciting newly learned Mandarin phrases to myself.

Done with the case and out of hibernation, I spent a half hour catching up on news. Shootout in Northern Mexico.

Protests in India over a controversial citizenship bill. New pneumonia-like virus emerging in China. All misery. All the time. The world's problems are endless and seem to have no solution. Unlike my cases.

When I see Detective Singh's name light up my screen, my heart skips a beat, then shudders to a stop.

"Hello," I croak, sounding like a wounded animal. I clear my throat. "Hello, Detective. I didn't expect to hear from you."

A brief pause, heavy with meaning. Then, he says, "We found Sharon's journals. I thought you'd want to know."

"Journals?" I forget all about my awkward confession at his office. "Sharon had journals?"

"Yes," Detective Singh says. "We found them in Alena's home, under a hidden trapdoor beneath her bedroom closet."

"Wow," I say. "I wonder if she stole them before or after Sharon's death."

"My guess is before - to strongarm Sharon to give back the money Alena thought she stole."

"Speaking of Alena, what happened with the life insurance payout for Sharon?" I ask. "Now that the case is solved, will the City get the money?"

"That's up to the insurance company."

But there's no one to file a claim. Alena is out, forcibly removed from her position, waiting to be indicted. Sharon and Sergio are both dead. Lake Templeton is in disarray.

The premier has touched down. City Council has been convened. New mayoral elections will take place. The insurance payout is an extra credit question at the bottom of a demanding exam sheet.

"There's one more thing bothering me," I say. "Where did Korinne Kendall get the video? The one from Sharon's office. That one that blew the doors off this case?"

"Alena," Detective Singh says. "We found it in her email's 'Sent Items.'"

Our archetypal villain strikes again.

"But why?" I am still puzzled. "Why would she share the video with Korinne? They did *not* like each other."

"Money. We found a wire payment from Korinne into Alena's bank account."

"One more corruption charge," I say. "Lovely."

"Alena says she wanted Korinne to share it with the police anonymously."

"Nonsense," I say dismissively. "*Alena* could've shared it with the police anonymously if she wanted to avoid questions about where she got it." I pause. "I want to read Sharon's journals,"

Detective Singh agrees readily. Why else would he have called me? He asks me to come to the RCMP detachment at Wesbrook Mall. The journals were sent by courier from Lake Templeton this morning.

The case is over but questions remain. Who was Sharon Reese? I never met her but her specter still haunts me.

Sharon, the shapeshifter, the woman who wanted no one to know her.

The flimsy answers in Korinne's book only offer a slice. They barely slake my thirst to learn about the dead woman's life. But her journals - they are a coveted entry ticket to her closed-off world.

I abandon my headphones, lace up my boots, and grab my keys. In twenty minutes, I am at the station.

I avoid Detective Singh's mystic hazel eyes as he leads me into the records room. Something smolders between us but maybe it's only in my head. When silence falls, I struggle to fill it. We are past the point of small talk and I've run out of inane questions about the case.

I sit down in the records room with a small pile of A4 sized dogeared notebooks. Detective Singh leaves me there by myself. I've earned the trust of the police department. And he has work to do.

The journals are written in accented cursive in blue ballpoint pen. Sharon's motivations, the thoughts that drove her, her fears, all are buried in these seemingly innocuous pages.

I flip a page. Sharon finally breaks her silence and starts speaking to me, as if from a time capsule. Uncorks the thoughts that she kept bottled up inside, buttoned up in a vow of silence, even as cameras flashed in her face and microphones were shoved under her nose.

After she left the cult, Sharon's mind was a convoluted mess - shock, shame, regret, anger, guilt. She felt adrift. Angry at Jefferson Wall, her jailer who became her mentor. Furious that he left her behind as he led his followers to the Pearly Gates. Confused at why.

Did she do something wrong? Didn't she follow in his footsteps, overlook his transgressions, join in with him? She was his right hand, the hand that inflicted pain on the others - so he didn't have to.

The day of the mass suicide was like any other day. Sharon woke up with no idea that her life was about to fall apart. Jefferson Wall trusted Sharon more than anyone else on the compound. But he told her nothing. That day, he handed her a goblet he had prepared himself, like he always did. Sharon didn't know it was mildly laced with poison. The same viscous poison that pooled in the others' goblets. Sharon sipped at it like she always did, not knowing hers was the only empty chamber in the roulette gun. It was specially prepared so she could sleep like Cinderella while chaos ensued around her.

When the cult members were doubled over in seizure, Sharon was lucid. The pall of death descended as she stumbled - on rickety feet - to Jefferson Wall's office. In a locked room, she found the TV and VCR, hefty magic boxes as big as her torso. And in a drawer which she jimmied open with the tools she knew were resting under Jefferson's bed - she found a VHS tape. She grabbed the tape, swept it into the folds of her toga, hooked it into the elastic band of her billowy jute pants. In the ensuing flurry of activity, it remained with her, its cold hard plastic reminding her to keep her wits, like a battery pack keeping her going.

In the days subsequent to her rescue and the discovery of the dead bodies, Sharon struggled to make sense of Jefferson Wall's actions. Why was she saved? What did it mean? Months after attaining her freedom, Sharon began to understand. Her page-ripping outburst of words mellowed into reflective understanding.

Jefferson Wall left her alive because she was his legacy. His actions were intentional. He shut her out of the mass suicide plan out of love. He wanted her to live. To rebuild. He didn't share his plans with her because she would insist on joining him.

But did Sharon want to continue Jefferson Wall's lofty quest?

Unbound from the shackles of the cult, Sharon realized that she didn't. She liked being free. She felt relieved to let go of the whip. She wasn't a megalomaniac cult leader. She was a normal woman who wanted a normal life.

And then, guilt started tearing away at her. It wasn't just survivor's guilt. It was deep regret for the things she did - was forced to do - while entombed in the living death of the cult. She needed penance. To comfort her mind. To relinquish the burden she carried constantly.

She wrote about the Thriving Mind Society. The place that took her in with no agenda, no prying questions, no demands. Enveloped in their walls, Sharon could finally breathe.

Weeks later, in the privacy of the media room, at two a.m. she watched the VHS tape she took from Jefferson Wall's office. Mouth gaping in baffled horror. Aghast. She didn't know Jefferson had been taping his flock. Whose hand did he trust the camcorder to? It wasn't his own. That shaky jitter was beneath him. And Jefferson was in many of the videos himself.

Why? Was it for posterity? To live on even after he died? For notoriety? To gain his rightful place in the cult leader hall of fame? Maybe Jefferson intended for the police to find the videos. But Sharon derailed him. It filled her with cold satisfaction.

There's nothing in the diaries about Lona. She and Sharon were passing ships in the night. They flashed their lights at each other, alerting their presence, then shifted silently to the side to make room. Maybe they shared a smile over breakfast. Chatted about the weather while sipping coffee on the lawn. But nothing more.

As she became an object of national curiosity, Sharon felt torn. She couldn't share her wild tale with others because she could barely make sense of it herself. In her most bereft moments, it all seemed like a bad dream. Sharon clung to the safety blanket of silence for the sake of self-preservation. She just wanted to be left alone so she could find herself again.

Until Korinne Kendall showed up.

The final page of the last journal is dated May 19, 2009. It was the day that Sharon met Korinne Kendall. It simply states:

'Met a journalist today. She wants to tell my story. Am I ready?.... I think I am.'

I don't know whether Sharon stopped writing after that. No journals were found at her home. Maybe lending her voice to Korinne, using her as a megaphone, slowed the tide of Sharon's emotions. Speaking through Korinne, she no longer felt the need to transcribe her thoughts to stem the conflagration.

Maybe Korinne nabbed subsequent journals before the police could get to them. Her winning book formula is taking a true story and telling it like a tabloid. She's writing a sensationalist tale of her friend's murder for public consumption, based on stolen evidence she did not share with the police. It's not like she has scruples.

Maybe I'll find out once the book comes out.

I close the book on Sharon Reese, snapping the journal closed. Sharon lived a tumultuous life. She had lots to atone for. But she was also a victim of her circumstances. She came to Lake Templeton for a fresh start. To get away from bright lights and city noise. But found that the quicksand of small-town politics wasn't any less treacherous than the big city's.

Hopefully, in her final days, when she stood up to Alena's bullying, when she refused to let Sergio get away with theft, she finally found the absolution she was looking for. Before her life was brutally snuffed out.

Sharon never knew that Alena tried to mousetrap her, even in death. Tried to pin the embezzlement on her. Played hide and seek with the Lake Templeton revitalization project file. Glossed over irregularities in the City's finances. Squirreled away the CCTV footage from City Hall which would have exonerated Sharon. Maligned her reputation. Tied her, toasted her, and served her on a platter to distract from Alena's own illegal activities. But ultimately, truth triumphed. As it always does.

I walk out of the police station, feeling content. Detective Singh's office is dark, and his door is ajar. Good, he's not there. That's a shameful page in my own book that I can put to rest.

The sun is starting to set as I slide into my Mazda sedan that patiently waits for me outside, as it has for so many years in so many cases.

The station recedes in my rear-view mirror as I drive away. Until next time.

ACKNOWLEDGEMENTS

This book is inspired by the majestic mountains and oceans of Western Canada, which I am pleased to call my home. The characters are based on the incredible ethnic and cultural diversity of our country.

This book wouldn't have been possible without the ongoing support and encouragement of my husband, my family, and my friends.

I also want to thank my editor, who enabled me to catch fatal flaws in my writing before they made it to my readers. And my creative writing advisor in college, who made me a better writer.

And finally, thank you, my dear reader, for coming along on this journey through Lake Templeton, with me. I hope you enjoyed the ride. I would very much appreciate it if you would consider leaving a review.